HEIST
OF
HAURES

HEIST
OF
HAURES

A Devil's Trials Novel

Stephanie Gluck

ISBN Paperback: 978-0-6454075-3-2

For Janelle, who supported every moment of this journey.
(Love you, mum)

&

For Mr. Puff, always

Also, by Stephanie Gluck:

THE DEVIL'S TRIALS
Feast of Samael

Heist of Haures

THE FOUR REALMS
Death's Stalker

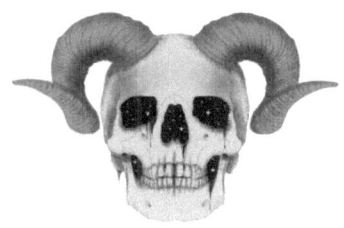

Chapter One

Visions of a vengeful, gluttonous angel ripping Ophelia's heart from her chest seared the back of my eyelids. Each time I'd close my eyes, the vision would force me to relive her final moments. An innocent girl lost too soon. Each haunting flash cast her contorted face, which flickered from contentment to betrayal to fear.

Gluttony's force snaps Ophelia's ribs with a crack that haunts my dreams, her bloody heart shuddering in his grip as he wrenches it free. Ancient magic refracts from Gluttony's eyes with intense satisfaction as he takes the first bite of her heart. His dark wings shudder with pleasure.

Everything in that moment had felt like a blur, but I then faced every sickening detail in my moments of recollection.

The train journey from Gula to Invidia took three long days, most of which were spent laying in the dark in silence. Shared trauma connected all of us, but we were still nothing more than strangers: five young adults, damaged by Gluttony and the emotional turmoil he had created.

I didn't want to share the details of what was tormenting me, disinterested in acquiring their pain on top of my own. We lay sprawled across different seats on the train, and as seconds ticked into minutes, into hours, more than one of us screamed or wailed with the nightmares. It seemed I was not the only one to wake up with a thundering heartbeat and fear in my veins. Different nightmares seemed to plague all of us, and pleas dripped from our lips, even in our sleep. Even in my waking hours, I was forced to listen to the whimpers drawn from their own experiences.

Finley whimpered in the corner; his entire body twitched in his sleep. With a sigh, I rolled on the seat and drew my legs tighter against my chest to block him out. The golden envelope lay unopened against my cheek. While I couldn't read or understand it – rendering the message inside useless – I didn't want to let it out of my sight. It would be the key to my survival, but I couldn't bring myself to worry about the burdens I had already been carrying.

I drifted in and out of consciousness, never fully rested, always waking with Phee's name on my lips. At some point through the journey, the men roused from their torment and pulled themselves together. I woke to their whispers at the back of the compartment. As I lay in silence, I listened to their soft words, wondering how they found the will to get up. A laugh grated my nerves, and I wondered how anyone could manage to feel joy in the tattered remains of the first trial. Still, I listened for anything I would need in their conversation, but nothing sparked my interest.

At the sound of my name, I cringed into a tighter ball and tried to block them out again. I prayed for sleep to claim me. I didn't want anything to do with them. Instead, I grieved for the bright-souled girl who should have survived in my place. I should have let Gluttony steal my heart instead; maybe he had, with the way my chest ached with raw grief.

Each time I woke, I cried until I ran out of tears, and my head pounded in chastisement for my emotions. The tears dried against my cheeks, then I cried again until the darkness swept me under. Grief was a living entity in my chest, determined to devour me from the inside out. It was easier, in many ways, to block out the reality of what our lives had become.

The world slammed into focus in the middle of the night as someone wrapped their hands around my ankles and lifted them from the seat. A squeal of terror tore from the back of my throat, and my heart dropped. On instinct, I lashed out. The side of my foot caught soft flesh. Frenziedly, I kicked out again and again and again. Gripping the side of the seat, I clawed at the fabric, writhing to get away.

"Devil be damned, Tav!"

Nash wheezed as if my foot had knocked all the breath from his body.

When I scrambled upright, head spinning, pushing myself into the corner of the seat, I realised he had his hands clasped between his legs, cradling his family jewels. Nash squeezed his eyes closed as pain twisted across his features.

A beat of silence lingered between us as I took in his state of distress. It was on the tip of my tongue to tell him he deserved it. He knew better than to wake someone up that way, not after everything we had been through.

"Sorry," I muttered.

"I think you've robbed me of the chance to have kids," Nash whined.

Neither of us commented on that. I never wanted my own family. The idea of miniature versions of myself running around turned my stomach cold. Nash would be a happy man, determined to show them the beauty of the colour in the world as he saw it.

He slumped into the space beside me. I drew my knees to my chest to pose a barrier between us, and we sat in silence until his breathing stabilised. Eventually, the pained tension faded from his features.

I felt the need to flee and put space between us. Although I knew Nash was a friend and ally and that every man in the train carriage was, fear tensed my body, my fingers shaking with anxiety I couldn't quite quell. Getting close and trusting any of them was too risky, not in the way that they could betray me at any time, but for the pain I would feel if the trials were to have stolen them. No. It was far better to keep my distance than feel this level of grief again. Never had I wanted so badly to take a dead woman's place in the world. Ophelia deserved to live on more than I did.

While Cyn had stressed at the beginning that each of these sins and the trials were deadly, I knew I had been flippant about the idea of oncoming death. The warning hadn't been taken seriously. When leaving Ilrea, it wasn't important. All that mattered was I'd lived longer than that first day, longer than if I had stayed behind. At an unknown point, however, I had come to believe that I could win these trials and live to see the Devil. There was some level of hope that I was worthy to receive his favour.

Since then, I understood I knew nothing in the scheme of things. The dangers of these trials were worse than I could have imagined. Gluttony was only the first of the seven deadly sins, and with six more to face, my chances of surviving were slim. We were racing across the Earth at Envy's demand, and at his mercy was the last place I wanted to be. My head and my heart weren't ready to face another angel any time soon.

Idly, I pressed my face against the cool glass window and peered out across the darkened plains, Kaida's overgrown ruins. These ruins displayed what was left of the little towns and whole societies since the angels decimated us hundreds of years ago.

What would happen if I ran away into the night?

We were suspended in a moment between the end of the Gluttony trial and the commencement of Envy's house of horrors. Which one of the two would stake their claim on my life and soul if I had fled that moment?

"Coin for your thoughts?" Nash whispered in my ear. He was too close, so I flinched away, my head banging against the glass.

"Ow!" I grumbled.

He chuckled softly, causing a smile to pull at my lips. Nash was not the ray of optimism he had been two weeks prior, not with the trial weighing heavy on his shoulders. But somehow, he still managed to conjure a smile.

"Well?" he pressed.

"I was thinking of running away," I admitted softly.

Nash was silent and peered through the window. I wondered if he was considering it, too. "Where would you go?"

That was a rhetorical question. Nowhere in the entirety of Kaida seemed safe, not anymore. Demons and other dangerous creatures hunted the shadows of the night. The angels dominated the cities, the biggest dangers of all.

Searching for an answer, I huffed a sigh. It would have been grand – exciting, even – to tell Nash a tale of living in the ruins of old human cities. To create a fantasy around collecting humans from the surrounding villages, pulling them from poverty, forging a path towards a safer world. Except we both knew that would be entirely fantasy. I could barely keep myself alive let alone lead a revolution.

I was no hero.

"Eternis," I told him finally.

In the window's reflection, his eyes widened. Nash lifted a hand and ran his fingers through his matted blonde hair. They snagged, and he winced.

"You'd go straight to the Devil?" Nash laughed like he thought I was joking.

This time, I didn't smile back. Slowly, the curl of his lips dropped away as he realised, I was serious. His lips parted on a sharp inhale, and he shook his head.

"Why not?" I asked.

His throat bobbed. "Because he's the one who set these trials? We're dying for his entertainment, Tav. He's not your saviour."

I thought of the way the Devil, Samael, had whispered in my ear through the Gluttony trial. The way his encouragement had kept me going and the way his hints had given us the answer to our survival. We were one member less than we should have had, but for the most part, we were here. Damaged but alive because of the Devil himself. Whether they knew it.

Nash was wrong, I decided, because the Devil wouldn't have saved my life if he didn't want to see me make it to his city. He wanted something, but it started with my success in these trials.

"Then, I'll sell him my soul," I declared grandly.

We had all heard the stories of bargaining souls to the Devil. It would be my last resort.

Nash's gaze dropped to the identical cuffs around our left wrists, and he didn't voice what everyone could have been thinking. We had already sold our souls to the Devil, in a way, and we were just playing his game to get them back.

"So, what if he opens the gates to Eternis and kills you on sight?" Nash asked softly.

I pressed my teeth onto my lower lip until it stung, and bitter blood coated my tongue.

"Then, none of it matters, does it?" I whispered back.

Nash reached out and grasped my waist. He pulled me in towards his side and anchored me beneath his arm. My heart hammered with alarm, a squeak echoing in the back of my throat, but I forced myself to stay still against him instead of wriggling away. The hug was needed, but my skin still crawled.

"It matters, Tav." He was firm.

The corner of my mouth dropped, I fidgeted with the ends of my sleeves. I wished I could have his sense of optimism, that I could see the world with the same certainty as Nash Wickham. As far as I was concerned, my life or death didn't matter at all.

"Nash," I said. I could hear it in my voice, an edge to my tone, like I was preparing to deliver bad news to a child who couldn't understand. He stiffened, his eyes narrowing on my face, as he silently dared me to continue.

"You were in the same feast as me . . ."

"And?"

I tilted my head to look at him, my nose wrinkling at the fact he was going to make me spell it out. "It's only going to get harder. Get worse. Nash, there's six more trials, and so many people died just in the first. I won't make it to seven."

His jaw sharpened with tension, gaze flaring with disagreement that he didn't voice. He couldn't deny the deaths, not when we had left Ophelia behind.

A near hysterical laugh rose in the back of my throat, dry and gravelly, loud enough to make Mikhael glance over.

"Nash." I shook my head. "We're all already dead."

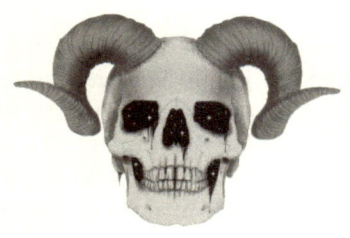

Chapter Two

Mikhael climbed over the seats and dropped onto the soft cushions across from us. In the carriage's low light, he looked haunted, with the shadows splashing across the sharp angles of his face. The first trial had eaten away at him.

"As amusing as your misery is, Octavia, I'd appreciate it if you didn't write us all off," he commented.

My head jerked to meet his gaze. He looked mostly unburdened by the Gluttony trial; if it weren't for the circle of bruises along his collarbone, the cut on his left cheekbone, and the deep circles beneath his eyes, I would have thought he hadn't participated at all.

"Excuse you?" I challenged him to repeat himself.

Mikhael steepled his fingers and leaned forward so abruptly I was forced to push back against the chair. He lifted a single brow, a sleek and patronising movement. He said nothing and let the silence linger until the urge to fill it became too much.

"You think my misery is amusing?!" I snarled.

Finley and Niklaus jolted from their sleep.

"Wass going on?" Finley yawned. His dark curls flopped in front of his face. He was a soft contrast to Niklaus, who had jumped to his feet, tension rippling across his body as he searched for a threat. When his gaze landed on me, I looked away quickly.

"In a way, yes," Mikhael answered. He ignored everyone else and held my gaze with an intensity that left me helpless to do anything except stare back. He was a man who demanded the full attention of those he spoke to, a privilege afforded with the status he had held at home.

A pained noise echoed from the back of my throat, half a cry of pain and a growl of frustration. My eyes narrowed on him, and for the first time in days, I broke through my mind-numbing grief for Ophelia and for myself. She had died, but I also mourned the parts of myself left behind in that first trial, any remnants of my naivety destroyed.

"I lost a friend," I muttered. "She was barely a kid, and she died, Mikhael! You can't just ignore that because it's inconvenient. Is it that you're scared of tears? Or that you don't know how to mourn a life?"

"You only knew her a week," Mikhael reasoned firmly.

He appeared so calm and unaffected, which left me fuming. He didn't understand, and for a moment, I hated him for that, hated him for not mourning her the same way I did. I envied the fact he didn't seem to have a hole in his heart.

"I didn't realise friendships had to be forged over a long time. What's the best length of time for a connection to be real? A month? A year?" I snapped, and Mikhael's lips twitched at the left corner – a smile or a frown, I wasn't sure. It was just enough that I took it as an acknowledgement of my point.

"Well . . . you're not doing the girl any good crying about it, are you?" It seemed Mikhael Heira pushed buttons as a skill. His brother came to stand behind him, a strong and constant presence. I shifted restlessly, but Nash's arm around my waist anchored me in place.

"*The girl* has a name," I spat.

"And?" In that second, he was worse than his brother, and I imagined how it would feel to punch him.

"*Ophelia.*" I retorted, glaring at him. "Say it!"

Mikhael remained silent.

My eyes flickered up to Niklaus, who stood tense beside him, and my jaw clenched. He watched me with a quiet, concentrated interest, but for all our turbulent emotions and our shared history, he said nothing in my defence. Family was everything for the Heira men. His apparent obsession with me was not enough to overcome his blind faith in his twin brother. Dismissing him, I snapped my gaze back to Mikhael.

"Nothing is doing her any good," I growled. "She's dead."

Mikhael had the audacity to laugh. A spike of hot frustration rolled through my veins, and I struggled against Nash's hold with the intense desire to lash out at him.

His laugh ended with a full grin, and Mikhael dipped his chin at me. "That's better."

My fingers curled into fists, the jagged ends of my broken nails digging into my palms with pinpricks of pain.

"What is?" I hissed.

"Finally." The green of his eyes seemed to glow as they lit up at the bite in my voice.

"What?!"

"You're completely useless if you keep crying. Don't be sad because you lost her, Octavia. Be mad that she died at all."

"I am mad," I insisted.

"Really?" Mikhael leaned in close. He smelled like the trees in the Gulan forests and the undertones of the soap he had tried to scrub it away with. "It doesn't seem like it."

My teeth gritted so hard a flash of pain flared in my jaw, the irritation of one of many injuries I had acquired in the forests. I prepared to argue, but he cut me off.

"Looks to me like you're just moping around, crying about it, instead of working out how you could avenge her death."

"You want me to avenge Phee?" I laughed hollowly. "You saw Gluttony. I bet the rest of them are even worse. How am I supposed to go up against that? I don't have magical powers."

"By winning," Mikhael announced, like it was the most obvious solution in the world. I rolled my eyes, and he scoffed right back. "You don't believe me?"

"How does winning hurt Gluttony?" I asked.

Mikhael didn't waver and held my gaze. The silence stretched between us again.

"Dying alongside her would only satisfy him."

Mikhael tilted his head and watched me closely, as if I were the otherworldly threat. For a split-second, I felt like one, anxiety thrumming in my veins as I debated between attempting to run again. Out of the carriage, off the train, and far from this torment.

Stubbornly, I pressed my lips together and denied him the satisfaction of an answer.

Mikhael watched me, and I stared back. It became a game to see who would look away first, and I was determined not to fail. An ominous quiet settled through the train carriage as everyone waited to see what happened next. Nash unwound his arm from my waist, and the palm of his hand rubbed soft circles between my shoulder blades. I winced as it put pressure on the small splinters still wedged beneath my skin. Pain prickled through my body, leaving me acutely aware of my own mortality.

"Stop!" I had meant to direct the words at Nash, but Mikhael narrowed his eyes.

"Tav," Nash murmured. I glanced at him sharply, eyes narrowed, as I waited to hear what he had to say to me. Words failed him when reassurance couldn't find its way to the tip of his tongue. Nash glanced down at his lap, and Mikhael stole the opening instead.

"Don't let Gluttony feast on any more of your emotions, Octavia. He's had enough."

I considered the emotional turmoil of the weeks before then. The highs and lows. Mikhael's hands around my neck, choking the life from the body, the feel of the rough rock beneath my fingers before I fought for my life, the way Niklaus had thrown me with ease across the forest floor. Time and time again, I had risen to struggle for my life, but I could barely find it within myself to move and greet the day.

He was right – not that I would ever admit it out loud. I was dying alongside Ophelia, as I allowed myself to drown in my grief and shock.

A heavy sigh rolled from me, and Mikhael's mouth twitched into a smile. We both knew he had won. His attention finally lifted, and I could breathe again. At least until he twisted in his seat to search out his brother and nodded sharply. There was no rest for the wicked.

"We should go through the clue together." His eyes flickered in my direction. Shame burnt in my belly as I realised, he was doing it for me. A silent apology. If we discussed the contents of the envelopes together, I wouldn't have to admit I struggled to piece together the simplest of words.

I didn't want to feel grateful to Mikhael, but I did.

Nash squeezed my shoulder. "Are you up for that?"

A grimace stretched across my face. If I were honest, I didn't feel up for anything, but I gave him a stiff nod and plucked my crumpled, unopened envelope from the seat. I twisted it between my fingers, then finally peeled back the black mark of the devil's seal. Inside was the same luxurious cream card as before. The same thick black lettering that meant nothing to me.

I stared at the words as if they would magically become recognisable. Mikhael gently cleared his throat. It drew my attention, and he unfurled his fingers to ask for my card. There was a beat of hesitation. I didn't want to give up my card, even if it was of no use to me. It was still mine.

Reluctantly, I placed it in his palm, and Mikhael's gaze danced over the words before he read it aloud.

> *DEEP BENEATH THE DARK CITY*
> *WHERE HUMANS FIGHT TO SURVIVE*
> *OUR LORD INVITES YOU TO A GAME*
> *BEST PLAYED IN TEAMS OF FIVE*
> *THE HEIST OF HAURES*
> *WHERE TRUE NATURE WILL THRIVE*

I tried to interpret it. My gaze travelled to each of the men to gauge what they were thinking.

Finley, with his dark Cupiditian looks, was an open book of expression. Trouble and discontentment splashed across his features, prominent in the descending slope of his lips, and his wrinkled nose.

As per usual, Mikhael and Niklaus gave little away. The latter had climbed over the seat to sit next to his brother, and they shared a quick glance, holding conversations the rest of us were not privy to hearing and that we would never understand.

Nash, however, grinned as if the clue had given him the world. The ease of his smile was not something I understood, not when the weight of our grief should have been heavy for his lips to move.

"Why are you so happy?" I asked as I jammed my elbow into his ribs. Nash grasped his side and gasped with a mock hurt, but then he laughed before I could feel bad. That sound brought another ghost of a smile to my lips.

"Isn't it obvious?" he asked and looked around. When silence met his question, Nash shook his head and raised a finger to poke me in the arm.

"One," he counted. "Two, three . . ." Nash pointed at both Heira twins, then jerked his chin at Finley Nightingale, whose eyes lit up with understanding. "Four." He stabbed at himself with the end of his thumb, then right above his heart. "Five!"

Nash beamed. "We have the perfect team already."

My throat tightened, feeling I was the one lacking in contribution to the team. Each of them had their advantages, but what did I have? Nothing.

"Five of us to do what, though?" I shook my head. "Play a game? I've never even heard of it."

The blank looks we shared showed I wasn't alone. None of us had any idea of what was coming next.

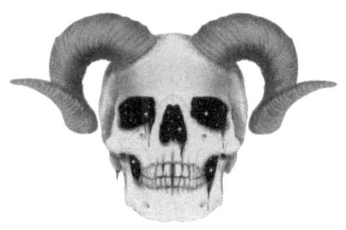

Chapter Three

Charon had appeared in the train carriage hours later to announce we were nearing our destination and to prepare to exit. He didn't waste time or pause for our questions but merely took off into the next carriage and left us with our racing thoughts.

Every now and again, someone would pipe up with the idea of what the Heist of Haures could be, and with each new pitch, the concepts became wilder. Nash had just finished describing his idea of breaking into city galleries he had heard about and stealing the most enviable art on display.

Niklaus had quickly shut the idea down by pointing out he thought we would struggle to find three other people who would be envious of a painting. The only thing we could all agree on was it would be considered theft of some sort. Mikhael had explained that a heist meant stealing for those of us who used a simpler language. Again, he slowed it all down for my benefit.

"You're a thief," Niklaus stated so abruptly I startled from my thoughts.

My chin jerked up, and I cringed away from the sudden attention. The last thing I wanted was to be the subject of their scrutiny. "So?"

"So," Niklaus stretched and sauntered in my direction.

I jumped to my feet to make sure he wasn't looming above me. He halted an inch from me, far too close, and the memory of his rage in the forest left my body trembling.

"Shouldn't you be leading this entire discussion, love?" he asked, the challenge clear in the feral grin that rolled across his face. "As our expert thief."

Heat burnt in my cheeks; I took no great pride in thievery in Ilrea. Even when thinking too long about a card game, I wanted nothing more than the comfort of the familiar and the high of the win, and my body ached not having had a fix in so long. Thievery had been a means to an end.

Niklaus Heira had no place to judge how I had survived in life when he had spent most of his time stealing the last few coins from the poor who struggled with rent for a place to sleep. He was as bad, if not worse, than I was.

"Stealing . . ." My tone was a fraction too high, nerves wound tight. Out of the corner of my eye, I noticed Mikhael step forward, and I wondered if it was to rein his brother in or egg him on. "Stealing coins, so my family can eat –"

"You mean for you to gamble away?" Niklaus said.

My face flushed brighter. "It's not the same!" I protested.

The corner of Niklaus' mouth curved his green eyes bright with victory. His brother took another step forward as I glared at Niklaus.

"Why are you doing this?"

He smirked. "Just pointing out your strengths. You have certain skills and could lead us to an easy victory on this one."

We both knew that wasn't true; the only place I could lead our ragtag team was into an early grave.

"You're just being an asshole, you mean."

Niklaus chuckled, the sound rolling from deep in his chest, and he leaned to whisper something in my ear. "Always, love."

"Nik," Mikhael said. "Enough."

I glanced between the twins. My hands fisted by my sides. "Can't you two just leave me alone?"

"We need to work together." Mikhael refused. "No more baiting each other. The clue says we need to work in teams. If we can't get along, we'll never get it done."

He was right, but it didn't make it any less frustrating. I glared at them both and dropped back down into the seat. My body ached with pain, and I wished we had a few more days to recuperate before facing the Angel of Envy and his trial.

I stared out the window, looking but not really seeing. I could feel Niklaus' heated gaze on the side of my face but forced myself not to look. Another small game I would determinedly win.

Instead, I focused on the one I thought could help and survive the second of the trials, the same thing that had helped me pass the first.

"Samael," I whispered as I gazed out at the darkening landscape. My breath felt short as I waited for the tell-tale signs of his presence, the way the rest of the world seemed to fall away as the devil turned his focus on me and me alone. A moment of complete quiet.

He didn't come. All I could hear was the Heira twins' heated conversation and Nash's faint snores, who had fallen asleep in the corner.

"Samael," I asked again. "Have any hints for me?"

I'd never truly been one for prayers to the devil – or anyone else that old souls believed in, but I could have put some faith behind it, if he had only appeared.

"Samael," I whispered a third time, eyes closed in reverent hope.

"Who are you talking to?" Finley asked.

My eyes snapped open to find him sliding into the chair Mikhael had vacated. He leaned forward with his elbows pressed against his knees and studied my face.

"What?" I asked stupidly.

"Who are you talking to? Yourself?" His brows drew together with a strange concern.

I blinked in the face of it and shook my head. "No."

"Then, who?" he pressed.

"I wasn't talking to anybody."

"You were redoing that conversation, right? With Big-Brute over there. In a way, so you win."

I scoffed, and Finley Nightingale laughed. His entire face lit up in a way I envied.

"Do you do that?" I asked.

Finley nodded, loose curls falling into his face. "Of course." He tilted his head and glanced at the Heira brothers from the corner of his eye. "I win all the arguments in my head. It's the home of my best comebacks."

Despite myself, my lips twitched. I couldn't disagree on that front; I rarely lost an argument when completely invested and undertaken in my mind.

He nodded in Niklaus' direction. "You shouldn't let him push you around like that. In Cupiditas –"

"Well, we're not in Cupiditas. We're –" The words died on the edge of my lips as the light outside cut off, and we were plunged into darkness. The ruins of Kaida disappeared as the train slipped into a tunnel. The tension in the carriage seemed to double in the dark, and my heart slammed so hard in my chest it thundered in my ears.

By the time the light had returned, and the train had started to slow, we were all standing by the windows, wound tight with apprehension. The weight of what was to come felt too heavy to carry.

"Teams of five," Finley said, and his voice rang with uncertainty for the first time since we'd met. He was the outsider in our little group of Ilreans, and I wondered if he was worried about whether we would keep him along for the ride.

"Right," Mikhael confirmed. "We work together, and we face the trial of Envy as a group."

One by one, we nodded in agreement. Although, any one of us could betray the rest.

The train came to a shuddering halt, and I sighed.

"I really hate this thing," I murmured.

Nash bumped against my shoulder as he stretched. "The train? Why?"

I shrugged. "We don't have anything like it at home; I didn't think they still existed, but the cities . . . they have . . . everything."

Finley's lips twitched. "The angels kept what they wanted from the old world to shape what existed into their vision. The rail is run by the devil himself. Charon is one of his favoured."

"Still weird," Nash hummed in agreement.

"Well." Finley shrugged. "I guess it would be to village plebians who don't have a lick of magic or technology at your disposal."

The tense silence proved that that was the wrong thing to say. The twins turned in his direction, their faces tense with mirrored displeasure.

"The same plebians you expect to keep you alive through this trial?" Mikhael asked as he looked down his nose at the curly haired man.

"It was a joke! *Relax!*" Finley grinned, and I realised the flippancy was a defence mechanism. If he didn't take himself seriously, neither could we.

The tension slipped away, whether it be from the ease of his smile, as if he had been joking all along, or from the fact that the doors on the side of the train eased open. The distraction we needed.

Mikhael was, of course, the first one out on the platform. Nash followed, Finley behind him, and Niklaus swept me a mocking bow to indicate I lead us before he swept through the rear of the group.

Nervous energy fluttered in my belly, and I inhaled before stepping onto the platform. We had been let out in the middle of nowhere. Reedy grass rose high along the edges of the platform, wild and unkempt. Nearby, the rubble of flattened buildings peaked into view, the ruins of the world before.

"Where are we?" someone shouted.

I twisted on the spot to look at the group of us who had exited the train. We were a mess. Guessing, I would have said a few hundred of us were crammed on the platform. Most of us were dirty and bedraggled, old horror etched into the lines of our faces, and I could no longer tell the competitors, who had hailed from the privilege of cities, from those of us who had scrounged our way up from the forgotten pockets of humanity. But we were all on the same playing field, stripped bare, thanks to Gluttony.

At the end of the platform, golden-skinned Charon cleared his throat. As I turned towards him, I caught sight of Helina out of the corner of my eye. Despite the turmoil of our relationship, I found my gaze tracked her in quick assessment, seeing she was okay.

Charon pointed to a great shadow in the distance. A beat passed as I squinted at it and realised it was a great, circular wall of black stone.

"The rail does not have permission to enter the city of Invidia," Charon announced. "Therefore, you will continue the rest of the way on foot."

A collective groan rang out.

It seemed strange the railway couldn't extend into the city walls in the same way it was slid beneath the heart of Glorae and arrived in the middle of Gula.

"Right." Mikhael pulled his shoulders back and stood tall, ever the leader. His eyes bounced over us as part of his internal ever-present head count. "Let's walk."

Nash slipped an arm around my shoulders and dragged me to the edge of the platform. He told a tall tale about the ruins in my ear as he forced me down the stairs.

"Stay together!" Mikhael called, and Nash flipped him off smoothly as we disappeared into the long grass.

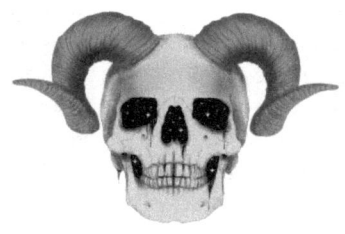

Chapter Four

With nightfall, the city of Invidia loomed, and if I had to guess that the Erlkangs had hailed from anywhere in particular, it would have been this stony dark city. Surrounded by a black, impenetrable wall, it was cold and uninviting. We approached the gate, a pathetic-looking group cuffed by the devil. With a rumble, the skies above opened, and rain poured to wash us away.

The city gates were made of black wrought iron, the pattern long, twisting serpents. Envy took his emblem to heart, and they writhed around one another in a complex pattern. I cringed backwards into Nash when I noticed that, within their open mouths, wedged between sharp fangs, there were human skulls.

It accounted for much of the bad smell. My stomach twisted, and had Nash not been standing solidly behind me, I might have run.

"This isn't going to be good," I said.

Nash tightened his grip on my shoulders. "I think you're right about that."

We peered in the rain and the darkness at a man who was approaching from the other side of the gate, lights flaring around him.

The toes of his shined boots peeked out from beneath his long, dark cloak. A lantern swung from the end of the carved cane he carried and splashed a glow against his path. When he stood on the opposite side of the gate, he was proud and tall. He pushed back his hood, and the material dropped to his shoulders.

He was not ancient, but the passing of time creased deep lines in his face. He had dark eyes under the glint of his swinging lantern, his chin covered in a close-cropped black beard marred by a silver streak. The same anomaly appeared in his right brow, both thick, black, and bushy, except for that silver streak.

We waited in expectant silence, a tense crowd on the edge of losing everything.

"I am Seamus." His voice carried in the night. "The devil's Chancellor of Invidia. I am second in command to the Lord of Envy." He paused to let this information settle. "Welcome to the trial of Envy. You may enter the city and follow me."

The iron gates groaned as they shifted. Squawks of displeasure echoed from the crows above, as the opening gate disrupted their feast. The gates slid outwards, giving way to the slippery rock-paved streets of Invidia.

Together, we shuffled forward and entered the next ominous chapter of our trials.

23

The chancellor led us through the city, where buildings darkened and only a few dim lights flashed off the slick surface of cobblestone paths. Invidia was a quiet place at night to begin with. Only as we turned and descended to a new world beneath the streets did I realise why the citizens didn't brave the world after dark – at least, not without some form of light. That was when the harpies screamed. Their high-pitched screeches of bloody murder rang in my ears long after we all wove through an alleyway, into an abandoned seamstress building that led down beneath the ground.

We pooled into a large space beneath the city's outer buildings. On one side of the room was a raised platform, the walls lined with discarded mannequins and cardboard boxes, scavenged out of anything of worth.

Seamus waited as we filed in and longer still for our whispers and jitters to settle.

"Welcome to the Infra." Seamus demanded our attention, and I leaned towards his voice, desperate to pick up every hint in what he had to say. I would take any clue as to how to survive the Envy trial.

Mikhael was truthful when he had said that I shouldn't let Gluttony feast on any more of me. I would miss Ophelia dearly, and her death would manifest a constant hole within my heart. But if I wanted to live, I couldn't keep grieving her so heavily. I had to focus on the one thing I had always managed well: scraping through.

"What's the Infra?" someone asked loudly.

Seamus dipped his chin in acknowledgement. "Invidia's underground. This is the biggest black market in Kaida. It is here that you will stay." Seamus held our attention, and he knew it. "You are not a guest of honour in our Lord Envy's house. You will not stay here as a burden on his coffers and his people. You will register as a visitor to our city and find your own way in this trial."

A heavy silence settled over the room. This was different from the few days with Gluttony prior to the feast, where we had lived in his crumbling home and eaten at his table. We had not been placed below everyone else.

Mikhael shifted at my corner and cleared his throat loud enough to draw the chancellor's attention. He didn't flinch away, as I would have, and lifted his chin.

"What is the trial?" He demanded answers with an ease I envied and given the expressions on the faces of those around us, I wasn't the only one who felt that way.

Seamus offered an indulgent smile in return. "Such impatience. You must do three things before we discuss the trial, and they will take you most of the night." Seamus' expression turned hard, unyielding. "We will discuss the trial in the morning, but for now, you must do as I say. You have not yet finished your previous trial."

"What?!" The gasp flowed not only from my own lips but ripped throughout the crowd of competitors.

Seamus' chuckle was dark and knowing. "You must receive a mark of completion for the Gluttony trial."

He swept his arm forward in a gesture to someone behind him, and from the darkness, Cyn stepped forward. The low light reflected off their smooth tattooed scalp. Irrationally, I felt a bubbling anger at them for Phee's death.

Cyn nodded their head. "As per the rules, you must receive a mark of completion."

Seamus nodded by her side and gestured with his other hand. From the shadows, a third person joined them, a woman older than any I had ever seen. She had dark, wrinkled skin. Her body was gnarled and stooped over, nearly doubled over. Her long, bright, white hair hung in lank, greasy sheets, which was twisted into loose plaits.

"This is Eadlin," Seamus said. "Lord Envy's favoured healer. You will be remedied in order to be at your best for his trial."

Nash leaned against my back, his breath hot against my ear, as he whispered, "It's a crone."

It was an ominous and fitting label for the old woman who seemed to radiate strange power strong enough I felt the instinctive need to stay away. An instinct that would prove hard to follow, as Seamus laid out the path our night would take.

"First, you will see me and register your entry to the city. Secondly, you will visit Cyn and receive a mark of completion. Finally, you will visit with Eadlin and be examined and remedied. You are expected to follow her instructions completely. There is a camp within these tunnels for those who sleep rough. It's here you will find your place to spend the night once you are finished."

He paused to allow time for protest or arguments, but none came. We all stood in tense silence. Cyn and Eadlin disappeared into the darkness again, and Seamus moved to a wooden table.

"Come forward, singularly, and we will register you." He didn't sound particularly happy that his entire night would be spent with us, and as the front of the crowd formed a line, I realised why we wouldn't have time to discuss the upcoming trial that night. The line was moving at a sloth's pace.

The five of us stayed close, pressed midway into the line, and while we didn't talk and joke around like some of the other competitors, we obligatorily took turns poking each other to stop ourselves from falling asleep.

Two to three hours must have passed before Mikhael stepped up to the desk and took his turn to register. Nash went after him before each disappeared into the darkness behind the chancellor. As they left, my palms slickened with sweat. I hadn't wanted them as allies and friends, and I didn't always trust them, but the fear involved in not knowing where they had gone and what would happen to them next crept in.

I didn't have long to think on it, as the chancellor flicked his fingers and beckoned me forward. My feet felt too big and clumsy as I approached the table, threatening to send me stumbling to the floor.

"Who are you?" Seamus asked.

"Octavia Emilia Nox."

"Where do you hail from?"

"Ilrea. It's a settlement out . . ."

"I know where it is, girl." He turned a piece of paper around. The words on it were illegible, and I hoped unimportant. He tapped a finger against a thick line twice. "Sign here."

"Uhh . . ." I glanced over my shoulder. My eyes connected with Niklaus, but he couldn't do anything to help me.

"Sign here," the chancellor repeated with a sigh. "Sign in as competitor of the trial."

I nodded and picked up the strange pen. It felt thick beneath my fingers and dripped ink when I lifted it, which smudged my name in black across the paper and down the side of my hand.

"There." I dropped the pen and hoped I hadn't forfeited my soul a second time. The chancellor nodded and gestured for me to move on. I huffed a sigh and stepped around the table to be swallowed by the darkness like the men and women before me.

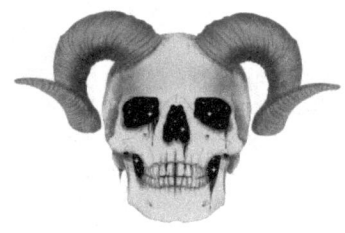

Chapter Five

I found Cyn in a dimly lit room at the end of a winding corridor. The armoured guard stationed at the door didn't let me through until Cyn called for the next participant, and by the time I had entered, Nash was nowhere in sight. Disappointment crested through me, and I realised how badly I had wanted a glimpse of him, just to be sure he was okay.

"Hello, Octavia." Cyn's voice was refreshing, a soft growl compared to the refinement and privilege that had rung in Seamus' tones. "How's the ribs?"

My hand drifted to the tattoo beneath my breast of my lucky dice, and for the first time, I wondered if it was that omen and a symbol of luck, which had kept me alive, and not the devil or fate itself. It would be nice to believe wholeheartedly in such things, and as a result, to believe I would survive the trials.

"They healed All right," I managed to say, shuffling farther into the room. "Considering."

Cyn's lips pursed. Beneath the sway of the overhead lantern, they had tattooed their lips an inky silver colour, striking against the swirling black lines that covered the rest of their body. "Normally, I wouldn't recommend rolling in the dirt for a week after getting my art."

I had shuffled forward enough to see the contents of the table Cyn sat behind. It didn't take a genius to realise I was about to receive another tattoo from the demon-born soul.

"I'll keep that in mind this time." My tone was dry, and the corner of Cyn's mouth twisted as they flicked their decorated fingers at the chair. It scraped against the cold concrete, too loud. We both sat for a moment, in critical evaluation of each other.

"You survived," Cyn growled as they lit a small flame beneath a bowl. I watched the spark dance lazily before the flame took hold. It was a strange blue colour.

"Barely," I admitted.

Cyn glanced up sharply, catching me beneath the weight of their gaze.

"Do you know why I come and speak at the little settlements, like your town?" they asked.

I pressed my lips together and shook my head.

"I visited seven settlements before your town. What was it called? Eshla?"

"Ilrea," I corrected firmly. It was strange to have a sense of pride for home I had never cared for before. Yet, I knew it was where my family would safely outlive me. So, somehow, Ilrea had become a more important place since I'd left it behind.

"Right." Cyn tipped a metallic powder with a violet tinge into the bowl. I scrutinised every movement closely. "Ilrea, then. I go to these towns because you need it more. Villagers come out here with a little more grit and a little more heart."

My nose scrunched. I didn't think I had much heart to give to this competition, and these trials were not after my heart. They wanted my entire soul.

"Would you enter the trials?" I asked Cyn, and their rough growl of a voice rolled into a husky laugh. "If you were human?"

"Devils, no!" Cyn shook their head, and light bounced off their perfectly smooth scalp, the inked design on it glittering. "There is some of all the sins in all of us, but I find there is always a lot of envy."

I stayed silent, as not to pull Cyn from this thought. Instead, I waited for them to continue, knotting my fingers to stop the tremors.

"Those in the villages envy those in the cities; they want the technology, the luxury, and what appears to be an easier life," Cyn said as they tipped a powder in the bowl and stirred it with a metal rod. I couldn't deny the truth of those words, having seen the peace of Glorae and Gula compared to the desperation of home.

"Those in the city Envy the Devil and the favoured and the prestige of Eternis. They are still restricted by the whims and wishes of their lords. Look at Gluttony. Gula is a thriving city, but he is a cannibalistic overlord, and the people still struggle."

My hands jerked as I cringed, the memory of Gluttony feasting on human flesh so vivid it may as well have been happening all over again. I swallowed roughly, my chest tight.

"Why didn't you warn me?"

It was an unfair demand. Cyn owed me nothing, least of all information about what the trial had entailed. Since I had learned what Gluttony intended to do with us, I found a place to lay blame for Ophelia's death and thought she would have been alive if we had known about this risk. Cyn ignored the question. Their dark and cursory gaze swept over me. They didn't ask for Ophelia's name, and I didn't offer it. I was sure she already knew, anyway; the city would have mourned one of their own.

"Anyway," Cyn continued flippantly, "villagers have the grit to do anything to survive. Citizens have very little idea of how comfortable they are. They have not suffered many trials of life before entering the trials of the devil. If I were human, I would be realistic enough to know that I couldn't survive outside of what I know."

That appeared to be the end of the discussion, as Cyn leaned in and blew out the flame.

"Your wrist?" Cyn asked, and I glanced down at my hands. My fingers were still knotted together so tightly my knuckles blanched. With a sigh, I unthreaded them and pushed my cuffed wrist across the table.

Cyn's fingers were cool as they upturned my palms. The pad of their fingers brushed over the skin of my wrist just below the shining cuff.

"Take a deep breath," Cyn instructed and pinned my hand with one of theirs, using their free hand to dip a small instrument into the hot liquid.

I inhaled slowly, muscles tensing with anticipation.

"Exhale," Cyn demanded.

As I exhaled, they pressed the instrument against my skin. It burnt the ink into my flesh, hot enough that a squeal tore from the back of my throat. I tried to pull my hand back, but Cyn held firm. They counted beneath their breath and kept the stamp-like tool pressed against my skin as the first tear leaked from my eye.

As soon as Cyn's grip loosened, I snatched my hand back and cradled it against my chest. I didn't touch the mark but held it tightly to the cuff instead. Still, my skin burnt with the memory of it.

"That wasn't a tattoo," I said, stating the obvious.

"It was a brand." Cyn agreed. "Keep it clean, Octavia. Envy's crone will not return to heal you a second time if you develop infection."

Cyn set their materials down and gestured to a door to their right with a quick nod. I had been effectively dismissed, and I didn't linger.

I had completed the trial of Gluttony.

Outside the second door, alone in the damp hallway, I had gathered enough courage to look at the brand I had received. Just below the tracking cuff, I had a small circle of violet ink branded into my skin, within which lay the symbol of Gluttony: his possessed, feasting little piglet.

For a second, I wanted to touch it, the damaged, inked skin and the flare of red inflammation that radiated out from its edges, but the warning of infection kept me still. Instead, I gulped down deep breaths of the disgustingly stale air and forced myself to continue down the hall until I arrived at the next guard. His lantern swayed light across snake-scale armour. He opened the door without a ward, and I entered the next room to meet the awaiting crone within.

No pleasant conversation flowed through the room. The old woman turned and straightened, her spine popping and crackling in protest. She peered at me from beneath her heavily lined brow, her old eyes assessing every inch of me. The sound of her bones cracking left me dry, retching as my stomach turned. Unwittingly, I glanced over my shoulder at the hall, wondering if I could retreat.

"Bah!" the crone called. "Get in here!"

There wasn't time to second guess, so I hurried forward. The half ajar door bounced closed behind me, and the clicking lock struck fear into my heart. There was nowhere to go, except to face the crone, and the chancellor had demanded we follow her every command.

I felt trapped.

Suspicion lit my veins, and I watched the white-haired woman carefully, keeping a decent distance between us both – not that there was anywhere I could go.

"Are you just Envy in disguise?' I blurted out my paranoid thoughts without pausing to think about the consequences of my words.

The crone watched me for a second that felt like an age before she cackled wildly.

"Me?! His Lord Envy?! Bah! Child, you're a funny one." The old woman shuffled towards me, closing the space between us. "I am Eadlin, twice Devil-cursed, and the best healer that Invidia has seen."

With a statement like that, I wanted to remark that the old woman might have been more at home in Glorae with Pride than in the dark underground of Envy's realm. Surely, it was the Prideful, not the Envious, who considered themselves the best of the best.

"What now, then?" I asked, only to break the silence. Eadlin waved her spindly hand at me.

"Bah! Strip down, girl. I can't assess you like this!" It seemed obvious when she said it, but I still felt the pang of embarrassment at the condescending edge to her tone. I didn't think I was stupid, but more and more often in these trials, it felt like everyone else had concluded I was.

"All right." I nodded and shrugged off my jacket, then the thin shirt, and peeled the warm leather pants over my thighs until I was shivering in the chill of the unheated room. "I'm ready."

I wasn't. That was the first lie I had told in Invidia but not the last.

Eadlin's inspection felt as if it took half a lifetime examining the bumps and bruises scattered across my skin with disapproving clicks of her tongue, punctuating it with sighs. I felt truly judged as she smeared a foul-smelling paste against most of the bruises and left it to soak. Its heady odour crawled up my nose and left me on the precipice of throwing up, but the paste worked well. One by one, she removed the Heira's fingerprints that collared my throat and had been pressing into my jawline; they disappeared from the places where Niklaus had grabbed my arms and pinched my skin.

The crone could do very little for cracked ribs, she informed me, except have me drink a pale orange concoction to numb the lingering pain. Some relief, however, was better than none, so I couldn't complain.

"It'll just last 'til morning," she warned as she cleaned the many cuts on my feet and wrapped them in soaked bandages. " You'll be feeling those ribs for days yet."

"Why are you doing this?" I felt compelled to ask after she instructed me to turn on the chair, my chest pressing on its cold back as she took a strange silver pick and forced every wooden splinter from beneath my skin. The process stung.

Eadlin hummed, and I wondered if she was enjoying the hiss of pain on the edge of each breath as she dislodged another splinter, which was something she had insisted on doing before she could wrap my ribs. It took a long time for her to answer the question, to the point where I thought she hadn't heard me.

"Lord Envy wants you all fighting fit," the old crone admitted, finally, as she reached for her basket and dropped the pick inside. She pulled out a cloth and solution before soaking the rag with it and turned back to me.

"Why? If the aim is to watch us fail, shouldn't we be broken before we start?"

I felt broken, no matter what the woman did in the name of healing me. Pieces of my soul would never come back together after that.

Eadlin rubbed a solution into the small cuts the splinters had left behind, and I hissed. It felt like a punishment for my words. "You think my lord wants you to fail?"

"Gluttony did."

"Envy is not his brother. Do not judge one sin by what you know of another, or you will fail quickly," Eadlin decreed, and I shivered. Her hands were surprisingly soft as she pulled me to sit up and fish a long bandage out of her supplies.

"Lord Envy wants you to triumph or fail on your own full merit. He does not want broken little playthings discarded by his brothers. He wants to see what you can really do and who you really are . . ."

The crone bound my ribs tightly, then tapped me on the shoulder with a short demand to redress quickly because she wasn't the sort of healer that dealt with a common chill.
Time posed too elusive for questions after my clothes were back on. Soft hands turned firm as she pushed me towards the door and exiled me into the night.

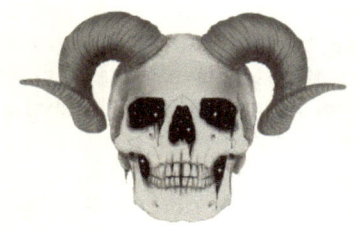

Chapter Six

The camp for those sleeping rough in Invidia wasn't all too different from Ilrea. If I closed my eyes, it was merely a square room with too many mattresses and blankets pushed into the floor and too many bodies tangled within. Just like home. The smell was worse, of course, and the people were suspicious as we entered their place of safety, but it was manageable. It left me with a strange ache in my chest, which made me miss my family more than ever before.

"I miss my bed," Finley grumbled beneath his breath. The simple comment reminded me that he was, as Cyn had called it, "a citizen and not a villager," so unused to the discomforts of struggle. "Plus, it smells."

"Shh," I replied.

Finley pinched his nose as if to make his point. The five of us had regrouped after our visits with the healer and had since picked our way through the mass of bodies to find a space where we would all fit.

"There's too many people here," Mikhael muttered as we huddled in the corner, too close for comfort without blankets and warmth. "It's not safe."

Sighing softly, I dropped to the floor and pulled my jacket tighter around my shoulders. He wasn't wrong, but his words irritated me. We had no place to complain, not when we had chosen to compete in the trials.

"It's no different to Ilrea," I hissed beneath my breath, unwilling to meet his eye as I spoke. The force with which Mikhael turned his head caused his neck to crick loudly. His eyes narrowed on the side of my face, and when I glanced out of the corner of my eye, I realised he was frowning with genuine confusion.

"What do you mean?" Mikhael asked.

After a beat, he seemed to realise how imposing he was, towering over me, his lean body blocking out everyone else. He fell to his knees with a heavy thud.

"I mean, there's plenty of people with nowhere to live at home, either." I lifted my chin stubbornly, jaw set. "I don't see you caring about how safe it is for them to be out in the cold." My eyes flickered past him and settled on his brother, the corner of my mouth dropping. "Especially not when Nik is making a pretty coin on it, too."

Niklaus' throat bobbed tightly. His jaw tightened with obvious displeasure.

"What?" Mikhael asked.

Niklaus clenched his fists at his sides.

Dread trickled down my spine as Mikhael turned towards his brother slowly, and I realised he hadn't known I had accidentally revealed a secret.

"Nik," he said, voice dangerously low. "What's she talking about?"

Tense silence ripped our group.

A muscle thrummed in Niklaus Heira's cheek. "Nothing."

I couldn't help but scoff. Niklaus sent me a look that offered nothing short of death before I said, "Three wrath coppers for a night on a smelly old bus . . . Sound familiar, Nikky?"

It was easier to challenge him than his brother. He had hurt me before. Niklaus was a danger I understood, and a touch of protection lay within his dangerous obsession with me, as if I knew he wasn't done with me yet. At least not nearly enough to destroy me.

"Is that true?" Mikhael asked softly.

Niklaus glared, gaze stony, first at me, then at Mikhael. Behind him, Nash and Finley shuffled away awkwardly, removing themselves from the confrontation. I couldn't blame them.

"Is it true, Nik?" Mikhael repeated and straightened until the two brothers stood nose-to-nose.

Tension radiated from them, enough of it that I huddled a little further into the corner. I wasn't sure which of them would snap first, as Niklaus remained stonily silent, and Mikhael stubbornly waited for his confession. Finally, the tattooed brother shoved his clenched fists into his pockets and jerked his shoulders in a rough shrug.

"Just a side business. People need places to sleep, and I have space to rent out."

"You're fucking kidding me." Mikhael growled. "You're charging homeless people to live in a bus that nobody owns?!"

Niklaus opted to stay silent, and Mikhael's chest puffed out as he crowded his brother, voice dropping to a whisper. "Do you ever actually think—"

Niklaus shoved him to the ground so quickly I didn't have time to prepare myself. Mikhael stumbled back over my feet and slammed against the concrete. The two brothers glared at one another as Mikhael slowly pulled himself upright, both seeming to have forgotten me.

"Stay out of it," Niklaus warned.

"Selfish prick," Mikhael snarled back.

They might have started swinging if Nash hadn't slid between their bodies with a forced too-cheerful laugh. He reached for my hand and forced me to my feet, pulling me between them, too, the last place I wanted to be.

"Settle, lads . . . You've got eyes on you," Nash stated as he pulled on my arm and out of the way of both Heira men. "If you're going to fight, do everyone a favour and go play with the harpies."

Nash wasn't wrong, either. Competitors and Invidians watched on from the dark shadows of the room, awaiting a seemingly inevitable fight. I thought about what the chancellor had said about the black-market trade and shivered. It was likely that was where the stolen organs in Ilrea ended up, and where others came from. That was the last place we needed to spill blood.

"Nash's right." I forced myself to speak up then, threading my arms into my jacket properly. "We're supposed to be a team, remember? We can't let them see us fighting."

Their gazes seemed to prickle against my skin, uncomfortable and too much. The thrumming tick remained in Niklaus' cheek, and there was a vein prominent in his brother's jaw. "Not so identical," as Mikhael had once said. Neither of them relaxed, not really.

I forced out the next words as if it pained me, choking on the sentiment I rarely voiced. "I'm sorry."

Niklaus narrowed his gaze on me, and I fought not to cringe away.

"No. You're not."

Mikhael sighed heavily and backed off, his fingers threading through his hair. It left me with the distinct feeling he was always the first to calm down and give in, the more rational of the two.

"I'm getting some air," Mikhael said, turning stiffly, then marched back through the tangled mess of bodies. His spine was ramrod straight; head held high like nobody had seen the fighting side of him.

Niklaus lingered. The full force of his stare pierced the side of my skull for a moment. He leaned towards me, and I shuffled back into Nash's chest.

"We'll chat later," he said, a threat and a promise. "You're more trouble than you're worth, Octavia Nox, I swear."

He carved a path through the bodies after his brother without another word.

The camp was not an easy place to sleep. The noise died down, but it was never truly quiet, and the air of suspicion never left. A few hundred newcomers with no explanation would have made anyone paranoid. More than a few of them took back to the streets for the night, shuffling away from us with glares and huffed grumbles.

I sat between Finley and Nash, my back against the cold wall, until the chill numbed my hands and feet. I couldn't quite bring myself to sleep, and I wasn't alone in the sentiment, as Finley told tall tales about Cupiditas Eylandt to us to keep us awake.

For hours, I waited for the signs of the Heira twins' return. I wasn't sure why it troubled me so much that they were above ground while we stayed below. Not when, half the time, I would have fed them to the harpies myself. Still, Niklaus wove his way back to the corner and said nothing to us as he kicked another competitor from his way and settled down to sleep, tension melting from my body.

Mikhael came back twenty minutes later, thin-lipped and disapproving in his sweeping headcount of us before he, too, curled up on the cold ground to sleep. It was in the time after that I finally gave in to the fatigue, my chin dipping into my chest as my eyes dropped to a close.

When I woke again, hushed whispers and rustling filled the room. The uncomfortable sensation of being watched skittered across my skin and pulled me abruptly into consciousness. I lifted my head off Finley's shoulder, and he grumbled unintelligibly in his sleep. My eyes darted around the room, catching gazes that turned away, until I caught a man's eyes, who stared back.

A groan caught in my throat as Niklaus held his gaze and jerked his head to the side in a quick, silent demand. The look in his eye told me there was no use in avoiding it, so I quietly slipped from the space between Finley and Nash and climbed to my feet. I moved with deliberate caution, half as not to wake the others but half because the delay, as I stretched my arms above my head, seemed to further agitate Niklaus. I knew I was potentially signing my own death warrant, but I liked getting a rise out of him, especially since he managed to rile me up, too.

Niklaus shifted away from the group, pausing to ensure I was following, and led the way through the twisting corridors. I couldn't match his pace and fell behind, but kept my eyes trained on his shoulders' broad muscles until he came to a halt.

We stood behind a strange tent made of black cotton sheets. A market stall, I realised at second glance, the black market startlingly more literal than I had first thought.

"Pay attention," Niklaus growled.

I'd missed what he had said, and the twisting confusion across my face didn't seem to amuse him. His lips pressed together. Up close, he looked fatigued, more so than I had thought, and it was on the tip of my tongue to jibe about his not coping without a goose-down mattress. The desire to comment faded when he offered me a warning look.

"I know what you're doing," Niklaus said. The tension in his fists, forearms, and shoulders reflected in his voice, causing wariness to roll down my spine.

I shifted. "Do you?"

"Yes." He turned, and I shuffled away, eager to keep the space between us.

"What's that, then?" I asked.

My only plan for the future was to survive, but Niklaus obviously attributed some half-mad scheme to me.

He twisted again, and I realised his own plan too late. The dance of his turning and my twisting left my back pressed against the cold cement pillar, and Niklaus stepped forward to pin me against it. The space between us disappeared.

"No!" I breathed the protest as the weight of his body pressed against mine. I shoved his chest, trying to wriggle out from under him, and he caught my wrists. I winced as his palm pressed to the still-tender Gluttony branding. He pressed against me, his body heat warm against the chill of the night before and the new day to come.

"Get off me!" I demanded.

"Settle down and listen!"

"Get off," I repeated, attempting to kick him.

Niklaus shoved his face close to mine. His lips pulled back in a feral snarl, teeth gritted and bared beside my cheek. His green eyes turned dark with anger, triggering every instinct in my body to obey.

"Stay still."

The fight fled from me, and I slackened against him, the survival instinct driving away all the tension in my body. I could feel the tickle of Niklaus' breath against my cheek, and I squeezed my eyes closed, waiting for his next move.

"You won't drive a wedge between Mik and me," Niklaus spat.

It was so unexpected my eyes snapped open. "What did you say?"

"You heard me," Niklaus growled. "Mik and I are brothers. *Blood*."

He was still too close to me, and spittle landed on my cheek. I went to wipe it away, but he tightened his grip. I grunted at the renewed pain in my wrist.

"I'm not doing anything to you or your brother," I stated. Niklaus' face darkened when it came across like I thought he was stupid.

"It won't work."

"You're causing damage all on your own," I snapped back. "That's what you do, isn't it, Nik? You break *everything*."

He let go so abruptly I sagged against the column; my legs unsupportive in the aftermath of his proximity. I wished my erratic pulse would slow.

"Nothing will get in our way!" Niklaus shouted so vehemently I felt he was assuring himself, not me. "Least of all you. I'll break you, Octavia."

"Is that a threat?"

"A promise, love."

Steadily, I pulled myself to my feet and glanced at the faint redness around the Gluttony branding. Thinking back to the forests of Gula, I knew this could have been a lot worse.

Niklaus paced from side to side, three steps one way before he turned and paced back again. He was a lion in a cage, riled with rage. I considered my chances of escaping when he spun back towards me.

"Don't try and get between us." He hissed a warning. "Or you won't like it when I come to collect what you owe." He stormed across the marketplace, which was slowly coming to life.

I fisted my hands into my hair, tugging on it with a frustrated groan. "I'm not going to like it either way."

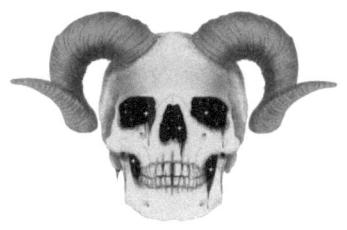

Chapter Seven

Invidia's black markets came alive in the morning's earliest moments. A man peddling human fingernail clippings informed me they did their best business when the gentlest of folk still slept. He also told me that the clippings were best used in curses and indicated I could use one on the man who had pinned me to the pillar, proving witnesses had seen Niklaus Heira's little temper tantrum.

I took my time exploring the market, all too confident in my assumption that the Chancellor of Invidia was a gentleman and that we competitors wouldn't be summoned until the sun had risen higher. Men and women without worries liked to lie in; they weren't called to duty by the lift of the sun.

The market sprawled across a widespread connection of tunnels and rooms, filled with a mixture of boring and insidious wares. Stalls with fresh meat proudly displayed skinned hares and freshly plucked birds, but only a few doors down, I found a butcher of another kind, who lined up jars packed with human organs. I had leaned in to inspect, not entirely sure what I was looking at to begin with, before I realised a jar of blue human eyeballs stared back.

The force of my recoil almost knocked them over. The peddler barely caught the rocking jar, a scowl twisting onto his thick lips as I retreated. My eyes flicked to the other jars and the contents within, morbidly wondering what organs they were. The sickening wonder of whether they had come from someone I knew plagued me. It was better to try not to think on it.

Eager to put distance between myself and the human meat trade, I hurried into the next section of the markets. It, too, contained a strange mix of wares, half of which I might have seen in Ilrea, the rest new to me. It was brightly coloured, inviting in a strange way. I couldn't quite look away. Spices from Gula sat in a stall next to love potions from Cupiditas; nothing seemed to go in order.

A man, a loud, self-proclaimed fortune teller, stood at the corner of an intersection and hollered at passers-by about his ability to see into the future. He was compelling as he spoke of a future of comfort. As his gaze pinged the cuffed wrists of competitors, the story morphed into one of triumph and achievement. The pillars were cold against my back as I watched one of the competitors steal away inside of his tent. I lingered long enough to see when they exited.

The man came out, looking grim enough to make my stomach churn, so I moved on.

Rugs and hand-woven blankets were displayed next to hand-stitched dolls, which the woman at the stall said were for laying curses on those who looked like the doll. I pondered them for a moment and inspected each doll to see if any of them resembled Niklaus. No such luck, although the woman pointed out a doll that looked suspiciously like me.

Behind a crudely built tent, I fished a coin from the heel of my boot, not managing to look at it properly until I had laced my shoe back up. A thin, silver Gluttony piece. A knot formed in my stomach; it was one of the handful I had stolen from Ophelia. I held it so tight I pressed uncomfortably against my palm.

"Thanks for breakfast, Phee," I murmured, as if her soul could hear me, and slipped back into the marketplace.

Over the past hour, the amount of people had doubled.

Amongst the weary faces of those who lived within the underground, people appeared of different casts. Women and men in soft-spun clothing, simple and comfortable, appeared for a variety of wares. People in finer threads carved their way through the crowd, careful not to touch anyone else.

It was a strange mix of souls that dared to slip beneath the city streets, and I found I could have wasted half my morning watching the way they moved. Quietly, I followed a woman through the twist and turns of the marketplace until I found the places boasting food. The smell of it left my mouth watering.

After the Gluttony trial, I thought I would never want to eat again, but after the three-day journey, when I had avoided food, my stomach grumbled with stubborn demand. I had become used to being fed well, and truth be told, I didn't want to starve again in this lifetime.

The truth of Mikhael's words settled heavily within me; dying alongside Ophelia had only given Gluttony more than he deserved. I couldn't go on a hunger strike on her behalf. I would have to eat, as my body demanded it, and I had a feeling I would need it for the upcoming trial.

As it turned out, Invidia's black markets were overpriced in all aspects, and my piece of silver could only buy a bowl of chunky, green vegetable soup and half a piece of a crusty roll. It was mostly stale, but the shopkeeper hadn't even paused for my protests.

A quick dunk of the bread into the soup softened it up, and I devoured it. As much as I might have liked something with sugar, like the candied butterflies of Gula, I couldn't complain, as it settled in my stomach.

Cradling the bowl, I took it with me as I strolled through the marketplace, wanting to see more before having to leave. Only a quarter of the bowl remained when a woman stepped into my path. I didn't notice her until our bodies knocked. The soup tipped from my hands, and the last remnants of soppy squashed peas splashed down her front.

We both gasped. Her hands shot to her mouth as she stepped back, and I fumbled to catch the bowl. It clattered on the stone floor and rolled away.

My fingers stayed outstretched, frozen in time, at the failed attempt to fix it. We both watched as the liquid seeped into her dress' fine fabric; splattered pieces of peas flew across the delicately boned bodice and at the slender hollow of her neck.

"Oh!" The woman fluttered her hands in front of her chest, a seemingly panicked movement, as if she didn't know what to do with them while she digested the situation. "Look what you've done!"

Her arms waved at me, then back at her bodice. With her next jerky movement, her hood fell to her shoulders to reveal her face.

When she shifted to glare at me, I realised she was a strangely fascinating woman. She was as pale as a cloud with delicate, birdlike features, a small nose, and fine lips. Even her hands were small and slender. Her skin looked almost translucent. She had thick eyelashes and brows and long loose curls, all completely white. Colour remained only in the piercing ice blue of her gaze and in the soft way her lips had turned a near similar hue in the cold morning. She was a woman of ice, entrancing me.

"Who are you?" I asked.

"You've ruined my dress!" Her expression turned fierce and sharp. "My favourite dress!"

Even her voice, laced with rage, was soft and lyrical. A shiver worked down my spine. A latent influence in the city that I hadn't noticed pressed against my nerves and senses as I received my first taste of Envy's power. It was not the punch of power that Gluttony had displayed but instead seemed to exist everywhere and applied pressure as needed. It slid against my skin and rubbed the edges of my nerves until a metallic taste burnt in my mouth. I shifted with erratic energy.

I wanted nothing more than to be that woman, to look that beautiful. I wanted someone to look at me with the awe I felt looking at her. I wanted her soft curves instead of the sharp, rough edges that defined me.

My throat constricted. The feeling seemed to possess me from the inside out, and I could think of nothing else beyond my longing to be someone else.

"Are you stupid?!" The woman raised her hand and snapped her fingers in front of my face. "*Hello*! I said what you are going to do about my dress?"

I swayed, my heart pounding, my mind spinning. I was possessed by the erratic thought of attacking her so I wouldn't have to compete and compare. If I raked the jagged edge of my nails across her face, she wouldn't be half as beautiful, would she?

"I . . ." My chest hurt. Stupidly, I asked again. "Who are you?"

Her petite lips twisted into an unhappy scowl, but even with her so angry, I remarked that this colour-leeched girl was not marred. She stepped forward, her pointed nose upturned, when a man swept between us and took her firmly by the arm.

"Margot!" he hissed. He wore black armour, and it gleamed with a snake-scale pattern. A city guard. He shot me a dark look and pulled the woman behind him. "You're supposed to stay unnoticed!"

Her head of white hair pushed around his shoulders, and she pointed a bony finger at me. Directed at my heart, it felt more of a curse than discarded toenail clippings or the strangely sewn dolls ever could have been. "That bitch ruined my dress; I demand a new one!"

The guard said nothing.

Margot turned her face towards the guard, her brows pulled together with a flare of distress. "He cannot see me like this. He'll know!"

Tension built and cracked as the guard nodded. "Come, Margot."

His grip on her arm didn't relent as he twisted and pulled the woman away. It was foolish to follow them, but that was exactly what I did. The discomfort beneath my skin mixed with the wonder at her appearance left me intent to see where Margot went next, determined to know more about the woman I wanted to be.

Deep within the twists of the paths, I lost them. I came to a halt at a junction, with the fortune teller on one side of me and a man selling dried chicken feet on the other. It was there I stayed until the strange feeling faded from my belly, and my heartbeat returned to a normal pace.

When I came to my senses, I no longer wanted to be Margot. Although, I couldn't quite get her out of my mind, nor did the prickling sensation of Envy ever completely leave.

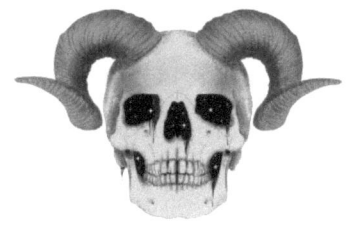

Chapter Eight

By mid-afternoon, we had all been summoned back into the large room that led out to the city. The Chancellor of Invidia stood on the raised platform and stared as we filtered inside. We neither looked well rested nor excited to be there. A new challenge loomed before us, and while I didn't know how anyone else felt, my stomach churned like a cage of thrashing serpents.

Inside the room, I set about finding familiar faces. Nash was easy to spot in the crowd, and I picked my way through the mass of bodies to his side. Finley rocked forward on his heels to look at me as I arrived.

"Seen the twins?"

I shook my head and shrugged. *Niklaus and Mikhael are not my problem*, I reminded myself. "They'll turn up."

Finley's thick brows knitted together. "They better. We need to stick together and be ready."

My eyes dropped to my boots, but I nodded in agreement. After that morning, I wasn't sure if having the Heira twins on my team would be a blessing or a curse.

"What do you think it'll be, then?" I asked.

It was a pointless question. If they had learned anything throughout the morning, I was sure Nash, at least, would have told me. Both men shrugged, and I huffed out a sigh. The cards introduced us to each challenge, but I thought they were not so much a clue but a way to raise our anxiety.

I felt the Heira brothers' solid presence behind me a moment later. Niklaus, as always, stood too close, and I couldn't have swayed on my feet without hitting his chest. Finley turned away quickly and began chatting, the tension of the night before entirely forgotten, but I kept my eyes on the chancellor. There was no point in riling up Niklaus again.

The chancellor, Seamus, stood tall and proud. A night of sleep had done a world of good for the dark circles beneath his eyes.

He wore a similar outfit to the guards, fitted leather breeches and a long, loose white shirt. The sleeveless tunic he wore over it appeared to be strange black metal. Tiny pieces overlapped into scales. It was belted around the middle and knotted with Envy's symbol, a coiled black and green snake, fangs bared to attack.

Chancellor Seamus cleared his throat, and all conversations died. The snake at his waist lifted my attention to his face, his cheeks red, his silver-streaked bushy beard smooth as if he had combed it.

"Welcome, competitors!" Seamus' voice carried. "To your trial of Envy. Our lord has decided that you will indulge in one of his favourite games: the Heist of Haures."

I bounced onto my toes, eager to know what the actual game was, and when my boots tapped back down onto the ground one, two, three times, Niklaus grabbed my shoulders, holding me in place.

Seamus reached past the collar of his tunic and withdrew a small, perfectly round, polished stone thread onto a leather strap. It glowed beneath his fingertips, and my breath caught in my throat at the sight of it.

The stone seemed to shift and move as if thick liquid green fire had been contained within and fought to escape.

"This is akelda," Seamus announced.

My tongue darted across my lips, and I subconsciously tried to move forward, despite the way Niklaus held me in place. I wanted a piece of this stone. Just the sight of it lit a fire in my veins; it looked valuable. More valuable than the fat diamond that glinted in Charon's ear or the pearls that the Chancellor of Ilrea's wife had worn.

"This" – Seamus twisted the gem between his forefinger and thumb, the light dancing off the flames – "is a piece of the Old World. A place where angels and demons lived in constant battle. Before our lord was dragged to the confines of our earth, he had the foresight to bring fragments of his home with him."

Seamus snapped the leather from his neck and held the akelda up. "Lord Envy keeps his treasures close, but when his citizens earn a place of prestige, they earn a piece of his home, a piece of a world beyond ours."

The smugness in his tone, as Seamus held a piece of another world, could not be mistaken for anything else. When I finally glanced up, I realised Seamus' entire face was bright. This piece of akelda elevated him above others, and they would be envious of his place in the world. Just as I felt the discomforting trickle of envy that he had a piece of akelda, and I didn't.

Seamus flashed a grin full of white teeth. "No other city possesses the akelda!"

The crowd seemed to have pulled in tighter as competitors moved closer to the stage. The Heira twins crowded at my back, pushing me forward with them. The uncomfortable feeling that had lingered beneath my skin since my encounter with Margot intensified, and a trickle of hot desire started at my scalp and rolled down my spine. I wanted that akelda more than I had wanted anything in my life, more than I wanted to win the Devil's Trials.

"The aim of the game is simple." An element of teasing seeped into Seamus' voice. He was encouraging the restless feeling and the uncomfortable need. "You must acquire a piece of akelda for yourself. You must each present a piece to trade back to Envy as he judges your nature and worth in order to win the trial."

I found myself nodding. My heart rate picked up as I realised what I wanted was what I had been needing as well. A false confidence pulsed through me. Niklaus had been right that I was a thief at heart and how different it could be to steal here than at home.

"Invidia's elite each possess their own pieces of akelda, and these are your targets – unless you are brave enough to take on the Angel of Envy yourself to get a piece directly." The way his grin widened and curled up at the corners projected his belief that none of us would survive that tactic. He wasn't wrong; the intense desire I had to possess the akelda cooled at the idea of facing Envy's attempt to obtain it.

"This is the first piece to come into play," Seamus shouted.

In a startlingly fast move, he flung the green gem at the crowd. A feral growl rose from amongst us as men and women rushed for it, and we were all crushed together in a wave of desperation, looking to obtain the first piece and win the trial before we had even begun.

The akelda disappeared into the thicket of bodies to the left of me, and the sound flesh and bone colliding rang out as a fight started.

To my surprise, it was Mikhael, not Niklaus, who dove into the thick of the fight. Those of us without the gall to exchange blows backed away, and I shrank behind Niklaus. He waited with his arms folded tight across his chest for his brother to return.

When the chaos calmed, a woman lay on the ground unconscious, blood smeared across her temple. Mikhael Heira stalked back to us, his face a blank mask of cold fury, jaw clenched tight, his split knuckles anchored by his sides. He did not show us a piece of the prize.

Calming took time as energy thrummed across the crowd; half frenzied by this twist. Seamus was patient as he waited for us to settle. When the tension smoothed out, I found my place by Nash's side again and reached for this hand. My fingers twisted around his, interlocked and waiting. My brain raced with the possibilities of how this game would play out.

We would have to stalk and steal from the privileged without getting killed or caught. It would be difficult.

Seamus cleared his throat. "Heist of Haures is a game best played in teams, and we have allocated these on your behalf."

My stomach turned to stone and sunk to my boots as dread pooled through my body. My eyes flickered to Nash. He was looking back at me, his mouth pulled down at the edges.

"No?" I said.

He jerked his head towards the chancellor, who had retrieved a piece of yellowed paper and begun reading out names in groups of five. Sweat seeped out of my palms. I wiped them against my jacket as I tried to gather my wits and listened for my name.

"Finley Nightingale."

My head snapped towards Finley; lips parted on a sharp inhale as the curly haired man nodded.

"Narelle Gardener, Aidon Reid, Billie Cowan, and Nash Wickham."

Finley and Nash were together, but I couldn't help the wave of disappointment and mounting panic that crested through me that we were separating. I had just become their opponent in this trial. Nash and Finley whispered to one another, and the five of them shifted to the space before the chancellor before they were directed from the room.

On his way out, Nash glanced over his shoulder and mouthed a soft goodbye. My hand half lifted in a wave, but he was gone too soon.

"Niklaus Heira," Seamus called next. I cringed to the side and out of his way, expecting Mikhael to need to move next. "Hollie Vale, Adam Leeds, Helina Archer, and Oskar Wallace."

The dread in my stomach turned heavy as I watched Helina pick her way through the crowd. She didn't aim for the door but for Niklaus. She caught up to him and grasped his bicep as she glanced over her shoulder. Helina looked right at me, the corner of her mouth quirking up. A misplaced possessiveness flushed through me, hot as a fire. It shouldn't have mattered they were on a team together and I was not. It shouldn't have mattered that she was so close to him, but it did.

In a fidgeting movement, I tucked my short hair behind each ear to keep it from my face. The next five names were called, five people who seemed to know each other, who cheered before disappearing. As more teams were called, the crowd thinned out, and my nerves grew. My eyes kept sliding towards Mikhael, the only of our intended group left, but he didn't catch my eye; his entire body coiled with tension, his troubles splayed across his face. I wondered if it was still because he had failed to get the akelda or because he had been separated from his brother.

On and on, Seamus droned, and we stood in silence, tense and waiting to hear our fates.

"Mikhael Heira."

We both startled, and he caught my gaze. Green eyes studied me as we listened for his group.

"Tristan Timbrell, Mark Meritt, Kale Nihil –"

I quickly muttered soft prayers to Samael for my name to be called and to be given a spot-on Mikhael's team for the safety of knowing just one person I could trust in this trial, but he didn't respond, no reassurance to soothe my fears. The disappointment of the silent devil worse than the feeling of loneliness that threatened to overcome me.

"Damien Voult and Kristoff Linell."

Mikhael didn't leave straight away. He turned to look at me, his penetrating green gaze shooting to me. I had a distinct feeling I was being judged. His lips parted softly, words on the tip of his tongue but then he shook his head.

"Bye," I said glumly.

He nodded tersely before following the rest of his team. When he glanced back at me from the middle of the room, the look in his eye left me nervous. I felt as though Mikhael Heira had already decided I would be dead before he saw me again.

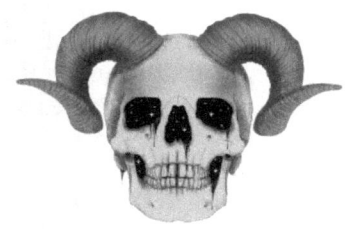

Chapter Nine

My name was one of the last called, with only ten competitors left. Five more names were called, and we were left in the quiet. Five of us, the chancellor, and his men. Seamus grinned down from the platform.

"Finally," – he looked relieved to be finished – "we have Benton Rumley, Octavia Nox, Kyra and Aureen Willett, and Monika Oster."

From the corner of my eye, I studied each of them. I couldn't judge whether I could trust them, so the safe bet was to trust nobody.

Benton Rumley was a solid man with a ruddy complexion. His eyes seemed too close together, his face, chest, waist, and hands all solid. He had thick red-brown hair, but his hairline was receding. His was beard wild and untamed, and he stroked it whenever he was thinking. It was his eyes, though, that gave me the shivers. Too dark, too black, too beady – they left me with the distinct feeling of nastiness in the way he looked back at me.

Aureen and Kyra Willett were, without a doubt, related. They had the burnished skin of Cupiditans, the same flattened nose and almond-shaped eyes. Aureen seemed to be older, more matured around the eyes and lips. Where she wore her long brown hair in a ponytail that swung with each step, Kyra had tamed and twisted hers into two plaits that hung over her shoulders, woven with golden wire. The younger of the two stood a step behind her sister, constantly glancing at Aureen for cues about what to do next.

Monika Oster reminded me of a rat. She had a face so gaunt that not even the spoils of the Gluttony trial had filled it out. Her skin was sickly, covered in irritated red spots that she picked at. Her limp, dark hair was knotted at the nape of her neck. She sniffled heavily and rubbed her nose with the back of her hand.

One moment, she was across the room, and the next, she stood beside my elbow, so quiet in her movements I hadn't realised it until she was there. It left me nervous. I folded my arms across my chest, hands jammed into my armpits as I looked around. I didn't like my chances with them. "I guess we're a team."

"Guess so." Monika had a reedy voice.

"Who are each of you?" Benton Rumley stabbed his thumb against his chest. "I'm Rumley!"

Seamus and his crew had left as the rest of us mumbled out our names and origins in awkward introduction. We stared at each other in suspicious silence, and I considered whether the teams of five were a recommendation rather than a requirement, not that I thought I had the skills to survive the trial alone.

"What now?" Aureen asked. Her tone matched the harsh, tense edge to her expression.

"Now, we plan a heist . . ." Monika muttered. "Obviously."

Aureen rolled her eyes. Her spine stiff with derision. "And you're the expert at that, then?"

"I'm good at gathering information!" Monika's voice had turned high and defensive. "People don't notice me much!"

Kyra stepped forward and placed a hand on her sister's arm, cutting off any terse retort. An awkward and unsure silence loomed again before Benton started laughing, a noise that rolled from deep in his chest, leaving his padded belly wobbling.

"Look at the lot of you." He wheezed. "Dumb as a box of rocks."

I frowned, confused. "What's wrong with us?"

Rumley laughed. "Well, you're never gonna make it."

"We . . ." Aureen said. Rumley grinned widely. "We're a team."

"Not me!" Rumley shook his head adamantly and reached into his pocket.

He flashed us a look at the desired piece of akelda. It was only then I noticed the red split skin at his knuckles and that some of the redness in his face was inflammation that would blacken with blood beneath the skin in time. He had been in the thick of the fight for the chancellor's first piece, and evidently, Rumley had won.

"Not me!" he crowed again and pocketed the stone before we could. "I've already won. Getting those stones sounds like your problem, not mine."

He turned his back on us and sauntered towards the door.

"W-wait!" Kyra called.

Rumley didn't slow. Instead, he flicked her a two-fingered salute off his forehead and strolled right out the door.

Tense silence filled the room in his absence. Nobody moved.

"Have you guys ever stolen anything before?" I asked.

Kyra hesitated. "Does a hair tie count?"

Aureen scoffed. "No, Ky, that doesn't count."

Monika rocked on her feet and shrugged. "Some stuff . . ."

"Like what?" Aureen pressed, and the rat-like woman shrugged again, unwilling to answer. We held our secrets close to our chests.

"I've stolen some coin, but never anything this big," I admitted.

Aureen stepped in the place of the leader. She straightened and tipped her chin up as she inspected each of us. "We start with a plan."

"Okay. A plan is better than nothing . . ." I agreed.

I wasn't sure if Aureen's leadership was the best thing for our group of misfits, but in the absence of people I knew and trusted, I had to have a little faith. Kyra twisted on the spot and took a seat on the platform Seamus had abandoned. She folded her long legs beneath her body and smoothed out the soft material of her shirt before beckoning us over. After a second of hesitation, I joined her, perching on the side of the platform, half poised to run. Monika crawled up beside me before drawing her knees to her chest. Aureen stood in front of us with her arms still folded.

"We need four pieces of akelda, so that's four targets," Kyra reiterated.

I nodded. "Do you think the families get more than one?" I sat straighter. I could imagine that, once they had a fragment of Envy's world, they would want more. That was how it felt when you won at cards. A small windfall needed to be doubled; the rush could only get higher. "We could rob one good group of a stash of four. Instead of having to, you know, do it over and over."

Aureen frowned. "I don't know."

Monika shrugged. "We don't know much of nothing, really. We don't even know where we are."

It was a good point. Invidia had looked enormous from a distance, and I hadn't seen much the night before we were led underground.

"So, we should map out the city first? Explore it all and work out where our targets would even live."

"We could do that this afternoon," Aureen stated, and Monika made a noise in the back of her throat, turning the full force of Aureen's gaze in her direction as she frowned. "Do you have something better to do?"

"No!" Monika was quick to protest. "It's only . . . that's what everyone is going to be doing, isn't it?" A lock of dark hair had fallen out of her bun, and Monika twisted it into a knot. "Everyone's going to be racing to an idea of what to do."

"Except Benton," Kyra muttered.

"We only have a month," I pointed out. If we had to plan and execute four separate thefts, then a month seemed like an impossible timeline.

"I know." Monika sniffed. "I'm just saying, two hundred of us flood the streets and people are going to get weary." She paused; her eyes flickered to Aureen nervously. "We should go at night, when everyone else comes back underground."

My breath caught in my chest and a thrill I had long since identified as fear. I locked my fingers together so that nobody else would see them trembling.

"At night?" I repeated. "With the screaming harpies and who knows what else?"

Aureen's face scrunched up with distaste. Her full lips dropped at one corner. When she inhaled sharply, I knew she was about to shut the idea down.

Monika beat her to speaking. "Yeah, when they don't expect us. We'll get better information that way."

Aureen's jaw closed with an audible snap. "Monika?" she asked, her tone sharp. Monika shrank back from it.

"Yes?"

"Have you ever seen a harpy?"

Monika's throat bobbed. "No."

"Right." Aureen leaned in. "Never seen one, never faced a harpy. Have you heard stories about them?"

Monika had gone pale beneath Aureen's scrutiny.

"No," she repeated in a soft whisper.

Aureen's full lips twisted into a wicked smile, sardonic and almost cruel, before she flicked her fingers in the direction of her sister. "Kyra tells it best."

An expectant silence fell over our group, and I watched the youngest of us all frown at the way she had been dragged into this mess.

"Harpies are Devil-cursed women," Kyra explained softly. "Barren, loveless creatures at maturity. When they hit puberty, they turn from girls into something more twisted. Their screams begin the night that wings tear from their backs, and they never stop shrieking in the night since . . ."

"Wings like the angels?" I asked, thinking of the Angel of Pride's glossy wings and the way we had spun in the air.

"No," Aureen retorted. Kyra shot her a look. "They're bony, leathery, sharp."

With every passing moment, I wanted less and less to go out into the darkness of the night with harpies circling above us.

"Anyway," Kyra continued sharply, "they have long, blackened nails, sharp claws, and profound eyesight. They nest in small groups, covens we call them, near Cupiditas. There are crops of them in the mountains of the mainland. Our village sits in the valley of their hunting grounds . . ."

Kyra looked glum. I realised her experience with harpies was not just a story told before bed but personal. The harpies had hunted people in her life. The way she described them was different to the way Mikhael had on our walk to Glorae, but I didn't know who was right.

Kyra cleared her throat softly, swallowing her emotion, and continued. "Harpies hunt in the dawn and the dusk. They eat only meat, animals, human . . . whatever they can find. They won't spare anyone, and they don't make death slow."

Monika gasped softly. "Oh."

Kyra looked up with wide, haunted eyes. "The only thing worse than the soul-chilling scream of the harpies are the screams of the people they're tearing apart."

I knew then that I wouldn't be entering the city at night if I could help it and that my imagination mixed with the Willett sisters' reality had put a new nightmare in my arsenal.

"Why are they here, then?" I asked. "If they're from out near your village?"

Kyra sighed. "Nerish."

"What?" I asked, confused.

"Nerish." Her head tilted to the side. "It's the name of the village we're from. It's a day west of the port to enter Cupiditas."

It was useless information that didn't answer the question, but it meant enough to Kyra that I made note of it. She glanced sideways at her sister for some level of guidance.

Aureen nodded. "They're loveless, so they haunt Cupiditian lands in search of it. I bet they're here" – Aureen waved her hand towards the roof in a vague indication of the city above us – "because I don't think there's a more envious demon on our earth than a harpy. Seems like a natural progression, don't you think?"

Neither Monika nor I answered, not when her tone showed that Aureen Willett thought that we were stupid.

"We still need to get a look at the city." Monika was brave enough to turn the conversation back to more important topics than folktales and Devil-cursed women. "Quickly."

I sunk my teeth into my lower lip. The need to act quickly leaned us toward using nights as well as the daylight hours, but the thought of walking through the streets as a potential harpy snack sounded like the worst of my options.

"Well –" I cleared my throat.

"We'll meet here tomorrow," Aureen declared. "Right here. Just after the dinner market starts!" Her heavy ponytail swung as she jerked her head in the vague direction of the Infra markets. "We come back here with every bit of information we can find to plan where we go next."

A shiver of upset curled down my spine at Aureen's interruption.

She paused long enough for us to protest the plan.

I had nothing to say and glanced away.

Aureen turned the full focus of her intense gaze on Monika. "That way." She stepped around me and closed in on Monika. It was designed to intimidate, and I shuffled away, wanting no part in it. "If you want to go play with the harpies in the dead of the night, you can, but my sister and me, we'll be using the daylight, and we'll come back with better information than you."

She laid out the explicit challenge, and Monika looked half ready to faint. If she hadn't gone out at night, or if those excursions into the deadly darkness weren't as fruitful as she had claimed, she would lose face. It was an uncomfortable position to be in.

It may not have been a big deal, but as the trust between us had barely formed, the last thing any of us needed was the others thinking we were weak.

I didn't wait to hear Monika's response as I turned towards the doorway. I sank my fingers into my jacket pocket and wrapped them around the folded piece of card that detailed this insane challenge.

There was no way I wanted to be out in the dark, and Monika's preoccupation with that risk wasn't my concern, but I didn't know I wanted to be out in this city alone at all.

"Tomorrow," I called back as I reached the exit. "Right here. As dinner starts."

"That's what I said," Aureen sniped.

I strode through the exit and chalked up my fear to ridiculousness. I would survive this city just fine.

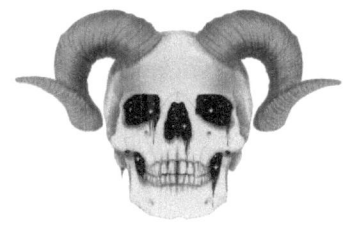

Chapter Ten

Dusk fell within the hour after I had found my way out in Invidia. Rich hues of pink and orange dragged across a cloudless sky. Quietly, I hoped Nash was seeing it, too. With the falling of the sun came the start of a bone-chilling scream.

It was enough to send me fleeing back to the Infra and below ground. The streets had gone deathly quiet by the time I found the abandoned seamstress' shop that marked the entrance. Newspaper covered the windows, but pieces had flaked away, the mannequins behind holes in the newspaper draped in tight dresses with flowing skirts. The cloth looked aged and forgotten, dusty enough to show a place long since forgotten for its wares and more known the world it hid beneath creaky floors.

It reminded me of the store filled with wood in a city of only metal and glass, unused except as a pathway to modifications and transport. I wondered what else in Invidia had been forgotten and if those things might not be my path to winning.

The aroma of roasting meat led me into the market. As I found my way to the makeshift eatery, Monika brushed past me, heading in the opposite direction.

"Good luck!" I called impulsively.

She turned and pushed a lock of dark hair out of her eyes. "Thank you."

An unsettling curiosity fluttered in my stomach about whether she would come back, but I didn't give myself a lot of time to stress about it.

The eatery was a different place again; humans from all castes crowded long tables with bench chairs and chattering. The subtle influences of the city's benefactor were only evident in the sidelong glances given.

I exchanged four copper pieces for a half stale roll filled with salted meat and some limp green leaves. I picked out the greens and dropped them as I searched the crowd for familiar company.

Nash was seated on top of one of the tables, eyes narrowed as he scanned the crowd, and he kicked over the chair to stop anyone stealing it. Finley sat next to him, wholly invested in his food.

I lifted my free hand. "Nash!"

His head turned, his narrowed gaze pinning me, so intense I faltered. It took a moment to find my breath and my confidence to move to his side. My boot landed firmly beside his on the chair, twisting as I planted myself beside him. Nash shuffled over.

"Did you eat?" I asked before I tore into the salty sandwich and bit down.

Nash shrugged. "Not really hungry."

I paused, holding out the roll. "Want some?"

"Said I wasn't hungry, Octavia."

It was on the tip of my tongue to remind him that he hadn't disagreed with Mikhael on the train about not letting Gluttony feast on our souls. My throat tightened as I leaned into the urge to avoid conflict. Nothing good ever came of it. We sat in silence for a moment, Nash surveying the crowd, his shoulders tense.

It was his tense stance, and the loss of the easy conversation between us that pushed me to the breaking point. I twisted and reached for him. My fingers clasped his wrist, and I tugged before slapping the rest of the bread roll into his hand.

"You have to keep going . . ." I stated firmly. "Don't let Gluttony feast on you, remember?"

The chair rocked as I stepped down and spun to face him. His face was scrunched, as if in pain, jaw tight and eyes ping-ponging between me and the food.

"Tav." Nash said my name as a gentle warning. He abandoned the food and followed me.

He grabbed me suddenly, arms wound around my shoulders, tight against his chest in a crushing hug.

"Tav," he repeated in a whisper, his cheek pressed against mine, his lips buried in my hair. "We can't spend time together."

"What?"

His breath tickled my ear. "We're on opposite teams now, Octavia. We're basically enemies."

My throat tightened. "Nash."

I struggled against his grip, but he held me tight. "My team has decided we're not helping anyone but each other. We're sticking together and doing whatever it takes. If you're hanging around, then you're in the way."

The implied threat lingered between us; dread pooled in my stomach.

"We're just having dinner, Nash."

"Stay away, Octavia," he repeated firmly. "I mean it."

"No!"

"Stay safe," he said, letting go. I jerked back. Nash's lips brushed across my forehead. "I'll see you at the finish line."

Nash pushed so firmly I stumbled a step. He leaned against the table and picked up my sandwich. His chin dipped before his teeth sunk into it. My fingers twitched with the urge to fight back, but a lump of defeat bloomed in my throat. Instead, I turned and fled.

I'd run past four tables before someone snagged my arm, wrenching me to the side. Too preoccupied to be on my guard, I went flailing and pitched in the direction of my attacker.

Helina's too familiar laugh rattled in my skull as my knees slammed into the ground. The cement scraped against my trousers and tore at my skin as I floundered to catch myself.

"Come to play, love?" Niklaus Heira purred.

I lifted my head from where I had fallen between his thighs and scowled as I pushed a lock of dark hair from my face. I lifted my hands from his thighs and wiped them on my shirt like he disgusted me.

"I'd rather die."

"Could be arranged," Helina piped up, laughing.

Something about it set my teeth on edge.

Niklaus shifted in his seat, leaning forward until I flinched back. His fingers brushed the curve of my jaw.

"Don't!" I snapped.

He didn't listen, still dragging his fingers across my skin. "I like you down there."

My face flushed red at the implication. I knew exactly how it looked. I forced myself to wipe the scowl of disgust away and moved into his space. I pushed myself onto my sore knees and pressed my palms against his thick thighs again.

Niklaus settled back. A smirk pulled at the corner of his lips as I tilted my chin up and held his gaze. A sigh slipped from my lips, and some of the tension rolled from my shoulders. His eyes darkened with anticipation as I slid my hands a fraction further up his legs.

"Nik," I murmured.

"Yes, Octavia?"

His smirk grew wider. He enjoyed taunting me, making me squirm. Niklaus reached out, and I fought a shudder as he smoothed his fingers over my hair.

"I would rather offer my eyeballs to Gluttony for brunch than spend time between your legs."

Silence fell around the table, lingered for a few beats, then he burst out laughing. I used my leverage on his thighs to push myself to my feet. When I staggered backwards, I landed against another body and instantly flinched away.

The man I'd hit stood three inches taller than me. He had a young face. He had to have been at least twenty but looked no older than fourteen. He had a rounded, cherub face and too-bright eyes. Messy brown hair fell over his eyes. His innocence reminded me of Phee, and that instantly soured my mood further.

"Who are you?" I snapped, suddenly alert. "Why are you touching me?"

My fingers curled into my fists, and despite myself, I edged closer to him. He was only one of them I could intimidate, the one moment where I could retain power.

Niklaus and Helina had stopped laughing. The silence damning. The chair scraped as Helina stood and leaned across the table, her plate clattering to the side.

"That's Oskar," Helina growled. The boy had paled. Niklaus shifted too close, his arms curling around my middle as Helina continued. "You don't touch Oskar."

Niklaus wrenched me off my feet and to the side. I stumbled when I hit the ground again, thrown off kilter.

"I wasn't going to touch him!" I protested.

Niklaus scoffed with disbelief.

Oskar glanced between us all but stayed quiet. His cheeks had gone pale and slightly green. Niklaus twisted towards me, and in assured, leisurely movements, he shuffled me back and away from them.

He had grown tired of playing with me, and instead had turned protective of his group. "Oskar's with us," he stated. "He's not part of your little game with me, and he's not a target for your group of gutter rats."

"I didn't . . ." The lie died on my tongue.

"Touch him" – he grinned, feral and bloodthirsty, a look I knew too well – "and I'll let Helina tear you apart."

He had crowded me towards the edge of the eatery. I couldn't see his table or his team behind him. He had herded me out of their social epicentre, where he had unceremoniously abandoned me.

My weight shifted from one foot to the other as I watched him go and took in Niklaus and Helina with their new baby-faced competitor to protect. In the distance, I could see Nash and Finley at their table; the blonde had relaxed, laughing.

Kyra and Aureen sat with a group of Cupiditan women. They didn't even notice me, completely unapproachable.

It felt as if the world was closing in on me, the air weighing down. Despite the amount of people in the marketplace, I had never felt so alone. My best friend didn't consider me worthy and stood with the man who loved to torment me. Nash had left me behind for his new team, and while it wasn't our choice, I felt betrayed.

As I scanned the room in a last-ditch attempt to find a place that I belonged, I caught a different green-eyed gaze. Mikhael stared at me. His face was void of all emotion. I considered stepping forward when his eyes narrowed, his expression cold. My heart seemed to clench tight and painful.

It was very clear that, in that moment, I was completely and utterly alone.

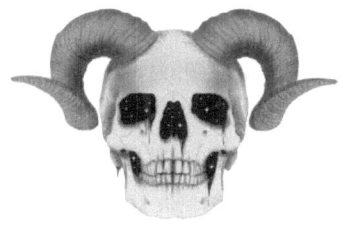

Chapter Eleven

Overnight, three people were murdered.

Screams of terror and pain echoed through the underground's twisted halls, and the silence that followed pounded in my ears, louder than their pain. I had barely slept, always jolting into consciousness with the fear that it would be my turn next.

As I fled the room of snoozing people, chilled from the temperature and the experience, I tripped over one of the dead bodies. I landed on top of her, her body stiff beneath me. A woman with a hole in her head. Her blonde hair matted with crimson. Horror tasted bitter at the back of my throat as I scrambled off her, and I willed myself not to cry. Her lifeless gaze penetrated me.

She was unfamiliar, and when my heart stopped racing, I crouched to search through her pockets. I found one silver coin and a metal hairpin. As I straightened, I twisted the dark locks of hair that framed the sides of my face around each other and secured them with the metal pin; it would be easier to hide if it looked as if it had always been mine.

By the time I left the tunnels, I had forgotten how her face looked.

Above ground, the last vestiges of early morning fog rolled around my ankles. It was late enough in the morning that the threat of the harpies had faded, and the first Invidians had risen for the day. The streets were quiet, the path still wet beneath my boots from the early morning rain. The air was thick with the threat of more showers, the crisp edge leaving me feeling alive. It was a world away from the stale, bloody underground.

After carefully noting how the seamstress' shop looked in the low light – in hopes that I could find my way back to it later – I took to the streets. My first point was to head out to the city's entrance. At the end of the path, I stared at the iron snakes that guarded Invidia and the rotted skulls mounted between their fangs. It was a miserable place to end up but an effective message.

I shivered, turning away. Instead, I stared back out at the city unfolding in front of me and walked the path into Invidia.

The outer buildings were a mix of size and height. They looked worn out and too close together, as if someone had been packing in more rooms as the population grew. Thin, crooked alleyways curled between the buildings, and garbage piled high permeated the outer parts of the city with a rotten stench.

Excitement curled in my belly as I explored, slipping through the alleyways and studying the buildings. The morning wore on as I wove out to the edge of the city, then back in towards the main street. As time slipped away, my stomach roared. I ignored it to explore further until I realised the city's overcrowded outskirts were villages crammed together. The people filling them weren't special, privileged, or any use at all. There were no treasures amongst Invidia's poor; they weren't blessed by Envy, just hungry, tired, and hardworking. Still, they seemed content in the way they filtered into the streets and went about their day. Content in a way I never had been in Ilrea.

Back on the curving main streets, I followed a girl in a maid uniform as she tied the apron around her middle. She led me down the street, unaware she had hooked my curiosity. The Heira family was the only family I'd known who could afford to employ the service of others to clean their home, but it was different in Invidia. Many girls from the outer district appeared in plain brown dresses and aprons cinching their waists. Their hair was taut, tucked under caps, erasing any sense of uniqueness.

They walked in groups of two and three, chattering brightly. As we moved deeper into Invidia, the buildings were spread farther apart, less crowded. We moved through an entertainment district with silhouettes of dancing women in the windows and pictures of drinks on their signs. It gave way to an idyllic marketplace, bright and open, compared to the Infra, with little shops peppered down the street.

As the maid paused, so did I. She had turned to talk to a friend, and I fished the silver coin from my pocket, buying a pastry with a sweet filling. The shopkeeper's eyes narrowed on me, and I lost my taste for conversation, stuffing the entire thing in my mouth. It didn't quite fit, and I struggled to chew it to a more manageable mouthful. It was nice, though, with its sugar melting across my tongue.

As I licked powdered sugar off my fingers, the maid disappeared. My heart raced at the abrupt loss, and I stumbled down the street in search of her plain cap. I found her in the next part of the city, as businesses gave way to homes.

Rather than rising high, people stacked on one another. The homes sprawled outwards on land. Fences separated them, protecting green grass and pretty flowerbeds.

Where the city's outskirts had been filled to the brim with families, these seemed calmer, with space to spare. As we walked, I could catch a glimpse of Invidians through an uncovered window or an open door.

The maid came to a stop, and I forced myself to walk past them casually. They didn't even notice. The girls hugged and disappeared in opposite directions.

With my fingertips, I brushed the fence's iron panels around one of the properties and nodded to the snake in the décor. Snakes were rampant in Invidia, an ominous warning. I lingered too long, watching the house, wondering what it would be like to live in the quiet and the calm. My gaze caught a woman in the window. Her head turned to look back over her shoulder. I was so focused on her apparent peace, swallowing past the lump in my throat that I didn't notice the man in scaled armour who marched along the fence line between properties.

"What do you want?" he barked.

I let go of the fence as if I had scorched my fingers.

"Nothing."

His face twisted in a scowl. "Little liar."

The guard took the hilt of his thin sword and tapped it against the fence's bars. It clanged, intrusive in the quiet morning. It attracted the woman in the window's attention, who then looked down at me, pale eyes wide and fluttering with an emotion I knew all too well. Fear.

She shut the window quickly, a barrier between us.

His sword smacked the iron bars again.

I flinched away. "I'm going! Okay? I'm leaving!" I stumbled backwards, noticing other guards had shuffled onto the street, the rising sun glinting off their snake-scale armour. Their faces were twisted with obvious disgust.

"Poisonous little trial rat!"

One of them spat through the fence at my feet.

"Piss off! You don't belong here."

I wanted to scream that neither did they. Hired guards in polished armour going through the same motions to survive. Insulting them didn't seem wise, though, so I backed away, hands raised, my chin buried into my chest to hide my face as I fled.

The noise had worked; when I walked down the curving street, guards watched on from each household. They stood stiffly, eyes narrowed and backs straight. Their hands rested on their swords. Other competitors appeared on the street, and they watched us closely, waiting for trouble.

It was an effort to keep my pace casual. I didn't want to stand out, so I kept to the middle of the cobblestone road and followed the path's curve until I found myself facing a second set of iron gates. The quiet around me was deafening.

With nowhere else to go, I glanced over my shoulder, confirming there was nowhere else to go. I had followed the gleaming black cobblestones right into the middle of Invidia and found myself in the front of the largest building I had ever seen.

It was built of black brick, looming and dark in the centre of the city. Invidia had been built around it. The large building had tall towers, and guards seemed to crawl out from everywhere. The insignia of Envy flew from the banners proudly. A giant castle in the middle of a city of sin.

The iron gate was cold as I grasped it, textured like snake scales beneath the pads of my fingers. This gate, I realised too late, was a replica of the one at the city's entrance – minus the human skulls, of course.

"Wow," I breathed softly. Something about that building, that castle, twinged an ache in my heart with an unfounded desire to enter; it was gated, and I couldn't go in.

"Wow is right," a voice said, startling me.

I pressed my back to the bars as I twisted towards the threat.

It was the baby-faced man, Oskar, who stood behind me. He looked quietly confident in these streets, hands slung in his pockets, shoulders slouched forwards.

"It's huge," I admitted slowly, wondering what he wanted. "What is it?"

My gaze swept over his shoulder for the threat of Niklaus and Helina, but the street was empty. I relaxed slightly. Oskar tilted his head, looking past me.

"Envy says his castle is the biggest and grandest structure in all of Kaida," he whispered. "Envy says he owns the most unique of everything. He has what his brothers can't have for themselves."

"Like what?" I asked, disbelieving.

Oskar hummed. "Like, everything . . ."

He flicked a piece of his hair from his eyes, then nodded at the castle. It was a bad idea to turn my back on him. He was my enemy of sorts, but I did it anyway. The need to know, the desire to understand had won the battle, and if he were to have slid a knife in my back, at least I'd know what he meant before I died.

My gaze roamed the castle grounds. Guards stood in gleaming armour, but it otherwise felt empty and undisturbed. Then, out of nowhere, a group of loud, giggling men and women strolled the gardens. They walked leisurely – beautiful, even from a distance, then disappeared behind a hedge.

Oskar's gaze pricked the back of my neck.

The men and women reappeared, closer, the whispers of their conversation carrying. They were, without a doubt, the strangest but most beautiful group of people I had ever seen. Identical men, some of fiery hair and others with burnished skin, always in sets of two or three.

Their beauty was their common ground.

Only one without a counterpart was not part of a set. She stood tall; her expression distinctly bored. My chest squeezed tight at her snowy appearance. Even from a distance, she was unmistakable. The Ice Woman. I could have sworn she'd caught my eye for a moment. My heart thundered. I let go of the bars and twisted back to Oskar.

"You mean he collects people?!" I gasped.

Oskar didn't have to reply, but he smiled like we had just shared a secret. Without a word, he backed away.

"Wait!" I protested. I wanted to know more.

Oskar didn't stop, and I started after him. "Oskar, wait!"

He paused mid-step, round face turned back to me.

"How . . . ?" I hesitated.

Oskar lifted a brow, waiting for me to continue.

"How do you know what Envy says?" A reedy urgency charged my voice that I hated, but I needed to know. "You didn't say it was stories or rumours. You said that Envy says . . ."

Oskar lifted a hand; he rubbed the back of his scalp and mussed his hair. It looked like he had just rolled out of bed.

"Why do you think your nasty friends are keeping me alive?" he asked.

I took a moment to appreciate him calling them both nasty. "I don't know . . ."

Oskar's laugh triggered anxiety. "Think about it."

An agitated sigh rolled from me. "I really don't know."

Oskar smirked. "I guess you'll see, then. Won't you?"

One day into the Envy trial, and I was sick of impossible questions.

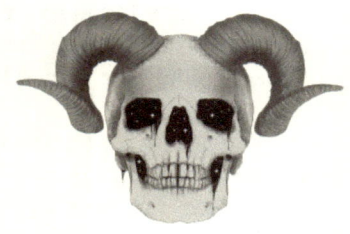

Chapter Twelve

I was fifteen minutes late for the meeting, my arms loaded with clothes, stomach growling as I burst through the door. I didn't apologise for being late, even though a tight-lipped Aureen's glare said she had expected one.

"I know I'm late," I said, "but I've had the best idea."

The clothes were offloaded on the platform. Benton hadn't joined the group, and Aureen looked less than impressed with me. Monika and Kyra shuffled to give me space to join in. The rest of the platform was covered in little black rocks.

"Mapping things out," Monika explained.

"Oh." There was a rock bigger than my fist in place of the castle. "Good idea."

"I thought so." Aureen sounded smug.

I blinked down at their map. "The city is a spiral?"

I felt foolish for not realising it when I had spent all day along the main street's curve.

"That's what we were discussing." Aureen's tone was sharp. "Which you would know if you were on time, Octavia."

Chastised, I sat down. Monika leaned forward and nudged the giant rock in the middle as she adjusted the surrounding buildings. Five of them made up the first ring of properties, and as the spiral widened, the rocks clustered with their respective buildings.

"It's smart," Monika explained. "With this layout, the castle is the most protected building in the entire city. It's surrounded by layers of citizens and guards. Not to mention the wall."

Wrapping my arms around my knees, I considered it, wondering what an angel of sin would possibly need to be protected from. Or if the city had been built that way to keep something inside.

My impressions of Pride and Gluttony had been that they were infallible, and not even the devil could match their power and claim their souls. Was Envy a little more mortal than the other sins? Was he afraid?

'*What a quaint thought.*' A sly chuckle echoed in my ears.

Samael was back.

A shiver pulled goosebumps across my skin. It was a struggle to not tune out Monika's report on guard stations at night, when Samael seemed to brush up against my very soul. My fingers brushed against the cuff around my wrist, and I swallowed roughly.

I couldn't say anything. Not when the others were so close. The rush of relief the devil was back felt intense. I wanted to demand to know where he had been.

Samael chuckled again, a low sound that caused my belly to flutter.

'*I am the most powerful being in Kaida, Little One,*' Samael said. '*You would do well to remember that. Do not indulge in silly fantasies of my owing you answers.*'

My throat tightened. It was disturbing, the way he rifled through my thoughts and combed my mind. He read my secrets like a novel, and I couldn't hide it. I had ignored it before, eager to survive, but since then, I knew he could pluck anything from my mind, whether I wanted it.

"Octavia?"

I startled and glanced up to the three women watching me. My face burnt. I had checked out and couldn't keep up. Aureen's lips pursed and turned downwards. I didn't need to be the devil to read her mind; it was written all over her face.

"What?"

"I asked if you found anything useful." Aureen's voice dripped with derision. Her gaze scanned to the pile of clothes. "Or did you just spend your entire day shopping?"

'*Stay alive, Little One,*' Samael said, distracting me and causing the hair on the back of my arms to stand up. '*I look forward to meeting you.*'

"Uhhh." I struggled to find balance between the two conversations and shook my head hard, as if it would dislodge the devil. "I didn't go shopping . . ."

"What about the clothes?" Aureen scoffed.

"I stole them."

"You stole them?"

"The entire trial is about stealing. Don't judge me."

Twisting, I jerked the clothes towards us and unrolled them for the other women to inspect.

"We stand out too much," I explained quickly. "We need to blend in. When I walked up to the castle this morning, all the guards could pinpoint me and then there's these ridiculous cuffs."

Kyra tapped on her cuff, face scrunched. "You're not wrong."

"I'm not," I said. "So, I thought we would be better off looking like everyone else."

The first outfit I held up was the plain maid's outfit, complete with the heavy apron. I hadn't been able to find any caps. Then I had picked my way into a clothing store and stolen three long-sleeved dresses in richer fabrics. They had the tight bodices I had seen in the upper-class sections of the spiral.

Kyra quickly snatched up one of the more elegant dresses in jewelled magenta tones. "I've never worn anything like this." She sounded so wistful I let go of the other side of the dress.

"It's yours, then."

She let out a breathy squeal that reminded me of Phee, and my heart wrenched. Kyra held the dress up to her body for a second, then stripped it off.

"Don't put it on yet," Aureen snapped.

Kyra froze. "Why not?"

"You'll get it dirty." Aureen climbed to her feet and snatched the dress from her sister's hands.

"Oh." Kyra's face fell. "But . . ."

Aureen twisted and pressed her forehead against Kyra's, nose-to-nose. She whispered. I glanced at Monika, who shrugged.

Aureen stepped back, clearing her throat. "You won't fit in if it's ruined from the underground."

I couldn't say anything else, so I gave Monika her pick and stared down at our makeshift map. It was good to see it laid out, but it yielded no clear direction.

"What next?" I murmured. Nobody spoke, and the silence was overwhelming. I glanced at Aureen, who watched Monika, who was staring at her shoes.

"We need more information," Monika muttered. "We need to each get into a house and work out what it's really like in there."

"Oh."

My stomach twisted, nausea turning to burning bile in the back of my throat. In theory, breaking into homes seemed to be an easy task. Dress as a village maid, get inside, and find the right opportunity to steal a piece of the old world for myself. The idea of doing it left me nervous to the brink of breathlessness.

What would happen if we got caught? I didn't realise I had spoken aloud until Monika shifted uncomfortably.

"We would probably die on the gate," she admitted.

"Fantastic," I muttered. Kyra smiled. "Let's not do that."

Silence lapsed again, proving we weren't a team; we weren't even comfortable in the same room with one another.

"Do you think they know?" Kyra spoke up. "Do you think they know we need to steal from them?"

I thought about it, twisting the thin, tarnished rings on my fingers. If they knew, it would be a lot harder and much more dangerous for us to achieve. If the Invidians knew, then our task would be almost impossible.

"No," I said. "If they did, the guards would be doubled. You would be able to see it. These people are too relaxed."

Aureen stepped forward. The toe of her shoe knocked into the map, scattering the rocks. "How long do you need?"

"Three days?" I suggested softly.

Monika didn't contribute.

"Fine." Aureen nodded before we could change our minds. "Meet here in three days."

Our plan felt thin, each move created on a whim, and strategy was a work of fiction. I wondered if the month wouldn't be up before we found a way to work together.

Monika was shuffling the little black rocks into the bag. Her face twisted, and I almost asked what her problem was when she spoke up.

"Be careful!" she called. Aureen paused in the doorway and glanced over her shoulder, confusion scrunching her features.

"What?" she asked.

"Be careful," Monika repeated.

Aureen scoffed. "Of course, we're not stupid . . ."

"I meant –"

Aureen and her sister disappeared into the hall before Monika could explain. She scrambled to her feet and rocks dropped from her hands. They bounced off the ground once, twice.

Monika turned to me. She stepped close, too close. My throat tightened, and I tried to tell myself she wasn't a threat.

"I meant, " she said, hands winding into the fabric of my jacket, where she had anchored herself so I would listen, "there's a group of competitors. They're attacking others."

Startled, I thought of the dead girl on the floor. Her slender metal hairclip felt heavy against my scalp. I frowned. I'd thought it was the Invidians who had killed her in the night.

Restlessness crested through me, my weight shifting to my back foot, but Monika didn't let go. Her grip tightened, and she shook my arm.

"Are you listening?"

"Why?" I asked. "Why are they killing people?"

Monika's eyes narrowed. Stark disappointment set in the hard lines of her narrow face.

"Why do you think?" It came out as a hiss.

"Well, fuck me . . ." I said bitterly. "I don't know."

Samael laughed, low and husky, and the sound haunted me for hours.

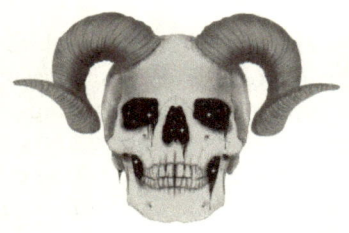

Chapter Thirteen

The harpies screamed above ground, and the competitors screamed below.

Many locals had disappeared in the past day, and a woman whispered that they had found other places to sleep, not wanting the bad luck of the competitors to taint them. Meanwhile, the competitors stretched across the large cavern, wall to wall, clustered in their teams or with friends. They created makeshift tents from blankets, along with pieces of wood and metal scavenged from the tunnels.

The tension didn't settle until the chatter died. In the quiet moments, I found Monika Oster had been right and resolved that, if I managed to get through the night, I would make sure to tell her as much.

Her warning kept me awake half the night and likely kept me alive. I had what felt like a thousand reasons to stress, a million thoughts in my mind, but it was her question and the tension on her face that haunted me. It left me fidgeting with the smelly, threadbare blanket I had stolen.

It smelled of old sweat, but it kept me warmer.

The makeshift tents rustled and fell. Metal bars clanged against the hard ground as some fell over. By the time the first scream of agony had erupted, I moved to the outskirts of the room, blindly searching for safety.

My spine pressed against the cold support pillars as I fought to remain out of sight. It chilled me through, damned with water that dripped down from the street, but I didn't dare move. My heart raced, and the noise grew louder and louder. I bit my knuckles hard to avoid making any noise. The pain in my hand grounded me. The sound of fists on flesh, of moans of pain, of gasping, left me shaking.

A pained groan echoed off the walls. I could hear the shuffling of bodies as more of us fled. Panicked, I tried again to orientate myself and to find a way out in the dark.

"They're coming," someone hissed.

The warning wasn't meant for me, but I took it. I twisted to get a better look of the danger heading my way, but shadows moved in the dark, threatening but unformed. I didn't know who I was looking out for and where they would come from.

"Samael." I whispered his name like a prayer.

The devil stayed silent. My teeth grit hard enough that my jaw ached.

"Come on," I pleaded, voice rising with my own rising hysteria. "Samael, help me."

A voice cut through my useless pleas. "Have you gone completely nuts?!"

My eyes opened to see Benton Rumley standing on my left. His face had turned red, splotchy. His eyes bounced from side to side, and he clenched his fists.

Dread and realisation washed through me. I couldn't be anywhere near that man.

"It's you," I said.

"What did you say?" His attention snapped back to me quickly.

"They're coming for you." Panic threatened to collapse my lungs. "For the akelda. That's what they want. Not me, *you*."

"Shut up," he hissed. "Shut up, or you'll call them over."

I needed to get as far away from Rumley as I could. The best path of action, I decided, was to just flee.

"Well." I gulped. A scream pierced the air, then died quickly. "That sounds like a *you* problem, not a me problem."

Before he could respond, I lurched off the column and shot in a random direction. I stumbled on my own feet, curses spilling from my lips as I flailed. By the time I had found my balance, Rumley's thick fist had gripped my shoulder, and he shoved me firmly backwards.

"What did you say?" he demanded.

I went from nearly falling onto my face to having all the breath knocked from my body when I collided with the pillar. I couldn't reply as my lungs struggled on my next breath.

Rumley crowded me in, his thick body and foul breath so close I gagged.

"You're not leaving me on my own," Rumley hissed. "Not in this mess!"

"I wasn't trying to." I lied. He grunted; his rotten breath hot against my cheek. "I was just —"

Rumley slapped a meaty palm across my mouth. I shuddered and retched at the taste of sweat and dirt. My belongings fell to the floor as I tried to shove him off me, clenched fists bouncing off his shoulders.

"Oh my, look what we have here . . ."

Helina's voice was the last thing I needed to hear. My body relaxed into a false sense of security, the familiarity reassuring before remembering her attitude throughout the Gluttony trial. Her presence wasn't good news.

Her face appeared over Rumley's shoulder. Her nostrils flared as she looked us up and down.

"Typical. Having fun?" She laughed.

"Piss off!" Rumley spat.

"Hmmm" – Helina pushed her wire spectacles up her nose – "don't think I will."

Three men closed in around us. Baby-faced Oskar, a man with a crooked nose, and Niklaus.

Rumley growled. He leaned right into Helina's implication like it was the lifeline. "We're *busy*. Now, piss off."

I wanted to gag at the implication. My fingers curled around Rumley's, pressed into the flesh of my cheek, and I wrenched them back as hard as I could.

Rumley swore. Split flecked against my face.

His grip loosened, and I sagged. "*No*. We're not."

"We *are*!"

Niklaus' face turned carefully blank. Rumley twisted and used the bulk of his body to pin me against the column before I could run, squashing me beneath the bulk of his body. He glared at Helina, picking her as the easiest of the four targets. If only he knew.

He grinned at her, and I squirmed away from him. Rumley growled and grabbed a fistful of my hair. He slammed my head back, and the sharp collision left the world spinning.

Helina folded her arms and watched him, unimpressed.

"Are you deaf, girl?" Rumley spat. Even in the low light, his spittle glittered on Helina's glasses. She didn't flinch; instead, she gnashed her teeth.

"Bite me," Helina spat back. "I –" She glanced over her shoulder at the three men who stood in stony silence at her back. "We don't listen to you."

Niklaus shouldered forward as I struggled against Rumley's grip in my hair. Helina glanced at him and slid a hand down his shoulder. Possessiveness rolled like an icicle down my spine, inciting a shiver and distracting me.

Rumley slammed me backwards with enough force my body crunched as I hit the post.

"Get off me!" I wheezed; I swung my fist at his flesh.

Rumley barely flinched.

A muscle twitched in Niklaus' left cheek.

He pulled away from Helina's grip and shoved Rumley to the side so sharply it ripped out a chunk of my hair. I grunted and barely had time to straighten before a different body, more familiar, pinned me back against the cold, stone column.

Same predicament, different danger.

"Don't move, love," Niklaus warned.

A frustrated growl rolled from me. I struggled against him, breathlessly spitting out every curse I could think of in the moment. It was easier to curse the life out of Niklaus Heira than anyone else. He made me bold, and the fury in my blood left me reckless.

"Why are you even bothering with her, Nik?" Helina's tone was low and soothing, a hint of promise in the way she said his name, laced with possessiveness that bit at my nerves again. Sharp and bitterly unpleasant.

Nik grunted; his hips pinned mine down.

"Search the prick," he spat.

He hissed as I sunk my teeth into his flesh like a rabid dog. I was bolder than I had been with Benton Rumley.

Helina sighed. "Fine."

The third man stepped to Helina's side. They stared at Rumley, and I watched as his chin dipped and sized up his competition.

"Nik," I breathed, blinking rapidly as I tried still to pull the rattled parts of my brain back together and find a new tactic. Niklaus shifted. His hand gripped my chin roughly.

"Quiet," he demanded.

Rumley charged forward. Helina's laugh grated against my skin, prickling against my nerves. I heard the impact of the first punch, but I didn't know who landed it. I couldn't see a thing between the darkness, and the way Niklaus forced my gaze upwards with his grip on my jaw.

"Nik," I grunted again, bucking my hips to dislodge him.

"Shh." He stroked his thumb up the column of my throat, a swift, ticklish move, and I squirmed. "Stay still."

Someone groaned. The sound of a beating filled the space. My heart was fluttering in my chest as I worried that Niklaus was just holding me in place until it was my turn. Benton groaned an unintelligible plea as I heard the sharp crack of a bone.

"Ha! Niklaus, look at this!" Helina's gleeful hiss caught Niklaus' attention.

His grip loosened as he turned away. I fought to drag a full breath of air into my lungs, and I slid down the column. From the floor, my head spun, but I gulped down as much air as I could.

With an erratic thought that I needed to take the maid's outfit with me, I snagged it and twisted onto my hands and knees. Niklaus was so distracted I had enough room to wriggle free. My palms and knees stung as I crawled away. I staggered to my feet and twisted to look back at them.

Benton Rumley lay curled up on the ground, his head cradled beneath his arms, blood smeared all over him. Oskar stood back, his eyes on me, but he didn't stop me. My eyes peered over to Helina and Niklaus, the main threats.

They were so close their foreheads were pressed together. Helina looked up at Niklaus, her lips parted a fraction as if she were about to kiss him. My heart squeezed at the thought, and discomforting heat flowed through my body. Niklaus' attention was not on her lips or her face but instead on the glowing bead of green fire that Helina held between her finger and thumb.

He stared, mesmerised. The corner of his mouth twitched upwards into a wide grin.

They had the akelda; Niklaus Heira couldn't look away from his prize.

I took advantage of his distraction and ran.

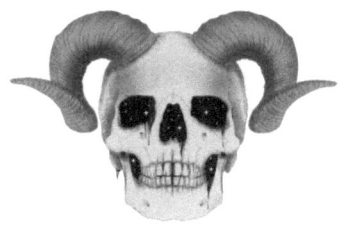

Chapter Fourteen

There was no shame in hiding from danger. Fleeing as fast as I could, I found myself back in the twisting halls of the black market. It was eerily void of life as it sat silent and sleeping. I found the deep blue tent of the fortune teller, and panicked by the sound of footsteps behind me, I threw myself behind it. Between the patterned fabric and the cold wall, I wedged my body firmly into the tight space and hoped that the bulk of the tent would hide me. The tight space felt secure in my panic.

STEPHANIE GLUCK

Too late, I had identified someone's soft snoring inside the tent. Too close for comfort, the shuffling footsteps on the concrete floor kept me from crawling out to find another hiding place.

I felt tense and pulled the dress over my body for some small measure of warmth in the cold night. Slow breathing helped me find some level of calm as I lay in wait for Helina and Niklaus to remember I existed.

They never arrived. With time, my body relaxed into a fitful sleep. I nodded back into awareness whenever shuffled footsteps sounded in the quiet night before exhaustion pulled me into sleep again.

Consciousness slammed into me as the fortune teller screeched his pitch across the noisy room. I shifted, disoriented and groggy. He hollered again and again for customers, so repetitive his tone was not enough to stave off exhaustion, and I slept again.

I didn't wake for hours.

Not until the gnawing hunger was so discomforting, so reminiscent of the Gluttony trial that I was forced to take properly and act. The dress was bundled and hidden behind the tent as I tentatively followed my nose on a path to satiation.

I had slept all day; the night market was alive.

The fortune teller offered me a startled look when I appeared to his left. He blinked rapidly, then flashed a wide smile. He had missing teeth.

"Come to find out how you'll fare in the Devil's trials?" He asked and moved close. His gap-toothed smile filled my vision, and I recoiled.

"No."

"You sure?" He reached out to touch me, and I jerked from his reach. "Let old Lenos tell you the ways you'll win or lose . . ."

"Very sure!" I swallowed roughly. "I don't need you to tell me that my luck is bad."

He called after me, even as I scuttled away.

His voice was lost to calls of fresh human kidneys for sale, and I didn't know which of the two was better to hear. Many of the makeshift tables in the eatery were full, competitors and Invidians alike crowded together and engaged in conversation. I watched the other competitors wearily as I edged around the tables and inspected the food.

Two coins pressed into my palm, and reluctantly, I handed them over to a woman who sold roasted meat. She wrapped it in a waxy scrap of paper and tossed it in my direction with a toothy smile and a sharp nod. "Thanks for yer bus'ness."

It wasn't hot, but I couldn't complain.

Few people paid me any mind; my gaze skimmed over them all as I assessed for danger. The best option, I knew, was to stay far away from Helina's little group.

Nash had explicitly told me to stay away. He caught my eye a split-second as he turned to cough into his elbow. He turned carefully, blank, and my heart sank. I decided to do what he had asked.

Rumley sat with two blackened eyes and an arm that didn't seem to hang right, the last person I wanted to be near. Aureen and Kyra sat together and leaned low over their food, while Monika was nowhere to be found. When I twisted around the table to approach them, Aureen glanced up sharply. Her mouth puckered, a frown creased between her brow, and I veered away at the obvious rejection.

It stung like a splinter.

In the end, I found a place to eat with surprising company. The old crone, Eadlin, sat at one of the uneven bench tables and said nothing as I dropped into the seat at her side. The bread rolled to the edge of the table, and I had to snatch it to stop it from hitting the floor. I smoothed the waxy paper, tore the roll in half, and pulled a strip of meat from the bone to lay it within.

At first, the silence felt uncomfortable, but as I chewed through the tough meat, I relaxed. The crone didn't owe me a conversation, and I had no right to expect one. Eadlin seemed to show no interest in me, not as she stirred a bent spoon through her bowl of greyed mush and watched everyone else.

"I —"

Eadlin slapped my knuckles with the back of her spoon. It stung. "Shh!"

I blinked. "Ow!"

"Bah! Be quiet, girl!"

The rejection from a Devil-cursed woman shouldn't have hurt as much as it did, but I couldn't fight the welling emotion. I bit the edge of my tongue to stop the tingling along the bridge of my nose to prevent manifesting tears.

My attention turned to my meal. I was halfway through the food when the crone turned and settled the weight of her judgement on the side of my face.

"What?" I bit out aggressively.

The crone hadn't wanted to speak to me before, and since I had mulled over my own feelings, I wasn't happy with being everyone's second choice.

The crone huffed. She rose from her seat slowly, her bones creaking and joints popping under the expectation of carrying her body. When she shuffled away, nobody claimed her seat.

Neither of us said goodbye.

Later, as I was chewing on the last crumbs of my bread roll, a dented metal cup hit the table in front of me. A dark leafy brew sloshed inside of it, and the crone dropped back into her chair, cradling the mug of her own.

I grunted and pulled the mug closer. The hot liquid inside warmed my hands.

"Bah! Most say thank you, you ungrateful brat." The crone snarked, and I lifted the mug to sip, more unwilling to thank her since she had asked for it. It was too hot and burnt the edge of my tongue, and it had a strange edge like soil had been dropped in with the bitter leaves.

"What is this?" I asked.

Eadlin huffed through her nose. She sipped the brew. "Mushroom herb tea."

"Mushroom tea . . ." I repeated, nose wrinkling.

Her eyes narrowed, the lines in her sagging skin shifting as she pulled a face. "Are you complaining, brat?"

"No," I said. "It's fine."

"Ungrateful brats always complaining . . ."

"How would you know?" I snapped as the accusation singed my last nerve.

She snorted. "A lot of secrets in the underground."

I rolled my eyes. "None about me."

"Bah!" Eadlin's spindly hand slapped my shoulder in a surprisingly solid thump. The tea sloshed precariously in my mug, threatening to spill. "Pay attention!"

I glared at the crone. I wanted to hit her back, but it hardly seemed fair, given the age difference.

"To what, exactly?" I asked and sipped the tea before she could knock it again. I wasn't going to waste anything that could keep me warm through another cold night.

Eadlin leaned close. Her hand pushed a stringy plait of white hair out of her face, and I was distracted by the curved hunch of her back. It looked painful.

"Pay attention to the people here . . ."

I did as she asked, set the mug on the table, and scanned the room. My eyes lingered, once again, on familiar faces. Niklaus, who tormented me. Helina, who had a newfound hate for me. Nash, who had abandoned me.

Eadlin nudged me again. "It's not all about you, brat. Look at the people you don't know."

I flushed at the fact she had called me out. "Tell me what to look for, then . . ."

The old crone watched me for so long I almost asked again. The heavy lines in her face shifted, then she rubbed the back of her fingers against her hooked nose and nodded.

Eadlin twisted. Her gaze bounced between person to person before she raised her wrinkled fingers and pointed someone out. "See them . . ."

"Monika," I said.

My rat-faced teammate sat alone, crouched with her back pressed to the wall as she wolfed down her meal.

"Her name doesn't matter, girl. Bah! Keep up, or I'm not doing this!" Eadlin snapped. "What is she?"

I hesitated. "A woman?"

The crone smacked my arm again, and tea splashed everywhere. I choked on my own exasperation.

"Look what you've done!"

"I paid for it," Eadlin snapped. "Now, focus."

A quick study of Monika again, and I saw she was at least a metre away from anyone else. Just like me, she was all on her own in this trial. I shifted with discomfort and drained my mug dry. When I answered, a sought approval in Eadlin's face. "She's lonely."

She snorted. "No!"

"What?"

"She's scared, girl!" Eadlin cried. "Pay attention!"

"She's not scared. She's sitting there, eating!"

Eadlin huffed. "You're a stupid one, brat."

My face heated. I clenched my fists around the mug. "Prove it, then."

The crone narrowed her gaze on me. Her lip curled, and she scoffed. "Just. Look. At. Her."

"All right . . ." Reluctantly, I forced my gaze back to my teammate. The crone leaned into me; the bulk of her body heavy against mine. Her layered shawls smelled of herbs.

"Look." Eadlin's voice dropped low. "Look at the way her grip trembles. Look at the way she's crouched, not sitting. She prepared to move quickly. Watch the way she watches them."

The path of Monika's gaze led me to Niklaus and Helina. My stomach twisted, and I wondered if she feared them due to the implicit threat, they posed to all of us with their cruel laughter and the way they made a display of targeting different competitors. Their team had quickly built a reputation just as dangerous.

"Oh," I said lamely.

"Bah!" The old woman rolled her eyes at me. She stretched out as if she were trying to straighten her hunched back. Her spine popped again. "Pay attention, and you'll find more secrets than you want, brat."

I watched Aureen and Kyra next, noting the way Aureen put herself between her sister and the crowd. I noticed a man who smiled too wide, too smug, and my heart raced; he looked like a man who had won, and there was only one reason for that. He already had a piece of the prize.

I made a mental note to see if I could learn his name.

Next was Nash, his mouth pressed into his elbow as he coughed again. Finley Nightingale had left their tight-knit group at the table and sauntered across the room towards a group of small children fighting in front of the food stalls. Little people smudged with dirt, their thin clothes riddled with holes, their fists clenched as they swung at each other with abandon.

They fought over a piece of cake that had already rolled to the floor and been squashed with their preoccupation. Finley spoke to them as he approached. His hand rubbed at the back of his head, mussing his dark curls before he crouched down. He didn't touch them, but whatever he said seemed to strike home, and they lowered their fists and turned their dirty, unimpressed faces to him instead.

"Hmm," the crone hummed. I glanced at her, but she didn't elaborate.

We watched as Finley straightened and pulled coins from his pocket to buy more pieces of cake. He took the pieces and broke them all down before handing a bit to each child.

"What do you see there, girl?" Eadlin pressed.

I shifted. I didn't want to tell her what I thought I knew about each of them. "I don't know."

Eadlin scoffed and leaned heavily against the table to get out of her seat. As she rose, a pouch fell from her pocket, but she didn't notice. I didn't bother to point it out; instead, I lifted my chin and met her lined eyes as she turned back to look at me.

"Practice it. It'll serve you well, girl . . ."

"Sure . . ." I shrugged. We both knew I wouldn't.

"Bah!" The crone shuffled from the room. I snagged her pouch from the floor and hid it in my lap. The crone paused in the doorway and glanced back at the lot of us. When she spoke again, her voice rang out, loud and clear. Damning us all.

"Ungrateful brats, I tell you."

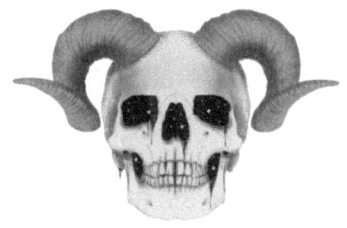

Chapter Fifteen

By the end of a week, I had a strange routine. At night, I hid behind the fortune teller's tent and slept in a nest of old blankets and clothes. I had met my team twice more, and each time, we failed to build a solid plan. Each time, we decided we needed more, more, and more information.

On the first day, I wore the stolen uniform. It didn't take long for me to work out that the little maids didn't work in the same homes every day, and I couldn't just appear at a gate and beg for a job. Instead, they reported first to a tall building with darkened windows and handed small plastic cards to a clerk with tired eyes. This clerk gave them a slip of paper and a house number in return, marking them down in his little book. The maids always laughed and compared, whispering advice to one another before they went into their daily assignments. Guards at the fences would study the slips of paper and let them inside the properties. The maids didn't seem to leave the estates all day, except for a rare errand. Just before the streets turned dark, they reappeared, the slips of paper clutched in their hands with a signature scrawled across it. They returned from the building each night, then to the clerk's office. There, they exchanged the slip for a single silver envy coin. None of them complained at the end of the day, even as their steps had slowed with fatigue.

On the second day, I dressed as a maid and walked into the clerk's office, brimming with confidence. I was knocked back instantly. The clerk behind the counter, a man with a bristly moustache, spoke without looking up and told me that if I couldn't find my city identification, I wouldn't get any more work. He barely even looked up, so I folded my shaky hands in my apron and slipped back into the street.

The third day, I didn't dress as a maid. I had hidden the cuff beneath my jacket's sleeve rather than pushing it to my elbows as usual. I wove through the streets and the maids until I picked one that looked most like me. It was a stretch, but she had dark hair and dull enough eyes that I thought we could pass as one another.

On the fourth day, I followed her specifically and realised she was much younger than me, only sixteen. Her name was Lillian Duncan, and she lived in a cluster of broken buildings by the outer gates of Invidia.

When she came home after work, three small children barrelled into her legs and cried her name. The sight made me uncomfortable. My siblings had never shown much enthusiasm to see me. I knew that was because I had never shown interest in them or had been happy to have them nearby. But my mouth still dried up with envy at the sight.

Her siblings became the best distraction, and I used them to stop Lillian from noticing my approach. One of the girls shrieked and ran about, so I pretended to stumble out of her way. A ridiculous gasp burst from my lips, and I waved my arms as I pitched forward in the fake stumble.

"Sorry!" I cried, slamming into Lillian.

She pitched sideways, struggling to stay upright. Panic flashed across her face as she tried to keep her balance for the small child perched on her hip. My fingers slipped into the pocket of her skirts, and I easily lifted the small plastic card off her body.

I had it in my own pocket before I straightened.

"I'm so, so sorry." I lied, reaching to steady her. "I'm visiting and not used to these stone paths. They make my feet hurt, and I keep falling right my boots."

Lillian smiled slowly. She rubbed circles across her sister's back. "It's okay. We were probably in your way. We're sorry."

My mouth quirked. I didn't bother with pleasantries as I turned and ran back to the Infra. My hand clenched that small plastic card as if it were the one thing that would save my life.

The next morning, I rose before the market became too busy. I washed with a tin cup with cold water and a stolen rag. The maid's outfit made my skin itch, and the long sleeves barely covered the cuff at my wrist. My mouth was dry, but I ignored it as I slipped around the tent and tried to settle into the crowd.

Even above ground, I couldn't breathe easy. A heaviness settled across my chest. I joined the line of other workers, listening to their conversations, fretting about the worn edges of my boots and the difference between Lillian and me. Not that it mattered. The clerk behind the counter barely looked up.

He snatched the plastic card from me and consulted it. Then he dragged the tip of his finger down his list. He consulted the card again, comparing it to a second book. All without looking at me. I shifted uneasily.

"You've been working well these last few months, Lillian. We're a maid short in the inner circle. Go to down to Lady Francesca North, in estate one-four." He held out the slip of paper with the details scrawled on it. I almost wanted to argue but instead whispered a quick thanks to Samael and snatched the slip and ID to flee. Stealing an identity felt alarmingly easy.

It took twenty minutes to find the right house, squinting at the silver numbers on the front fence three times to make sure they matched the paper. I stood outside for an extra five minutes, fretting that the house wasn't too far down the spiral from the looming castle. We'd identified these as some of the wealthiest.

Someone cleared their throat delicately behind me. "Hello?"

I turned to find another maid behind me, her apron tied tight, her hair hidden beneath the cap, exposing all her face, including the thin pink scar that ran down her cheek and puckered at the edge of her lips.

"Hello." I parroted back, feeling foolish.

"Are you new?" Her eyes whipped to my uncovered hair.

My palms felt sweaty, and I bit my tongue hard to stave off the impulsive desire to defend myself. My chin dropped into a sharp nod. I didn't trust myself to speak, and the other woman's face relaxed into a smile.

"I'm Rowan." She stepped closer, and I tensed, but Rowan didn't notice as she glanced at the basket she carried.

"I'm Tav," I answered, stealing the nickname Phee had given me.

"Well, Tav." She fished a scrap of material from her basket. "Lady Francesca will have a fit if you walk in there without your cap. You can borrow my spare."

Relief cooled the nervous heat in my blood as I realised how close I could have been to being called out. This kind stranger had unwittingly saved me.

Rowan set down her basket and twirled a finger in indication that I should turn.

With the smallest of smiles, I did as she asked. I jolted when she touched me. Her fingers pulled at my hair as she tugged it into a knot at the back of my neck so tight it flattened my ears against my head. The pin scraped my scalp as she forced it to hold the knot in place with expert ease. Her palms smoothed my hair one final time.

"Put the cap on, quickly!" Rowan advised. My fingers shook as I tied it loosely at the back of my head, but Rowan laughed and tightened it. It pressed uncomfortably against my skull.

"Perfect," Rowan stated, tucking a flyaway piece of hair beneath the cap.

"Thanks, I'm so . . ." My hands fluttered in front of my waist as I smiled, tension pulling my brows in. "Flustered."

"Don't worry about it. We're all nervous on the first day." She stooped to pick up her basket, then took my hand in hers. Gently, Rowan squeezed my fingers.

Again, the fact she was a thousand times kinder than me had stricken me. I felt a strange sense of relief that I wasn't going to be stealing from someone like Rowan. The hardworking maids wouldn't be the victims of the Heist of Haures. Which, of course, made sense; the game wouldn't be fun for an angel filled with power if he would be using it to kick those who were already down.

The front gate squealed as it opened. A pudgy guard in the signature snake-scale breastplate beckoned us inside.

"Hurry! Hurry, girls. Lady Francesca is just waking," the guard said with a chuckle.

The change in demeanour hit me from the other day. The guards were much friendlier with the maids.

"Thank you, sir," Rowan murmured.

I dropped my gaze to my boots as I realised that, despite his friendliness, we were still expected to defer to the guards. She pinched the slip of paper clenched between my fingers and handed it over with her own. Her firm grip on my arm pulled me inside.

It closed behind us with the same squeal.

The guard squinted down at the paper, then nodded firmly. He seemed to check only the house number and the clerk's signature at the base before he returned them to us and gestured to get a move on.

"Duncan, you're new?" he asked. I nodded. "Welcome, welcome. Hurry inside, ladies. There's a whole lot of trouble around these streets now. With that damned trial coming up, who knows what they're all doing? But you don't want to be caught in it. Death follows that competition."

A shiver rippled through me as Rowan tugged me towards the thin-lipped housekeeper's disapproving gaze. I glanced back over my shoulder at the guard and wondered if he knew trouble had just walked right through their front door.

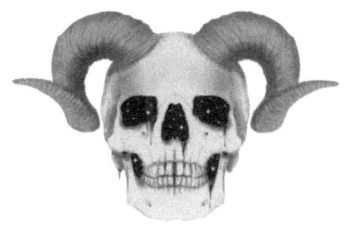

Chapter Sixteen

The housekeeper didn't offer a warm greeting. Instead, she glanced at the clock on the wall and hissed. We were a minute and forty-five seconds late. She took the slips and scratched a note of our tardiness in black marker before stowing them in her pocket. I stood stupidly, with my hands clasped behind my back. The housekeeper narrowed her eyes at us and hissed at us to get to work.

"Sorry, ma'am." Rowan stepped swiftly into the line of fire. "Miss Duncan is new. I'll show her the way we do things here."

The unfamiliar surname startled me. It belonged to Lillian, and Rowan had taken it from the guard. I swallowed roughly and pushed down a strange pang of loss at the warped identity I had assumed to survive. I had gone from Octavia Nox to Tav Duncan too quickly, and it left me uncomfortable. I had never had to pretend to be someone else to steal before; my transgressions had always been my own. I had never had the weight of such high stakes on my shoulders, either. Rowan reached back to clasp my hand and dragged me to a small door near the base of the stairs.

The door creaked as it was opened. Rowan bundled me inside. It led to a narrow hallway and a set of stairs that we clambered down. The space below the house was a maze of narrow corridors and small rooms.

"This is where the housekeeper and children's maid lives, but you can keep your things here during the day, so it's out of sight," Rowan explained and stowed her basket. I shrugged awkwardly. I hadn't thought to bring anything with me.

Rowan blinked. "You didn't bring lunch?"

As if condemning me, my stomach growled.

"No lunch," I admitted. "I guess I wasn't thinking straight . . ."

"We'll share," Rowan assured. "Now, let's go. Lady Francesca will be up soon, and we'll have to prepare the sitting room before she rises and then move to her bedroom once she's out."

The morning disappeared swiftly. It quickly became apparent how unskilled I was for both the lives of the rich and the lives of the maids that kept their lives running smoothly. We cleared the old ashes and built a fire in the sitting room, which was easy enough, so I was pleased with my accomplishment. It fell short when we entered the master bedroom, and Rowan instructed me to change the sheets with a fresh set from the trunk at the end of the bed. It was simple enough to pull the current set free, tearing them from the mattress, then replacing them with a crisp, ironed set. Pressing them flat, I smoothed them down with a sweep of my palm.

When I stood back to inspect my work, Rowan giggled.

"What?" I frowned. A quick glance over my shoulder revealed wide brown eyes, and her fingers pressed to her lips to stifle the noise.

"Tav." She giggled again. "You haven't tucked them in."

"What?" I repeated, confused.

My hands settled on my hips in protest, and I glared at the bed. "They're nice and flat like the other ones . . ."

"Oh. Yes. They are . . ." Rowan nudged me out of the way. She reached over to pluck at the side of the sheets, which spilled over the edge of the bed and hung to the floor. "You need to tuck these in."

I grimaced. "Tuck them where?"

"The bed."

"What do you mean?"

"You tuck them in the bed, same as at home?"

"Oh." I blinked and shifted my weight.

The mattresses spanning the floor at home hadn't been covered in crisp linens. I felt incompetent, embarrassment rising hot in my cheeks. Rowan's smile dropped as she studied the mortification on my face.

"It's okay." She breathed, kind as ever. "I'll show you."

It seemed like a painstaking process, one which turned a quick placement of sheets and blankets into lifting the heavy corners of the mattresses, pulling the sheets tight and creating sharp corners. By the time we had finished Lady Francesca's bed, though, I had enough of an understanding that, as we moved to the nursery, I could slowly make each of the children's beds.

Lunch was a twenty-minute break taken beneath the stairs, where Rowan offered half of her cheese sandwich and explained that she had been assigned to Lady Francesca's home for almost three years and worked in the city maid's service for almost five.

Her parents had died of the slow cough many years prior and had since raised a little sister.

Rowan had, in many ways, managed to become a better person than me under much harder circumstances. By the end of our lunch, I knew her better than I knew most people, as she filled the silence with easy stories. It was very easy to grow to like Rowan.

The afternoon passed with buckets of hot, soapy water and scrubbing brushes. By the time the dusk drew to a close and the housekeeper called that it was time to leave, my back ached, and the skin on my hands was red and wrinkled from constantly being dunked into the water. I was more exhausted than I had ever been in my life, and I couldn't believe people willingly got out of bed each day to work so hard.

I swiped my hands down the front of my apron, leaving dark smudges on the material and stowed the bucket below the stairs. Rowan took one look at me as she collected her basket and giggled again. The infectious sound left me smiling.

"You're a mess, Tav."

I felt it, too.

At the top of the stairs, the housekeeper handed back the slips we had given her that morning; they were adorned with her signature and a scrawl of words along the base. I couldn't read them, so I didn't bother trying. The guard bid us goodbye, and I lingered by the gate, taking in the city at the cusp of twilight.

My eyes strayed towards the castle, and I blinked as I noticed the familiar silhouette by the iron bars. Strong, broad shoulders that belonged to one of the Heira brothers. I squinted, trying to pick which one it was. A cloaked figure stood on the other side of the gate. Their heads bowed in close conversation, and their fingers linked around a bar of iron.

An acrid discomfort burnt within my gut, and my lungs tightened.

"Ready?" Rowan asked, and I startled. I glanced between the figures at the gate and the woman beside me.

"Yeah, ready for bed." I smiled and decided to forget about Heira troubles.

We walked side-by-side back down to the city maid's office, where I handed over back the slip. The office clerk blinked at it and cleared his throat. He did it again until I looked at him. "Well done, Duncan. It seems they were happy enough with your efforts."

The praise, rare enough for me, seemed to warm me up. It was a strange feeling, and all I knew was that I wanted to hear it again. A single silver coin slid across the counter, snake-side up. I stared at it for a beat, then snatched it to bury it in my pocket. When we spilled back out onto the street, Rowan paused, that same smile that had kept me moving all day on her lips.

"Want me to walk you home?"

My smile dimmed. "That's okay."

"It's no hassle," Rowan assured. "I'm sure it's on my way."

"Actually" – I cleared my throat – "I'm . . . uh, going to go down to the Infra for dinner."

The fear that flashed in Rowan's eyes was unmistakable. Not everyone braved the underground. The edges of her smile turned stiff, but she still nodded as if it were the best idea she had ever heard.

"Okay, I can't come, but that sounds wonderful." She hugged me tightly, quickly. "Be safe?"

My chin dipped, but I didn't say a word. I didn't like making promises I couldn't keep, not after I had told Ophelia Bell that nobody would die and failed to make that true. Weariness slammed into me when I entered the markets, and I changed clumsily behind the fortune teller's tent. As I moved to the eatery, I turned that single silver coin over and over in my fingers. It was the only coin I had ever earned through legitimate hard work in my life. I clutched onto that coin as if it were the most precious thing I owned.

My stomach rumbled in demand for something more than half of Rowan's cheese sandwich, but something a lot more enticing than food caught my eye. All too soon, I was settled on a large brown rug just outside of the eatery, my legs folded, the coin clenched tight in my fist.

For the first time since arriving in Invidia, anticipation overwhelmed me, and it momentarily drove away my fatigue and fear.

"What's the game?" I asked, breathless and excited.

A snaggle-toothed woman grinned. "Deceiver's Dice."

"I don't know it," I admitted. That didn't mean I didn't want to play more than anything in the world. More than that, I wanted to win.

"It's easy," a boy on the other side of the circle piped. He was smug beneath the dirt smudged on his face. He pushed a cup containing black dice in my direction. "Everyone has five dice. You roll but keep what it comes as a secret. Check your roll, right? First loser of the last round goes first. Do you understand?"

I tipped the dice into my hand, testing their weight, and nodded. "I think so."

"That person makes a bid. He's goes . . . Uhh, we got two fives. So, he's saying he rolled two number fives. So, we go around this way" – he twirls his finger clockwise – "and you up the bid. Next guy, he says we got six fives, and the next says oh well, I got ten."

I nod slowly.

"You can either raise the amount of the number or the number on the die or call out the lie. If you cry liar, everyone lifts up their cups, and we count from everyone. If there's less than his bid, the bidder loses and gives up one die. If there's the same or higher, the challenger loses one die. Then we roll again."

My eyes drop to the dice. "Okay."

I'd never heard of Deceiver's Dice, but it seemed simple enough, more a game of guessing and math than real luck, which meant I could win, even if Lady Luck wasn't on my side.

"How do you win?" I asked. These were the important questions.

Snaggletooth grinned again. "You become the last woman left."

The dice clacked together as I rolled them between my fingers. I had work to do, but one game couldn't hurt. It would be energising to take a moment to do something fun – or so I told myself.

"I'm in."

"Buy-in is one silver piece," the boy said quickly.

My right hand uncurled around the coin I had worked so hard to earn that day. A sharp feeling stabbed in my chest at the idea of letting it go, one which warred with the impulse to play and win. Reluctantly, I tipped the coin into the middle of the rug, and it fell flat. The boy had it in his cup before I could change my mind.

"Anyone else?" he called brightly.

The other four players chuckled as they reached into their pockets and shilled out coins.

He nodded a directive to start.

Quickly, I pushed the dice back into the little cup, covered the top with my palm, and shook it. They rattled around before I overturned the cup on the man, trapping them to settle.

Six, four, three, three, one. I peeked beneath the cup.

My fingers stayed pressed against the cup, nails drumming against the side anxiously. New excitement had me energised, and the hard day's work seemed far away. I could practically taste the win in my future.

"New girl first!"

It took a moment to realise he meant me. Everyone else's eyes prickled my skin, and despite myself, I smiled. My gaze flicked to the snaggle-toothed woman, and I nodded.

"Three of three –" I declared.

"Four of three." The man to my left was quick.

"Six of three." The snaggle-toothed woman beamed.

"Seven of three." The boy didn't miss a beat.

"Nine of three," said a quiet girl.

The man on my right hesitated. He checked his dice twice, then nodded. He smiled softly; the sort of smile that hinted at a secret nobody else knew. "Twelve of three."

Too soon, it was my turn, and my heart fluttered in my chest. My fingertips tingled, and I couldn't manage a full breath as I worked out what to do next. Thirty dice were in play; I had two threes, so only twenty-seven in total could be threes, and that was if we'd only rolled that number. Half of the rolls could be three, making it possible, but it still felt impossible. My throat felt tight. I turned my head to meet the thin-faced man's gaze on my right.

I studied his expression for a moment. "Liar!" I shouted.

Six cups raised, fingers with them, as players indicated how many threes were in their cups. Catching on, I raised two of my own. My eyes flickered around the circle as I tried to count.

"Ten threes in play." He raised a finger at the man on my right. "Challenger wins, you lose."

The man on the forfeited one of his dice with a laugh.

Twenty-nine dice left in play, I reminded myself. We rolled again and reached a pinnacle of challenge or be challenged time and time again until the dice ran out. With every round, the stakes rose, and with every dice lost, I could have choked on my disappointment.

I didn't win the pot of coins.

They went to the quiet girl, who said nothing as she tucked them into her cloak, bid us goodnight, and disappeared without risking her win. That night, I curled up behind the fortune teller's tent with my mind stuck on how the game would go the next day and how my luck would turn.

I would win before the trial was up. It was only as I drifted into sleep that I realised I had been so busy all day that I hadn't even thought to look for the akelda.

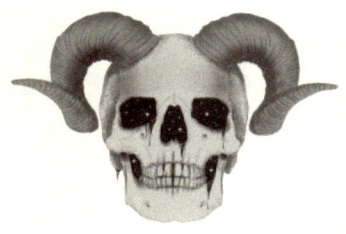

Chapter Seventeen

Another day of hard work left me swaying on my feet by the time I was below ground again. Irritation sparked through me when Aureen cornered me in the eatery with her sister.

"Go away," I demanded, the metal spoon in my mouth muffling my words.

Aureen scoffed and set her bowl down. She was eating the same strange grain and mashed vegetables that I was, while Kyra dropped quietly into the seat beside her, carrying drinks.

"Unlikely." Aureen twisted in the seat until she found Monika. She stared intently at the smaller woman until, paranoid, Monika turned away. With a jerk of Aureen's head, the entirety of our team sat around my table.

I huffed, unamused, and dragged my mug of bitter tea closer. My hands wrapped around it firmly, and I sipped in silence.

Before long, Monika had joined us and sniffled as she slid into the seat beside me. Rumley had caught sight of us, too, and his stare burnt a hole in the side of my head.

A flick of my fingers untucked the hair from behind my ear, and I used it like a shield to help me ignore the intensity of his gaze.

"So," I hummed, "what's going on?"

"I want to know what you're up to," Aureen demanded.

"It couldn't have waited until tomorrow?" I asked.

I wanted them to leave. I wanted to eat and find a spot in the little round of Deceiver's Dice. I wanted to win and wanted to sleep like a baby basking in my success.

"No."

"Why?" I asked, setting my mug down hard.

"Kyra and I" – she glanced at her sister, who remained quiet – "we're making a move tomorrow. You and Monika need to pull it together."

"There's no rush," I stated.

The bronzed woman looked like she wanted to pull the dark locks of her hair from her head. The corner of her mouth curled up in a sneer. "Tomorrow, we're a third of the way through."

"I know that!" I snapped. "I'm not stupid."

"Sure."

"Say it again!?"

Aureen huffed out a frustrated breath, her dark eyes flickering.

"We're making a move tomorrow," she repeated. "You two need to hurry up, or we'll leave you behind."

Her palms hit the table, and the chair fell backwards when she stood. Aureen was three steps away before she glanced over her shoulder, pushing a braided lock of her long hair to the side, and snapped at Kyra.

"Come on!"

Kyra flashed us an apologetic grin and scurried after her sister.

Silence lingered as I stared down into the murky mug of tea. A headache pulsed at my temple, incessant, irritating. Eventually, Monika cleared her throat. I tilted my head, just enough to show that I had heard.

"Have you made it inside a house?" she asked.

I nodded. I was irrationally angry, even though she wasn't the one who had destroyed my mood.

"I haven't." She pressed on. "But I can help you . . ."

For the first time, I looked at her properly. There was tension in her jaw, defensiveness as she braced herself for rejection. An unfamiliar feeling twisted my stomach as I realised, I hadn't been kind to Monika, and she hadn't deserved it.

"Okay," I sighed heavily. "But I need one more day. We can't strike tomorrow; I don't know where it is yet."

"I'll go out tonight." Monika nodded as she rose. "I'll find out a little bit more about the night security."

I blinked. "I don't think that's a good idea."

"You don't get an opinion."

She wasn't wrong.

I sighed. "Well . . . don't die, I guess."

Monika didn't reply. She didn't make promises she couldn't keep. Instead, she had already scurried away by the time I could think to say goodbye. The three of them had effectively ruined my appetite, so I abandoned the remnants of my tea and rose from the table, too.

I was halfway through the eatery before the first interception.

Benton Rumley's breath reeked of stale beer and onions when he crowded in on me. I wasn't sure why he'd picked me to come, but I hated him for it.

"What are they planning?" he hissed; spittle flew against my face.

"Nothing." I raised my hand, wiping the side of my face. "We don't have a plan."

I wasn't lying. Not really.

"Tell me!" he demanded. "I'm a part of the team!"

I glanced to his reddened face and the wildness in his eyes, the dark shadows a bruise still curled around the edge of his eye.

"No," I said and shoved forward. My shoulder slammed into him. "You're not."

"Nox!" he yelled. "Get back here!"

I didn't stop. I lost him in the thick of the market, amongst the citizens that had braved to come down close to dusk for the end-of-day sale prices.

I was in search for the dice game when the second interception came.

Nash Wickham grabbed my arm and pulled me quickly to the side. I staggered but managed to find my balance. Straightening, I gathered the last few fragments of my dignity as we stood shoulder-to-shoulder and stared at piles of brightly coloured Gulan spices.

An impulsive thought flitted through my mind to knock them all over and watch the colours merge.

Samael laughed, an echo in the back of my mind.

"Are you okay?" Nash asked, startling me from the thought.

"Do I look okay?"

He pinched his lips together.

"Nash," I hummed. I missed his cheerful attitude and the comfort of his presence, and I wanted to tell him that, but I couldn't find the words. "Never mind."

"Do you have a piece?" he asked, filling the space.

"No."

"I do."

"What?" Startled, I turned and stared at him. Nash didn't look at me. Instead, his gaze stayed on the spices, his hands buried in his pocket. "How?"

"Luck. A man in the market dropped a purse," he admitted. "There was a piece inside."

A shiver worked itself from my crown to my tailbone, like the soft tip of a finger trailed along each knot of my spine.

My throat felt tight. Panic threatened to spur on tears.

I wanted to be the one with the akelda, with the ticket out of Invidia, and the promise of safety in my future. I wanted to be good at the heist because, as Niklaus had stated, I was the thief.

"You need to find a piece quickly," Nash said.

Irritation sparked through me, fuelled by the bitterness I felt at not being the first.

"I know," I hissed. Too sharp.

Nash turned and squeezed a hug out of me. Despite how tense I felt, despite how annoyed I was, I relaxed in Nash's grip and sunk into his arms.

"We're going to make it through this, Tav. Just do whatever it takes to win, okay?"

I nodded.

"Say it," Nash demanded.

"Whatever it takes."

Nash disappeared, and I snuck to my nook behind the fortune teller's tent, slipping between the heavily draped fabric and the cold stone wall. His story had reminded me of another purse dropped.

Inside the tent, I could hear the fortune teller weaving a fanciful tale, his voice rough and gravelly as the man spoke of a girl who met a charming young man from the inner spiral. I tried to keep quiet so he wouldn't hear as I rifled through the nest of odds and ends accumulated over the past week.

Beneath food, blankets, and my carefully folded uniform, with Rowan's cap pressed on top, I found the woven purse.

The crone had dropped it just as Nash had mentioned in his story, but that night, I was too tired to do anything more than hide it away and sleep. By morning, it had been forgotten.

I knelt in my little nest of blankets, fumbling with the silver latch. My fingers shook.

Had the crone given me a way through this competition days ago, and I had just never known? Could I be so lucky?

Of course not.

When the latch gave way and contents spilled out, it contained nothing more than a handful of silver envy coins and a small bundle of dried herbs.

My excitement ebbed away, and I became aware of how the concrete floor pressed into my knees until they hurt, and I began to shiver. The cool night pierced right through me.

I stared at the coins until the fortune teller was done with his client. His footsteps shuffled out the front, and his gravelly pitch started again. Never had I been so disappointed to see a handful of coins; I had really thought I would find the stone of green fire in there.

My throat tightened as I bundled the herbs back into the purse. The clasp clicked closed. I had given myself false hope. I pocketed the snake-stamped coins and decided to repurpose them.

I had a game to win, and they wouldn't be so disappointing if they'd doubled.

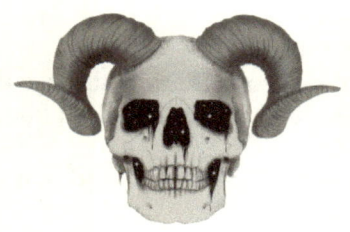

Chapter Eighteen

True to her word, Monika allowed one extra day of reconnaissance. I woke before the dawn, dressed as a maid, and despite the growing desire to go back to bed, walked up to the office. Rowan met me outside, and with a small smile, I handed her a wrapped pastry.

Finally, I had managed to win one of the rounds of Deceiver's Dice and had impulsively spent half my winnings on the soft, buttery pastry. It wasn't often I did things like that, but it felt like Rowan had kept me afloat for the last few days, and for that, I was grateful.

Once again, we had both been allocated to the North residence, and when I questioned it, Rowan giggled that Lady Francesca and her housekeeper liked consistency. If a maid performed well, they were allowed to stay. I greeted the guard as if I knew him well, although his presence left me skittish. It was only a matter of time until he realised, I was a fraud. Until he called me out and skewered me through.

The day followed a familiar pattern. We set the tables and lay the fires in the sunroom for Lady Francesca to have her breakfast. As she ate, we slipped into the bedrooms to tidy up after the family and prepare them for the night.

"I'll take the master bedroom." I blocked the door, facing Rowan with an uneasy smile. "You can take the nursery; we'll divide and conquer, so we can have lunch earlier?"

Rowan, sweet and trusting, didn't hesitate. "That's a great idea!"

My heart had been racing in my chest, hammering with a mixture of fear and anticipation, unsure if Rowan would trust me enough to go her own way. I waited until she was in the nursery before I entered the master bedroom.

It looked as it always had, with the strange, slippery cream sheets that needed to be smoothed and tucked back into the bed. The heavy blanket pushed completely off one side of the bed and rumpled on the other. At least three of the pillows were scattered on the floor. I tidied the bed as quickly as possible, settling the last of the pillows before I glanced at the fireplace. The ashes needed cleaning, but they could wait. Instead, I tiptoed across the room, glancing at the door nervously, and approached the large vanity.

The sight of me was startling. It wasn't often I had the opportunity to catch my reflection.

The sleeves of the dress fell past my palms, and the cap smoothed away my hair, which rounded my face.

I didn't look like myself.

123

It was easy to imagine I was just Tav Duncan, who worked for an honest coin each day. A woman who lived a simpler life. The harsh reality, though, was that I was not Tav Duncan. I was Octavia Nox, and I was not a maid but a thief and a competitor in a foolish trial that would surely kill me.

It took effort, but I tore my gaze from my reflection and settled into the cushioned seat at the vanity, a luxury after sleeping in the Infra.

A soft groan of joy slipped from my lips.

Samael greeted me with a low chuckle in my ear. I had gotten used to his laughter, but as I opened the jewellery box and started to rifle through it, he started a conversation.

'*What are you up to now, Little One?*' he asked.

I scoffed, pulling out every compartment of the jewellery box that I could find, the obvious place to keep the akelda.

"Trying to win."

'*Winning is very important to you, then?*'

"Winning is important to everyone." My nose scrunched. "Anyone who tells you otherwise is a liar."

Samael was silent.

The akelda wasn't inside the jewellery box, but a glittering jewel encrusted comb had caught my attention. My fingers drifted towards it, the pad of my thumb tracing over the large stone.

'*Tell me*' – Samael's voice was so demanding that I stilled – '*are you a liar, Little One?*'

My throat tightened.

I wasn't sure what the right answer was, not for the devil, so I settled on the truth. I lifted my chin to stare into my own gaze, imagining I was meeting his eye instead.

"Yes."

The devil laughed, a strangely rich sound that relaxed me. It reminded me of the way my hands had slid against the silky sheets on the bed.

'*Good.*' He sounded amused. '*I like that.*'

I curled my fingers around the comb as I lifted it from the box. It was tucked in the pocket of my dress before I set about putting everything back in order.

"Do you have any advice for me today, Samael?" I asked.

There was a fatigue that lined my face with shadows and wondered if the devil was not just my soul splitting in two. What if his dark shadows were coming out?

'*Hmm.*' He took his time. '*I have something for you to think about, Little One. If you possessed something that everyone coveted, would you hide it?*'

"Yes."

'*What if you wanted everyone to know that you had it? What if you wanted them to envy your fortune? Would you still hide it?*'

I didn't answer immediately, and he hummed again, a soft sound. I shivered as the feeling of his presence in my mind intensified.

'*Something to think about, hmm?*' Samael repeated. '*Until next time, Little One.*'

Protest pricked my lips, but he was gone before I could find the right words to put behind it.

The doorknob squeaked, and I jumped from the chair in a rush three paces towards the bed before the door opened and Rowan poked her head inside.

I twisted to face her and hoped I didn't look half as guilty as I felt. The comb felt too heavy in my pocket.

"All done?" she asked, not noticing anything amiss.

"Not yet." I gestured towards the hearth. "I couldn't find one of the pillows. It was underneath the bed. So, I still have the fire . . ."

Rowan blinked; her eyes darted to the clock on the wall. She pushed the door open wider and stepped inside. "I'll help."

I shook my head. "You don't have to do that."

Rowan scoffed. "It wasn't a question. Come on."

Between the two of us, we made fast work of the fire, and we raced down the stairs only to be waylaid by the housekeeper. The old woman put us to work to polish cutlery for the best part of an hour.

The entire time, Rowan spoke of her little sister, recounting stories, and I hummed and nodded in all the right places. It wasn't that I didn't want to hear her stories, but I was stuck on what the devil had said to me. It felt like he was giving me a hint, and I wasn't about to question the validity of his advice; it had been true in the previous trial. I just had to find the answer to his question.

"Rowan?" I interrupted.

She paused, waiting.

"Can I ask you a question?" After a breath, I clarified. "A pretend question."

"Anything." She beamed.

"Say . . . say you'd met a man" – I struggled to find the right scenario, the heavy weight of the jewelled comb in my pocket giving me ideas – "and he bought you a *very* expensive gift. A . . . a hair pin, and it was gorgeous but very costly."

I paused, and Rowan nodded, her eyes alight, a knowing smile on her lips.

"People will want it. They might try and steal it, but you also . . . You want people to know you have it. You want them to know this man spoils you. So . . . what do you do? You don't want it to get stolen, but still, you just want your friends to know what you have it . . . How do you tell them?"

Rowan grinned widely. "Tav, you wear it."

It seemed like the most obvious answer in the world, but for all the spoons I had just polished, I couldn't think of an alternative than hiding it away, protecting the precious jewel.

Rowan rounded the table, and her hip bumped into mine.

"Tav," she cried in a happy, hushed voice. "Did you meet someone?"

I blinked and dropped a fork. "*What?*"

"You did, didn't you?!" she gushed, a bright smile stretched across her face. "That isn't pretend at all. You have an admirer buying you pretty gifts. From the inner spiral? Is it a lord?!"

Belatedly, I could see how she might jump to that conclusion, and I couldn't see a way out of it.

"I . . . I . . ."

Rowan pressed a finger to my lips to silence me quickly.

I blinked at the intimacy of the movement. Guilt swirled in my gut at my many lies.

"It's okay." She grinned. "Your secret is safe with me."

True to her word, Rowan didn't mention my supposed admirer again. Not as we finished with the silverware and slid it back into the drawer, and not when we huddled downstairs and unwrapped the cold pastries to let flaky pieces melt on the end of our tongues.

As I sucked a drop of the filling off my thumb, I was reminded of the haunting moment before Gluttony had stolen Ophelia's heart. She licked her fingers; blissfully unaware her death would come so soon.

The pastry dropped back into the wrapper as my appetite fled. I wrapped it and placed it in my pocket, my fingers brushing against the heavy comb.

I wasn't sure why I had taken it; the impulse had been brash and stupid but one I couldn't ignore.

Not when my hands had essentially been in a treasure trove. Not when their trust for me was built on the record of another girl.

As Rowan hummed a song, I wondered what Lillian Duncan was doing in that moment, out of work just because she lost her identification. I couldn't bring myself to feel sorry for her, since her misfortune granted me a chance to survive.

I shifted where I sat and closed my eyes, listening to the rise and fall of Rowan's song. Guilt for befriending this woman swelled inside of me, especially after what had happened to Ophelia. She was too nice, too innocent, to get tangled up with someone like me.

The door at the top of the stairs banged open. It bounced off the wall and slid closed again. Shuffling sounded before the woman's face appeared over the banister.

"There you are!" she cried.

I blinked and glanced at Rowan, who looked towards the clock. I knew we had that long until lunch, when the fat line on the clock pointing downwards, and it was only two-thirds of the way there.

"Did you need something, ma'am?" Rowan found her composure first. She brushed crumbs from her fingers and stood.

The housekeeper sighed heavily. "You need to get up here! Fast!"

"Uhh." I hesitated.

"Now, ladies. Clean yourselves up. The gates are opening! They're coming," the housekeeper stated. "Lady Francesca wants the whole household out. You have five minutes."

Rowan grasped my hand and squeezed so hard my protests of lunch were lost. She squealed, startling me.

"What's going on?" I asked.

Rowan shook her head and smiled at me like I was being foolish, then her smile slipped. It seemed this was something I should have known if I'd lived in Invidia. Hastily, I tried to smile and find enthusiasm, as if I knew what they meant. My crooked, toothy grin relaxed Rowan back into her own excitement.

"They're coming out!" she cried. "I've never been this close to the gates before."

She packed her lunch and jumped up to turn to the small mirror and fixed the way her cap settled around her head, tucking away wisps of hair that had managed to escape.

As I stood and brushed off my skirt, I realised she meant the castle's gates. A strange sense of foreboding swept through me, violent enough to leave me light-headed.

I wasn't sure I wanted to see what would come out of them.

Five minutes later, along with the rest of the household, we tumbled into the yard and stood by the fence line as we waited for the gates to open.

The feeling of impending doom never left me.

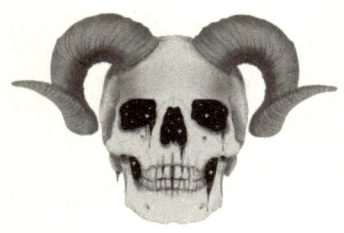

Chapter Nineteen

The castle gates groaned as they swung open, a violent protest of having been closed for so long. The North residence sat just around the first curve of the street, so gathered in the front yard, we held a prime view of what was to come.

It was not the looming castle or the marching guards that held my attention, not at first. It was the family in the yard with us, and as I stood quietly by Rowan's side, I realised this the first time I had seen Lady Francesca North and her family.

The lady was tall and regal, with chestnut curls of hair pinned up to display the length of her neck. Her husband stood a few inches shorter than his wife, with thinning dark hair, thick spectacles, and a fine moustache. Their children stood so still, so quietly, that, had I not picked up their toys from the past three days, I would have thought they had never known joy. They looked so serious, solemn, that the sense of foreboding I felt intensified.

The castle guards found their posts, spaced along the spiral, extending as far around the curve as I could see. A gentle wind blew through the spiral, and rain sprinkled. It seemed as if it always rained in Invidia.

Still, we didn't move. We stood as a household and waited.

Lord North murmured words too faint for me to hear, and my breath caught in my chest when Lady Francesca turned to look at us. Her pale gaze was critical and assessing, as how we presented mattered to this woman: two young maids, a housekeeper, the cook, and the nursemaid of her children, those in servitude to her status in this city. When she turned, I couldn't tear my eyes away. I wasn't taken by the severe angles of her face, or the sweep of pink powder brushed across her cheekbones but on the silver chain at her neck.

Rowan was right.

The luminescent akelda sat on proud display, nestled right in the hollow of her throat. The stone had been cut and polished in a unique shape with sharp points, and the liquid fire centre threw a soft glow against her skin. Every so often, Lady Francesca fidgeted with the piece, settling in the right place.

Such was the vanity of the rich.

I felt as if my veins had been lit on fire. I couldn't stand still. My fingers bunched into my apron and grasped tight as the jitters flowed through me.

I knew where the akelda was; my goal was literally in sight.

It was a heady sense of achievement. Yet, I wrestled with a growing hopelessness at how I would literally steal something from around a guarded woman's neck.

The theft proved to be much more difficult.

"They're coming!" Rowan breathed excitedly.

Her voice drew my focus away from my problems. I shifted my weight from one foot to the other, then leaned against Rowan. She grasped my hand, fingers linked through mine, anchoring me in place.

Voices rose from the castle.

The guards straightened, and through the hazy rain, a rainbow appeared.

A group of people pooled into the street in a mass of rambunctious laughter. A beat later, I realised I was seeing Envy's prized collection of people. Just like Francesca North and her gemstone, the Angel of Envy liked to show off what he possessed.

They walked the spiral in sets of two.

First, a man and a woman with the fiery-red hair of Desidia. Freckles smattered their pale skin, their movements languid. They had all the time in the world, and it showed as they linked arms. The woman leaned into the man, whispering and laughing.

They walked through the rain, uncaring of the way it clung to their skin and their hair.

Their carefree energy left my heart squeezing in my chest.

The next two people had dark, burnished skin and strong features linked to Cupiditian islanders. They were mesmerising. Taller than the couple before them, their long dark hair had natural waves that the upper-class women of Invidia must have envied.

These two were Lust's perfection.

I could see why Envy had stolen them.

I knew Lady Francesca had artificially curled her hair; soft foam rollers were often scattered about her pillow in the morning. I imagined she must have burnt with bitterness at the sight of this woman.

Behind the Cupiditans were a set of identical triplets. Short and slender, lean men with hauntingly identical stares and tousled dark hair.

These three did not laugh; there was no joy in their movements, they just walked through the rain as if it pained them to be outside. There was something strange about the way they moved. Occasionally, one of them would tilt their head or lean towards another, as if they were having a silent conversation, but their lips never parted. Their hands moved rapidly, as if they were talking, too excited, but that didn't reflect in their faces as they trailed across the cobblestones.

When the triplets passed through the gate, I craned my neck for a better look at them. It was only then I realised the man in the middle had milky-white, sightless eyes. He walked without aid, though, unhindered by his lack of sight as he moved between his clones.

"He's Devil-cursed?" I gasped.

Rowan sighed softly; her eyes flicked to Lady Francesca to ensure we wouldn't get caught chattering.

"Some say," she said, "that every piece in his collection is Devil-cursed. Each of them unique in the way the demonesses left their touch."

"You think so?"

"I don't know if it's true."

"Wow." My teeth clamped down on my lip, and I turned my gaze to the final woman to walk out of the gates.

It was the woman from the markets.

Margot.

I remembered her name as clear as day, as well as the curled sneer on her face. A sharp ache rolled through my chest as I remembered how beautiful her features were up close and how badly I wished I looked as striking as she did.

"Oh," I muttered. Rowan gave a tiny nod. "She's . . ."

"The jewel of his collection. There's none other like her –"

I leaned forward for a better look, and the housekeeper clicked her tongue, warning me to stay in place.

Many people would have said Margot looked strange and out of place, but something alluring in the affliction had robbed her of all colours.

Rowan nudged me.

"Yeah?"

"People say she was cursed by the demons of winter themselves," Rowan muttered. "You know, to look be as cold and unfeeling as snow."

"Bullshit!"

Rowan inhaled sharply.

I shook my head. "Nobody could be cursed to be unfeeling. Or else we would all seek out demons and ask for it . . ."

There were many things I wished I didn't have to feel. I'd sought out a demon to curse me if it were that easy. Many people would sell their souls for an unfeeling existence.

"Quiet, ladies!" the housekeeper hissed.

Rowan and I exchanged a look but fell silent.

Margot walked slowly and deliberately through the spiral. She didn't stray from the middle of the cobblestone. She didn't spare a glance for the families lined in their yard, who looked tense as they waited.

A strange feeling rolled through my body, a chilling and possessive desire to be that woman, to have people look at me the way they looked at her as she passed. As if she were everything. As if she had everything.

Margot wore a thin veil to protect herself, but I could still see the smooth perfection of her pale skin at the flash in her wrists and the slender length of her ring-adorned hands. Real gold and silver circled her fingers. Not like the foraged pieces of thin metal I had twisted and worn around my own.

I glanced at my hands, my skin so many shades darker than her own, but lighter where I had shucked off my rings and stowed them in my boots to hide away as a maid.

The jealousy for what she had was inescapable.

With every inhale, I found myself comparing my image to hers. My dry, dark hair, which was never really washed properly, seemed dull compared to the glossy curl of her blinding white locks.

Margot wore a gown likely valued at what it would have cost to feed my whole family for an entire year, and I felt starkly inadequate standing behind a rich family in a plain uniform, with most of my identity hidden away. Standing there as someone other than myself.

I was suffocating on my own insecurities.

It only worsened when a cry of joy echoed from the skies.

The collection of people stopped walking. Margot was two houses down from the North property and tilted her head to the side. She waited, and we waited with her as the angel in the sky circled above his city.

Then he plummeted from the skies to land by her side.

Envy was different from his brothers, and I noticed immediately. Even though his glossy black wings shrouded him from my view.

He felt different.

His influence was not the sharp punch to my gut that Gluttony's had been. Nor the prominent guiding hand I had felt with Pride.

No. Instead, Envy's influence had invaded my blood, and each time my heart pounded in my chest, it intensified.

A poison I hadn't known that I had consumed.

My grip tightened around Rowan's hand, anchoring myself as we both trembled under a wave of nausea and despair, the side effects of the acute envy consuming me, until I was trembling.

My eyes flicked to Lady Francesca, noting the tension that had wound into her stance, the vein throbbing in her slender neck, having appeared when Envy landed in the streets.

We were all strained and silent, waiting for their lord's acknowledgement.

They seemed to be watching each another as well, and I realised that, with the proximity to the castle, they must feel this all the time. This intoxicating desire to be better than the person next to me; to be the centre of the world.

The suffocating insecurity that followed my envy threatened to close my lungs. Or maybe it would claw its way from out my insides out into the world like a dark and deadly demon.

I felt irrationally angry at myself, at the world, and mostly at Margot.

My gaze skimmed across the street, and I noticed a familiar person.

Mikhael Heira stood tall in a crisp white shirt, sleeves rolled to his elbows, his head held high. He didn't bother to hide the cuff at his wrists as he stood on the side of the street. He waited as if he had belonged there, ready to move into one of the sprawling properties and take his place amongst Invidia's elite.

I watched him and realised he wasn't watching the angel. No, his eyes didn't stray for a moment from Margot. Curiosity burnt through me as Envy turned on his heel and glanced back at the families behind him.

My heart shuddered in my chest. This was my first real look at the Angel of Envy.

He was far younger than his brothers. Tall and lithe, Envy had the face of a man my own age. He was filled with the signs of arrogance and youth.

As Lady Francesca's husband bristled, I realised this was part of it all.

He was a baby-faced angel who ruled an entire city and manipulated their emotions as if it were nothing. A child on a throne and the old men in his inner circle wanted nothing more than to be him, to be younger, to be powerful.

Envy was dark-haired like Gluttony, but that was where their similarities ended. His eyes were a light green, and his hair lay in a way that made it seem like he didn't care to brush it, ruffled from his flight.

The way he moved, as he took Margot's arm and circled her back to speak to man who lived in the house next door, reminded me of the snakes that represented him. His body was sleek, smooth, and inexplicably dangerous. His wings shifted with every step, strong and powerful.

He used them in every movement, an extension of himself.

While Envy stopped to talk, Lady Francesca whispered to her husband. The muscles in his shoulders rolled and tensed. I wondered if it pained the man that his neighbour held Envy's attention.

The longer we stood, the more I felt I should leave, that it was too dangerous to be this close to the angel, but Rowan kept me in place.

She hyperventilated; her eyes cast down.

"Are you okay?" I asked.

She shook her head.

I held her hand tighter, my thumb brushing circles on the back of her hand.

Envy lifted his gaze to Lady Francesca and her family. His thin lips pulled back, and he nodded sharply at them. My heart skittered, skin tingling, and I wanted nothing more than for him to look at me properly.

The North family seemed to relax for a moment at this acknowledgement. Even the housekeeper straightened, basking beneath his gaze, as if they held more power than their neighbour.

He may have been at the neighbour's gate, but Lady Francesca had stolen his attention.

Envy's eyes flickered over the children and the help. For a moment, I worried that he would see me for the liar that I had become.

He barely seemed to notice me, though, which caused as much disappointment as it did relief.

I sighed as the angel and his collection moved on, tailed by their guards as if his power couldn't deter an attack.

We didn't move from the lawns of the property for the best part of an hour. My feet ached. The farther that the angel moved through the spiral, the more the knots in my stomach loosened. The tremors in my hands settled.

That was . . . until they made their way back.

His influence was so strong I felt faint and that, just like Rowan, I had to stare at the ground and focus on my breathing to control myself. I didn't know if I wanted to pass out or run for the fence, lunge at it, and attack Margot to take her place.

The envious desire to put myself in front of that angel to steal the adoration was too much. The way the angel looked at Margot was like she was the beginning and the end of his day.

I wanted to be the centre of someone else's universe.

The desire squeezed my heart so firmly my chest ached until they were safely back behind their iron gates.

Lady Francesca stalked back into the house, brushing past us without a word, her husband and children trailing in her wake.

The housekeeper turned in our direction, dropping her hands into her white apron's pocket, and pulled out our work slips, brandishing them at us quickly.

"Dismissed, ladies."

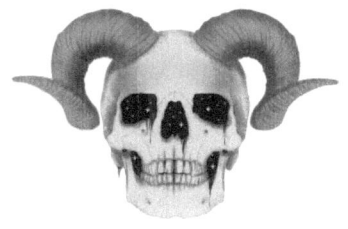

Chapter Twenty

Monika sat beside me at dinner. We didn't speak as we inhaled a bowl of chicken and soaked grain as fast as we could, leaning so low over the bowls we could have been trapped back in the Feast of Samael.

My spoon clinked against the bottom of the bowl. I dropped it, pushed it aside, and nursed the large mug of bitter alcohol that I had spent too much coin on. I needed it, though, after that day, after Envy.

It felt like his poison still coursed through my veins. I would never be rid of it, just like I would always fear starvation since then. The angels of sin were more of a curse than I had expected.

They had promised we would never go hungry again if we passed the Gluttony trial, but I had realised now that was not due to magic but from our own fear of the feeling after the first trial and the cemented need for satiation.

What scars would Envy leave on my soul?

I lifted the mug and drained it almost dry. A shudder rolled through me at the tart taste.

"I worked out the guard schedule." Monika broke the silence. "They switch over just before dusk, and the night guard works from inside a posting house between two properties. Instead of one to each."

She paused.

I waited out her silence.

"That's probably the best time," she added.

A nervous energy fluttered in my stomach and twisted around my heart like a vice. I glanced into the frothy drink and wondered why I was fool enough to be there. I had wanted to survive, and then Monika proposed a plan that would put me in more danger than ever.

Every day felt riskier than the last.

"You want to go out at dusk?" I croaked.

"It's the best time."

She was probably right.

Beneath any bravado I might have presented, I was nothing more than a coward who didn't want to brave the night and the demons within it. I chewed on my lip, then clutched my mug like a lifeline.

"Tomorrow, then." I reluctantly agreed.

"Which house?"

"North residence. One-four from the castle."

Monika's nose flared, and she nodded sharply. "Go to work tomorrow, finish the day, then circle back afterwards and meet me there."

"I —"

Aureen Willett slapped her palms against the tacky surface of the table and leaned over us.

I snorted a frustrated breath and tilted my head to meet her gaze.

Kyra lingered two steps behind.

"Yes?" I asked pointedly.

"We got one," Aureen announced, eyes bright. "Hurry, hurry, ladies."

"We're supposed to be a team," I pointed out roughly.

"And?" Aureen lifted a brow.

It was a fluid movement I envied, but I had to push the thought down to focus on the problem at hand. "You should be helping us!"

Aureen scoffed. "You didn't help me."

I rolled my eyes to the old world and shook my head. "You didn't even give us the chance. This is bullshit! They said we needed to work in teams, and you've not helped us at all."

Her nails tapped against the tabletop, her nose flaring.

"Fine." She sighed. "We got one without you. You get one without us, and we'll get the last two together."

It wasn't the best deal, but I knew it was all I would get from Aureen Willett because, while we may have been allocated as a team, we weren't friends.

My friends were trying to survive without me, and I had to do the same.

"Fine."

"What about Rumley?" Monika piped up.

"What about him?"

Her eyes flickered to the side. Sure enough, Rumley was watching us again. A scowl curled on his lips, and his brow furrowed.

"He's always watching."

The statement was ominous and undeniable. I realised I hadn't told the others that Rumley had lost his akelda.

"Be careful of him," I said. "He's a desperate man."

Desperate people took dangerous chances – I knew that.

Light flared in Aureen's eyes, immediately understanding, and she glanced over her shoulder at her sister. She straightened, her shoulders rolling back before she gestured at Kyra. The younger girl huddled close.

"Don't go near him," she commanded. Her word was law, and her sister inhaled sharply.

Aureen, dismissive of Monika, pinned me beneath her gaze and peered down the slope of her nose. The silence between us felt like it stretched an eternity.

"Find me when you get it."

"Right."

She wrapped her arm around Kyra's shoulders, and she steered the girl away. I watched them leave and wondered if the woman would carry her sister through each of the seven trials.

Monika picked up her bowl and stood. "Tomorrow?"

"Yeah," I confirmed. "Tomorrow."

I stayed put until I had finished every drop of the heady drink, and my gaze strayed across the room to where Helina and Niklaus were sitting with their team. They sat on top of the tables, elevating themselves and holding a form of court. Other groups seemed to grovel around them. I considered the way Aureen carried her sister through each day and studied the side of Helina's face. We had such a long history that the guise of competition had shattered. We weren't carrying each other anywhere.

It hurt that Helina Archer threw me away so easily, to know that I had never been in the long-term visions of her future.

If we had entered this competition side-by-side, instead of filled with strange animosity, I was sure the trials would have seemed much easier. We could have risen to the challenges with Helina's smarts and my willingness to do what needed to be done.

While I could understand the way she thought I was taking her glory, I still didn't like the assumption and how her suspicions and wounded pride had driven us apart so quickly.

Helina glanced up.

Our gazes met, and from behind her crooked spectacles, she frowned at me. I could hold her eye for one beat, two, three, then I glanced at the empty mug and sighed.

My chair hit the ground as I stalked away.

I slipped into the Infra and tucked my hands into my pockets as I started to inspect the stalls to pass the time. The vendors seemed reserved today, talking and watching their patrons instead of the way they normally called out for their sales.

Their change in attitude left me on edge.

In front of one of the stalls, a benchtop without a tent, I picked up a small glass jar that contained a swirling liquid, a near black blue. A man appeared behind the bench, moving quickly after I picked it up and showed interest.

"Fifteen envy coin," he advised.

I blinked at the exorbitant price and lifted the jar to the artificial light for a better look, even though I had no intention of buying it.

"What is it?" I asked.

The man stroked his beard. "Demon ether."

With a clatter, the jar returned to the bench quickly, and I wiped my fingers against my shirt, in case I might have caught something from touching it.

A raspy laugh barked from behind me.

I twisted to find the crone standing a few paces away.

"He lies," the beady-eyed crone announced.

My gaze swung accusingly towards the man. His lips twisted into a smirk. He raised both hands and shrugged. "Visitors of the Infra will believe anything."

Eadlin shuffled closer. "How many have you sold today, old man?"

"Three." The man laughed, and I watched as the old woman handed over a small pouch of herbs. He didn't offer payment.

"What is it, really?" I asked.

"Ink and water, girl." The crone hummed. "Ink and water."

I snorted, shaking my head.

"Can you stay here a moment?" I asked the crone, deciding their trade was none of my business.

She nodded.

I twisted on my heel, looked for any landmark to find the stall again, then paced through the market to the fortune teller's tent. After a quick, paranoid scan, I slipped behind it. My arm brushed the cold wall, and I couched in amongst the pile of blankets, sorting through my possession and snagging the woven pouch.

It took longer than expected to find my way back to the crone.

Her eyes narrowed on me as I approached. I had the feeling a twice-Devil-cursed woman was not the sort to keep waiting.

No apology was offered, but I held out the purse to the old woman.

The crone pushed her long braid over her shoulder in an impatient movement. She snagged the pouch and weighed it in her palm.

"Bah! Took it all, did you!?"

"Can you blame me? I'm playing the strangest game of theft of my life."

Unexpectedly, the crone grinned. It was an unsettling look against the wrinkled lines of her face. In truth, I had only given her the pouch back due to growing paranoia that the herbs inside of it would leave me Devil-cursed in the same way she had been.

I wasn't sure how someone came to be that way, but I would do anything in my power to avoid it.

The crone watched me, and I wondered if she could pluck the thoughts straight from my head as part of her curse. As this occurred to me, Samael's smooth laugh echoed in my ear, just as Eadlin's eyes narrowed further.

Someone was in my head, but it wasn't the old crone.

"Careful, girl."

"Huh?"

The crone was gone before I could get an explanation.

I glanced to the vendor, who gestured to his fake demon ether, and with a snort, I turned and stalked right out of the Infra's central hub. I twisted away from the path to the surface, not looking to be out after dark, and avoided the encampment as well.

Instead, I turned into one of the long tunnels beneath the city.

They were damp. The ever-falling rains of Invidia had soaked right through the buildings and dripped beneath the Earth to settle in the strange world that existed below. I hadn't dared to venture this far out before, and I couldn't deny my nerves as I edged into the Infra's dimly lit, crate-packed sections.

At a crashing sound, I froze.

I inhaled sharply and pressed myself against the cold wall of the tunnel. The damp seemed to seep through the back of my clothing, chilling me through. I stayed still, head tilted, and face screwed up as I strained to listen to what was happening up ahead. Good common sense said that I should have turned and moved quickly back into the safety of more familiar ground.

A familiar voice, however, coaxed me forward.

Rounding the corner, I pressed into the shadows and squinted through the darkness at the sight of Niklaus and Mikhael Heira standing nose-to-nose, their fists wound in each other's shirts.

Tension radiated from them, their grips twisting each other that neither could move unless the other allowed it.

Muscles bunched in their forearms, along their shoulders, in their necks.

Mikhael's teeth flashed a snarl as Niklaus hissed at him, the words low and full of vehemence.

"You need to stop, Mik." Deadly fervency filled Niklaus' voice. "Now."

"Fuck off, Niklaus."

"I mean it." Nik pushed forward. They both shifted a step. "Don't go near what doesn't belong to you."

"You're not our father." Mikhael snarled. "You don't tell me what to do."

"Listen to me, you idiot."

Mikhael shoved forward. They shifted again, Niklaus closer to the wall.

I knew I should have left, but I was drowning in my own curiosity, in the need to know what or who they were fighting over. I crept forward, crouching beside one of the wooden boxes.

"Mik," he warned.

Mikhael's lip curled, pulling back to bare his teeth. "You're just the younger brother, Nik. Not the heir. Not important. You're *nothing*."

Niklaus growled, and it echoed down the tunnels. The sound was so feral the hair on the back of my neck rose, warning me to stay away.

I huddled behind the boxes.

"Mikhael." He slammed into him hard.

They crashed into the wall. They tumbled, and my breath caught in my throat. My eyes flickered to the tunnel's mouth as I tried to decide if I could get out before they noticed me. After shifting, and Niklaus let go of his brother's shirt to grab him by the jaw, pushing his head back against the wall, I froze again.

I could see the way Niklaus' nails dug into his brother's skin.

With a sharp crack, Mikhael's head collided with the wall, and his grip went slack, face dazed.

Niklaus leaned in, spitting a warning. "Stay away from her, or you will die."

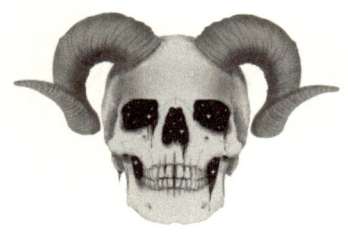

Chapter Twenty-One

Their argument turned into a complete brawl. Away from the main hub's bustle, the brothers spewed insults at each other, each jab an attempt to raise the other's insecurities.

They beat on each other until their breath came ragged, blood pooling on the cold floor, swaying on their feet before an unspoken truce occurred.

Niklaus stormed off, his left eye swelling.

He bypassed me without noticing, and I breathed easier once he was gone. I couldn't bring myself to move and watched as Mikhael massaged his jaw.

He paced back and forth in the tunnel, his shoes scraping the wet ground with each turn, tracking bloody footsteps.

Warily, I watched him, my mind spinning as I tried to work out which woman they were talking about.

Arrogantly, I allowed myself to consider the idea they were fighting over me. Niklaus had warned me I couldn't get between the Heira brothers, even though they caused enough of their own trouble.

But I remembered Mikhael in the street. The way he had stood tall and stared at Margot as if he would walk through those gates, march up the castle's steps, and steal the jewel of Envy's collection for himself.

The remnants of Envy's power pulsed in my blood, and my stomach acid turned bitter. It rose, stinging the back of my throat, until I tasted bile and felt that I could have spit fire.

Of course, it was her and not me; of course Mikhael Heira – a man I had had no interest in before – would look at her before considering me.

My jealousy was irrational, but it heated my blood and put colour in my cheeks.

I watched him from behind those wooden crates and resented him for it, even though my thoughts were theoretical.

A huff of frustration muffled behind his clenched teeth and twisted on his heel. He slammed his fist into the wall so hard his bones crunched as they shattered.

It snapped me out of the simmering anger in my blood, and my sharp inhale bounced off the walls. Nausea rolled through me just from the sound.

Mikhael spun, and I shrank back.

He stalked two steps towards the crates, his jaw tight and gaze searching. I pressed back against the wall, stomach flipping with fear. I knew it wouldn't end well if he had found me there. Given the ferocity with which he had attacked someone he supposedly cared for, his own flesh and blood, there was no way I wanted to step into the path of his anger.

It felt like a stand-off. I huddled into the corner, cold and barely willing to breathe too loud, and he glared into the space, suspicion and coiled tension buzzing in his gaze.

Three minutes felt like three hours.

He kicked out at one of the crates. It shifted, and I flinched, but Mikhael took the same path as his brother back to the markets without a glance my way.

My heart took a few moments to slow and dislodge from my throat.

'*What are you doing, Little One?*'

"Suffering."

I drew my knees to my chest and rested my head against the wet wall.

Samael laughed at my pain, and I scoffed.

Of course, the devil relished in the suffering of humankind, even mine.

"Fuck you," I told him. "And fuck your trial."

'*You'll be fine, Little One.*'

"Another one of your promises?" I spat.

A sense of despair threatened to overwhelm me.

'*Are you calling me a liar now?*' Samael asked, a dangerous edge accompanying his tone. The soft amusement that was usually curling at the edge of his words had disappeared.

I wondered what it was the devil could do to screw me over anymore. What he could do from such a distance while he sat in Eternis and waited for us to destroy ourselves on our path to him. I forced myself onto my feet.

"Yes."

'*The devil does not lie!*'

Samael sounded affronted. I scoffed at his words, lifting both palms up.

"I won't be fine," I spat. "I'm already not fine. Gluttony may as well have taken a bite of my heart."

Samael chuckled in cruel amusement. '*These trials will better your soul for Eternis, Little One?*'

I leaned against the crates, and the lid of one shifted to the side. I glanced inside and frowned at the assortment of weapons within. They felt out of place underground. Dangerous.

"Better for who?" I asked. I shifted the lid back in place, ignoring the contents and turned to follow the Heira brothers. Samael's last remark haunted me all night.

'*For me, of course.*'

The next morning arrived too fast. I woke late to the marketplace's early bustle. In a panic, I dressed and escaped Infra with my cap in hand and apron still undone.

Rowan greeted me at the office, smiling and seemingly recovered from her anxiety the day before.

"Tav!" she cried. "You're a mess!"

"Good morning to you, too." I laughed, and we joined the line. "I overslept."

As we shuffled farther down the line, she twirled her finger in indication that I should turn around. I spun, and she tied the apron tightly, all while recounting a story of her sister's antics the night before.

The transaction in the office was quick, and before I knew it, we were walking down the wet, cobblestone path towards the North residence. We greeted the guard, checked in with the housekeeper, and went to work.

Halfway through the day, I realised it would be the last time I'd see Rowan. She was so cheerful, chatty, and blissfully unaware, but I knew I couldn't return to this house after I had stolen one of Francesca North's most prized possessions.

I would have to leave her behind.

As much as I wanted the day to last forever and enjoy Rowan's simple happiness, the afternoon raced by, and we were dismissed.

At the office, I took my silver coin and tucked it in my pocket.

Rowan beamed and offered, as she always did, "Do you want me to walk you home?"

"That's okay."

"Are you sure? I mean . . ."

The edges of her smile had slipped, and guilt threatened to turn me inside out. I was no real friend. I needed to remember that. I had been manipulating Rowan since the day I met her, and she would probably be better off the next day, when I was no longer in her life.

"Seriously, it's fine." I hugged her quickly. "Go be with your sister. I have some errands to run."

"See you tomorrow!" Rowan called as she started down the street.

The edges of my smile slipped. "Yeah. Tomorrow."

I waited until she had walked out of view and turned to walk slowly through the spiral again before turning into the middle. I paused in the entertainment district, standing in front of one of the stores. My eyes travelled over the outfit on the mannequin.

Dusk came, and the sky turned different shades of pink and orange.

While the sun slipped away, I became more and more anxious, rubbing my hands across my thighs. I had bitten so hard into my lip it beaded with blood. With a wistful glance at the clothes, I turned and dragged my feet to find my teammate. As the screeching of harpies started in the distance, I picked up my pace.

"Wow." Monika cackled when I approached. "You actually look like a hardworking member of society."

That was the first time I had ever heard her laugh.

"Shut up!" I grunted.

Monika mimed zipping her lips but still snickered at me from behind her pursed mouth.

She gestured for me to follow. I shook my head at her antics, begrudgingly slipping into the thin alleyways between the buildings. They were narrow pathways, twisting strangely between the towering, dark buildings that created Invidia's spiral. Thicker in the outer spiral, packed with structures and people alike. It was harder to stay hidden, as the houses sprawled farther and farther apart.

Every so often, I glanced at the sky, my stomach twisting as the darkness came.

More dangers riddled the night than I wanted to confront.

We crouched low and slunk behind the back fences of the properties. Monika tapped the pads of her fingers against each bar, counting beneath each breath. She paused behind a large stone pillar at the edge of the property and glanced back at me.

"Two more houses down," she said, and I nodded. I had to bury my fingers in the thin dress' pockets to hide their shaking. The harpies grew louder.

"It –"

"Shhh!" Monika hissed, and my teeth gritted.

I didn't like being told what to do, but it seemed childish to say something. So, I clenched my jaw and rushed to follow her. My eyes flickered to the sky as I searched for the danger to come. I was so focused on it I didn't notice when Monika stopped, causing me to slam into her back.

"Oof!"

"Shit!" I muttered. "Sorry."

"Just get through the fence, Octavia."

I blinked at her and glanced at the cold metal bars with the spikes on top. "What?"

Monika's lips twisted into a sly smile. "You heard me."

"Just giving you a chance to say you were joking." I scoffed and wrapped my hands around the bars, inhaling sharply at their frigidness.

"I won't fit." I hedged.

"You're as skinny as a rat," Monika hissed and shoved my shoulder.

A whine rolled into the back of my throat as I scrunched my nose. "Fine."

I tightened my grip on the bars, staring dubiously at the thin space between them, and I pressed forward, forcing myself between the cold metal.

My skull felt stuck, and anxiety wrapped around my chest, like a tightly laced corset. I struggled, sucking in a lungful of the cooling air like my life depended on it. Just when it felt like my chest would cave in, I slipped free and fell to my knees in the soft, green grass.

"Praise the devil." I gasped.

Monika slipped through with ease.

'*That's right, Little One. Praise me!*' Samael purred in my ear.

Monika wrenched at my arm.

"We need to go," she hissed.

One foot after the other, I staggered upright and followed her to the next fence, internally groaning at the sight of the next gap she wanted me to force my body through.

It was a tight squeeze, but I managed to slip through and went stumbling against a whitewashed structure. It occurred to me that, if I had been one of those competitors planning to enter The Devil's Trials, I would have spent the years beforehand making sure I was fit.

As it was, by the time we pressed our backs to the guard's hut between properties and listened to the faint rumble of conversation within, my breath came in short bursts, and I rubbed at the tension in my chest.

Monika had her head cocked, and her brow furrowed as she listened. I marvelled at the fact that she could hear them, when, to me, it all sounded like background noise behind my own struggle to breathe normally.

"First guard is leaving," she said.

"Okay."

"We'll give the second guard a few minutes to settle and then get inside the house."

"If you say so."

I slid down the side of the building and pulled my knees to my chest as we waited. The closer we got to our first, real attempt at the heist, the more I decided it was a very bad idea. I was a petty thief; I wasn't ready for the enormity of this task.

Monika slid down beside me. A moment of silence rested before she jabbed her elbow into my ribs.

Irritation skittered across my skin. "Don't!"

I shoved her hard enough that she toppled to the side slightly, her hand sinking into the grass to catch herself. "We need a plan."

My lips pressed together. I suppressed the urge to tell her she had brought us all the way out here so she could figure out the rest.

Instead, I grunted.

"Where's the akelda kept in the house?" Monika asked.

My throat tightened. "Around her neck."

"*What*?!" Monika hissed. "She's wearing it?!"

I nodded, looking away from Monika. I could almost hear the way she gnashed her crooked teeth and turned this new information around in her head.

"Okay."

This time, I twisted to face her, stunned by her casual acceptance of the new challenges and the determined looked that had creased across her face.

"What?" I asked stupidly.

"We get in the house now," Monika stated. "Before it gets too dark and then we hide out until they go to sleep. That will be the best way to get close enough."

It was a simple plan, lacking enough details that I couldn't poke firm holes in it. My belly fluttered and rolled, assuring me it was a bad idea.

The passing of time was measured in two ways. The darkness that crept around us, then the rustle of the guard as he set himself up and settled, the soft clanking as he adjusted his armour, and the snuffling sound that drifted out the cracked window once he fell asleep.

"Why do they even need night guards?" I asked, irritated with having to wait for him. The feeling doubled when I realised, he was sleeping, guarding nothing. It was just another means of showing off in this city.

"Harpies," Monika answered.

They seemed to cry in time with their name.

I looked to the sky and shivered.

The temperature had also dropped as the minutes wore on and the sun sunk lower, shadows rolling from the horizon's edge to steal the orange glow.

"They're coming, aren't they?"

Monika glanced up and nodded abruptly. "Yes."

Part of me wished she had lied.

"In fact," Monika continued, and I tensed, "we need to go soon before they get more active."

My heart squeezed with fear as she nudged me, and I forced myself upright. I staggered through the grassy yard behind Monika, slipping around the side of the house until she stood at the plain wooden door that led into the kitchens.

It was in a place I had rarely been in.

Monika fumbled at the lock with the sharp edge of a knife. She swore beneath her breath when it refused to budge.

An icy feeling crept down my spine, the unnerving awareness of being watched, and I shoved her roughly out of the way. "Give it here!"

"It's mine," she protested.

"Shut up."

I wrenched the knife from her grip and slid it in the gap at the edge of the door. My breath held for a second as I tried to find the right spot and leveraged it with as much strength as I could muster.

A loud crack echoed from the door, and we fell inside.

Above us, the first of the harpies swooped over the city in search of prey.

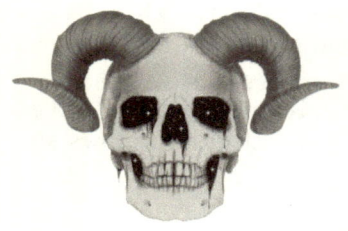

Chapter Twenty-Two

The kitchens were mercifully quiet as we crept inside. They were still well-lit and smelled of the dinner the cook had spent most of the day preparing. I didn't feel safe lingering and instead reached for Monika's hand to pull her towards the closest door. Monika snatched her knife back as we moved, and I wished I had thought to bring a weapon.

The next hallway was familiar. A lump formed in my throat as I glanced towards the little nook where Rowan and I had nestled for the past few days to eat lunch and chatter. Strangely, I realised I was going to miss her a lot.

"We need somewhere to hide," Monika stated.

I shushed her when the floorboards above us creaked, my heartbeat doubling its pace. It felt enormously risky.

"Down here!" I directed.

We twisted down one of the service hallways. I peeked around the corner before opening one of the closets where the guest linens were kept and bundled Monika inside.

Nobody would disturb the cupboard, as the fresh sheets had been folded the day before, and the North family never had guests. They simply emptied the closets and had everything washed weekly on the off chance they did. Besides, Rowan and I were the only ones to have made beds.

"Stay here," I warned Monika. She forced the sheets to the side and crawled into the space. "Don't move, and I'll come back for you."

Her rat-like eyes blinked at me. I closed the door quickly, shutting her within, and fled further down one of the halls.

Three people lived in the service level, as far as I knew. The housekeeper, who would recognise me on sight and call the guard, the cook, who had never looked up when I scurried in and out of the kitchen during the chores, and the young woman who looked after the North children each minute of the day.

She had the worst of all tasks, I thought; earlier that day, I had witnessed a meltdown from the youngest, which had resulted in the sharp corner of a wooden block bouncing off the nursemaid's cheekbone. A bruise bloomed by the time Rowan, and I had left.

She was the one member of the small servant team I thought wouldn't raise the alarm if she found me in the halls. Which was why I turned left towards her small room and pushed my way inside.

She wasn't there, probably still wrestling the children to sleep. A small blessing.

The room was bare. A single bed with paint-stained white sheets. A small wooden dresser with a worn leather-bound book on top, a chamber pot, and a large ceramic jug of water with a rag beside it. A neat uniform swung from a peg behind the door, and an acute sense of panic arose at the lack of places to hide.

Out of options and unwilling to brave the halls again, I dropped to my knees and inspected the space between the bed and the floor. It was a dusty, tight fit but empty enough I lay on my belly and wriggled beneath it.

The dust rose as I moved and I coughed twice, burying my face into the crook of my arm to muffle the sound. My nose itched, and I sneezed violently, glad she wasn't in the room to hear it. Then I lay there as quiet as I could, counting the too-long minutes before the household went to sleep.

The door to the bedroom slid open, and I startled back into consciousness. It was only the sleeve of my dress pressed against my lips that muffled the sharp inhale of awareness.

The back of her shoes and her black dress' hem moved into view from beneath the bed. I tried to quieten my breathing, my spine ached from lying in one position for too long, and the urgent pain in my bladder begging me to relieve myself.

The woman, whose name I had long forgotten, leaned out the door, and I could see the way she balanced on her toes, arching her foot. Her shoes slipped off her heels and called out a goodnight to the housekeeper before closing the door with a firm click and shuffling around the room.

At any moment, I thought she would look under the bed and find me there, that she would scream in surprise, and our heist would be over before it truly began.

The woman flung her apron to the floor, items jingling in its pockets. I flinched and closed my eyes. She groaned, and I heard the clatter of her long metallic hairpin on the top of the dresser. It was silent for a second too long, and I opened my eyes again, just in time to see her black dress pool around her ankles.

Swiftly, she stepped out of the material and kicked it into the corner. Water sloshed and splashed, and I sighed softly, relieved, as I pictured her getting ready for bed.

Before long, I could get out of there.

That was until she dropped to her knees beside the bed, startling me so badly I tensed, inhaling a lung full of dust before biting my arm as my body spasmed with a coughing fit. The sound felt too loud in the quiet, but she didn't seem to notice. My eyes watered.

Oblivious, the nursemaid recited prayers and pleas to Envy, begging the world at large he would deem her worthy of his collection. I was privy to her whispered dreams of being swept away and elevated in status until even Francesca North looked at her with green-eyed adoration.

It was a startling insight into how much people adored and envied the collection the angel held. His collection was not just the most unique, the most beautiful, but the most privileged in the Invidia.

When the woman exhausted her pleas to the angel, she turned her murmurings to the devil. She called him by three names, Great Devil, Samael, and Lucifer, begged him to save her using all three.

It was a struggle not to scoff.

I wanted to tell her the devil didn't save people, not without a price. He would be collecting from me, if I were to have won my immortal soul, until the end of eternity. I closed my eyes and reminded myself to stop listening to his whispers. It wouldn't be long until I had nothing left to give, if I even had anything anymore.

Above me, the springs of the bed frame squeaked as the woman rolled onto the mattress.

I waited and waited and waited until her breathing evened out. I counted the sounds between each exhale to make sure she wasn't pretending, and with a soft groan, I shuffled out from beneath the bed.

Dust clung to the front of my dress. My eyes flickered to the woman on the bed, her face relaxed in sleep, unbothered since she had offloaded her pleas of desire for more.

It felt invasive to watch her sleep, so I crept to the door before holding the frame carefully as I pulled it open, my breath suspended in hopes it wouldn't squeak.

The hallways were darker, soft lanterns dimmed for the night. I had to move slower in the low light. With every step forward, I worried about being caught.

The anxiety wasn't unusual. Every time I had slipped my hand opportunistically into a pocket or found a way to jam a lock, I thought I was on the edge of the end. It left my blood running hot and a bitter taste on my tongue, both of which kept me going.

I scratched the linen closet's wooden door and threw it open. "Monika?"

A blanket shifted, and she blinked back at me. I stepped back and glanced down the hall wearily.

She shifted and rolled out of the closet. The sound of her shoes hitting the floorboards halted the breath in my throat.

"Quiet." I snarled.

She sniffed and straightened quickly.

We left the closet door open and tiptoed past the housekeeper's room. A flickering light thrown from within the kitchen glowed beneath the door, so I led Monika to the stairs that led into the main part of the house.

The stretching corridors and wide rooms felt so much bigger in the evening, without the soft rumble of busy lives filling the space. The *tick, tick, tick* of the clock sounded so much louder in the room.

We delayed our task only long enough to slip into the servant's bathroom so I could take care of business. Then I beckoned her to follow me through the house.

Monika followed quickly, so close behind me her breath tickled the back of my neck.

I wanted to growl at her to back off and give me space, but I worried she would disappear, and I wasn't sure I could do this alone.

We climbed the stairs, Monika mimicking, as I deliberately stepped over one that squeaked underfoot. I shifted onto the plush rugs that ran down the halls on the upper floor to muffle our steps.

"Which room?" Monika asked.

With a quick glance back at her, I lifted one hand and pointed at the double doors at the end of the hall, which was large, with gilded décor painted onto the carved ridges. No mistake, it was anything other than the master room of the house.

I wondered if the Lord and Lady of the North house slept with their doors locked or if they were so secure, with the snoring guard outside, that anyone could walk into their room. The door handle turned easily, and that invisible corset cinched tighter and tighter into me, since the workday had ended loosened just a fraction.

Monika nodded as I glanced back.

I gulped before I pushed open the door. It whispered across the carpet as I pushed it open, and we entered.

Both bodies on the bed snuffled in their sleep, and I watched them wearily before turning to Monika.

"Where" – I didn't dare talk louder than the softest whisper – "would you keep your jewellery if you took it off at night?"

Even in the dark, I could see the way she looked at me, like I was the dumbest person she had ever met. Monika came from the same type of town I did, rough, underfed, and well below the city's privileges. Nobody in our town wore anything of value unless they were the chancellor or so dangerous nobody would think of stealing it.

I huffed out a sigh. "Check the vanity."

Monika didn't move, so I pointed at the large, mirrored table.

She shuffled across the room, lifting the lids on pots and setting them down gently.

I turned back to the bed and tried to steel myself for the next possibility that the akelda didn't leave her neck during the day or the night. Anxiously, I adjusted the cap on my head and pulled it down to my brow. The thin, gauzy curtains were pulled closed, and when I approached, I could see the outlines of their bodies, two distinct shapes sprawled across the bed.

Fingers outstretched, I took a handful of the curtain and dragged it slowly out of the way. Days of making the bed meant I knew I was on Francesca's side of it, and unlike her staff, she looked tormented in her sleep.

Her hair had been tucked under a cap like mine to sleep, but hers was silky and tied loosely enough that strands escaped and clung to her neck. Francesca North gasped in her sleep, snuffled softly, and twisted beneath the covers.

Beads of sweat glistened across her forehead.

She shifted again, rolled onto her back, and the cover slipped off her body, showing the way her nightdress – also silky – tangled around her long pale thighs. My eyes dragged up her body, tension coiled in my muscles. At the base of her throat, tight against her skin, lay the akelda.

It taunted me, green fire contained beneath a cracked, polished rock.

It should have been obvious this woman would never let go of the thing others envied about her, the favour she had received from the young angel who ruled their lives.

These people burnt with envy, with the same intensity that the akelda burnt with light, but they wanted to be envied, too. They wanted everyone below them on the spiral to look up at them and see how much better their lives were, how much more privileged and favoured they had become.

"Octavia?" Monika's voice startled me out of the strange trance I had been in. I glanced back at her, and she gestured. "It's not here . . ."

"I know," I whispered. "It's here."

I leaned over the bed, my eyes stuck on the stone.

It would be our saviour, my ticket through to the end of this Devil-damned trial.

I needed it.

My fingertips brushed the soft skin on Francesca's throat and curled around the piece of akelda. My heart fluttered in my chest as I gripped it, preparing to rip it free.

Awareness rippled through my body, and my gaze swung up from the hollow of her throat, one last look at her face before stealing her most precious possession.

Her eyes were open.

She stared at me as the sleep cleared from her hazed gaze.

I inhaled sharply, unable to look away.

Her lips parted, and Francesca North screamed.

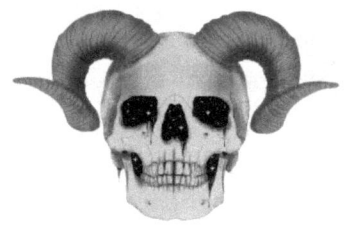

Chapter Twenty-Three

I reeled backwards, startled by the noise. The dainty chain around her neck shattered with the force of my movement. The akelda went flying, then rolled across the soft, carpeted floor.

"Intruder!" Francesca shrieked. "Thief!"

Her husband roused groggily. I staggered backwards, almost falling right over Monika, who was on her hands and knees, chasing after the akelda as it rolled beneath the bed.

"Mon," I gasped.

Lord and Lady North rolled from the bed and started towards me. Francesca wailed loudly, and heavy footsteps thundered up the stairs.

"Mon," I repeated shrilly, backing towards the window. "Time to go."

The door to the bedroom burst open, and Francesca screamed again, covering herself as the scale-armoured guard burst through the door. The cook followed, waving a wooden spoon.

Mon scrambled upright. The guard spun, but she managed to twist around him and find her way behind me.

"Gee, thanks," I muttered as she used me as a human shield.

Her body wedged between me and the wall as I backed up.

The guard had settled in front of Francesca, and I shivered as he pulled the sword at his hip free. The metal snicked, and the sharpened tip levelled at my heart.

A nervous laugh bubbled over my lips.

"This isn't funny, girl!" the guard hissed.

"I know that. I honestly don't know why I'm laughing . . ." I babbled.

He took a menacing step forward.

I raised my hands, placatingly.

Monika squeaked at my back, but I ignored her, unable to look anywhere but at the blade.

"It's just a misunderstanding."

The guard laughed, a cruel sound. He appeared a lot more vicious than the guard I'd met each morning. "City law says I can run you right through, thief."

"I think you'll find I haven't actually stolen anything."

Francesca fluttered a step forward. "My akelda is missing."

She had unstuck her throat long enough to throw around accusations.

The guard closed the space between us, the tip of his sword pressed against my chest in threat, right on top of my thundering heart. I felt like I was going to faint.

"Hand it over," the guard hissed. "And I'll make your death quick."

"I don't have it."

"Liar!" Francesca hissed. "You ripped it from my neck, you greedy bitch!"

I had stolen a lot of things in my life: coins, food, and even a pretty comb from this woman, but it seemed strange and disorientating that I was on the precipice of death for something I had only failed to steal.

"I don't have it," I repeated with a whine.

Behind me, something clicked.

I couldn't turn to see, but the old night air rushed into the room and stole my breath away. I felt Monika shift at my back. She reached out and firmly tugged at the ties on my cap, which unravelled and slipped off my head. Dark hair swung into my eyes.

I groaned, not moving my gaze from the sharp sword. "What?"

"Back up and jump," she breathed.

The weight of her presence disappeared, and I took a step back. It put a little space between me and the guard who intended to pierce my heart. A fraction of space between myself and death.

The windowsill pressed against the back of my thighs; the cold air left me shivering. I glanced between all three of them.

"I don't have it."

"Face your sins," Francesca spat.

Such a brave woman, hiding behind the guard's armour and weapon. I glared at her defiantly.

"Octavia!" Monika called. Moving one hand, I felt for the window frame. My fingers found the edge, and the guard stepped forward again, forcing me back. I pushed myself into it, half hanging out into the cool night air.

If Monika had survived jumping the window from that height, then I would, too.

I just had to find an ounce of my courage.

"Don't you move," the guard hissed.

I wished Monika had given me her knife, anything to defend myself with if I couldn't get free.

Samael counted with me. '*One, two three!*'

Without time to overthink it, I shoved myself back through the window.

The night was frigid, and the fall felt like the longest part of my night so far.

The ground came as a shock. I landed hard on my back. My lungs spasmed as the impact knocked air out of my body. I wheezed, struggling for a full breath.

Monika swam in and out of my field of vision. Her hands flapped around her face.

"You need to get up," she hissed.

"Try-ing . . ." I gasped, blinking rapidly as she took my hand and pulled to help me to my feet. The world spun when I clambered upright, my body aching. It had not been the best idea of my night, but it was better than dying at the guard's hand.

Monika tugged me to the side.

"Oi," the guard shouted. In the time it had taken her to get me focused and upright, he had come outside. "You stop right there!"

Monika ran, dragging me with her to the fence. She squeezed through, and I flailed in her wake. The guard let out a furious growl, too close by the time I slipped through.

The heel of his sword rapped against the iron bars, again and again, a loud signal, and all along the spiral, lights flared inside the guard's huts as they followed the call to arms.

"Run!" Monika screeched.

Above us, another screech chilled my blood.

I struggled to follow her as she twisted through the properties and spilled out on the cobblestone streets. My legs and lungs burnt as we ran. It had started raining while we hid in the house, leaving the stones of the paths slippery. Monika slipped, and I fell on top of her, slamming into the ground so hard my teeth pierced my upper lip, blood filling my mouth. Pain ripped a whine from my throat, and I spat blood onto the stones.

I staggered upright, out of self-preservation, reaching for Monika's jacket and twisting my fingers firmly into the fabric. I used it to leverage her towards her feet, and we pressed into one of the thin alleyways between the more crowded buildings on the outskirts of the entertainment district.

We moved as quickly as we could, even as my head pulsed, and I had to pause to spit out more blood. Garbage overflowed on either side of us, tightening the passage, but if we would have kept going, we would make it back to the main street of the spiral.

From there, we could find our way back to the Infra.

A small spark of hope bloomed through my panic.

We lost the thundering sound of guards behind us. I knew they would spread through the city quickly. But our luck was doomed, and one danger gave way to another.

Dark wings beat above us in the sky, dark leathery wings, and the harpies circled the city. I wondered if they could taste the blood dripping off my face.

They screeched, and my heart skipped a beat.

We had to elude the city guards and the screaming harpies to survive. Two deadly options, none of which I wanted to face. Ideally, neither.

"This way." Monika seemed to find her senses. She pushed on a door halfway down the alley. The wood splintered and gave way under her weight. She scrambled inside, and with blind faith, I followed.

The room smelt wet and rusty, and it was hard to see properly, but Monika slammed into another door and broke through into another alley.

"How are you doing this?" I gasped.

"I have good eyes," she admitted, "especially in the dark."

I took her word for it. "Can you get us back to the Infra?"

"Yes."

"Are you sure?"

"If we stay between the buildings, we can avoid them all," Monika pointed out. When she glanced back, her eyes were bright and determined, enough so that I didn't argue. "Besides, the guards are too fat, and the harpies' wings are too big."

"I'm not arguing, Mon."

A feral light glinted in her eyes, a strangling grin on her lips. "Good. How else do you think I survived the nights out here?"

Her confidence was infectious, despite the way I ached and the way my body burnt with demand for air. I followed her lead through the twisting alleyways of Invidia until I begged her to stop, wheezing and sliding to my knees and leaning against the wall as I gasped for air. I was unfit, and my body felt too broken to keep going.

My hands pressed against the wall as I tried to suck in air and vomit up the contents of my stomach. My entire body trembled.

Monika chuckled, a dark and desperate sound. "You've got about thirty seconds before we go again . . ."

"I need to rest."

She shook her head. "We can't stay still too long."

"That's not enough," I muttered. "I feel like I crushed my lungs jumping out of that window."

"It looked bad."

"It felt like it."

I rubbed at my sternum; a dry retch shuddered through my body. I squinted at her in the dark. "Tell me you got the akelda, Mon."

Guilt flashed across her face, a crack of lightning in the sky illuminating it.

My heart turned to stone and plummeted to the pit of my stomach. All that effort, all that danger, and we hadn't managed to get the prize. I wanted to cry, as hopelessness overwhelmed me.

Monika said nothing but glanced at the sky. Worry creased between her brows. Neither of us said anything more about the failure.

"We need to go," she stated.

Swallowing the lump in my throat, I nodded.

"Just . . . one second." I gulped down deep breaths as the first fat droplets of rain fell from the sky. I still didn't feel right, disoriented and three steps behind.

Monika Oster didn't wait for me as she scurried down the alleyways. I squinted after her in the dark, the worn soles of my boots unable to find a grip on the slippery cobblestones. The rain came down harder, plastering my hair to my face, and blinding me with its intensity.

"Mon?" I called out. "Mon!"

The hiss of my voice bounced down the alley, and I fought to hear a reply through the sound of the storm. I wasn't sure if I heard her voice or not.

Thunder rolled overhead, and it drowned everything else out.

I staggered to the alley and twisted left; my hand dragged against the side of the building to orient myself. I pushed my soaked hair from my face, struggling not to trip as the sodden skirts of the maid's uniform weighed against my legs.

"Monika?"

I lurched blindly into the next alleyway and slammed right into her back.

"Oof," Monika cried as she fell to her knees.

I would have reached for her and pulled her back up if I hadn't been distracted by the same thing that had stopped Monika in her tracks.

At the end of the alley, a shadowy figure moved.

It slipped through the rain, and my heart leapt to my throat. My first thought was an Erlkang, and I shuddered at the memory of them attacking after I had left Ilrea.

Could they form in the flash of lightning?

It tore across the sky, illuminating the city for a second before we were plunged back into the darkness. I backed away; my building distress too distracting to reach for Monika now.

"Erlkang," I gasped, wrapping my arms around my middle and squeezing tight. I was a coward, but I couldn't get out of my head.

Monika edged backwards, crawling across the cobblestones towards me, dragging herself closer and closer to me. "Worse," she corrected as she tried to pull herself up by my apron.

The material ripped loudly, and the creature paused. I squinted through the rain, my pulse thrummed, and dizziness swept through me. This night was never-ending.

"Worse?" I breathed, my throat tightening.

Monika held onto me as she found her feet, thin face pale and dark eyes shining with real terror. I felt like I went numb as I took in her fear.

"Harpy!" she cried.

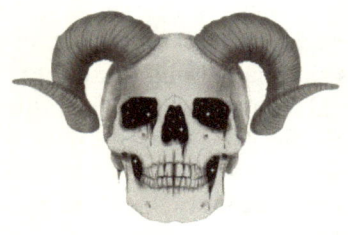

Chapter Twenty-Four

The more we ran, the faster it followed. Newfound fear overpowered my exhaustion, and I fled, deciding I would rather be run through by a pompous, armoured man with a sword than fall prey to this creature.

I would rather a lot of things than to face another of my nightmares in the flesh. Devil-cursed women who looked like hunched crones or colour-leeched ladies were nothing compared to the curses on the harpies. The way the different descriptions from Mikhael and Kyra mixed in my head to create a whole new horror.

Neither would be right, I knew, since the stories were that nobody saw a harpy and survived. They hunted down every soul who laid eyes on them, anyone who dared look in their direction.

I wished I'd never set my sight on the end of that alleyway.

"Go, go, go . . ." Monika urged at my back.

"I'm going," I hissed.

The creature crashed down the alleyway behind us. Where we climbed over old crates and dodged piles of garbage, it barrelled right through at an unstoppable force.

"I thought you said they wouldn't fit," I gasped, accusation clear in my voice.

"I was wrong."

"Shit."

An indigent squawk came from Monika's throat, half a laugh, half a protest, and I realised I had misjudged her as weak and quiet. Stupidly, I had deemed her as rat-like as she looked, but once she started opening, she had more attitude than I could have imagined. There was nothing that would bring two people together more than multiple near-death experiences.

"Left." Monika gasped.

I obeyed without question and flung myself around the next corner.

The alleyway opened to a large cement rectangle between the towering buildings. We were in the outer spiral, packed full of broken high-rise homes, and shattered, abandoned toys filled the square. Children lived here, and a strange fear pulsed through me that we had brought a monster to their homes. If they were to have died that night, it would be my fault.

Only the children of Invidia were not foolish enough to be outside after dark, not like us. They would only be in danger if we'd entered the buildings. A tempting thought, to hide away, but I couldn't guarantee the harpy wouldn't follow.

"See the alley on the other side?" Monika panted.

"Next to that pink thing?"

"Yeah," she confirmed. "That way."

We made it halfway across the square before Monika slipped again. Her feet went out from under her, and I heard a cracking bone and a scream as she landed awkwardly.

The harpy screamed in response and burst out of the alley.

I was half twisted towards Monika, half turned back to help, when I got my first real look at the demon-damned creature. One day, nothing in this world would make me afraid, one way I couldn't be weak with terror, but not that day.

I was frozen in place as the harpy shook off easing rain droplets and stalked towards us.

It was somewhere between the stories from Mikhael and Kyra and what I had fabricated in my imagination.

I couldn't deny this creature was once a human woman. She stood tall and proud, with womanly curves that were voluptuous and strangely perfect in a horrifying way. Huge, leathery wings stretched from her back as the harpy shook off the water again. Unlike the angels, these wings formed points. The pointed edges looked sharp beneath the next flash of lightning.

The harpy had ashy-grey skin, like she had died, had been buried, then had risen; her fingers were blackened where fingers extended into long sharp talons, the same deadly weapons extended where her toes once were. Her hair was long, dark, and limp from the rain. It hung in front of her body and stopped at her navel.

As she stalked closer and closer, lightning lit up the world again, and I got my first real glimpse at her face. Her nostrils flared, and a pointed tongue swept across her blackened lips, sharp teeth flashing. It as if she were already tasting us, preparing for the meal she had hunted.

For a moment, I was struck by how human her face felt, reminded that this had once been a girl, cursed before she grew into a woman.

Monika groaned as she tried to move. The harpy's head tilted sharply. I didn't take my eyes off it and didn't move. As Monika shifted, and it shifted, too, I realised it was listening to us.

I had not wanted to encourage it to come for me and see the end of my life in its eyes or a void that might curse me, too. But somehow, I gathered the strength to look death in the eye.

It had a milky-white stare, not focused on me at all as the harpy listened to each pained whimper from Monika and stepped forward deliberately again.

I had seen eyes like those before, in Ilrea, when old man Jilk had not paid his debts and had been blinded by the hot coals of the fire where he cooked his dinner. Nobody thought he'd survive, but he did, only with white, sightless eyes. I had seen them before, two days before, in Envy's collection.

The harpies were blind.

It listened so intently, the only way to track us, with our crashing run in the winding alleyways. We had given it the perfect way to find us.

"Shush," I whispered at Monika.

The harpy's chin tilted as it located me.

Although I knew it couldn't see me, I felt like it had focused on me all the same. I became acutely aware of how loudly I breathed and how loud my heart must have sounded as it tried to beat its way out of my chest.

"Octavia," Monika groaned. "Run."

The harpy's lips drew back into a wicked smile, wide and flashing sharp fangs. It let out a loud shriek, in a different pitch than before.

My stomach bottomed out as I realised it sounded victorious.

"No!" I gasped as it darted forward and foolishly grasped for Monika as it struck. Talons raked through clothing and flesh, blood spilled onto the concrete, and Monika screeched with pain.

"No!" I screamed again.

I lunged forward, my fists finding a grip on her shirt as I tried to pull her back to me. It was useless; the material ripped with the force at which the harpy dragged her off the ground, lifting Monika by her damaged leg.

A sob burst from my lips as I watched Monika's eyes roll back in her head, succumbing to the pain.

"Give her back," I pleaded.

I knew it could hear me; I had no idea if it could understand me.

"Please." I begged, fingers scrabbling against the wet stone ground as I reached for Monika again. I didn't know why I was begging for her life instead of fleeing for my own. Maybe because I thought the chase would make me a more enticing target, maybe because Monika hadn't left me at the end of a sword to fend for myself without a plan.

Strong muscles bunched beneath the harpy's ashen skin. It shook Monika, who was blessedly limp and unconscious.

The harpy dropped her with a proud shriek, and she crumpled onto the ground.

A breathless whimper rolled over my lips, pained for her, and I scrambled forward, reaching for her again. The harpy was quicker. It moved with surprising speed and grace as it dove on top of Monika.

The sound of the creature's sharp teeth piercing into her flesh was one I would never forget, and my sense of self-preservation finally kicked in.

As quietly as possible, I edged, backwards.

"I'm so sorry, Mon."

An amalgamation of the storm fall and my salty tears soaked my cheeks. I tried to slowly pull myself to my feet, and the harpy's head lifted.

The full focus of that unseeing attention moving from Monika to me so quickly my heart felt like it faltered. I was frozen on the spot, my body tensing with fear.

I had been close to death more than once in my life by then, but I had never thought it would wear this face. The harpy's head tilted, and it straightened slowly. I pressed my lips together to try and stifle the sound of my erratic breathing.

I rose my hands in defence as the harpy's pointed tongue flicked over its bloodstained lips. It stepped over Monika's limp body, and for the first time, I noticed the scrape of its claws on the stone.

Dread filled me, my lips trembling, and I tried to stifle the pathetic whimpers that built in the back of my throat.

The harpy loomed closer, and my fear melted into an eerie calm as I squeezed my eyes closed and accepted my fate. Alarm pulsed through me; it was too close.

The tip of its pointed tongue flicked down the side of my cheek, its breath putrid of rotted flesh.

Crying, I waited for death.

"Well, well, well, gentleman . . . we've caught ourselves a beasty," a man called out, his voice jarring me. The harpy screeched and spun towards the new sound so quickly her leathery wings knocked me to the ground. Pain seared through my head, and the world spun on impact. The cut in my lips reopened until all I could taste was blood.

I was battered, bruised, but alive. My ears rung from the scream of the harpy.

Slowly, I pushed up onto my hands and knees, panting and collecting myself. I coughed up a mouthful of blood onto the stone.

When the dizziness eased, I lifted my head. I realised these were not gentlemen at all.

The guards of the spiral surrounded us, laughing and taunting the harpy. One held the tarnished lid of a garbage can in his hand, and he raised the hilt of his sword to slam the pommel against the metal.

The loud noise caused the harpy to flinch and shriek, a warning call that caused the hair on the back of my arms to stand on end.

It crouched low and backed up closer to Monika, protecting its kill from the intruders.

The guards laughed, and one scraped the end of their sharp sword against the stone. The harpy hissed and spun. The garbage can lid clanked again, and it turned again, hissing with confusion.

Monika's blood seeped beneath its feet.

That was why the city guards caused such a ruckus when the alarm was raised for any reason. In the dead of the night, they protected their citizens from the harpies by confusing them, using loud noises and misdirection.

The harpy stepped over Monika swiftly and charged at the next one to make a noise. They closed in around it, laughing and jeering. Stupidly, I dragged myself over to Monika's body.

Her clothing was shredded, her arm lay in the wrong angle. Bloody marks stood out where the harpy had bitten her, and I reached to push her hair from her face.

My fingers fumbled at her neck, searching for a sign of life in the way my mother had taught me in Ilrea. Panic rose in my throat as I touched her cold skin, but as my fingers pressed firmer against her neck, I could feel the faintest, fluttering beat of her pulse. The tiniest sign of life, but enough that I couldn't leave her behind.

I felt like I was about to vomit up my own heart as I struggled with the fact that, after all this, Monika Oster had survived.

Pain lanced through my head as I glanced at the guards surrounding the harpy. The scaled look of their armour flashing beneath the next flash through the sky. They created so much noise I couldn't focus.

My breathing came in short bursts, and I watched them wearily, but the guards were no longer searching for us. They were too enthralled at being the ones to slay the beast to look back at discarded women, too preoccupied with their pending kill to care if Monika was dying.

They were the perfect distraction.

As one leapt forward, swinging their sword and catching the side of the harpy's wing, the harpy screeched, and I teetered on my feet, dazed and nauseous. I glanced between the guards, the harpy, and a broken Monika, sucked in a deep breath, and crouched to slide my hands beneath her armpits.

"Time to go."

When the guards yelled and surged forward again, tightening their circle around the harpy, I pulled backwards. I focused on each step at a time, moving slowly, steadily, until I had dragged her broken body to the edge of the square. The night would be over by the time I had found safety; my movements felt painfully slow.

It was a struggle to pull her through the thin alleyways and over the accumulation of rubbish and forgotten items. Once clearing the alley, I caught my bearings enough to realise we were close, so close to the entrance to the Infra. Monika had almost managed to get us home.

If it could be called that.

Dragging in a deep breath, I grunted and stepped back again, dragging Monika. At any given moment, I thought more harpies would come, swooping into the aid of their sister, who shrieked and hissed in the distance. If not them, I was sure the guard would realise we were the ones they were hunting and would come to claim blood.

Paranoia left me skittish. Fear left me cold, neither of which disappeared, even as we descended safely below ground.

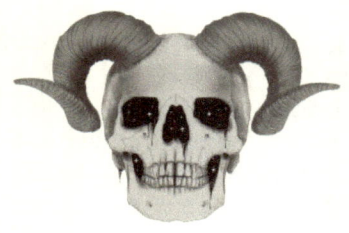

Chapter Twenty-Five

I fled through the marketplace, having left Monika sprawled by the platform, broken, bloody, and barely alive. It was empty aside from the few broken souls who raided the closed stalls for wares left behind.

Rather than hiding in my little nest and blocking out the rest of the world, I ran through the next corridor and burst into the encampment. The normal residents had thinned out, and the competitors slept in groups, bundled into their teams, with each giving the others a wide berth. It was a strange place, neutral enough to sleep if not to relax.

I stood in the doorway, practically vibrating with anxiety as my eyes darted from group to group, trying to identify each one. Most were asleep and hard to pick, curled into protective circles, but every now and again, I met a suspicious gaze and shivered. I looked as bad as I felt, soaking wet, covered in dirt and blood, with half of it splashed across my face. Self-consciously, I lifted a hand, wiped my sleeve across my mouth, and shuffled farther into the room.

I didn't feel safe, not even close, but it was undoubtedly safer than aboveground.

It took too long to find Aureen, and I was unsurprised to find her wrapped protectively around her little sister. Tiptoeing around the groups, I edged closer to her and knelt.

Aureen's eyes snapped open, and she moved before I could comprehend what was happening. She had rolled me, pinned my body on the floor, and held the sharp edge of a blade to my throat.

"Ugh," I grunted.

Aureen blinked. "Octavia?"

If I could have nodded, I would have. "It's Monika . . ."

"What happened?" Aureen was on her feet quickly. She lifted her weight off my body and nudged her sister into awareness with the side of her foot. "Up." She hissed at Kyra, who stumbled to her feet.

They pulled their shoes on in the time it took me to find my way upright again. Bile rose in the back of my throat, and my body ached in warning at the fatigue I felt. Adrenaline might have kept me going, but it was fading fast. "I . . . we . . ."

Aureen sighed heavily and pushed her hair behind her as if I had just rested the weight of the world's problems on her shoulders. I knew how that felt. She stretched and pinned me beneath her gaze, which felt almost as lethal as her knife.

"Where is she?" She spoke too loudly, and I shuffled nervously.

My head jerked to the side. My gaze swept the room, connecting with a familiar green for a moment before I led the Willett sisters on a path back to our fallen teammate. Monika had not moved since I had left her; she was too still, too pale, her breathing too soft.

Aureen didn't hesitate as she marched over to the smaller woman and crouched over her, Kyra and I shuffling up behind. With her fingers, she pressed Monika's jugular with more confidence than I had, pushing the edges of torn fabric to assess her injuries.

She twisted, her dark eyes finding me, her full lips pressed into a grim line. "Harpies?"

"Just one," I admitted.

"She's been bitten at least twice," Aureen said and blew out a slow breath. "She's pale. Looks like she lost of a lot of blood. That arm is broken and" – she pressed along Monika's torso – "her ribs feel shattered."

I nodded, swallowing hard at the memory of the way Monika had crashed back into the ground, of the blood that had pooled beneath her body. I was surprised her neck wasn't broken – or maybe it was I didn't know how to check, and Aureen hadn't inspected it.

"What do we do?" I asked.

Kyra was whispering a soft verse beneath her breath, her hand over her heart. When I noted the devastation on her face, I knew what Aureen had not yet said.

"Nothing."

"What?" The exclamation sounded as raw as it felt on the edge of my tongue.

The truth was hard to hear after I had dragged Monika through the wet night in the hopes that the women would know to fix her injuries. In the hope that our team could survive as one. Rationally, I might have known that was what it would come to, but it was a night for rational decisions. It was a night for emotion and struggle, another one I would never forget.

Aureen wiped her hands along the front of her thighs; her nose wrinkled, and the action infuriated me. It felt like she was wiping Monika off her, dusting her hands of the problem.

She raised her chin and proclaimed, "She won't live until dawn."

"Aureen!"

She twisted to face me; her gaze fierce as she came so closer that I could feel the flush of her breath against my tear-stained cheeks. "Did you get it?"

"No."

Aureen scoffed. "Then, she died for nothing."

The rest of the sentence hung between us, unsaid but ringing in my ears all the same: she died for nothing, and it was my fault.

They left me alone before it occurred to me to move her somewhere more comfortable. My hands fluttered in front of my ribs, anxious and unsure of what to do next. Panic threatened to overwhelm.

I crawled into the space between her body and the platform, stretched out my legs, and used the last of my strength to pull her head into my lap. My fingers shook as I pushed blood-matted hair from her face and marvelled at how the look of impending death did nothing to help her features.

"It's okay," I whispered finally. "You can let go."

Stubborn to the very end, she held on longer than I expected. Death did not come swiftly.

Soft pants of breath turned into a strained rattle for air. The blood seeping from her body soaked into my dress, and I tilted my head back and whispered pleas to Samael to help her die. For all those hours, I remained awake, exhausted, and waiting.

Nobody deserved to die alone.

Monika's last breath passed just as the first few stallholders crept past us with their carts of wares to set up for the morning. Each of them deliberately didn't look at the broken and dead women in the corner.

At a break in the foot traffic, I rolled Monika's body off my legs. My stomach twisted unpleasantly as I reached over and closed her eyelids, not something I had ever expected to have to do.

I searched her pockets, in a vain hope she had lied about not finding that piece of akelda to keep it for herself, but it wasn't there. So, I took her coins and knife, all she had left to offer me.

Then I stood, stretched, and stared down at her body. I had no clue what to do with her next, no means of burning or burying her bones, and so, with a heavy sigh, I left her there, at the mercy of those who wanted to loot her remains.

The fortune teller was still snoring when I crept behind his tent. He stayed that way in the time it took me to collect my clothes, collect water from the leaking taps, and find a private space in the tunnels to strip down and wash the gore from my skin. My unwashed clothing from the end of the Gluttony trial left me smelling ripe, but it was better than spending my days wearing Monika's dried blood.

I curled into a ball behind the tent and succumbed to my own fatigue.

A sharp kick roused me from a too-deep sleep. I shot upright, groggy and disoriented, staring into the angry face of the crooked-toothed fortune teller.

"This isn't working out, darling," he announced.

I blinked. "Huh?"

"I was all right with your little hidey hole when you were quiet, but . . ." He waved a hand sharply.

"You knew I was here?"

"O' course."

"The whole time?"

"I'm old, not stupid, darling," he snapped. "But now you're screaming in your sleep, frightening away all my customers, so you go to go . . ."

"You're kicking me out . . ."

"Yeah." He grinned. "'Less you want to be paying me rent, darling."

It took a moment to find my feet, my hand on the cold wall for balance as I processed the quick change in my circumstance. "Uhhh."

"Didn't think so."

"But . . ."

"Out you go!" He jerked his thumb over his shoulder in a clear direction and backed out of the small space for me to shuffle out.

I moved erratically, snatching the blankets, and the glittering comb bounced onto the ground. I swooped for it and tucked it into my pocket, then shuffled out into the open. The ruined uniform was left behind.

It felt as if everyone was watching as the fortune teller evicted me, even though half the day had passed, and we had entered the slower, mid-afternoon market lulls.

An antsy anxiety filled me at what I perceived to be their stares, and I chewed on my sore, split lip. "Where am I supposed to go?"

The fortune teller scoffed. "Go and sleep in the encampment with the rest of the death-fated fools."

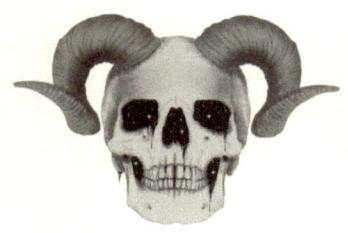

Chapter Twenty-Six

Thankfully, many of the competitors had fled the underground for the day, continuing their heist in the light of day. Without Monika, I realised I might be completely without allies now. Aureen did not stay for her death and wanted nothing to do with me until I found a piece of the akelda to match the one she had stolen. Kyra followed her lead.

Helina and Niklaus were too dangerous and disdainful to approach. Nash had declared himself off limits, Finley with him, and Mikhael Heira was an enigma I didn't want to be entangled with. He would bring more trouble than I needed.

I was alone once again; it was becoming a familiar feeling, and I was slowly beginning to realise I could count on nobody but myself. I picked my way through the littering of belongings and settled my blankets close to where I had found Aureen and Kyra the night before.

I kept my coins and the comb in my pockets, valuables not to be left out in the open. I was tired enough to want to sleep again, but I didn't trust the rest of the competitors and the few homeless Invidian's who lingered about not to attack me.

For that reason, I forced myself back above ground, even though every time I'd glance at the cobblestone streets, all I could picture was Monika, bloody and broken on the ground.

Instead of turning to follow the tight spiral to the castle, I turned in the other direction. After wandering aimlessly for twenty minutes, I tapped a man on the shoulder and asked where to find Rowan's home.

The old man raised the stick he was using to prop up his weight at a nearby building and waved it about.

"Little Rowan lives down there with her young sister. Fourth floor, left door," he croaked.

I nodded. "I'll wait for her, then."

He shook his head, white hair flopping across his forehead. "She's home today – came running back in tears this mornin'."

Guilt pinged my nerves, a deep intuition that Rowan's tears were, in some way, attributed to me. I didn't voice this concern, though, and nodded again, marching towards that building like a woman on a mission.

The building was creaky and falling apart on the inside. No better or worse than our homes back in Ilrea, which gave me the startling realisation that poverty existed, even in cities that appeared shiny and enviable from the outside.

By the time I had climbed the four flights, my thighs burnt, and I was struggling to breathe smoothly. I stood, glancing between the two identical doors, and tried to recall which one the old man had told me she lived behind.

I hesitated, hand raised, then turned and rapped my knuckles against the door. The sound seemed too abrasive and too loud in the quiet corridor.

It seemed like she wouldn't answer, and part of me hoped she wouldn't, but footsteps sounded from within. The door creaked as she swung it open. Rowan appeared in the gap between the door and the wall. Her hair swung over one shoulder, her face pale, and her eyes rimmed red as if she had been crying.

Just like the old man had said.

"Hello," I said.

Rowan pulled the door closed tighter against her body, a subtle sign I was unwelcome.

"Is your name even Tav Duncan?" Fury tainted her tone.

"It's Octavia . . ." I bit my sore lip. "Tav."

"Duncan?" she pressed; her nose scrunched.

"No."

She flinched back. Splotches of red rose high on her cheeks.

"What happened?" I asked.

"They fired me, that's what happened!" All her natural happiness from the day before had evaporated, and her teeth clenched with building anger.

My lips parted to ask why, but I couldn't bring myself to. Not when I was sure I knew the answer.

Rowan looked devastated, dark eyes wet, lips twisted down with devastation. "Apparently, one of the North maids robbed Francesca at knife point last night –"

"There was no knife."

Monika owned a knife, but we hadn't threatened anyone with it.

"Because I couldn't prove it wasn't me, I was sacked on the spot," she continued, like I had never spoken. Her face turned a deeper red as she spat the words.

"Rowan . . ." I said, and she scoffed.

"Don't!" She shook her head.

Behind her, someone was making a noise in the apartment, and Rowan pulled the door tighter against her body. "We've got nothing. *Nothing*! I don't even have a job anymore because you couldn't keep your hands to yourself."

"I . . ." My lips clamped firmly closed. I could say very little to make this better. "I'm . . ."

While I felt sorry, she had lost her job, I realised I wasn't sorry about what I had done. I had to survive somehow, and Rowan had been caught in the crosshairs. I sighed and pushed at the sleeve of my jacket. I tugged it back over the iridescent cuff and turned my wrist to show Rowan the mark of Gluttony.

The little purple piglet was stark against my skin, having healed in the days past and shimmering with a magic.

Her eyes widened a fraction. "You're one of them."

"You don't need to make it sound so disgusting."

She looked nervous. "You need to leave."

"Look." I slapped the wooden door, using the leverage to stop her from closing it. "I just want you to know why I did it."

"Because you're selfish!" Rowan stated shrilly. "Anyone who enters those stupid trials is selfish! They go off to die and leave people behind!"

Such hurt laced her voice that it occurred to me I had never asked how Rowan's parents died, and she had never volunteered the information in her chattering.

"Oh." I breathed as the pieces fit together. "Rowan . . ."

"Just go . . ." She shoved my chest, and I stumbled back. "*Go!*"

The other door creaked as it opened, and a dark gaze watched me from within.

Quickly, I hid the cuff and my tattoo. Chin lifted and eyes narrowed, I stepped towards Rowan, and she slammed the door in my face.

Just like that, I had lost another friend.

I thundered down the stairs again, four flights down, far easier than climbing them. By the time I burst back into the streets, my chest ached, and confusion left me dizzy. It hurt to lose Rowan as a friend. I didn't know why, but once again, someone I had barely known left an impression so deep my emotions had become a tangled mess.

I sighed. I had nowhere to go and no idea what to do next. The prize we all sought wouldn't fall into my lap the way it had for Nash. I was over a third of the way through this fool's trials, and already, any spark of hope I had felt had dimmed out to barely a flicker.

Before I knew it, I was back in the underground, hovering at the strange invisible line that separated the marketplace's viciousness and the eatery's implied truce. My coins weighed heavily in my pockets. They needed to be spent – or better yet, they needed to be doubled.

I bought a slice of sticky lemon cake covered in icing that needed to be licked from the sides of my fingers, then I gravitated to the woven rug and the sound of dice clattering inside a cup.

"Afternoon," I squeaked.

I tried to ignore the tension in my body as I lowered myself to a place in the circle. I couldn't gamble my way to a successful end in the trial, but I was willing to pretend there was a chance. Other players shuffled to the side to let me in. I tipped coins from my pockets and dumped them in a cup in the centre before I snagged a cup of dice for myself.

They were electric-blue, like the ones tattooed across my ribs. The dice made me think of Niklaus Heira, of his rage, of his tenderness, of the kiss in the Gluttony trial.

Quickly, I pushed them back into the middle and swapped them out for red dice. A better colour, a little luckier than anything the memory of a Heira brother could bring. The game commenced, and the play zipped around the circle again and again, until I lost the first round, stuck in an impossible situation with the final three.

My palms pressed into the woven carpet, and I leaned all my weight back on them as I waited for a winner, but more importantly, for another chance to play. We were four rounds deep before the newest of players joined us.

Finley Nightingale shuffled into the circle and folded his long legs. He paid his coin, took his tie, and rolled them around in the palm of his hand.

He grinned as I glanced up at him, and my heartbeat raced. Finley liked a fanciful bet as much as the next man, and I knew he knew exactly where a piece of akelda was, where I could find my salvation from Envy.

I'd have to get him to tell me where Nash Wickham kept his piece.

Slowly, I resettled myself on the mat and wriggled into a more comfortable position. My hand drifted to my pocket, toying with the weight of the coins there, more than enough to keep playing, and I had won the quick rounds of Deceiver's Dice twice, filling me with an arrogant confidence that I could do it again and again.

My chin lifted, and I forced a fake smile on my lips.

Just for him, as if I wasn't drowning in shock and emotion after the last day. Or the last month.

"Well, well, well . . . if it isn't Finley Nightingale the Second."

His lips twitched. "Octavia Nox."

"Here to lose all your money?" I asked.

He laughed. "Hardly."

I lifted a brow and waited.

Often, I found that, if you let silence linger, other people liked to fill it. The host set up the next game, redistributing the dice.

"Betting money is boring," he added after a beat.

I weighed my red dice and glanced at the crudely carved dots on each side. I counted to the beat of three in my heat, making him wait, before I tipped my chin to catch his eye again.

"What do you want to bet?" I asked, reminded of that night full of confusion and butterflies that melted on the edge of my tongue, making all words sweet and dizzying. "Not another kiss."

He laughed loud enough that it implied it was a possibility, and I blushed.

Snickers rolled around the circle.

My throat tightened, and my spine straightened.

"What do you want to bet?" I repeated, tone harsher. Finley pulled at one of his stringy curls. It straightened, then bounced back, tight around his face.

"The second-best currency, of course . . ."

"Which is what, exactly?"

"Information." Finley smiled as if I should have known.

I knew then he wanted something from me as badly as I wanted something from him. The problem was, I didn't know what he would want from me. I didn't have anything of worth.

"Fine," I said. "The person who outlasts the other wins one question, answered truthfully."

The game host cleared his throat, nodding.

I tipped my dice into the cup, and we rolled.

Finley grinned broadly and lifted his cup to inspect his dice. "You have a deal, Octavia Nox."

Each round of Deceiver's Dice went as fast as the round before, truths and lies zipping around the circle, accusations flying. The stakes felt higher this time. There was a little more on the line now.

Finley outlasted me in the first round. My next coin hit the cup, and he did it again. Round three, and I came ahead of him – more out of luck than skill. In round four, I won the whole thing.

It was then he stretched, rolling his shoulders and pulling himself to his feet. "Four coins is my limit."

My heart pounded. I glanced between Finley, who watched me carefully, and the collection cup waiting for the bet of the next round. I wanted to keep playing. I'd just won, and I was sure I had another win. In that one win, I had turned one coin into eight.

They weighed heavily in my pocket, begging to be played.

"Octavia?"

I glanced at Finley, tormented by the choices in front of me. I wanted nothing more than to lose myself in this game, easy to play and surprisingly fun, until I had a hundred coins in my pocket. More than I had ever won before, and a lot less than I had lost in my lifetime.

"You owe me three questions, Octavia." His tone was a little more urgent.

My eyes shot back up to his face, noticing the way his lips pursed, unimpressed I hadn't instantly joined him.

A deep breath later, and I was on my feet, swallowing the longing feeling that all I wanted was to play a little more. "You owe me one."

The tension in his jaw lifted, and Finley laughed. "One question is nothing. Let's get a drink."

He led the way into the eatery, which smelt like roasting meats. He greeted the stall owner as if they were long-lost friends, and I caught myself glancing back to the dice game as he ordered two mugs of sweet cider.

When Finley turned back to me, the tin mug outstretched, my nerves fluttering.

What could Finley Nightingale want from me to the value of three questions?

He moved to a small table in the corner. It sat crooked, and the moment I put my mug down, it started to tip. It stayed firmly clenched in both hands as I settled on the overturned crate and stared him down.

"So . . ." I hedged.

Finley leaned back and sipped his cider. He was taking his time, and it felt uncomfortable. I envied the way he looked so relaxed, as if this trial didn't take anything away from him. It wasn't long before I couldn't wait any longer.

"What's your first question?" I demanded.

He hummed, and it sparked fury in my blood.

I tapped my nails on the mug until it grated on my own nerves.

The longer we waited, the wider Finley's grin became.

"Tell me," he said. I leaned closer. "Are you the one they're talking about?"

I tilted my head, confused, and waited for him to elaborate. I had no idea what he was talking about.

"Did you kill the woman in the foyer?" Finley clarified.

My stomach twisted and turned, a tight band cutting into my chest. Procrastinating the chance to answer, I lifted the mug to my lips and gulped down the too-sweet contents. Finley grinned wider.

"No," I protested. "No."

"She's one of your team, though, I know that" he pushed.

"Yes." It was easy to be honest. "She was on my team."

Finley Nightingale said nothing for a moment and stared into his cup of cider. A crease formed between his brows. I wanted to question it, but I only had one, and unlike him, I wasn't willing to waste it away on useless topics like underground gossip.

"You have one question left," I told him.

"You can learn a lot in one question, if it's asked right," Finley told me, and I silently agreed.

I was counting on it; I had only won a single honest answer from him, and I needed it to be worthwhile.

"Go on . . ." I prompted.

"You first, Octavia."

"No. I don't know what you're getting at. All you know now is that I didn't murder a girl I knew." I narrowed my eyes. "If it helps, I've never murdered anyone."

His lips pursed, then he laughed. "I never thought you did. You're not that sort."

"Then –" I clamped down on the question before it could slip out and steal my one truth from him, even though I burnt to know why he would ask if he didn't think I was capable of it. "Just ask, Finley!"

He put down his cup, and it inched to the left. It slowly slid along the table.

"Some say it was a harpy." He studied my face carefully as he leaned too close to me. He stayed there, close as he waited for what he wanted to see in my face. Finley didn't even flinch as the cup fell off the side of the table, clanging as it bounced off the concrete. I don't know what he saw in the twist of my lips or the flicker of my eyes, but he grinned widely, like a cat who caught a mouse.

"Tell me, what was it like?" His final question asked me to relive a nightmare, and for a moment, I thought my throat was closing in. It was hard to breathe, and emotion tingled the bridge of my nose, threatening tears.

"Pick something else."

His brown eyes widened; the corner of his grin dropped on one side. Finley's sharp inhale felt like a slap to the face. "You did see it!"

"I don't want to talk about it."

Finley reached for me. His hand caught my arm and held tight. The abrupt movement knocked my hand, and I dropped the mug. Sweet liquid splashed to the ground, wasted.

"Octavia." He shook his head. "You promised."

"I . . . I can't . . ." Emotion thickened my voice, fear inducing tremors in my words. Beneath his grip, my fingers trembled. The first of my tears rolled down my cheek. "I can't . . ."

Finley blew out a slow breath. "Octavia . . ."

I shook my head and tried to pull my arm from his grasp. It was a foolish idea; I wasn't in any state to trade information and secrets.

"Just tell me how to survive one." He changed his question.

I stared at him, wide-eyed, with trembling lips and cried harder as I shook my head.

"You don't."

"You did."

"I wish I hadn't," I admitted.

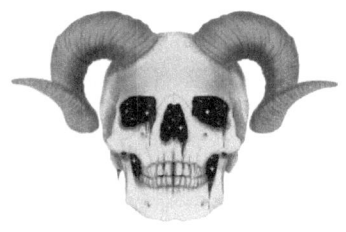

Chapter Twenty-Seven

I wrenched my arm back again, and this time, he let me go. The momentum almost sent me toppling right off the stool and onto the floor. I turned my hard gaze on him and stared until his smile dipped. The harpies were no joking matter.

"Just don't go near one, Finley," I told him firmly. "That's my only advice. Don't go out after dark, and you'll survive the harpies. Don't take the risk."

He gaped at me. He ran his hand through his thick mop of curls, and I watched as his throat bob, like I had crushed all his plans.

A sharp kick moved the stool out of the way, and I brushed at the drops of cider that had landed on my leg. Finley's hand flapped, as if he was trying to mentally put something back together.

When I stepped back, he looked up sharply. "You still have a question."

I paused and fidgeted with the thin pieces of wire wrapped around my fingers. Although I hadn't recounted the experience with the harpy, all I could imagine was its ashen skin, the sharp points on its wings, and the way its claws had raked through Monika's skin like it was nothing more than wet tissue.

I felt too frazzled, dizzy, and out of sorts to put together a proper question. I wanted to craft the perfect question, give the perfect details to walk into their team and snatch up a piece of victory from right beneath their noses. When it was gone, Finley would know, he would know it was me.

He would know he had led me to this point.

But right then, I couldn't remember how to breathe properly, let alone how to work out what I needed from him.

My voice trembled as I finally asked, "Who has the piece?"

He didn't even blink. Finley screwed up his lips but answered. "Nash, of course. Who else?"

I cursed beneath my breath as I paced through the tunnels and tried to tamp down on the rising panic in my veins. I didn't know how to survive on my own – not really, especially not in that city. I was a world away from Ilrea, from familiarity and safety.
A demonic danger aboveground loomed, along with an immediate danger below.

On my own, I didn't know how I was going to get through a night in the encampment, let alone infiltrate Nash's space. He wasn't Niklaus Heira; I couldn't pretend I wanted to seduce him to get close. Nash had eyes on for his goal of finding a cure for Alby, and I was just another traveller going the same direction. We may have been from the same small town, but we hadn't known each other before this trauma.

It was too cold to camp out in the tunnels. They dripped with moisture, carrying the stench of mould. Once the temperature dropped far enough to make my teeth chatter, I ventured back out into the main hubs. Dinner had come and gone while I dried out my tears and pulled together the frayed edges of my psyche.

I slipped around the edges of the market, reserving a glare for the fortune teller who had put me in this position, and crept to the entryway of the encampment. Lines were drawn again; groups formed in their own spaces.

The structures were improving day by day. Tents and hung blankets sectioned the space until it had become a little city of its own. Unable to linger too long, I stalked through to where I had left my belongings. Two of my three blankets had been stolen, so I snatched up the last one and wrapped it around my shoulders.

Aureen glared at me from three steps away, daring me to come closer and the message couldn't have been clearer, so I sat on the floor, crossing my legs, searching the crowd for Nash.

He wasn't hard to find, too tall for his own good, and strangely, he was laughing again.

He always seemed happier than he should have been, and an acidic twist in my gut seared me as I realised how much I wish it were me he was talking to, me he was laughing with. I missed him. I wanted to be his teammate and survive with him more than anything – well, almost. Not as much as I wanted to survive.

I watched him closely, battling guilt that left me nauseous – that, for me to survive, I had to risk his failure.

If I had stolen the akelda from Nash, and he couldn't find another piece, I would be leaving him behind. I wrestled with that idea long after the chatter died down and the lights dimmed.

It would have been better if we were teammates, and we could have figured out this problem together. His optimism might have carried me through. The second-best option would have been if my own team were better than they were, cohesive and willing to trust. Instead, Monika was dead. Aureen was waiting for proof that I was worth her time. Kyra didn't have a thought of her own rattling around in her head. And Benton Rumley?

I could feel his gaze on the back of my neck.

He watched every one of my movements, waiting for a moment to strike. He was a danger in wait. I didn't know when or how to be ready for his attack.

Huddled beneath the blanket, I wished for more protection, time, and choices.

I listened to the way the whispers turned into snores, trying to convince myself I could get through this trial another way. By the time I had found the courage to move, half the night dragged on. I was lucky the devil made us face the worst of humanity's vices and not prove ourselves to courageous, brave, or selfless because I couldn't fit myself into those boxes, no matter how hard I tried.

It took a long time to get from my side of the room to where Nash and his team slept. I moved slowly, more than aware that not everyone was asleep, and some were watching my every movement. The closer I managed to get, the more my heart thundered in a desperate plea to flee.

Panic was a poison in my veins, though, and I could do nothing to stop the path I had chosen.

I crouched down beside Nash, his blonde hair sweeping his face, and counted the time between his slow and even breaths. I had to make sure he was really sleeping. When I was satisfied, he was asleep, I let my eyes avert to his teammates, marking the place of all four.

I wasn't surprised to see that Finley grinned, even in his sleep.

He shifted restlessly, twisting and curling an arm around one of his teammates, pulling her close. My heart stuttered as I thought she would wake, but she sighed and moved closer.

The little time I had to do this was running out fast.

With a renewed sense of urgency, I reached for Nash's jacket and started rifling through all the pockets. There was a crumpled piece of paper, but as I smoothed it out, I realised it was worthless, the slanted writing not something I could decipher, even if I had all the time in the world. I picked up his boots, loosened the laces, and felt inside. Both were smelly but empty. I dropped them and immediately regretted it when they thunked hard against the floor.

Time suspended for a heartbeat, tense and frozen as I waited for them to wake, but Nash just frowned in his sleep.

"Alby." The name was a whisper on his lips. My heart squeezed in response. I was drowning in my own guilt. I wasn't just robbing Nash of his chance to win but his lover of the chance of survival. "Alby. No."

The ring of urgency in his voice made me move; if Nash had the akelda hidden anywhere, it would be on his body. Just like Francesca North had kept her valuables close, so would everyone else. Searching for his pockets, I skimmed my fingers against his hip, accidentally brushing regions I really didn't want to touch. When I couldn't find what I wanted, I moved to see if there were pockets in the thick sweater. He was bundled into it to fight the cold. My fingers grazed exposed skin, and he shifted restlessly. I gently patted his chest, my hands moving frantically higher as dread and desperation set in.

His hands wrapped into shackles around my wrists before I had even registered that Nash was awake. The wind knocked out of my body as his long legs caught my waist, and he rolled me quickly.

"Uh!"

My back hit the cement hard, my head bouncing off it with such force the world went fuzzy. I blinked rapidly, breathed shallowly, and tried to focus on Nash's furious face.

"Tav?!" he growled.

The girl in Finley's embrace woke.

"What's happening?" she asked sharply. Finley grunted when she elbowed him awake and crawled to her knees. Her body wavered in and out of my peripheral vision.

"No," Nash rebuked as my gaze strayed. "Look at me."

I couldn't refuse his request, even though I didn't want to look at the dark accusation in his eyes. His mouth turned downwards; I had only seen him unhappier than he had been screaming for Alby, the mercy of the sweet river.

"You were stealing from me."

I focused on breathing and refused to answer him.

"Octavia!" he hissed furiously, his cheeks turning pink. Nash pulled me up by my wrists and slammed me back onto the floor. The air rushed from my chest again, and I whimpered at the pain that zipped down my spine. "What were you doing?"

"Why are you asking if you already know?" I spat, bitter.

The last of the anger drained from his features, and he looked sad.

I closed my eyes, not wanting to look at what I'd caused.

"Nash?"

I peeled my eyes. His four teammates had surrounded us. They blocked out everyone else, faces impassive.

He sighed; his breath tickled my cheek. "What, Billie?"

The girl shifted and held a knife out to him. My stomach twisted with dread.

"That's a big knife."

"We made a deal," Billie said. "We gut anyone who comes for the akelda."

Nash had his eyes on the knife. A lock of blonde hair fell across his face as he tilted his head, considering it.

"Octavia," he said, and I tensed.

"Yes?" I asked after I found my voice, the single word infused with a tremor.

"Tell me why I shouldn't."

He let go of one of my wrists. Relief filled me for a moment, before I realised, he had only let me go to take the knife from Billie, who grinned viciously at me. From this angle, her teeth appeared pointed, and it reminded me so starkly of the harpy that I shivered. It felt like I was always in some level of danger, that it haunted me, the ghost of my past sins.

Nash turned his wrist, capturing my attention in the way he moved the sharp blade.

I swallowed.

"What did you say?" I asked faintly.

He leaned over me, careful with the weapon, and whispered in my ear. "Give me a good reason not to gut you like my team wants."

Billie shifted, bloodthirsty and impatient.

"Because it's me, Nash?" I searched his face intently for some hint as to the right answer. "We survived Gluttony together, Nash, you and me. We're going to make it to the end together. We got through Gula . . ."

He shook his head. "This is a whole new trial."

"So?"

Nash waved the knife at his teammates. Finley stiffened at the casual swipe of the blade. "This is a whole new team, Octavia."

Dread pooled in my stomach. This wasn't going in my favour. Foolishly, I hadn't even considered what to do if I was caught, too focused on the need to get the akelda and save myself instead.

"This is *my* team." He pointed at them. "My team is going to victory, and we made a pact. Anyone who came for our pieces, we'd run them right through . . ."

He had offered up a nugget of information I didn't already know. They had more than one piece, which meant Finley could have given me a different name, but he had chosen to give me Nash.

My gaze flickered to him, and he turned sombre, as if he knew what I was thinking.

"Do it, then." I found my voice.

Nash paused. "What?"

"Do it," I said. "Just fucking kill me. I'd rather die here than out with the harpies."

That was the only other fate I could see for myself here in Invidia. I wouldn't let an angel take me at the end of the trial. Not like they had taken Ophelia.

Nash twisted the knife. It sliced a hole through my shirt and pricked my stomach's soft skin. I inhaled sharply; acutely aware I was less ready for this moment than I had let on.

Pain spiked through my body as Nash applied pressure, drops of blood pooling from the cut he created. My eyes closed tightly.

The knife clattered against the ground, and I heard Billie whine.

Nash grasped both my wrists again and shifted. As he stood, he pulled me to my feet.

"Get out," he demanded.

"Nash." I breathed his name as a prayer of faint disbelief.

"Go, Octavia, before I change my mind," he demanded.

"Why?" I was the fool to question blessings. I needed to know why, and I couldn't go anywhere, considering he hadn't released me.

"Because it's you, and we did survive together, and that does mean something. But this is the only chance I can give you," Nash hissed. "Don't do anything this stupid again, do you hear me?"

The urgency in his voice struck a chord, and I nodded quickly.

"Wait!" Billie cried. "You made an oath."

Nash whirled, his face pinched. "Now I'm changing my mind, Billie. So, shut it, or I'll . . ."

I used their altercation as a distraction enough to scuttle away. I moved through the encampment and ran blindly, looking for the way out. Closer to the door, I slammed into another body.

Benton Rumley grasped both my hips roughly. He looked at me and laughed, loud enough to draw attention. I shrank back from him.

"Aren't you a lucky little rat?" he snickered. "I'm watching you, Nox, and the moment you have a piece, I'll slit your throat and take it from you as you bleed out."

"You're all talk, Rumley." I bluffed.

He grinned viciously. "We'll see about that."

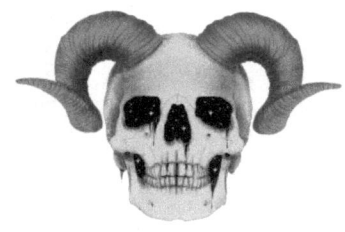

Chapter Twenty-Eight

I felt as though my blood had been poisoned, as though I'd been injected with fear and desperation that blurred my vision, leaving my head spinning. Huddled deep in the tunnels, I shivered through the cold, too scared to go back to the encampment. The list of people I had to be wary of had grown immensely. I was sure Nash's team would be out for my blood.

The moment I heard rustling in the markets, I prised my cold body out from behind the crates, teeth chattering, hair stuck to my face, and hid amongst the slow foot traffic of the early morning risers. I dawdled past bench after bench of fresh produce, my gaze wearily bouncing around to make sure danger had not come to find me.

I paused in front of a stall and fished a bronze wrath coin from my pocket as I picked up an apple.

The severe-looking woman shook her head at me. "We don't take that coin here."

"What?" I glanced at the bronzed coin and flipped it to inspect the lion carved onto one side. "It's real, though."

"I know it's real, lovie." The woman sighed. "But we don't take anything from the Wrathlands in Invidia."

I blinked, my brow creasing. "Why?"

The woman's lips curved into a sly smile. "Why do you think?"

Another of those questions that threatened to make my blood boil. Just like Oskar had so many days before. I still didn't know the answer to his question.

"I've got no idea," I told her bluntly, the ends of my nails biting into the flesh of the red apple.

She laughed, and I tried not to take it personally.

"My dear" – it was hard not to cringe at the nickname – "even the Angel of Envy is envious of something . . ."

"Oh . . ."

I pushed my hand into my pocket and dug out a fistful of mixed coins. "I . . ."

The woman reached over and plucked two sloth coppers from my hand. "These will do."

My eyes narrowed. It was overpaying for the fruit, but she had already tucked them away in the pocket of her apron. I quickly stowed the rest of the coins and took a large bite from the apple with a loud crunch.

"Thanks," I said around the mouthful of fruit. When I passed through the tunnels and rooms that would lead me into the city, my eyes flickered to the corner of the room where I had left

Monika Oster. Her body still lay there, picked clean of clothes, her skin pale and grey beneath the low light.

Exposed.

A lump formed in my throat. I glanced away and strode past like I didn't know her at all. If only my demons could be left in the shadowy corners with her body, forgotten between one day and the next, instead of haunting the recesses of my mind.

I had no idea what to do next. I couldn't return to the maid's office and find a new target within the job. I had ruined two women's reputations in my quest to find the coveted jewel – three if I counted myself – but my reputation wasn't worth talking about.

Out of options, I pushed my hands into the pocket of my jacket, hiding the competitor's cuff as I strolled through the streets and decided to explore the city properly. It was bigger than I had realised in the past twelve days, where I had scurried through the spiral to find my target and inspect the castle, but I hadn't paid much attention to how wide the city was. Even as we had weaved through the little alleyways, fleeing danger. The Envylands were one of the biggest states in Kaida, and I realised that Invidia was in proportion to that.

I took my time, since I had nowhere else to be and no plan to speak of and inspected the weave of alleyways through the slums flooded with lower-class citizens. The width of the spiral was huge but didn't thin as it curled inward, but there were fewer people cramped in wider spaces. By the time I had wandered back and forth for hours on end, I found myself in the thick of the entertainment district.

It was mid-morning by the time my stomach growled with the need of something more than the juicy apple. I had no desire to subject myself to hunger again. Huddled into my jacket, I turned into one of the bars on the side of the street, squinting at the sign out front.

I couldn't read the specials, of course, but I paused as if I knew what they advertised, then pushed through the door.

The pub smelled like old cider and sweaty boots. All the furniture was worn and repolished wood and leather. A man stood behind the bar and dried glasses.

"Mornin'." He grunted. "What you after?"

"Uhh . . ."

I edged up to the bar and shuffled out of my jacket to throw it over the back of a nearby chair. The floor was tacky beneath my boots. I leaned my elbows on the counter and pretended to read the scrawled words on the blackboard behind him. He set down the glass when I took too long.

"Well?"

My gaze flicked to his face. "What would you recommend?"

"Pie," he answered. I nodded.

My eyes dropped to the glass he had set down on the bar. "And whatever's good and cheap to drink."

I didn't want him robbing me blind, and I didn't know what a pie was, but it was probably expensive, considering this was aboveground. He looked at me and muttered an amount. I scrounged in my pocket to pay and watched as he filled my glass with a frothy substance. Small bubbles floated to the top, and he pushed it along the bar to me.

It was bitter on the end of my tongue but better than nothing, so I sipped slowly as he shuffled away. It didn't take long before I was no longer alone in the bar. First came businessmen at lunch. They crowded into the booth tables, calling orders over the top of me. The bartender nodded at each, turning to holler at a woman named Mary in the kitchen with each one.

Then came the rush of guards on their lunch breaks, their armour clanging, their swords in place as they laughed brashly and hovered around the tall tables in the middle of the room. They made me nervous, and I hunched over my drink, unwilling to make eye contact.

A woman bustled out from the back of the bar. She was ruddy-cheeked, heavyset, and cheerful as she beamed at the patrons. She dropped a plate onto the bar beside me and turned to deliver the other two she held without waiting.

"Mary," the barman called to her, and she glanced at him. "Music!"

The woman moved to the back of the room and kicked her foot sharply against a large box. It shuddered and coughed before a jaunty tune floated through the room. The guards raised their drinks and cheered brightly.

Mary beamed at them and continued her tasks, delivering food to businessmen and the few stray families that had wandered in. I turned my attention to the rapidly cooling pie by my elbow. It was a pastry, I realised, fired until golden, alongside a lump of mushy green vegetable on the side of the plate. The barman had dropped a fork in front of me while I had been distracted watching Mary.

I picked it up and twirled it between my fingers, scooped a large portion of the mush on to the fork, and swallowed it before I could second guess it. I gagged. My entire body shuddered, and the barman let out a rumbling laugh, watching me from the corner of his eye.

"You all right?"

"Salty," I gasped.

He chuckled, poured another glass, and set down on my right.

"You'll be fine," he said. "Eat your pie."

He reminded me so starkly of my dad in that moment. The sheer number of times he had told me to eat my dinner, and it would all be okay in the morning. Loneliness and a longing for my family, even the annoying siblings I barely knew, overwhelmed me. Unwilling to drown in it, I gulped down the brew to settle the taste, directing my attention to the pie.

It had cooled enough that I could lift it to my mouth without burning the tips of my fingers. I blew out a breath, tamped down on my apprehension, and took a smaller bite. Much to my surprise, the inside was a chewy meat with a thick gravy searing my tongue.

It dropped from my grip, hit the plate, and fell apart, the insides spilling out. I sighed heavily, picked up the fork, and dissected its innards.

The businessmen left before I had worked my way through it, pausing every so often to suck the fatty gravy off the fork's tines. I had just pushed the vegetable aside and scraped up the last of the flaking pastry when the door flung open again.

A group of competitors barged into the bar, cheering, and the pie in my stomach turned to stone. I knew those voices. The rough huskiness of Helina's tone, more prominent when she was excited. Niklaus Heira's refined pronunciation a strange and unwanted burst of energy from my head to my toes. I closed my eyes and counted to three, wishing they would disappear or prove to be nothing more than my imagination.

I was not so lucky.

They crowded into a booth, all five squashed in together, and I dragged my second glass towards me, leaving dregs in the bottom of the first glass. I hadn't paid yet, and I couldn't leave, so I tried to make myself as small as possible and avoid their attention. All the while, I couldn't stop paying attention to them. The way they laughed, the way they cheered, nudging Oskar and grinning at him.

"Three of five!" they cheered.

Oskar beamed broadly under the attention, his rounded face bright and excited. It took a beat of watching them before I realised what they were celebrating.

They had three pieces of akelda.

Deep-rooted envy flushed through me, hot, then cold.

I forced myself to turn away again, clenching the glass so hard my knuckles blanched. They were almost done, having stolen the first piece and gained two more over halfway. I was floundering with a dead teammate, one who was ready to kill me should I persevere, and two who couldn't have cared less if that happened. I burnt with a bitter desire to have a better team, to have been dealt a better hand.

"You just keep turning up, don't you?" Helina Archer sighed as she stood beside me at the bar.

I had been so focused on trying to quell the rage that came with feelings of bitterness that I hadn't noticed her approach.

I pursed my lips. "I was here first."

"You shouldn't be."

"What?" I scoffed. "I can go anywhere I want."

"You shouldn't be in this competition at all, Octavia. I've said it before, and I'll say it again: riding on my success is pathetic. You should have stayed safe and sound in the gutters of Ilrea."

My knuckles whitened as I clenched the glass between my hands. I stewed on her words while she ordered four drinks and then set the glass down hard. Beer slopped over the sides, and the bartender grunted a warning about his bar top.

"Who are you?" I twisted on my stool to look her in the eye. Helina twisted, too. She had no hesitation in holding my gaze, in assessing me.

"Hmm?"

"Who are you?" I repeated. "Where's my best friend? Did you get knocked in the head while I was in Glorae? Did someone give you a new brain."

Her face had turned hard. Helina pushed her spectacles up the bridge of her nose. She inhaled sharply, but I cut her off.

"My best friend would *never* act like this! Sometimes, she was the worst, mocking, blunt and knew too much, but she was never a Devil-damned bitch," I spat. "So, where's that Helina?

Where's the woman who tried to teach me how to read? Or tried to become self-sustainable and grow stupid little plants; because, if one person could do it, Ilrea could dig themselves out of being the Devil's arse of Kaida?"

Emotion flickered across her face. She slapped coins down on the bar, and the bartender snatched them up, lining up the drinks on a wide tray.

"That Helina deserved the world, you deserve . . ." I scoffed, bitter and angry, raw and hurt. "Nothing at all." I leaned into her space, close to her face. "Not to win. Not to be remembered. Not even a glorious or whispered about death."

Helina had gone pale.

Swiftly, she pushed one of her dreadlocks over her shoulder and reached out to grasp my chin. Her fingers pinched at my skin.

"That Helina," she hissed dangerously, "didn't sign up to watch her best friend die. She signed up to win and come back to her and make their lives better. She signed up, so she could bring the luxuries of Eternis to her only friend and her entire family. She signed up so we would never feel poverty again. I was leaving to make both our lives better in a way I couldn't do in the archives of Ilrea, pretending the stories in my books would become my reality."

Guilt joined the writhing mass of emotion in my belly at those words.

"Then you followed, and at first, I thought I would work with you; we would win, even though I didn't want you there. But I didn't sign up to be left behind while you danced with angels because that was when I realised, I would carry you through this competition, Octavia, and you could spend two days forgetting all about me because someone better came along . . ." Helina scoffed, shook her head, and glanced back at her team.

"Helina," I said. "You –"

"Go home, Octavia, you selfish bitch." She knocked my glass over. The glass shattered, and the beer spilled down my front.

"Whoops." Helina lifted the tray of drinks and turned away. Her dreadlocks flew with the abrupt movement, almost slapping me in the face, which felt worse of an insult than the drink I wore.

Gingerly, I pushed at the fragments of broken glass and cringed at the mess. As I stumbled to my feet, I gripped my shirt and squeezed, beer dripping. It was already drying, sticky against my skin, and I huffed with frustration.

The bartender tapped his thick fingers against the bar top and whistled for my attention, like I was a wet hound misbehaving. I flushed indignantly, chin jerking as I met his gaze.

"You'll be paying for your meal now, then." He nodded. "And my broken glass."

As predicted, he robbed me blind.

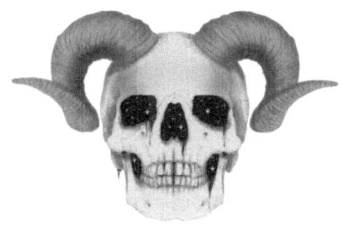

Chapter Twenty-Nine

A ny remaining wealth I had in my pocket disappeared as the afternoon wore on. I traipsed through the entertainment and business districts until I realised the drink in my shirt had dried. It shrouded me in an odour, like I had spent a fortnight sleeping on the tacky floor of a tavern. It would attract more attention than I wanted.

When it started raining, I ducked inside the nearest clothing store and tried to ignore the disapproving looks that the matron gave me for dripping all over the soft carpet. I raked my fingers through my hair, wincing as they caught on tangles.

"How can we help you?" The woman's voice was brusque, and I swallowed roughly.

My eyes dragged over her merchandise, and I shrugged.

"I, uh, I need a new shirt."

She looked me up and down, assessing and disapproving. At first, I thought she was going to turn me back out into the drain, but instead she clucked her tongue. A damning sound.

"I imagined so."

My face flushed.

"You smell like a brewery," she added.

"A what?"

"Where they make beer, girl . . ."

For a moment I stared her down, but the woman didn't flinch or apologise. She merely swept around the counter and looked me up and down. "A new shirt and a pair of boots."

Her hand waved to the young girl lingering in the corner, who scurried to find some options.

"I don't need boots," I protested.

I knew shoes were expensive. It was why I had been living in this one pair of boots for years, and why my younger sisters always went barefoot at home.

"Yes, you do." She turned away from me.

"No." I planted my hands on my hips, pouting. "Stop trying to con more coin from me."

The woman white-knuckled the coat hanger, and a beat passed before she seemed to pull herself together again. She turned me abruptly, sharp eyes sweeping me up and down, lingering at my feet.

"You have a hole the size of a devil's coin in your left toe . . . Not to mention the blood."

My eyes followed hers, and I realised she was right. Monika's blood was still all over my shoes. A wave of sadness rolled through me, a strange longing not to give to give up on those boots. They were mine and only mine – for years. Not

218

handed down from my older brothers, not stolen from someone else, already worn in at the soles, but bought new from the markets with a windfall at my favourite card game.

Even before the trials had started, I had known they were wearing thin, every uneven surface and loose stone pressing through the soles to cause me pain. But still, I didn't want to let go.

I sighed heavily. "All right, and a pair of boots."

The sharp way she smiled was as if she had known I would give in all along. "This way, then, behind the curtain."

The curtained enclosure cut off my view of the street and left me feeling claustrophobic. The shopkeeper joined me a minute later, a hanger in each hand and another cluck on the end of her tongue.

"What are you waiting for?" she asked. I blinked. "Strip off that disgusting shirt."

Hastily, I dropped my jacket by my feet. My fingers wrapped in the soiled material of the black shirt, and I paused. I had taken it from a dead friend's room at the end of Gluttony's trial, and it felt like I was leaving the last of Ophelia behind as I peeled it over my head. It hit the floor, and guilt weighed me down. I folded my arms over my chest and forced my gaze back up at the woman.

"Oh, my," she said as she inspected the faded scars and fresh bruises marring my skin. "You're a rough one."

I didn't disagree.

The woman frowned at the two shirts on the hangers. I went to reach for one, and she jerked it from me. "Neither of these are right."

"But –"

She was gone before I could tell her they were fine.

I stood alone and cold in that little room until she pushed her way behind the curtain. The small face of her assistant pushed in after her, and with a giggle, the girl dropped a pair of boots.

"Here." The woman held out a plain olive-green shirt, her lips pursed in a manner suggesting I shouldn't argue.

Ever foolish, I hesitated. "I don't really like green."

Her brow rose. "In Invidia, you'll wear it."

Although, I had noticed the citizens of Invidia favoured shades of the angel's colour, I had thought it was just another way to gain his favour.

"I really think . . ."

She lifted a brow and took the shirt off the hanger. "This is your only option."

"But you have a whole store full of clothes!" I protested. I had never shopped in a traditional storefront like this, but I had assumed every piece inside was for sale.

"This is the only piece I'll sell you." She tossed the shirt at me and snatched up my old shirt from the floor before tossing it out. "It's this or you can go back outside."

I swallowed. "Without my shirt?"

She smiled, and I was reminded of the snakes that decorated the city. Invidia had more reptiles than those of wrought iron displayed on banners.

Gritting my teeth in protest, I pulled the shirt on. The woman chuckled as the material obscured my face. I hated that it fit well, a strange, ribbed material that clung to my ribs. Long sleeves covered the evidence of the trials, with a high-enough neckline in which I didn't feel uncomfortable.

"Well?" She fished for praise.

"It's okay," I grunted.

"Sit."

Mentally, I reminded myself that the only beings I couldn't deny were the angels of sin. I obeyed and dropped onto the stool, tilting my chin up in question.

"Boots off," she demanded and picked up the pair her assistant had dropped on the ground, who unlaced them efficiently for me to try on.

"Can I ask a question?" I asked as I took a moment to check the hollowed-out heel and retrieve the coins I had stacked in there.

"You just asked one."

"You know that's not what I meant."

A pause lingered.

"Ask, then."

"Why doesn't Envy like Wrath?"

The woman said nothing while I battled with the triple knots in the laces of my right boot and slowly worked it loose enough to free my foot.

When I looked up, her face was pale, her lips pursing in disapproval.

"That's a question for the angel himself," she said finally, passing the new boots over. "If you're stupid enough to ask."

It was frustrating to know that the people of this city had information that could help me survive but who were also so reluctant to share. I didn't bother giving her an answer. The new boots' leather was much softer than my last pair, and my stomach twisted as I realised how expensive they were going to be. One glance at the woman's face, however, and I knew it would be useless to argue.

I slid my feet into the boots. The soles were strange, well-cushioned and longer than my last pair, hugging my calf halfway rather than my ankle. They took longer to lace, but when I stood and wiggled my toes, it felt like how I imagined standing on a cloud would feel.

The woman was already watching me closely when I turned my gaze back to her and nodded. "I'll take both."

She offered that sly smile again. "I imagined you would."

The curtain was thrown back as I stooped to collect my jacket and the few stray coins, I had dropped on top of it. My old boots had disappeared by the time I straightened, and I was ushered to the counter.

It cost a small fortune, and I was left with a handful of wrath coppers – apparently useless – and two Pride silvers by the time I had paid my dues.

The woman deposited me back on the street before I could grumble or consider thanking her for her time, not that I would have. The only sweet relief to the whole ordeal was that it had stopped raining.

My jacket still smelled like beer, and I was in desperate need of a bath, but I felt marginally cleaner.

The afternoon light was fading, but I still walked out of the entertainment district and followed the cobblestone path that led right to the gates of the castle. The castle grounds were huge, a world of their own within the city, with fountains and little bridges, grand steps, and tall towers.

As I lingered by the iron gates, I stared at the distant windows and the stone walls and wondered what it might be like to live within the castle. Those within were coveted by everyone who lived on the outside, and I found that I, too, burnt with desire for a permanent, luxurious home like it. I burnt for a desire for more.

My fingers trailed along one of the snakes designed into the gate. It was a replica of the one at the front, designed the only way behind the grand stone walls that surrounded the entire city. The snakes writhed out from a knot in the centre. Their eyes polished and gleaming, jaws open, fangs bared. I pressed my finger against the tip of one of those fangs and found it sharp enough that it pricked me. A bead of blood pooled on the pad of my thumb.

I inhaled sharply, and snatched my hand back, cursing under my breath at the devil and his angels. It was only then I realised how long I had been preoccupied by my thoughts.

The sun had begun to sink.

It was hard to decide which was worse: the idea of having to back below ground and survive another night in an encampment full of people likely to murder me for their own or to spend the night above ground, trying to be as quiet as possible and avoid becoming harpy food.

With every quick step I took, relishing in the feel of my brand-new shoes, I tried to debate which of the two bad choices I would take. As I strolled back through the business district, it was empty, the smarter middle-class Invidians already tucked away in their home behind the buildings, safe and sound for the night.

The entertainment district had thinned out, too. As I passed the bar from earlier, Mary was pulling the sign back inside, calling out to the bartender over her shoulder. Her smile didn't look like it had slipped since lunch. If only I could find a way to be that joyful.

My pace dragged as I wove into the slums and came closer to the tailor that would lead into the world that wove belowground. The sky was stained orange and pink by the time I neared, but it was the sight of Mikhael Heira that stopped me in my tracks.

Almost instantly, I veered off course, hiding around the corner of a building and peering back at him. He stood with a woman, his arms wrapped around her body, holding her against his chest.

My eyes lingered on the pale fingers that pressed against this back. Her hood fell back, and I wasn't surprised to see Margot with her face buried in his chest.

My throat tightened. I had no interest in Mikhael at all, but I wanted someone to hold me that tight. I wanted someone to cling to me as if I were the sole reason for living.

The sky darkened further as I tried to wait them out, but the fear of the harpies became too much, and I edged my way around the building, determined that I could slip past without them caring. Just as I tried to move by, the woman pulled her head back, her clear blue gaze pinning me.

"Margot." Mikhael said her name like a caress.

I shivered. It pulled her gaze from me, though, and with a shaky breath, I tried to keep moving to give them a moment alone.

"Mik!" I froze because she had not said his name back. It had been a deeper, rougher voice, echoing from a distance. "Mikhael!"

I turned.

Niklaus was running down the spiral, heading for his brother as fast as he could. Two of his teammates paced behind him. The air seemed to leave my lungs; this was not a good place to be.

"Mik!" he shouted again.

Margot pulled herself free of his brothers' arms. Tension tugged at the corner of her lips, her eyes snapping to the skies.

She reached for her hood, covering her face quickly.

"Go." Her voice was as melodic as I remembered.

I shifted out of the way, pressing against the rough brick of the building as she glanced to me and Mikhael before shoving him. "*Please*. Just go."

"Margot." He sounded broken.

She shook her head, fingers threading into the end of her long, white hair, and she twisted the pieces between, plaiting it nervously. The shadow of wings appeared on the cobblestones.

Fear slipped like ice down my spine. Niklaus slammed into his brother, shoving him past Margot, forcing him away from her. They both came barrelling towards me.

"What's going on?" I hissed as I shifted out of their way.

Niklaus had Mikhael by the scruff of his shirt. His muscles bunched, straining to hold him as he pinned Mikhael to the wall. Niklaus held him against the brick, spitting back a curse for everyone that Mikhael growled at him.

"What's happening?" I demanded again.

The shadow of wings flashed across the street again, distracting me from the brothers. Panic tightened my windpipe as I searched the skies for the imminent death that awaited us. The harpies were early. They would come, swoop in, and take us all. I would have survived being prey for only a day longer.

Instead, an angel fell from the sky.

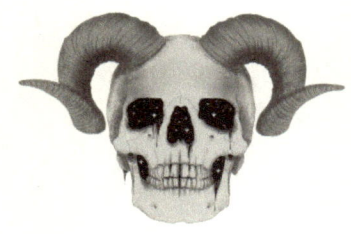

Chapter Thirty

Envy dropped from the skies so heavily I thought the stone street would shatter, but his landing was deceptively quiet. He was quick, light-footed, a predator.

As he straightened, sleek wings rustling and stretching, his power seemed to curl around me, tightening its grip like a serpent strangling its prey. The effect was nauseating. My blood seared my veins.

The angel stood with his back to me. His full focus on Margot, who stood frozen in the middle of the street. His back rippled, his lithe body built of lean, strong muscle. His wings shuddered, and he pulled them in tight. The wind played with tendrils of his dark hair as he tilted his head, waiting her out.

Niklaus gripped my arm and yanked my attention from the angel of sin. He all but dragged me to his side, green eyes wild, jaw tense as he tried to pull me out of the path of danger.

I couldn't tear my eyes from Envy for long, though. I twisted in his grip for a better look, even as a strange bitterness sparked and burnt deep in my heart. I wanted Envy to look in my direction, to see me.

A glimpse at Margot over his shoulder showed that her snowy skin had turned sickly as she paled in his presence. Her chin dropped, eyes cast down, slender hands threading together in front of her body. She presented a picture of innocence wreathed with guilt.

"My Lord."

A tremor charged her voice, and those soft words echoed in my ears as if she had shouted them, ricocheting through my head. It left me dizzy. A sour taste burnt my throat as my gaze boomeranged between the angel and Mikhael, who had fallen still but stared, face pained over his brother's shoulder.

Envy stalked forward. He moved with a slow, predatory grace as he closed in on the woman. Margot's head bowed lower with each step. His hand shot out; fingers clamped around her chin. Her entire body jolted. I could almost feel the bruises that would mark her skin.

The angel tipped her gaze up to meet him, and it felt like my ribs tightened around my lungs to the point of pain.

This woman, Margot, had everything I wanted. She had the very embodiment of Envy shaking the streets with an old-world power, sweeping through the city to find her. More than that, Mikhael looked as if he was dying as he watched the angel touch her face. She had woven him so tightly around her slender fingers he was completely and utterly trapped.

A possessive shiver rolled through me from head to toe.

When Envy spoke, I felt like I'd faint. "You've been naughty, Margot."

She shivered. Her eyes dropped from his face to the stone floor as if ashamed. An admission of guilt before swallowing and speaking.

"No." Margot breathed. Her ice-blue eyes fluttered. She forced a soft smile and corrected. "Not unless you mean my adventure from the castle."

She giggled while I choked on Envy's power. It seemed to pulse through me until its poisonous desires was poised on the end of my tongue. I swayed forward on my toes. Niklaus gripped my arm tighter. I was dizzy and overcome with emotions I couldn't control, sick for all that I wanted and all that she had.

"Liar!" I hissed out of nowhere.

I had become the snake, not Envy. Coiled and sharp, striking out at the woman who had everything I desired. It drew the attention of the angel and his prized jewel. Beneath their gazes, I wilted.

Mikhael let out a huffed groan and pushed forward.

Niklaus slammed his elbow back, catching his brother in the stomach. His fingers loosened on my arm. I swayed, tempted to lurch forward and scratch out Margot's eyes so she would feel even a fraction of what I felt. I wanted to ruin her perfection, so she was not unattainable or special. The envy inside of me felt like pain.

"What did you say?" Envy asked, voice deceptively soft.

His vibrant green gaze was narrowed, and his high cheekbones appeared sharper as his mouth twisted in to a tight, displeased line. The angel's youthfulness had stricken me again, compared to his brother's, and the power and status he held despite it. The Heira brothers stiffened beneath his inspection.

"Well . . . ?" Envy didn't have to raise his voice to make an impact, his tone silky and demanding.

"Nothing." Niklaus clamped his calloused hand over my lips.

"Mmhfm!" I cried against his fingers.

"She's confused, sir." Niklaus glared at me, a demand to be silent. "She has nothing to say."

I could see the shadows within his tormented gaze. He struggled to contain his own envy; it threatened violence if not tamped down, hinting at pain, but I didn't care for his envy, only for the fire of my own.

I looked to the angel and shook my head behind Niklaus' tight grip. My gaze narrowed as I tried to tell him the story he wanted to hear because they didn't deserve their secrets, their infatuation, and manipulation, when I had nothing of the sort. If I couldn't have it, I would ruin it for them, too.

Envy closed the gap between us a little more, and his tight grip on Margot's jaw dragged her with him. He didn't wait for her to find her footing, only expected her to keep up. It showed that, for the adoration he reserved for her, she was nothing more than a possession. In my turmoil of envious desire, I paid no attention to it. I saw only what I wanted.

My vision was tainted green.

"Release her!" Envy demanded of Niklaus.

The tension between us escalated tenfold. The angel waited, assured in obedience, until Niklaus fell into step with the most impactful rules of these trials. We may not refuse a direct order from an angel of sin.

His fingers peeled away from my mouth, and I sucked in a dramatic lung full of air, acting as if he had been suffocating me with the forced silence.

Envy whipped his head around. The full force of his attention zeroed in on me, and some of the weighted pressure on my chest eased a fraction. I preened beneath his attention, a small smile at the corner of my mouth. My attention flicked to Margot to ensure she was watching.

"I said –"

"She said nothing," Niklaus retorted.

"No, he" – he stomped on my toes – "Ow!"

His attempt to silence me was futile in the end. Envy tilted his head, and his gaze flicked between the three of us. I had the distinct feeling that I would only be confirming what he already knew.

His power was well beyond what I could understand, and it wouldn't surprise me if he couldn't taste our jealousy in the air.

"Which one?" He let go of Margot, and she stumbled forward. Her thin hands raising to rub the red marks left behind. She didn't answer him immediately.

The angel reached for her throat; his grip tight.

My breath hitched, my heartbeat accelerating as it thrashed beneath the confinement of my ribs. I watched on, burning up with emotion. Envy stroked his thumb along the column of her throat, a tender movement.

Mikhael growled softly, drawing all of our attention.

Niklaus quickly pressed the weight of his body backwards, pinning his brother harder against the wall to muffle the sound.

Mikhael's face twisted with pain.

"Margot," Envy warned. The angel's fingers squeezed her throat; her body shuddered. His wings unfolded, rustling and stretching. Tension rippled through the muscles in his back. "Speak up."

Envy's power intensified, and nausea followed, my stomach rioting against the intensity of what I felt. I trembled.

Niklaus' fingers trailed down my arm, and he grasped my hand so tight my bones crunched. His neck was taut, jaw clenched. After joining hands, I could feel his hands trembling as well. Behind him, Mikhael slid down the wall and groaned, unable to hold himself upright in the face of the angel's power.

Margot whimpered.

"Envy," she rasped. "Envy, my love . . ." Her hand pressed to his, a plea for him to let go.

"Which one?" He didn't falter.

My head swam. Above us, a scream rolled through the sky. I forced myself to glance at the now darkened sky. The harpies circled in the shadows of the night but didn't descend when the bigger threat stood right before us. Even the cursed cowered from the angels.

My gaze dropped to the guards who had swarmed around us and waited.

Until a voice finally cracked through the silence, shattering the tension in the streets. "Me!"

I was starkly reminded of the enrolment for these devil-forsaken trials, when Mikhael had proclaimed his own intent to enter, proud and loud. Only this time, the cry had not come from him but from Niklaus. His tattooed counterpart let go of us both, his fingertips brushing my wrist softly before he dragged himself forward.

"It's me," he stated. "I was with . . . her."

Mikhael let out a pained noise of protest and dragged himself upright.

Niklaus stubbornly ignored him. He clenched his fists by his side, lifted his chin, and placed himself firmly in his brother's way. A shield between his brother and the angel.

Envy let go of Margot.

She crumpled to her knees, hands massaging her throat. I knew how that felt; both Heira brothers had strangled me in the thick of the frenzy of our first trial. But any sympathy I held for her was lost beneath a fresh wave of bitterness.

"Explain yourself, human." Envy stood eerily still, head cocked, teeth bared.

Niklaus' throat bobbed. He had to look up, as the young angel towered over him.

"I'm the one who coaxed your woman." Niklaus glanced at Margot, a quick flick of his eyes and his upper lip curled up a fraction. I wondered if he hated her because she had stolen a part of his brother away, the same part he had been trying to protect.

"You're . . . Margot," he corrected, butchering the soft nuance of her name. "From your ridiculous castle and into the streets."

"Is that so?" Envy questioned.

The angel nodded at Mikhael, who staggered forward, his lips parted in protest.

Impulsively, I grasped Mikhael's wrist and used all the strength I had to wrench him back towards me. Out of the firing line.

"Octavia!" Mikhael hissed.

"Don't!" I said. "Don't do it."

Envy offered me a scrutinising look.

Niklaus glanced over his shoulder at us, his attention moving to the place where our bodies met. His expression darkened, reflective of the ever-present thunderclouds rolling above.

"Yes," Niklaus said stonily. He set his gaze determinedly on Margot. "We're in love."

His voice trembled over the word, and I thought bitterly that Niklaus Heira didn't know how love felt. I was sure that Envy would see right through it.

Jealousy lacked perspective, however, and even gods of an old world were prone to the sins of which they ruled.

Envy's face tightened with distinct bitterness. His lips thinned and eyes darkened.

He didn't move to manhandle Niklaus in the way he had Margot. Instead, he bared his teeth, dark wings flung wide.

A shiver worked down my spine at the threat he posed. My grip tightened on Mikhael's arm, and his muscles bunched beneath my touch.

"Have you touched what is mine?" the angel asked. His deadly tone rang through the spiral.

The guards' armour rustled as they shifted their weight, reacting to the rise and fall of his overwhelming power.

Niklaus gritted his teeth, refusing to answer. His silence descended through the streets as an admission of guilt. Envy's face darkened. Lightning flashed across the sky, illuminating the demons above, who waited for their chance to strike.

The angel's wings flapped, creating a gust that smacked against me. I rocked back on the heels of my brand-new boots and tried to not to cringe. Pressure weighed on my chest, in my head, in my veins.

The angel was overwhelming as his own emotions ran wild. For a moment, I thought he would strike as quick as a cobra and take Niklaus' life right then and there. But it all melted away when Margot found her feet and slid her hand up his arm. She curled against his body, so small in comparison to a vengeful angel, but still somehow fitting perfectly.

Margot tilted her head upwards and murmured something to him. She was a master of not just manipulating Mikhael but had one of the invisible ribbons tied to her fingers, within all the strings she could pull, and Lord Envy was included.

Margot was not just a pretty jewel in his collection; it was obvious she knew him well, and the sweet words she whispered in his ear settled the envy in the angel's ancient soul. The otherworldly beast slackened.

Envy nodded sharply. His arm banded around her waist, pinning her close, before he pinned Niklaus beneath his dark glare.

"You will not struggle when my guards take you." Envy knew how to wield the rules of our trial. His demands were firm. "You will be judged for your sins, human."

Niklaus nodded.

"Take him to the gate," he commanded of the guards.

"Yes, my Lord!"

Envy held Margot tight. His wings rustled, and he was momentarily breathtaking before he shot into the sky. Harpies scattered, screeching, and he turned into a speck amongst the clouds, stealing the woman away as easily as that.

My chest ached for the loss of him.

The guards marched forward, and two took a hold of Niklaus' arms before they led Niklaus Heira to the early judgement of his soul.

Mikhael's face had twisted into a picture of shattered desperation, for himself, for his blood, and for the woman he had failed. A broken noise rolled from the back of his throat, a cry that threatened to shatter my own heart. He was not my friend, not really, but his pain reached me.

Helina crept forward, and I flinched.

I had forgotten she was even there, bearing witness to Mikhael's shame, to Niklaus' sacrifice, the bond of brothers and blood.

"We need to follow them," she said, pale-faced with her arms wrapped around her middle. Helina looked shaken.

Mikhael nodded, tearing from my grip as he started after the guards at a run.

I exchanged a glanced with Helina. Her eyes dropped away first. Neither of us knew what to say. All we could do was follow silently in their path to the iron gates of the city.

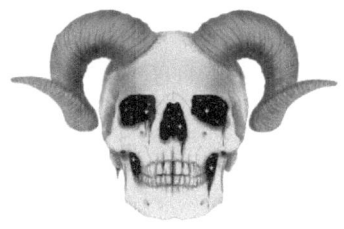

Chapter Thirty-One

Invidia looked even more intimidating that night. We followed the guards along the curve of the spiral until we moved past the looming wall surrounding the giant city. Outside the dark stone walls, it felt as if my lungs expanded properly for the first time, as if I could breathe again.

I stared into the pitch-black night with thoughts of a train I couldn't see. It was nothing more than a fantasy to run away from Envy, from the trials, and from the retribution due, but I still entertained it.

Helina hovered by my side. Our feud and nasty words were forgotten for the moment. She pulled her spectacles from her nose, cleaning them repeatedly on the grimy hem of her shirt. I knew this was a sign she was nervous, unsure of how the night would unfold, and her nerves only added to mine.

Envy touched down on the ground. He kept a tight hold on Margot, his treasure not to be let out of his sight, to be coveted but not touched by another.

The guards held Niklaus still, and he stared straight ahead.

I tried to catch his eye, but he wouldn't look at me – only at his brother, who hovered uselessly amongst us, strained in the way he held himself.

"Close the gates," Envy called.

A soft wind pushed his tousled dark hair across his face.

"Yes, my Lord." The guards hurried to obey.

The iron groaned an ancient protest as it moved. With every inch it crept forward, the dread in my heart doubled. My attention wavered between the two brothers, each tortured in a different way. I clenched my fists, stubbornly attempting to quell my untethered emotion.

With the gate shut, Envy turned to whisper in Margot's ear. One of his slender fingers pressed against her lips, as if she were a child, hushing her as the adults spoke.

Envy let go of Margot, and she stumbled back a step. Her pale hands raised to her mouth to stifle any noise. From behind the angel, she looked to Mikhael and stared intently. Her angel didn't notice, not since his bright green gaze had turned on Niklaus.

Envy's upper lip curled back in a sneer. "Who are you?"

A loud growl rolled from the back of the angel's throat as he waited for an answer. His dark wings rustled. The guards, responsive to the moods of the creature that ruled them, shook Niklaus hard.

"Tell me!" Envy growled.

His hand shot out and wrapped around Niklaus' throat. The guards' grips fell away as the muscles in the angel's arm clenched, and he lifted the tattooed man off the ground by his neck.

"Nik!" Mikhael yelped.

Helina and I lurched forward at his cry. My hand curled around Mikhael's arm, anchoring one side of him to keep him still. Helina held his other side. We mirrored the guards that had held his brother. Except we sought to protect him, where they had held their captor in offering to the angel and his whim.

Niklaus watched us, expression darkening, his eyes shifting with emotion before he growled his name from behind clenched teeth.

"Niklaus Heira," Envy repeated. A deadly caress because I was sure whatever came next would be the end of Niklaus. This thought caused my heart to trip in my chest. It stumbled, skittered, then raced as if it could catch back up. I pressed my sternum, rubbing at the discomfort.

"What?" Niklaus found his tongue and spat the word.

Envy's eyes glowed in the night. "You will be judged for the sins in your pathetic human heart."

"You said that before."

Envy noted the cuff around Niklaus' right wrist. "A pleasure to come early; it seems."

Mikhael's arm tensed beneath my grip, but he stayed silent. We watched as Niklaus rolled his eyes at the angel, insolent and rebellious until the very end.

"Seems to me that the only sinner here is you . . ." Niklaus drawled, and my heart dropped. "Envious that your sweet, little bitch doesn't want you anymore? You that bad in bed, *Lord Envy*?" A mocking edge dripped from his tone as he dared the godly creature to answer.

I flinched, whispering, "He has a death wish."

Helina nodded.

"No." Mikhael denied it. "He's just making sure it's quick."

Niklaus wasn't done. He held Envy's gaze with such confidence that, if I couldn't see it, I wouldn't have thought that he was being held in the air by his throat, at the mercy of an unhappy angel.

"Greedy to keep her all to yourself . . ."

Envy's face darkened, his power shivering through the air. The world tipped sideways, and iron bands wrapped around my lungs as, irrationally, I resented that Niklaus spoke of Margot and not of me. Envy's power snaked through my veins until I was so wrapped up in myself that I let go of Mikhael.

He staggered forward a single step. "Shut. Up."

It turned Envy's head, even as his fingers flexed around Niklaus' throat, squeezing it harder. Otherworldly green eyes focused their full force on Mikhael. His brow furrowed, and Mikhael shuddered.

"Don't speak of her." Mikhael's hands fisted by his sides, and he stepped forward again. "Or I'll gut you myself."

"Hmm." Envy smirked, young and wild. Without warning, he moved. The muscles in his body rippled, and his dark wings snapped open and stretched wide as he flung Niklaus to the side. He went flying, crashing against the gates and crumpling to the ground.

Before I could inhale again, the angel towered over Mikhael, too close to all of us. His proximity left me trembling, and it was only as a tear slid off the end of my nose that I realised I had been crying for a while, both my cheeks wet. I dared not to move, in case his attention turned to me. This was not the way I had wanted him to notice me.

"How do you know my treasure?" Envy asked. He seemed to assess Mikhael quickly, looking outside and in, before he scoffed dismissively. "She wouldn't touch you. A quiet copy of a bolder man."

Mikhael shuddered as if he had been struck.

I realised that, with these words, he had stricken true, Envy had looked inside of Mikhael's heart and judged what he envied most, his brother. Twins who looked so alike, striving to stand out, envious of one another.

"Margot and I –"

A body slammed into Mikhael hard enough to steal the words from his lips. Niklaus shoved his brother to the side. Caught unaware, Mikhael dropped to the ground like a stone.

He collided with me, the force of him knocking me into the soft grass. I yelped as pain ricocheted through my elbow and radiated through my shoulder. Beneath his weight, I struggled to move.

"Mikhael." I gasped, digging my fingers into any part of him I could reach. My nails bit into his collarbone's soft flesh.

He growled, his flailing elbow catching my already sore shoulder, and I screamed as he used that leverage to climb to his feet.

I struggled to sit, blinking through tears and pain.

Niklaus squared up against Lord Envy again.

He rolled his shoulders back and lifted his chin. He breathed heavily, pain flashing across his features. An arrogant smirk pulled at the corner of his mouth, all the same.

"Your final sin angel –" he jeered, never knowing when to stop. "Wrath; for needing to punish my sins with such rage."

The angel backhanded him so hard Niklaus crumbled at the entrance to the city. His head bounced off the first black stones of the spiralling path through Invidia. He lay so still my heart clenched, and I found myself trying to crawl across the grass to his body.

"Don't be dead, you bastard, don't be dead," I whimpered.

Envy spun, a growl rumbling from deep in his chest. His wings flared, his face a thunderstorm of emotion. It was enough to freeze me in my tracks, halfway to Niklaus' body.

"Does anyone else have anything to say?" Envy sneered.

The guards bowed their heads.

Margot said nothing, carefully looking anywhere except Mikhael, who stared at her without a care for the consequences.

"No." Helina's voice cracked the night. "Render your judgement, Lord Envy, so we can sleep."

I hated her for those words. I hated the way she turned the angel's attention back to Niklaus just as he stirred. I imagined it was his thick skull that kept him alive, the same thick skull that had him stuck a mess of his brother's making.

I waited as Envy stretched his wings, then pulled them closed. He surveyed Niklaus and swept his hand almost lazily, his eyes flaring bright with power.

In some sense, I knew magic existed.

Without magic, there were no angels, no devil, no demons. Without it, Gluttony couldn't have induced the never-ending hunger or stolen away our daylight hours, but it had never seemed quite as tangible as the moment Envy manipulated the city gates.

The iron snakes writhed and twisted, the magic heavy and paralysing in the air. Every instinctual warning sign in my body told me to run and get as far away from it as I could. Yet, I remained on my knees in the grass, stunned stupid.

The snakes' eyes glowed emerald with his power. They shifted and curled from the knot in the centre of the gate, their jaws stretching and closing. The iron's movements a strange hiss of its own.

"Get him up," Envy demanded of his guards. They hesitated for a single beat before they shuffled forward and pulled a dazed Niklaus Heira up onto his feet.

Envy's fingers twisted, directing his iron emblem. The two bigger snakes slithered along the gate and coiled to strike. Deadly, dangerous snakes.

The guards let go just as they shot forward, iron fangs piercing into Niklaus' back. Their jaws locked around him tight.

His scream pierced the air, full of violent pain; from the skies, the harpies screamed wildly back.

I sat back on my heels, reminded starkly of the penance wall on Ilrea and how the faceless man had been mounted on spikes. Niklaus was suspended just off the ground, mounted on iron fangs, his face pale, blood dripping down his back. He was facing his penance.

"Here, you will remain through dusk and dawn," Envy announced. "And the demons of this world will strip your sins from your flesh, Niklaus Heira. Only if you survive may you continue your path through my city to end of your trial."

Helina opened her mouth, and I wondered if she wanted to protest that dusk was almost through. The words never seemed to come, and she just watched, open-mouthed, horrified.

Mikhael had torn his gaze from Margot and watched his brother with nothing short of torment.

"Nik," he growled.

"Shut. Up. Mik," Niklaus rasped back.

There was no way I knew Niklaus would last the cold night in the snake's jaws, with or without the harpies – or the hellhounds that would come for his bones.

Fresh tears rolled down my cheeks.

Envy, apparently done with us, turned back to Margot. When his attention wavered, we found the strength to move. Mikhael approached Niklaus first, Helina on his heels, and I staggered to my feet behind them.

A guard cleared his throat. "Gates close in five minutes."

It was a clear warning to be inside in time.

I paid little attention to the way Envy stalked towards his treasured prize; I had little care for whether Margot lived. This was all her fault.

I stumbled forward to where Helina grasped Mikhael's arms and murmured a thousand soft apologies to his brother. Pain coursed through my body, accompanied by a wave of sadness, as

I looked up into Niklaus' face and wondered about things that could have been.

He didn't deserve this; even though he deserved a lot of misfortunes, he didn't deserve to die for his brother's sins.

"Mik, shut up," Niklaus said again, his voice so full of pain I cringed. "Told you I was here to keep you safe."

He glanced to Helina. "Take him back in."

Niklaus Heira was no sin borne angel, no real leader at all, but Helina Archer still nodded her head and tightened her grip on his brother's arm.

"May your spirit rest a lifetime in Eternis." She whispered the age-old prayer that, if we didn't visit the Eternis paradise in this life, we would see it in death.

I shuddered at the thought.

With more strength than I thought she had, Helina shoved Mikhael towards the guards, who waited to close the gate. The fight drained from Mikhael's body as she led him away.

When I looked up again, Niklaus was watching me. His gaze heavy, as it always had been, and I struggled to inhale over a sob.

"Crying over me again, love?" he teased.

I swiped quickly at my cheeks, my shoulder screaming with the movement.

"Only that I didn't get to kill you myself."

The way he laughed told me he didn't believe it, and I was grateful for that, for I had never told a bigger lie in my life. Even after it rolled off my lips, it felt wrong and left me flooded with red hot fear that he would believe it.

"Why, Nik?"

"He's my brother."

"No. Tell me why?"

He blinked slowly, and I sniffled. Niklaus sighed heavily, a sound tinged with pain. "Because sometimes you do shitty things for the people you love, Octavia. Sometimes it's just worth it."

I considered the sentiment. "Is dying really worth it?"

Niklaus' eyelids drooped. "I'll let you know in the next life."

"Can't you be serious, for once?"

Nik was quiet, his next breath heaving, and my heart jumped up, lodging hard in my throat. My fingers trembled, my pulse pounding in my ears. I glanced to Mikhael for help, who seemed to not want to stay to bear witness to his brother's pain, then to Helina, who pulled him onto the cobblestone streets as asked.

"Nik? Niklaus?" I breathed.

His eyes fluttered open, catching me, before they closed again.

"Go on, love," he rasped. "Only one of us needs to die tonight."

I felt as though I was going to turn myself inside out. My entire body filled with nervous energy. When I looked up at him, I saw other people's pain. Deadly punishments for sins that weren't really their own.

A body in the alleyways of Ilrea, organs missing.

A girl in the forests of Gula, stepped over and forgotten.

Ophelia Bell, her heart removed too soon.

Monika Oster, cold, dead, and left in a corner.

Too many people had died already. Each of their faces seared inside of my mind, and Niklaus Heira would join them. Another name on a never-ending list of people who didn't receive their final respects.

Panic clawed at me with talons as sharp as any harpy, and all sense of rationality seemed to flee my body. Impulse and adrenaline saw me through.

I moved before I could think better of it. The toe of my boot wedged against of the curling iron snakes, and I launched myself up onto the gate. The iron was cold beneath my fingertips, but I found my grip and scaled two steps up towards Niklaus' body, and in that moment, I couldn't think of anything else.

When I reached him, I saw how he was mounted on the fangs, the sharp points that had torn through flesh and muscle. I touched his back, and he whimpered. My fingers stained with his blood.

"Shhh." I hushed him quickly. If he kept groaning in pain, I would lose my nerve. "I'm getting you down."

"Octaviaaaaa," he groaned.

I tried to shift him on the spikes, with no luck. Searching for another option, I clung to the iron serpents with one hand and rummaged through my pockets with the other, searching for Monika's small blade.

Niklaus watched me beneath hooded eyes. He didn't look nervous, which could have been the pain and the adrenaline. I pretended it was that he had faith that I wouldn't carve out his heart, like he had threatened to do to me. I hoped that he knew it had been a joke about wanting to kill him myself.

The edge of the blade slid through his shirt, and I scrabbled at the edges of soaked material, pulling it free of his skin, blood smeared across the pictures inked into his chest, and it fell to the ground.

"All right," I breathed. "You can do this . . ."

"Octavia." He groaned again.

"Hush."

I shivered and shifted to find a different foothold on his other side.

"You . . ."

"Don't," I said. "I just need to figure out how to get you off this thing . . ."

"Why?" Niklaus croaked.

My heart thundered harder in my chest. I didn't have an answer. I had no idea why I was wrapped around him on the gates of the city instead of fleeing to safety. I was no hero, but I couldn't stand the idea of losing someone else right then.

My entire body rejected the possibility of more grief.

"Freeze, human!"

Envy's command startled me, and the blade slipped from my fingers.

Instinctively, I obeyed.

Niklaus and I were nose-to-nose, my breath flushing across his lips when his green eyes opened again. I was drowning in them and in my own fear as I clung to him.

I feared what the angel would do next. I didn't want to draw the attention of the Angel of Envy, but the consequences of my actions had been the furthest thing from my mind when I had climbed to free Niklaus.

He left me still long enough that my weak muscles trembled with exhaustion. I stuck to the command and the letter and stayed frozen in place against Niklaus' body. If Envy left me there all night, the harpies would have to tear through me to get to the man.

A deep sense of intuition told me that punishment wouldn't be so easy.

"Get down." Envy's power curled around me, infusing the command. Niklaus and I watched one another.

"Goodbye, love." He sounded miserable.

I shook my head. "Breathe deep, Nik."

"Wha –"

The word turned into a scream of pain.

I had wrapped my arms around his back, his blood soaking through my sleeves. I tensed my legs and pushed up as hard as I could. He was heavier than I expected, and I struggled to push us both higher on the gate. A scream lodged in my own throat.

Slowly, he moved, his body sliding off the fangs. The moment he came free, his weight overwhelmed me, and I plummeted the short drop back to the ground, taking all of Niklaus' weight with me. He landed on me, pinned me down, heavy and unmoving.

"Nik." I wheezed his name.

He didn't respond.

"Nik?" My fingers curled into his hair, and I tugged hard. He was dead weight, and I gasped, shuddering against the possibility that I might have killed him faster. "Wake up!"

Mikhael rolled him off me, concern etched into his face for his too-still brother.

I barely had time to consider that nobody was concerned for me when the clank of armour signalled my next problem.

The guards wrenched me to my feet, and I squealed in pain. My shoulder hung too low.

Envy stalked close. His wings blocked out my view of the twins, of the city, of everything except him. There was nowhere else to look. I studied his wings' glossy black feathers until he gripped my chin. His fingers were surprisingly soft, but his expression was not. Envy's eyes were a portal from this world to the last. He stared through my own and right into my soul.

My body shuddered in the grip of the guards.

"How dare you think you can overturn my justice?" the angel hissed. I could feel my life shrivelling in my veins. I was stupid – I could have survived the night if I'd only left Niklaus alone.

"No . . ." I stammered. "I . . ."

His face moved close. We were sharing air, and if he didn't kill me, I was sure my heart would just stop. Fresh tears pooled in my eyes, rolling down my cheeks. "I . . ."

"Wait!" Helina Archer's voice snapped through the air, stealing everyone's attention.

Beneath the angel's influence, I couldn't help but burn up over the fact that she had stolen my focus, even though I didn't want it in the first place.

Helina was pale and twisted and turned her spectacles in her hand. I had never seen her look so nervous.

"She did nothing wrong!" Helina protested. "You didn't lay down any rules for this trial. You didn't say we wouldn't interfere with your punishments. You didn't say we couldn't do stupid

246

things, only that we needed to get the akelda, *no matter what it takes.*"

Shock seemed to restart my heart.

Was she defending me? Helina, who had more than once implied she would prefer it if I was dead?

Envy had straightened. He turned the full force of his attention onto Helina, and she seemed to fortify herself. With slow, careful steps, she pushed her way over to Niklaus and crouched beside him.

Her fingers pushed into his pocket, and she pulled free a glowing piece of the old world. My heart clenched at the sight of it. I had been so close to it, so close to victory.

Helina nodded at me. "You can't kill her for doing what needs to be done."

"I can kill her for any reason that I choose." Envy refuted, his eyes whipping to me, and I dropped my gaze to the ground. "She is not sinless."

Helina's laugh wrung out my nerves.

I struggled to work out why she was helping me.

"She is riddled with the guilt of her sins; I assure you that much –" Helina lifted her chin. When I peeked at her, I realised the akelda was gone. She had stolen it for herself. "But she's just playing your game."

My blood burnt with resentment as she had walked through this night unscathed. Envy watched us, and I wondered what went through the head of an angel that had seen countless lifetimes and who saw humans as insignificant. Did he resent having to waste his time and energy on us?

Envy turned on Margot, who bowed her head at his attention. "You."

I sagged in the guard's grip, filled with a rush of relief that his attention had been diverted. I lifted my chin enough to glance at Helina, who offered only a solemn look at me.

247

"I need to deal with you, next." Envy stalked back to Margot. His arm snaked around her waist, and he pulled her into his side, securing her. His gaze swept across us; it felt like competitors and guards alike had stopped breathing as they waited for his mood to switch again.

Envious eyes seared into my soul, and as the angel smirked, it brightened his youthful face.

"Take her to the dungeons."

He shot into the air before I could protest. The guards' hands around my arms tightened to the point of pain, and I could do nothing more than look back at Niklaus, Mikhael, and Helina as they dragged me away.

I didn't have a chance to see if Niklaus had lived or died.

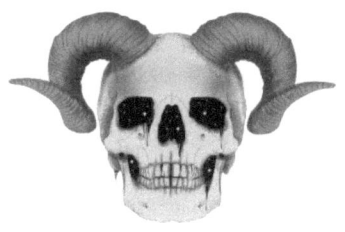

Chapter Thirty-Two

Days passed in a blur, and I marked time only through the changing of armoured guards at the end of the hall. Twice a day, one left and another arrived. I marked it mentally as morning and night. Every so often, they'd bring food and water, although I quickly learned it didn't equate to everyday, only when they remembered.

Nobody emptied the steel bucket in the corner that I used to relieve myself, but the entire dungeon reeked enough that my shame didn't stand out. I was lost to the insufferable stench.

Envy's castle had a dusty, dirty dungeon, and I was not alone. A woman lay in the cell next to me, the slow cough hacking through her body, and whenever she lay still, she moaned softly in pain. She was deteriorating in front of my eyes. Whenever she shifted, dragging her body across the floor, my heart skipped a beat. I kept as far away as I could from her infectious cough, huddled into the corner of the cell, unmoving as I waited for Envy to come and exact his punishment.

He didn't come in the hours after I was thrown to the ground or in the days that followed.

It was cold beneath the city, much colder than the streets above. The longer I stayed in the dungeon, the less I could feel my fingertips. Heat wouldn't stay in my body, and I knew that, inevitably, I would catch my prison mate's slow cough. She moaned at the edges of her cell, crying to the guards in a litany of a single repeated word. "Mercy. Mercy. Mercy."

I didn't know who she prayed to or why she thought she needed mercy, but I found myself repeating her words in a soft whisper. My head pressed against the cold stone walls, eyes on the ceiling, as I begged Samael for much of the same.

He remained quiet in my head, and I cried for the sense of abandonment that swelled through me, distinct and undeniable. I shouldn't have been surprised; everyone abandoned me at some point. I wasn't worth their effort.

With each new day, I was sure Envy would come for me, and his wicked, ancient smile would stretch across his face as he judged me to be insignificant. The truth was slow to come to me. The angel was not going to appear and dangle my insignificance in front of me because I was worth so little that Envy had placed me deep in his dungeons and had already forgotten all about me.

I was unworthy and alone.

The realisation rocked me. In the chill of the long daylight hours and dark night, I couldn't help but obsess with how I had come to be there. I was a fool for having tried to help a man who had died all the same. I was a fool for clinging to the notion that Niklaus had deserved my fragmented loyalty and for thinking that the world would align in my favour.

As it turned out, I deserved nothing more than what I received.

After a while, I dozed through the guard changes and lost track of the days. My stomach roared with hunger until I dreamt I was back at the Feast of Samael, struggling to quell the demands of my body and the appetite that would eat me up. Within my dreams, I was so hungry I climbed onto Gluttony's dinner table and joined him in feasting on Ophelia's heart.

I woke disgusted with myself, retching at the place my dreams had taken me. I wished I would rot away in the cell a little quicker, as quickly as the woman beside me.

When I woke the next time, she didn't beg for mercy; she didn't cough up half of her lung. I edged towards the bars separating us, and saw her unmoving on the ground, too thin, grey, and forgotten.

In this corpse, I saw my future.

My eyes opened to a face between the cold, iron bars. A pale young man with dark eyes watched me from between them. I shifted from the corner of the cell, tried to cry out, but I hadn't used my voice in a long time.

I didn't remember falling back asleep, but by the time I woke again, he was gone. I was sure I had dreamt it all up. That night, I received a meal, and for the first time, it was hot. I swallowed it down so quickly it burnt a trail from my throat to my stomach.

The bread singed my fingertips. It warmed me long enough to fall asleep but did nothing to stave off the cold. By the next morning, my nose was dripping, my teeth chattering, and I felt like that meal had set me on fire. Sweat beaded at my hairline.

Bundled in the corner, I whimpered and begged Samael to take me away. I had no idea what the devil looked like, but as my fever grew, I pictured him as a thin man, with sharp and pointed features, with thick dark horns curling from his head. His face was always blurry. I couldn't quite make him out. Mindlessly, I found myself on my knees, murmuring pleas to the faceless ruler of us all.

"The devil doesn't do self-serving favours," someone commented from the door. They crashed through my visions. The world spun sickeningly, my fingernails scrabbling against the stone floor, scraping for a grip on reality.

"What?" I rasped.

The barred door slid open. The pale, angular face from days before appeared in my line of vision. The milky eyes of a harpy flashed in my view, and a strangled cry echoed from my throat.

"No," I pleaded, scrambling backwards. "Harpy! Demon!"

The world spun. I was seeing two of him, then three.

"Huh?" His head tilted.

I couldn't bring myself to move, frozen in fear. Every time I looked at him, all I could see was the blind monster.

"Oh," he laughed. A wide grin split across his face. "I'm blind, but I'm not a woman cursed. Imagine, brothers!"

All three of my hallucinations laughed.

My teeth chattered; unintelligible sounds spewed over my lips. All three of the men tilted their head. The world spun, and I whimpered, trapped in my own skewed reality. I didn't move, breathing heavily, watching the triple vision of this man.

"I am Zeres, the eldest," the middle one announced, and the copy on his left jammed his elbow into Zeres' ribs. He coughed, a rueful grin pulling at the edge of his lips. "This is Ciris, the middle one, and . . ."

I lost focus of what he was saying as I tried to process that my vision had not tripled, but there were, in fact, three different men standing in front of me. They were so similar in the eerie way they moved, and my mind rejected its reality. Surely, it was just a vision brought on by sickness.

"Eros," Zeres announced. He tapped the man on his right, who shifted and turned his head. Zeres' hands shifted in rapid movements before his attention turned back to me. "Who is the one who is going to get you out of here?"

Eros shifted towards me slowly, as if he thought I was the threat instead of him. A feral animal liable to bite. In a way, I probably was, because I practically vibrated with nervous tension as neared.

A cry rolled from the back of my throat, but he ignored it. His arms banded around my back and beneath my legs, holding me solidly.

He was real. The truth of it settled firmly within me as he lifted me off the cold, dirty floor, darkness crowding the edges of my vision.

They were real, and they were taking me away.

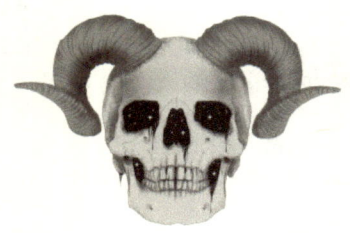

Chapter Thirty-Three

The atmosphere was crushing me. I was tangled in sweat-soaked sheets when I woke. The room was too hot, the air too thick, and I choked on it, crying out. Three identical faces blurred in my vision; thick wrinkles creased heavily at their brows. I stared into sightless, white eyes before my own rolled back.

My dreams were bright with colour and nonsense – but of what, exactly, I couldn't remember. The details slipped away like sand through my fingers as life pulled me to the surface again.

This time, the crone hovered over me. She sniffled loudly; her wrinkled fingers pressed against each side of my temples, foreign words flowing from her mouth. Her grip moved, and a sticky residue slid across my skin. She felt to the corner of my jaw and pushed it forward. I cried out softly, the sound reedy in the back of my throat.

"Bah!" Eadlin stared down at me. She released me and pressed one hand to my burning forehead, her palm cool against my burning skin. The crone smacked me on the end of the nose lightly. "Hush, girl! Rest. You've a long way to go."

I closed my eyes, content to obey.

Faint rustling and a sharp inhale of breath sounded. I hovered just between sleep and awareness.

"Will she survive?" someone asked.

My eyes blinked open again, even though every fibre of my being winced away from the idea of facing the brightness of the room. I didn't know who was asking or why they cared. Blearily, I made out the side of Eadlin's wrinkled face. She was staring off to the side, her ancient face twisting into an expression I couldn't identify. My head ached, and I had given up on hearing when she huffed out a sigh.

"Well, enough if she wants to," she stated. "Now, get. I have work to do."

Two voices spoke at once, one lilting, the other a harsh, flat monotone. "You have our many thanks, Eadlin."

The world was quiet when I resurfaced. I had been cleaned. The sheets felt cold and crisp beneath my body instead of soaked through. The air was cool and had lost the weight I had felt before.

I was alone.

That shouldn't have surprised me, but it was an internal pain I had tucked away all the same to agonise over later. Slowly, I sat up on the narrow cot and cradled my head in my hands as the world spun. It took time for everything to settle before I could inch to the edge of the bed and swing myself unsteadily onto my feet.

My legs wobbled with weakness; the nightgown I wore tangled at my knees. I stumbled and toppled forward until my chin hit the floor hard. Stupidly, I noted the floor was covered with a plush rug. It ran from corner to corner of the room, and it cushioned most of my fall.

Silence stagnated with my cheek pressed into the rug, and I realised my boots were sitting within reach. A strange wave of relief rolled through me, and the sight of them provided the motivation I needed to move, albeit slowly.

The hinges on the door squealed as it opened. One of the three men from my fever dreams stood in front of me. I stammered, shocked, and he paused in the doorway.

"You're up," he said.

"Guess so."

"Want help?" he asked, and I blinked. I had never heard a voice like his before, flat without inflection.

My teeth scraped my lower lip, and slowly, I nodded.

He stepped forward, his thin body folding as he crouched in front of me. I tried to think of his name, but he looked so startlingly like his copies that I couldn't remember which one of them was which. As he stood close to me, I recognised him, one of the three identical men that had walked through the spiral on display, part of Envy's desired collection.

Although I could rationally determine that it probably wasn't his choice to be one of Envy's coveted few, it was a position that left me suspicious of him. He could have been using me, like it felt like Margot had used the Heira twins.

I steeled myself to ask. "Which . . . which one of them are you?"

His chin dipped. "Eros."

It meant nothing to me, his name, but since he hadn't hesitated to answer, I took his offered hand. He straightened and took me with him. My legs wobbled again.

"I'm Octavia," I supplied when Eros turned away.

"I know."

"Oh." I entwined my fingers nervously. "Well . . ."

"Follow me."

He strode away, and I hobbled after him on weak legs. I fell farther and farther behind.

"Wait!" I cried.

His heavy sigh led me back to him, and when I collided with his back, I realised we were the same height. Eros glanced over his shoulder, and I blinked at the strange, slightly asymmetrical look of his features.

"Hurry up," he chided, watching me closely.

"I'm trying!"

"Try harder." Eros left me behind again. Two hallways later, I found enough energy to catch him. I nudged him for his attention. His head turned, eyes on my face intently.

"Do you always only speak in two-word sentences?"

"No."

I rolled my eyes. When he glanced back, he had a toothy grin stretched across his face, wide and free. It distracted me enough that I didn't realise he had stopped and tripped over his foot. Eros barely caught me in time.

"Feeling weak?" he asked.

Pink shame fused across my cheeks as I straightened up and leaned against the wall. "No, I'm fine."

Eros smirked. "Be careful."

"I swear I'll die if you say three words," I muttered.

When I looked up, his gaze was fixated on my mouth. The redness in my cheeks deepened.

Eros didn't comment but turned to stroll the remainder of the corridor. With a huffed sigh, I followed him and paused in front of a set of large, gilded doors. Apprehension pooled in the pit of my stomach. I didn't know what was behind the door, and I didn't want to go through.

"I think . . ." I backed off a step.

Eros twisted, watching me carefully.

"I think I'll go back." Fear laced my words and my thoughts. I wondered if they had pulled me from the depths of the dungeon for something much worse. I was in unfamiliar territory with new faces, and I wasn't sure how to keep myself safe.

"Octavia?" Eros reached for me.

I shook my head sharply, a warning not to touch me. "Don't."

He fell still. He looked at me as if I might bite, and it brought up the fuzzy memory of the three of them when they had appeared in the dungeons.

"I just . . ." I sighed.

"I know."

I watched him, scrutinised him carefully. My voice was raw as I asked, "Do you?"

His palm wrapped around the gold ringed door handle, and he pulled hard at the gilded doors. They swung outwards without a whisper or a groan. Eros was no longer giving me a choice; I would face my fear of what existed behind those doors whether I wanted to.

"Welcome to the collection, Octavia Nox."

The doors opened to an apartment. Wide-eyed, I stared around the mix of colours and cultures that decorated the new space. I realised that half of Ilrea could probably exist there. It was full of plush couches, soft carpets, and small symbols of wealth, the luxury that left me breathless with desire. Jewellery littered the tabletops, crystal-embedded earrings lay forgotten in the carpets, and silk throws hung over the back of the couches.

Wealth was nothing to the people who lived here, and I itched to take it all and stow it in my pockets. Each piece would accumulate a small fortune at the table. I could play for days with the earrings alone.

I staggered forward a step, caught on that single, driving thought, but Eros reached out and caught my hand.

At the brush of his fingers against my wrist, I glanced over my shoulder. He lifted his chin and pressed a slender finger to his lips. "Quiet now."

Despite myself, my lips twitched. We were back to two-word sentences. "Why?"

"It's early."

Six grand doors led from the main rooms, and he took me to the one farthest to the left. It was dark, decorated with painted whorls of black and silver. When we burst through the entry, two men sprung to life. One had been dozing in a chair and jumped to his feet, a silver blade clenched in his fist, his sightless eyes wide as he waited for approaching danger. The other had sat up in bed, dark hair tousled and sticking up at all odds and ends.

For the first time since they had arrived in my fever-hazed visions, the three cloned men had never looked so different.

My throat bobbed as my nervousness grew. I shifted to stand behind Eros. He grinned at his brothers, unspeaking, and the silence was so intense that, when the door clicked shut, I startled. The gasp on the edge of my lips turned the attention of all three towards me.

"She's up?" the one by the chair said.

I remembered which one he was: Zeres, the one with the harpy's eyes. His voice softer, more lyrical than the man by side.

"Obviously," Eros droned.

The one on the bed said nothing at all. I studied him carefully from behind Eros, apprehensive about what he might say. Silence lingered, the men glancing between each other, until I couldn't help but fill the silence.

"Hello," I greeted cautiously.

Three grins, eerily similar, grew wider.

"Hello, little criminal," Zeres greeted.

His brother chuckled, dropping to sit on the edge of his bed. I shuffled from foot to foot, anxiety sparking in my veins, until I rubbed my fingertips against my thighs and rocked back onto my heels.

"Are you brothers?" I asked, stupidly.

"Yes," they answered with startling synchronicity.

My tongue ran over my lips as I struggled to fill the quiet that they seemed to be so comfortable within. "Who . . ."

Eros raised a thin, dark brow. Two slender fingers tapped against his chest twice. "You know me."

"Yes," I replied dryly. "Mr. Short-Sentences . . ."

The man with the blade slid it into the sheath at his waist and nodded firmly. His fingers slid through his inky hair. "I'm Zeres, and that's Ciris."

"Oh." I swallowed. "Okay. You're all so . . ."

"Similar?" Zeres asked.

"Different?" Eros deadpanned.

Ciris remained quiet.

"Well . . ." I hesitated, unsure I wanted to offend them. "Both."

Zeres laughed again and shuffled away from the plush, grey couch he had been sleeping on. He swept an arm towards it. "Have a seat. You must feel half dead."

"Was I?"

"Huh?"

"Was I half dead?"

"More than half, I'd say." He chuckled darkly. I thought I must have been lucky to be standing on shaky legs. He perched beside his brother on the large bed.

For the first time, I noticed it was big enough to hold all three of them. I wondered, fleetingly, if they shared everything. These three strange clones.

They watched me closely, their dark stares intense as they waited for me to act. I shivered and dropped into the chair, my body finally relaxing as the cushions cradled me. It was softer than many of the beds I had slept on in my life. When I glanced to the high ceiling, I realised it was covered in tiny little gems, which glittered beneath the lights.

A replica of the stars on a clear night.

I could have fallen asleep there, if they hadn't been watching me so closely, if I hadn't been so hyper aware of their stares. It was so unnerving I steeled myself to stare back.

"How long have I been here?" I asked.

Zeres glanced down at a timepiece on his wrist. "It's twenty-two days into your trial."

My mouth dried out with fear. "I only have eight days left?"

They all nodded in tandem.

My hands trembled, and tears pooled in the corner of my eyes. "I'm dead."

"Actually" – Zeres' grin was all pointed teeth – "you're alive. Eadlin made sure of that."

Confusion left me off kilter. "Why?"

All three of them shrugged, and I wished they wouldn't move at the exact same time.

Zeres glanced at his brothers. "Margot wanted it."

A stone formed in the pit of my stomach as I thought of Margot; it seemed she held a power I couldn't even imagine if the others in Envy's collection moved at her will.

"Does Margot always get what she wants?" I asked, strangely apprehensive of the answer.

It was Eros who screwed his face up. His eyes caressed the line of my jaw again. "Normally."

I flinched under the intensity of his stare. I didn't know why he watched my face so intently, but my thoughts raced with the idea that he was pulling me apart with his gaze.

"Don't," I said finally.

"What?" Zeres frowned. Ciris moved next to him, mirroring his confusion.

"You" – I glared at Eros – "stop staring at me."

"He's not –" Zeres started.

"Yes, he is!" I stated. "He's *always* looking at my mouth. Cut it out!"

Eros' eyes dropped quickly.

Zeres and Ciris both snickered, until Zeres was flopped back on the bed, clutching his stomach with the intensity of his mirth. The tips of my ears turned red.

"What's so funny?" I demanded.

It took him more than a minute to calm back down, wheezing his way back into the quiet. When Zeres sat back up, his milky, sightless eyes were wide, a grin splitting his face.

"Maybe we should introduce ourselves properly." He glanced towards his brothers, and they nodded.

I closed my eyes, silently counting to three, reminding myself I couldn't make too many demands of them. "Go for it."

They all stretched and stood by the side of the bed. They were startlingly similar, exact images of one another, if not for Zeres' white eyes. Their skin paled and looked soft, their features not quite aligned in a way that stopped me from staring too long. Their dark hair tousled and fell over their foreheads. They all stood at the exact same height.

It didn't help they all wore the same outfits, loose linen black pants, and a white shirt with polished buttons, which hung a touch too big on their lanky frames.

Ciris and Eros looked the most alike, since Zeres' milky gaze set him apart. They pulled themselves up to their full height, which admittedly wasn't any taller than they were before.

"We're Zeres, Eros, and Ciris."

I nodded; they had told me this already.

"We are Envy's three-cursed." His thin lips quirked, the hint of a smirk, before he presented a mocking bow. "The devil cursed us for the audacity of our mother, so we were born both completely identical and very different."

I shifted uncomfortably. "I don't understand."

The three men tilted their heads as one. I shivered, my teeth pressing into my lower lip until it stung.

Zeres stepped forward, the obvious leader of the three, and his body folded as he crouched in front of my cushioned chair. He dropped to his knees, pale palms set against each arm, and I was reminded of when I had fallen to the floor between Niklaus' knees and his rude comments.

My face heated, with Zeres perched in the same position, between my knees, too close to the naked skin of my legs.

"W-what are you doing?" I asked.

His chin lifted, and I imagined that, if he could see anything, he would have been staring right into my eyes. It caused my breathing to turn shallow, and I watched cautiously as he sat back on his heels and cleared his throat gently.

"Amara was a human girl born in Eternis, blessed by the devil within her first hours and raised within the real luxuries of his world. But for all that she had, like many human souls, she grew restless with age and explored the limits of her life," Zeres said. "At the edge of the Devil's Lands and the Wrathlands, she met a man. He was a warrior named Perich, and such is the beginning of all sad stories; they fell in love."

A noise rolled from the back of my throat, half a breathy scoff.

Zeres' lips quirked, a silent agreement. "Amara did the unthinkable. She snuck a human, uninvited, into Eternis. His soul had not been challenged, his nature not accepted by the devil, and he brought his sins with him. At first, all was well. His sins spread only to Amara. They spent days cooped up in her home, indulging in the sin of lust. So, it continued until Amara fell pregnant, and with her pregnancy of three came trials of illness and fatigue. As she struggled with this new situation, Perich's attention strayed to humans and souls that lived within Eternis. Ever a greedy man."

I bit down on my lip to stop myself from commenting. Zeres paused for a second, as if giving me permission to do so, but I had no idea what to ask. "Go on . . ."

Zeres wet his lips. "Perich's lust was out of control, and he found himself enthralled by the Wildlings of Eternis, daughters of the devil, said to be demons borne of his passing thought, but they rejected his advances. Some said they could smell the taint of his humanity and that they knew he had not been blessed by the Devil. Lust gave way to wrath, and Perich turned into a wild being himself. He was fuelled by his anger and turned it on Amara, who fled to the strongest being of her land for protection."

"Samael," I breathed.

"Yes," Zeres agreed, his brothers shifted. "Amara went to the devil himself and begged for his aid. The devil is not a forgiving being. He is the worst of the angels who dominated our lands, the most mercurial of all. He was displeased with the fact that Amara had thought her boredom such a priority that she brought tainted humanity into his land. A soul to corrupt all others. After two days of deliberation, the devil agreed to deal with Perich, but by then, the influence of his sinner's nature had spread. They found him indulging in the feasts of the forests by Solis Lake, watching with glee as the wildlings fought amongst themselves and tried to drown one another in shallows."

I leaned forward, closer to Zeres, desperate to know what would happen next in his tale. "Did Samael kill Perich?"

"Yes," Eros stated flatly from the bed.

Zeres hummed an agreement. "It is said that the devil commanded his wildlings to take Perich to the very base of the lake and offer his soul to the Mellish demon who resided there.

The demon was an ancient soul, a water spirit who took his cheeks in hand, and kissed him gently. In that moment, she stole every memory from him. His mind was intact to know he needed to breathe. His lungs still burnt for air, but the spirit stole his knowledge of how to swim or that he couldn't inhale the water. Perich didn't struggle for the surface. As she let him go, he sunk to the bottom of the lake and drowned."

I knotted my fingers in my lap. I swallowed roughly. I wanted to know more of this story, not out of concern for Amara or Perich, but to know the swaying moods of the devil, to learn more of Samael himself.

"Then what?" I prompted.

Zeres shifted. "The devil turned his displeasure on Amara. He reassessed the worth of her soul and decreed that she would die in childbirth but not before all three babies lived. Each child would bear the mark of her transgressions, her sins, for all to know that human children shall be judged for the actions of their mothers and fathers. He told the wildlings to take her hand and toss her onto the borders of the Wastelands. It was there that Amara of Eternis gave birth to three identical boys."

He paused and twisted to his brothers, both of whom had moved to stand at his side, all implying they were the three identical babies of his story, cursed by the devil before they even breathed, left to struggle for the factions of Amara of Eternis and Perich of the Wrathlands.

"First born was Zeres, who knows too much but sees nothing; he would never use his eyes. Then came Ciris, with too many thoughts but unable to voice them. Finally, Eros, who feels too deeply but cannot hear the voice of another."

It took me a slow moment to catch on. I studied them one by one. Zeres saw nothing, his eyes white with blindness. Ciris couldn't voice his thoughts, and so far, had been strangely silent. He flashed me a smile, his mouth opened wide, and I saw he had no tongue.

Then, I glanced back to Eros, who held my gaze again, studying my eyes for judgement, not the curve and tilt of my lips as he had before.

"You can't hear?" I asked.

"I can read your lips," he explained, and again, his voice struck something within me. The words felt misshapen and not quite right, and it struck me it was because he had never heard how they should sound. Never regulated his voice by his own ear. Not in the way I had learned the soft vowels of my own parents' speech patterns.

"But . . ." I struggled to reconcile the story with the three men who stood in front of me. There were a lot of unanswered questions, specifically around how three babies in the Wastelands with a dead mother managed to survive to adulthood and how they came to be a part of Envy's treasured collection.

I found my breath and sorted my thoughts. "How long have you lived here?"

Zeres smiled sadly. "Our whole lives."

"Oh." I blinked. "How do you communicate if Ciris can't speak to you and Eros cannot hear you and you cannot see if they wrote it all down?" I asked.

Eros laughed bluntly, and Zeres smiled, too. He answered me, and I knew now why he took the lead and spoke for all three.

"The world is a quiet place for my brothers, but our heads are not. Our curse left our minds linked and so our thoughts swim in a shared pool of constant communication."

I struggled to accept this wild idea, and my head spun. The men all stilled.

"How silly of us." Zeres clapped. "We should have given you food before we laid all of this on you. Imagine digesting all of that without breakfast."

He nodded to Ciris, who moved to the door and pulled it back open. It showed me a glimpse of the original apartment and let in the soft murmur of movement as life filled it.

"Let's have breakfast with the entire collection." Zeres held out a hand. "And we can discuss this more later, okay?"

I didn't take his offered hand but instead gripped the sides of the couch to push myself to my feet. My weak legs shook, knees knocking, and Eros caught my arm. I blew out a small breath. Eros let go once I had my balance, and the three men walked out of the room with the expectation that I would follow.

My gaze drifted up to the replica of the glittering stars above us. I closed my eyes for a moment and tried to quieten out the rest of the world.

"Samael." I breathed his name, a plea for a response. "Was that story true? Did you give that man to a spirit to kill? Do you hate us so much?"

'*Oh, Little One,*' Samael purred in my ear, his voice husky. '*You have much to learn, and I have much to teach you about humanity.*'

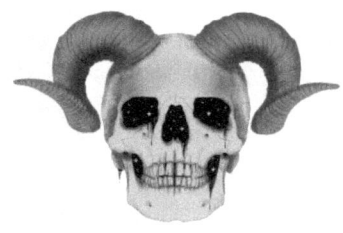

Chapter Thirty-Four

Envy's collection contained eight treasures and several silent servants. I knew four of them, and I stayed close to Eros while sliding into a chair at their long, lavishly set table. Every plate, bowl, and teacup were delicate and thin, covering in floral patterns with accents of green. The cutlery shined, freshly polished. I could see my reflection distorted on the back of the spoon.

As I inspected my own image, it reminded me of Rowan and the way she told stories about her life while we polished silverware. I dropped the spoon back against the table with a clatter, and a woman across from me scoffed loudly, muttering under her breath about manners.

Eros cleared his throat, and Zeres hummed in agreement. "You're right, E, as usual."

He was silent as servants pressed to the edges of the table and set down trays of breakfast. A boiled grain, creamy milk, soft granules of sugar, and freshly toasted bread. The smell of it left my mouth watering.

The woman with the red hair snatched a slice of bread and lifted her knife to the preserves across it. I copied her actions. The toast burnt my fingertips, and I dropped it with a soft hiss.

One of the servants muffled a laugh as she set down a bowl of ripe fruit.

I braved the toasted bread again, slathering it with bright yellow butter and a chunky spread before tearing the slice in half and chewing through it. It sat strange and heavy in my belly. I knew I hadn't eaten in days, so I should have craved food, but by the time I made it through half a slice, my stomach was revolting.

It didn't eat a bite more.

"So," Zeres drawled, clearing his throat, "Envy tends to collect in pairs."

"I can see that," I said dryly. "Except you three."

"And me, of course." All eyes turned to Margot, who sat at the end of the long table. Her white hair lay twisted into two soft plaits over each shoulder. She was still dressed for bed, and her mouth stretched open with a yawn.

"I am the one and only . . ." Margot told us, stirring a silver spoon idly around her drink. She proclaimed it with such self-assurance and haughty confidence that I had to believe it to be true.

Zeres chuckled after sucking porridge from his spoon. "You know Margot, of course. Envy's little queen, and devil-above does she act like it."

"*Hmm*, aren't you precious this morning, Zee." Margot threw him a sardonic smile. She pushed her chair back and stood, taking her cup with her as she left, heading for the biggest set of doors. Margot disappeared before anything more could be said, and everyone else relaxed without her presence at the table.

"As I was saying," Zeres continued. "Pairs. We have Nadiya and Aeron." He nodded towards the man and woman with dark features, and glossy hair that hung in distinct clustered spirals. Both had dark lashes that most women would envy.

Pale, metallic blue ink decorated their skin, marking symbols of the sun at the centre of their forehead, along with a pattern of dots down the bridge of their noses. Beneath their right eyes, a line swept from the fullness of their lower lips, which were painted to match the curve of their chins. The pale ink formed a V over their throats, ending at a sharp point in the hollow of their collarbones.

A heavy gold emblem sat below the hollow of their throats, pinning the material draped across their bodies in place. The depictions on their skin were strangely haunting. I had the strong feeling they meant more than the fanciful art that Niklaus had covered himself in. I was staring, but I couldn't help it.

Nadiya's full lips shifted, as if she might have laughed, but caught herself just in time. When she spoke, it was never above a whisper, tones soft and gentle as not to disturb. "We are . . . the last?" When she moved her head, the heavy pieces of gold jewellery hanging from her ears, they tinkled, sun symbols brandishing. "The newest."

Aeron chewed on a piece of an apple. The markings circled his wrists and curled around his strong fingers.

"Where are you from?" I asked, eyes darting away.

"The Silheim Temple in the Eastern Lustlands."

I blinked; another bedtime story came to life. "Temple dwellers are real . . . ?"

Aeron gave me a hard look.

"Of course, we're real. We're people of magical faith, not temple dwellers," Nadiya said sharply.

I flushed with embarrassment.

The Silheim faith believed that, if the devil had come to earth hundreds of years ago, then a higher power would follow from the old world in time and save us all. They believed that sins were just humanity's ultimate trial, and if we could survive it, our future generations would thrive with a resilience our forefathers never knew.

They didn't believe that the old world had perished with the devil and his comrade's departure. They acted in faith that the humans could capture the magic that had infiltrated this world and use it to their own advantages. They believed they would be the first to be blessed with this power.

My mother was the one who called them temple dwellers, and it was always her worry that one of her children would become one.

"So," I hesitated. "Why does Envy want you?"

Nadiya's face scrunched. "That's a personal question, don't you think?"

I bit my lip; I guessed I would never know the answer, then.

The woman to her left, regal with fiery hair and smattered with a dusting of freckles, snorted loudly. "It's because they're beautiful; that's why he wants all of us." She leaned over the table as if she were sharing a secret. She winked over the rim, her fragile teacup in salute.

"This is –" Zeres stated.

"I'm Viktoria, and this is Tomas." She flicked her fingers at the man on her other side. He was strongly built with a cleft chin, covered in the same strange freckles all over his skin, but in a vastly different pattern from his counterpart. I wondered if a picture would arise if I joined the spots on his skin.

271

"We're from Northern Wastelands." He commented and seemed to enjoy the shock that splayed across my face at this revelation, and I almost dropped my cup.

"There are humans in the Wastelands?!" I gasped.

"You don't know much, do you?" Viktoria mused.

"There's a heap of us, whole pockets of rebellion in one place," Tomas crowed. "Envy plucked us up before he decimated our village, mostly because he liked the patterns on our skin."

They shared a look, private and haunted, before Zeres cleared his throat roughly. "Let's move to lighter topics . . ."

I glanced at Ciris, who sat on my other side, and he pulled a face, lifting one hand and tapping his thumb and fingers as if he were mocking everyone for talking too much. A laugh caught in the back of my throat.

"So," I said, searching for a better topic, "what does Envy's collection do all day long then?"

Nadiya shook her head, her heavy jewellery tinkling again. "We wait."

"Wait for what?"

"Envy to make his pick."

"I don't know what that means," I admitted.

"That doesn't surprise me." She smiled. Nadiya plucked her napkin from her lap and threw it down on her plate. She walked away, and with a half-smile, Aeron followed her down the hall.

Tomas sighed. "Want to walk gardens, Tori?"

Viktoria nodded so quickly I knew there was no room to me to intrude, and before I knew it, I was alone with the three brothers again.

Anxiously, I tapped the edge of my spoon against the tabletop.

"Do you ever feel like the dumbest person in a room?" I asked glumly.

They all snickered, even Ciris shook with silent laughter.

I huffed.

"Let's find you something to wear and then we can go about our day," Zeres declared and leapt to his feet. As we left, I looked at the mostly untouched and completely wasted food. Gluttony was not present in this group, not even slightly.

Twenty minutes later, I stood in the main room, dressed in warmer clothing, with my hair scraped back from my face. "What now?"

"Now we do whatever we want. Envy won't be here until later."

That felt like an ominous prospect. I didn't want Envy to be here at all. I had visions of the young angel sweeping into the room, head high, full of bold arrogance, looking at me only once before he declared I should be rotting down in his dungeons. A place I never wanted to return.

The brothers sprawled across the couches, their eyes fluttering closed.

"What are you doing?" I frowned.

"Relaxing." Eros yawned.

"We have all day to relax," Zeres agreed.

Ciris had picked up a book, flipping idly through the pages, with one foot kicked over the other.

My hands fluttered. Lost, I huffed through my nose, before I turned on my heel and walked towards the doors to the apartments. I couldn't believe that this was what they did all day in the castle, lounged around in a fit of nothingness.

"Where are you going, Octavia?" Zeres called.

"Anywhere," I shouted back over my shoulder. "You said I could do whatever I wanted, and what I want is to explore."

That was a lie; I didn't really want to explore for the sake of it. All I could focus on was that I had escaped one death, and the next loomed. It felt like a never-ending cycle. In eight days, the trial would end, and in eight days, I wouldn't have the akelda I needed to pass my second trial and move a step closer to Eternis.

The castle was cold and quiet. I became more of a ghost than I had ever been before. I wondered if only the collection and Envy himself lived within these walls, making it a mass of wasted space while the Invidian's in the outer spiral crowded on top of one another.

I followed the halls until I found stairs. I climbed them to the tallest tower I could find. Halfway up, my thighs screamed, my body trembling from sheer exhaustion. By three-quarters of the way, I had no idea what a full breath of air felt like anymore. When I staggered to the top of the tallest tower of Envy's castle, the entire world spun.

My back hit the wall, and I slid down the side until I was seated on the floor, desperately willing my heart to slow just a fraction and reinforcing the idea I needed to be much fitter to live my life the way it had turned out.

It took me too long to realise I was not alone.

A large, semi-circle hole was built into the wall, and the floor extended onto a large platform.

Envy stood out on the platform. The angel was naked from the waist up, the muscles in his torso flexed and braced as wings shuddered and snapped out to their full wingspan. Alarm trickled through me; my too-fast heartbeat seemingly lodged solidly in my throat. I pressed myself against the wall and inched towards the stairs.

There was no chance of him noticing me, though, as his wings flexed, flapped, and he dove from the platform, falling out of sight. A sigh of heavy relief followed from my lips, but I choked on it as he soared into view again, flying high into the sky above his city.

A long minute passed before I found my feet, and on shaky legs, I staggered through the opening in the wall. Envy was long gone, and from his vantage point, I could see the entire spiral of

Invidia. In the vast distance of people milled around, going about their day as if nothing had changed. I imagined I could see the people I knew, and see if they were safe, but it was really no use.

It was a mistake to look down. The ground was so far away, and my head spun again. I gasped for air, chest tight, and I staggered back to the doorway. It was a quicker path down the stairs than it had been to climb them.

At the base of which I ran into a familiar face, her spindly but soft hands caught me by the elbow as I tried to flee right past.

"Bah! No running!" Eadlin chided without missing a beat. Her fingertips tightened on my elbow and pinched my skin. "Where are you going, girl?"

"I . . ." Heat crawled up my spine, leaving me flustered and confused. A growl of frustration rolled from the back of my throat. "I don't know! I don't know where I am! I don't know where I'm going! One minute, I'm in the dungeons dying, and the next, I'm having tea with eight of the most stuck-up people I have ever met."

The crone cackled loudly and held tighter to my elbow. There was no consideration of my waiting or what I wanted, and she dragged me down a hall, taking a hard left into a little study that smelled of roots and mint. It was a cloying scent that overwhelmed me, and I couldn't escape it. Something bubbled softly in a silver pot suspended over a flame, intensifying everything.

"Bah!" she cried. "Sit!"

I sat. Right on the edge of the chair, my fingers curled around the arms. "What do you want?"

The crone turned her wrinkled gaze on me. It was sharp and unimpressed with my attitude.

"Bah!" She spat, and spittle flecked across my cheek. I cringed back into the chair. "Have some respect for the old woman who saved your life."

I pouted in silent apology. As the crone bustled around the room, I thought of all that I had learned that day. The story of a woman and her children cursed by the devil. I wasn't sure how much of it had been a pure story, but it had me studying the crone a little closer again.

"You really are twice-cursed, aren't you?"

The crone froze with a fistful of a leafy green plant. "Aye."

I tapped my bitten nails against the arm of the chair, waiting for the rest of the story.

The crone stared at me; I stared back, each waiting for the other to fold.

She scoffed. "Once as a baby, again as a winner of the Devil's trials."

My jaw dropped. I leapt from my seat and was two paces closer to the old woman. I braced myself against the table, leaning close. "You won the trials? The devil's trials?"

The handful of greens fell into the bubbling pot, and she tinkered through little glass vials to look for what she needed. "Said what I said now, didn't I?"

"When?"

"One hundred and twenty years past now."

I frowned, counting it up in my head. "So, you're . . . one hundred and fifty?" A laugh bubbled over my lips before I could stop it.

Eadlin's hunched spine stiffened, and she spun towards me. A heavy brow lifted, and the laughter died in the back of my throat. Suddenly, it wasn't so funny.

"Something to say, girlie?" she barked.

I was considering the crone in a whole light. Only a few short years after I was born, she had been suffering through trials. This woman, this old, decrepit soul, had prevailed where people I had known had not, any remaining mirth fading.

"You just . . ." I hedged. "Look a lot older."

She cackled again, a hollowed and harrowing sound. One of her spindly fingers pointed upwards. "I was cursed as a child to be able to investigate the heads of man and see their true intent. Cursed as a victor to live nine lifetimes in an aged body. Bah! I'm one century and forty-seven years on this planet, girl. Not quite one-fifty yet."

"And you'll live . . . how long?"

The crone rolled her eyes and flicked a rope of greasy hair over her shoulder. "I have . . . five hundred and eleven more sun cycles to suffer through."

It seemed like an overwhelming amount of time. I couldn't imagine how it would feel to live through those years and watch the people she came to know thrive and wither before her eyes. All while she stayed in an aged shell that belonged to someone far beyond her own years.

When I thought of this and the three lanky men downstairs, I realised the devil was indeed a mercurial man.

I corrected my own thoughts a moment later. He was not a man at all, so his moods would have to be unpredictable, wild to the human soul.

"What if . . ." I hesitated. I swallowed over the nerves this crone instilled in me and voiced my thoughts all the same. "What if you just ended the cycle yourself?"

She scoffed. "I am immortal until my time comes, child."

From the corner of the room, a clock ticked away. The rod the crone used in her potions pot clanked against the side before she reached for a spoon. She let me digest this information, pouring a thick elixir into a mug.

I broke the silence with another question. "Why did he curse you the first time?"

Eadlin hummed. "It's a common tale, for the sins of our fathers."

The corners of my mouth dragged down. For the first time, I was glad my father was a boring, hardworking man. I held the mug she offered but didn't sip straight away. I wanted to know more, to have a little piece of information to understand the ruling force of our world a little better.

I wanted Samael to become more than the whisper in the shell of my ear, he who offered secrets and hope, but laughed at my naivety.

"What did he do?"

"Drink up," Eadlin demanded.

"But –" I protested.

"Drink, and I will tell you, girl."

It was bitter on the edge of my tongue and burnt my throat. I choked on the greens that hadn't stewed right through. A shudder of disgust rolled down my spine at the texture of the drink, but I chewed on one of the leaves and waited for my answer.

"My father led one of the northern rebellions." Eadlin shifted and stretched. Her joints crackled and popped before she sat heavily in a nearby chair. "He marched from the base of the Greedland Mines and onto the Devil's lands. Bah! Full of bright demands of a better life for humanity. He was full of hope. Full of vengeance. He wanted better for me."

I had heard, as many had, of the dangers of rebellion. The ways that the angels of sin hung men or fed them to the shadowy demons that roamed through the lands for such fanciful thoughts. Even knowing the danger, many men drank bitter home brew and became loud about their desire for bigger and better things. I had never known someone to act on it.

"He got caught?" I surmised.

"He failed on the borders." Eadlin nodded gravely. "His entire band of rebels wiped from the Earth, and my father, as their leader, was taken to Eternis itself to meet the devil for this final judgement."

"Oh." I held the mug tightly. "And . . . ?"

"He died there, but vengeance is not found in death, not truly, girl. Vengeance comes from suffering, and so the Devil cursed his only living blood, a girl aged five, to see the true, despicable nature of man."

My throat felt tight. "What does that mean?"

"It means I woke the next morning, unaware of losing my father, and could hear the thoughts of the people in my village. So loud that I screamed for days, and they locked me in the potato cellars until I could calm. If they came too close, I could feel the overwhelming nature of them. Men who smiled but wanted to slit their friends' throats. Women stood tall but quivered inside with deep fear. Children who cried even though their faces remained carefully blank."

My lips had parted with awe and horror.

"How . . ." I struggled to find the words, and my eyes landed on the old crone, wondering idly if she could feel the conflict within me. Suspicion twisted across my features before I could stop it.

Her aged lips rolled into a sad smile. "I have been in this world a long time. I have a handle over what I choose to see."

"Was that hard?"

"Everything is hard, Octavia Nox. Ease comes only with practice."

Yet, another person who loved to answer a question with words told me nothing. I huffed, and she chuckled roughly.

"I didn't gain control for two decades."

She nodded firmly at the cup, and even though it tasted like bitter vegetables and rotten tea, I sipped at it, attempting to stop a grimace from stretching over my features with each taste. The crone didn't continue until the cup was drained dry, and I didn't have the gall to ask what it was supposed to be; sometimes more harm lay in knowing than not.

"The second time, I was cursed . . ." she said.

I sat a little straighter, leaned forward, ready to hear more on this topic, ready to know the history of the twice cursed and the being that had rendered judgement on her soul. "Yes?"

"I had just won The Devil's Trials, broken and battered from facing the seven sins." Eadlin offered me a hard look, as if she were warning me. "I walked up to the devil with my head held high, ready for him to render final judgement and offer his favour. He stared into me and saw the mark of his curse, his signature on my eternal soul, and when he did, I plunged a knife into his chest."

I gasped.

The crone continued, "Actions have consequences, even his, even mine."

The mug had slipped from my fingers. It shattered against the stone floor, my fingers raised to my mouth instead, stifling my gasp of surprise. "You tried to kill Samael?"

"Samael?!" The crone laughed; the sound high-pitched in disbelief. "You call him Samael? As if he is your friend and not the devil who stole our freedom? Bah! Girl, you best get your head on straight."

She rose from her chair and hobbled towards me on sure footing. The shards of her ceramic mug cut into the soles of her feet, and blood seeped against stone, but the crone didn't falter, she didn't flinch.

"What?" I asked.

Old hands grasped the arms of my chair; she leaned forward and forced me to sit back, her aged face studying me intently. Dread pooled in my stomach, and bile burnt my mouth. I knew she was using her curse to look into my soul and truly see who was beneath every brave face I had put on, like a mask of protection.

The old crone scoffed, the sound damning in the too-quiet room. One of her hands grasped my cuffed wrist, aged fingers tight across the mark of Gluttony as she pinched my skin in warning.

"The devil is not your friend, girl; he is a being from another world. Forged in fires we do not know. He takes what he wants and acts for only his own pleasure. You are a plaything in his game, and he will toss you away when he finished with you – if you even manage to survive long to meet him."

I shivered.

"You are not special, Octavia, the devil does not care for you, he does not want to see you win, he wants you to dance like a little puppet on strings for his amusement."

My face had turned a violent shade of red. Unbidden tears pooled in my eyes, and my nose tickled as I tried to hold them back. "I'm not . . ."

She shook her head, silencing me, and let go. The crone shuffled back and gave me enough room to stumble to my feet and flee for her door. I didn't bother to thank her, for the tea or for invading my mind.

"Octavia!" Her tone was so sharp I hesitated at the top step. I glanced over my shoulder to meet her hard and knowing stare. "Don't trust the devil."

Softly, and for my ears only, Samael laughed.

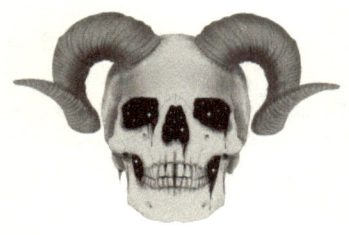

Chapter Thirty-Five

Hour after hour, I lost time wandering through the dark stone walls of Envy's castle. Samael's laughter haunted me. In the shadows of each corner, I saw the crone and the way her eyes had flared with raw disappointment as she had investigated my mind. The horrors she must have seen when baring her senses to my emotionally ravaged state.

Dusk had fallen by the time I found my way upstairs, and the collection was sitting around the same long table with a mountain of untouched food in front of them.

I burst through the doors, frantic and out of breath, shattering their quiet piece, and Nadiya looked ready to flay me alive for it. Her eyes narrowed, fork hovering near her lips, before she placed it back on her plate.

"There she is!" Zeres cried.

I relaxed slightly. At least someone was happy to see me.

The only free chair was between him and Margot, and I slipped into it. She ignored me, and Zeres tapped me on the arm. His sightless eyes were crinkled at the edges with a genuine good mood that felt slightly infectious.

"What did you do all day, then?" Zeres asked cheerfully, his fork sliding into a piece of meat, which he piled onto my plate. Ciris handed him bowl after bowl of vegetables, and within moments, I had a full meal in front of me. Hunger curled in my belly at the sight of food, and I reached for the cutlery.

"Just explored," I hedged.

"The gardens?" Eros asked, his flat tones jarring.

I glanced up and shook my head, swallowing a mouthful before I could answer.

"Upstairs, and well . . . everywhere, I guess." My knife scraped the plate. "I had tea with Eadlin."

Margot sucked in a sharp breath. "You saw the crone?"

"Uhh . . ." I glanced at her from beneath my lashes.

Tension grappled her jaw, displeasure in the twist of her mouth, and I wondered if she knew how much I hated her for having so such beautiful clothes, for having days that could be wasted away like that day, for being beautiful, and for having Mikhael Heira and an angel eating from the palm of her hand.

As if she could read my mind, Margot sneered. "I asked you a question. Are you too stupid to understand it?"

I sucked in a sharp breath, on edge. My fingers curled a little tighter around my fork.

"I just said I did," I bit back. "Is that a problem?"

"You should stay away from the crone. For your own good."

"Really?" I asked.

"Yes," Margot snapped. "You will stay away from the old bat."

"You don't tell me what to do!"

Margot's nose flared, looking terrifying instead of beautiful, a cold fury that radiated from her features. "I think you'll find –"

Tomas shouted, "Ladies!"

We turned. My eyes narrowed, jaw aching and half ready to slap Envy's most prized jewel. Tomas withered beneath Margot's haughty stare but caught himself after a breath.

"It's almost seven," Tomas said, nodding at the large carved clock in the corner. Much like everything else, it was decorated with serpents.

I stared at it for a moment, trying to determine the significance of seven in the evening.

Everyone else discarded their plates, gulped down the last dregs of sweet wine, and stood. They buzzed around like angry bees, their hive disturbed, while servants took the food.

The collection disappeared in and out of their rooms. I sat at the table, alone and dumbfounded as each came out in a different outfit. Pressed linens and dresses in varying shades of green, their hair fixed, and a soft pink applied to the women's cheeks. They were so preoccupied I may as well have been invisible.

They had reconvened in the main room by the time the clock struck eight.

It was only then the three brothers remembered I was there. Margot scanned the room, her icy gaze slicing through me, then hurried to shift me out of her view.

"Keep her quiet and out of sight," she demanded. "Or better yet, go hide away."

Eros and Ciris helped me from the dinner chair. A servant rushed in to straighten it.

They led me to a plush couch in the corner and gestured for me to sit. I fell into the soft cushions, more confused than ever.

Eros pressed a sold, slender finger against my lips. His dark eyes beaming with a message I didn't understand. He stared at me as if he could speak inside my head the way he did with his brothers, but when I blinked and frowned, he whispered, "Be quiet."

"I will."

"Good."

I felt a strange need to please him in this command. Not because of the way Margot had demanded it first, but for the way the soft pad of his finger had brushed my bottom lip. He glanced to his brother, concern blatant in the pull of his brows, and disappointment felt bitter when I realised, he was questioning whether I could comply.

"Like Ciris," he pressed, and I nodded.

I would stay as silent as his cursed brother. "I promise."

My reward was a toothy grin. Then Eros rose, and with his brother, moved back into the fray of activity. With their backs turned and attention diverted, I felt insignificant and forgotten. My emotions ran wild as I watched them all flutter about and stand in a straight line along the back window. Women so distinct and beautiful, so regal, everything I could never become.

Many people had told me, in this lifetime, that I was not special, and as I watched Margot, Nadiya, and Viktoria preen under the soft light of the setting sun, I realised just how true that might be.

The men were something else altogether: Tomas and Aeron stood tall, strong and attractive, and while I hadn't looked twice at them before, it ate away at me. I was not the type of woman that would catch their gaze.

"It's my night tonight." Nadiya laughed, her voice carrying. She pushed a soft, springy curl over her shoulder and preened.

"Ha!" Zeres countered. "Not a chance. He'll pick us."

They fell into softer bickering, each one perfecting their appearance as they stood with their back to the glow of the disappearing day. Tension developed, thick and unavoidable, leaving me breathless. It was coiled tight within me, too.

The three brothers stood as if they came only in a package. Viktoria kept brushing her hair back to show off her slender neck. Even Margot stood with a haughty and quiet confidence, ready for what would come. Something else existed in the room, though, in the way they darted their gazes at each other, overly critical, and offered sharp comments to bring others down.

Jealousy ran rampant inside this castle as much as it did in any other part of Invidia, and these beautiful creatures battled amongst themselves.

The doors flew open.

Envy radiated tension as he stepped inside. His glossy wings rustled; footsteps too quick as he blew into the apartments without regard for anyone inside. Black pants slung low on his hips, his shirt buttoned crookedly, flashing his muscled torso.

In his presence, the sickening bitterness in my gut doubled. I pressed my knuckles to my lips to stop myself from crying, biting down hard to keep my promise to Eros.

There was enough self-preservation beneath my stewing emotion to know that it wouldn't be good if I turned Envy's head now. No matter how much I wanted to be picked above the beauties he had before him.

I had a bigger desire to avoid rotting in the dungeons on the precipice of death.

The angel circled them. His long fingers sweeping his hair, a smirk lazy on his lips. Envy knew he held all the power, and the tension built as each of the men and women in the room shifted. Their chins lifted, their eyes wide, trying to seduce an angel of sin.

His influence felt heady from a distance. I didn't know how they weren't choking on it up close.

Envy leaned in, he whispered in their ears, and it stirred them. I could see the way they glanced at one another out of the corner of their eyes. Their noses flared, jaws sharpened, and I waited, just as invested in the outcome as the eight gems in his collection, as he walked a slow circle around them again.

Envy waited them out with more patience than I had expected him to possess.

Until one of them broke, and Tomas stepped forward.

"It's my turn," he said roughly, emotion thick in his voice. "Pick me. You want me."

Envy stared him down, lips twitching with soft humour. I wondered if he would kill him for the boldness of this statement or if that was what Envy liked, his little jewels fighting to be the centre of his attention.

The angel's tongue flicked over his lips; his eyes hooded as he gazed at the strong, fiery-haired man. "Do not presume to know what I think, precious."

It was a rejection, no matter how pretty the endearment might have been at the end, and Tomas wilted beneath it. As he turned smaller, Margot stood taller. She didn't look at Envy directly, but she waited for attention she knew would come, and it did. The angel turned his sights on his prized possession soon enough.

He turned to her, grasping her jaw with surprising force, and he turned Margot to face him. They stared at one another for so long it seemed they had forgotten the rest of the room, but Envy's lips drew back in a disgusted sneer.

"You are not yet forgiven." He sounded like a petulant adolescent, fitting in his youthful image.

"Envy . . ." she whined.

"Check yourself, Margot," he growled.

"It's been well over a week! What can I do to show you that I think of nothing but you? Envy, my day begins and ends with you! As it always has!"

"You think of nothing but me?" Envy hissed dangerously.

"Yes," Margot sighed. "Only you."

"Did you think of me when you were in his arms?"

Margot cowered.

"When you allowed him to touch you?!" Envy roared. His wings snapped open and almost swept Zeres off his feet, who barely caught himself mid-stagger.

Nadiya smiled slyly and slipped forward. She ran her hand along the angel's forearm soothingly. Envy calmed a fraction, his jaw tight as he stepped towards Margot, who, to her credit, didn't cower.

"You are mine!" Envy hissed.

"I am yours," Margot repeated.

"And you will learn your place."

"Yes, my Lord."

Envy spun. His wings knocked Zeres down this time, but he paid it no notice. I bit harder on my knuckles, forcing myself to stay quiet.

The angel grasped Nadiya by the throat. "I didn't invite you to touch me."

I bit down on a whimper, desperate to flee before he noticed me, but Envy had eyes for nothing outside of his collection. He squeezed Nadiya's tattooed throat, stroked it softly, and let her go to grasp her dark-eyed counterparts by the back of his neck. A strangely intimate gesture compared to the violence of a moment ago.

The man straightened, a smile pulling at the edges of his full lips.

"Aeron," Envy decreed. "You'll spend the night with me."

The angel dragged him from the room, Aeron glowing beneath his attention. They were gone before I could fully process what had happened. Silence stunned the room.

Managing my emotions was a struggle, even as the angel's influence faded. I was crying, bitter with resentment that I hadn't even been a choice for Envy.

"What . . ." I swallowed. "What just happened?"

Nobody answered.

Nadiya whimpered, burst into tears, and fled. Ciris and Eros were helping their brother to his feet before they turned away, cheeks coloured with splotches of pink.

Tomas hugged Viktoria tightly; they murmured to one another, and before I knew it, I was alone with Margot. She cleared her throat purposefully, lifted her chin, and shook her hair back into place.

In a few short strides, she stood in front of me, her icy gaze narrowed. Suppressed tears glimmered in her reddened eyes, the mark of embarrassment burning against her colourless skin.

"What –"

"Quiet," she snapped. Despite the reprimand from Envy, she spoke as if she were the queen of this castle. "You will be quiet; you will say nothing of what you see here when you leave."

I sucked in a breath. "And when will I leave?"

Her attention averted. "Meet me in my room after breakfast tomorrow, and I will explain why you're here."

"Tell me now?" I asked.

She scoffed. "Not a chance."

Margot swept away, and her door slammed.

Outside, the harpies screamed. I shivered and pulled my knees to my chest.

'*I suppose*,' Samael said as I entered the liminal space between consciousness and sleep, '*mercuriality is a family trait.*'

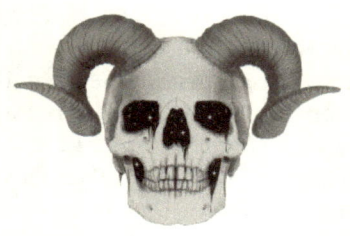

Chapter Thirty-Six

Margot's quarters were not what I had expected; I had imagined they would be as lavish as the rest of the apartments. All throughout breakfast, I had envisioned emeralds dripping from her ceiling and bed covers of silk and velvet. Instead, I had felt like I had stepped from one world to another passing through her door.

Margot didn't live in the luxury of wealth behind closed doors. Her rooms reflected the inside of a small cottage, and they reminded me starkly of home, with rickety furniture, a carved wooden bedframe covered in chips and creaking with age. The small table in the main room was balanced out by a novel wedged beneath one side, keeping it steady and even.

One of the doorframes had knife marks carved into it. A line a whole way across and a small number etched in beside each one. I had seen this before; Helina had something similar in her parents' home. A child had grown taller, and measurements had been taken, the last of which I would bet lined up to Margot perfectly. She had grown in this room, so out of place in this castle.

In that doorway, I hesitated to watch the woman in question as she set out an old painted teapot and chipped cups, so different to how she had presented at breakfast, haughty and regal.

"What –"

Her gaze shot up, and I shifted my question. "Where is this?" Margot ignored me, of course.

"Why am I here?" I asked.

Met with silence again.

She waved a hand at a chair, and when I slumped into it, it creaked in protest.

Margot sat slower, properly, wiping her thighs with her palms. I wondered what she had to be nervous about when the world seemed to exist at her beck and call.

"This is my home," she stated.

"Obviously," I huffed, rolling my eyes.

"No, Octavia." Margot's tone was hard. "This is my home from before Envy took me. He brought all of it here."

I studied the room again, reassessing the fact Margot seemed to come from humbler backgrounds than I had assumed.

"And?" I asked.

Margot stared and said nothing.

"Do you want me to feel sorry for you?" I continued harshly. "That this angel moved every one of your familiar creature comforts into his giant castle of luxury, so that you would still know your home."

Her white brows drew together, her lips thinned. I distinctly felt she didn't like me.

"You mean after he stole me away?"

I didn't flinch. "I don't see you crying into your golden handkerchief, Margot."

"It took five years to run out of tears. I am so sorry that I don't have any for you now."

"Yeah, well as Envy's little—"

"Shut up!" Margot snapped. "Don't talk about what you don't know."

My teeth ground together, fingers twitching, and I stretched as I pulled myself from the chair. "I have better things to do than this," I told her. "See you at dinner, princess."

Margot let me get halfway to the door. "Don't you want to know how to get out of here, Octavia?"

I froze. "Doubt you'd know."

"I was in the streets, wasn't I? You've seen me more than once."

With a sigh, I turned, leaning against the markers that showed how this woman had started a child and turned into an idiot.

"Maybe I'll just stay here. It's nice, and I'm being fed."

It was a far cry from the chilled tunnels and noisy markets below the city. There were far worse ways to live than being ignored in luxury.

Margot scoffed. "Just to die in seven days?"

"What?" I sneered back.

"That's all you have left." She smiled like we were playing cards, and she had called my bluff. "Seven days until Envy decides if you passed his trial."

I swallowed.

"Do you have your pretty piece of the old world, Octavia?" she taunted and reached for a small box on the table beside her, one I had assumed was filled with biscuits. From it, she retrieved a carved piece of the precious akelda.

It was the biggest piece I had seen. My body flushed hot with possessive desire.

"Do you need this to win your little trial?"

My heart had lodged itself in my throat, the flare of desperate hope heady enough to leave me dizzy. "You'd give it to me?"

Margot tucked it into her pocket. Out of sight, out of reach.

She pointed at the chair, a silent demand.

I stomped back to it, dropped down heavily.

"I'll give it to you." Margot nodded. "But not for free."

"Of course not," I said. "And what does the woman with everything think she needs?"

"When you leave, you'll take me with you."

"What?!" I spluttered. "No!"

Margot smiled. "For the akelda, and besides, you owe me."

"I owe you nothing."

"I convinced them to save your life, Octavia." She smirked and picked up her teacup. "I'm the reason you're sitting here, alive, instead of dead and forgotten in the dungeons. I saved your life, and you owe me mine."

"I never asked you to do that," I protested hotly.

She didn't flinch. She had stood toe-to-toe with an angel of sin and lived more than once. I paled in comparison. No threat I could make would leave Margot quivering.

"Don't you want to stay here?"

"No."

"Why not? It's . . . *perfect*."

"Looks can be deceiving," Margot stated.

"What's so hard about your life?"

Her lips thinned, and she seemed to be in two minds about answering me.

I shook my head. "Just tell me."

"What we think we want and what we actually want are two different things, but we can't see past what we think we want," Margot whispered. "That is the basis of envy. I thought I wanted to be loved by an unstoppable force, an angel, whisked away and cherished in his moments of devotion. I wanted someone who wanted me for the very reasons that others loathed me."

I raised a brow.

"That's not what I became. We are treasures in his collection, and I am not cherished unless the moment and his mood align. I want to be seen, but he picks me less and less, and even when he does, I am a fleeting moment forgotten about in the troubles with his sister. I am discarded like I have no brain, and no heart . . ."

I blinked, distracted. "Envy has a sister?"

"Pay attention!"

I snorted softly and nodded.

"What I thought I wanted, what I thought was love from him was actually becoming a possession, a doll to be used and tossed aside . . ." Margot's clear eyes had turned troubled and dark. When she looked at me, I could see the truth in her words. The reality she had so coveted had not been what it seemed. "What I really want is my village and my freedoms. Margot Galatea is not a possession for a broody angel. I will not be owned, not even by him."

Silence ticked between us as I weighed her words. I struggled with how to approach what I believed to be pure delusion from his woman.

"I'm not the right person . . ."

"No," Margot agreed quickly, too quickly.

I bristled. "You need –"

"There's nobody else. I tried Mikhael, but he's not here – you are. And in seven days, many of you will be evicted from the city. I need to be amongst you. You need to make that happen."

Margot sipped at her tea as I considered it.

I let mine go cold.

I looked at her closely, the humble beginnings she once wanted to be free of and wanted nothing more than to go back to them. What would I give to return to the familiarity and safety of Ilrea?

"Tell me," I said, and Margot dipped her chin, listening. "What's stopping me from taking you from here, then passing my trial but telling Envy that you're with us? That you're trying to run from him? I could take that akelda, pass and win, and still leave you in his clutches."

Margot had gone very still, and for the first time, I noticed the tiny gold serpents painted on the tips of each of her nails.

"I suppose . . ." Her features flared with panic, then smoothed out.

"Hmm?"

"I'll have to have faith."

"In what?" I scoffed.

"In your desire to live, Octavia Nox." I blinked, but she continued before I could question it. "Mikhael spoke of all of you, you know. His little group from home. Ilreans are made of thin dreams and hard work, he told me. He told me of the brother who would save him, until his last dying breath, of a bright-eyed boy who he thought couldn't face the darkness to come. He told me that he would crumble if not for the friends he had created, and he told me of you, Octavia . . ."

I almost didn't want to ask. It bewildered me how Margot managed to get opinions from Mikhael, who had seemed like the strongest of us all.

"What did he say?"

"Mikhael told me you didn't enter the trial for glory or because you have good morals. He told me you were different, that you hadn't come forward with hope. He said you were a girl with a cold, black heart, who thinks of nothing, but her own survival," Margot murmured, and my chest ached with a sudden and sharp pain. "He told me you would stop at nothing for your next breath. You would take from anyone you needed to in order to survive. You would even steal the air from his brother's lungs . . ."

"So?" I ground out. It hurt in an unexpected way that this was how Mikhael Heira thought of me, even though his opinion had never meant a thing before. "So what? It's just one man's opinion."

"If you betray me, Octavia, Envy will take your life, too."

I wanted to deny Mikhael's assessment of me, but I knew anything I said would sound childish.

Her chair creaked as Margot stood. Pink had appeared on both blanched cheeks, and she moved towards me at a slow pace. She was a queen, and I was the woman with the blackened heart. I flinched at the thought.

She lifted a pale hand and pressed it against my cheek, her fingers cold and soft against my skin. A lump had formed in my throat, and it was hard to swallow it down.

Margot smirked triumphantly. "How badly do you want to live?"

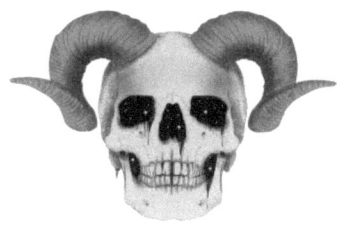

Chapter Thirty-Seven

I was left with three major problems. The first was that I had only seven days to find a path out of the castle for us; the second, I would need to ensure Margot was safe until the end of the trial, and the third was that I needed to ensure she would give me the piece of akelda that would save my life.

I didn't trust a single soul in Envy's collection, least of all the queen of the castle.

Before leaving her quarters, I had tried to question Margot on the ways she had slipped free of the castle before, most of which were unhelpful, since she had charmed a favourite guard to letting her straight out of the front fence or through the servants' quarters. When I'd asked where he was, Margot gave me a flat, hard look.

"Dead."

I shouldn't have been surprised, but I still flinched, wheeled around, and strode from the room with a bitter taste on the edge of my tongue, my heart beating at a furious pace, reminding me I was probably making one of the worst mistakes of my life.

Humble beginnings or not, Margot was a spoiled child and would throw me away as quickly as she had that guard when I had served my purpose. I had to figure out how to protect myself.

Wandering footsteps led me down flights of stairs until I tumbled out into the gardens. I had seen from the other side of the wrought iron gates. The pale pink flowers, the shaped green hedges, and the fountain looked so different from the inside looking out.

It was easy to imagine the collection deemed it a place of peace, with trickling water, the background chatter of birds, and the fresh air. I couldn't relax here, not as I counted a handful of guards within my first six steps.

They stood tall in their heavy armour, scales glinting in the light. They didn't move a muscle and stared straight ahead. I wondered if they not only kept intruders out but also us inside.

I wove through the garden path, set on reaching the iron gate, when I noticed Eros stretched out across a stone bench beside the fountain. I strode over to him and leaned over his body, watching the rise and fall of his chest.

"Still alive?" I asked and nudged him with my knee.

Dark eyes snapped open at my touch; Eros squinted at the sun behind me. Once his gaze fixated on my mouth, I repeated the question slowly.

"Barely," he groaned, throwing an arm over his eyes.

"What are you doing?"

"Self-soothing."

"Which is what, exactly?" I pressed.

Eros said nothing, I assumed, because an explanation would require more than two or three words. I nudged his feet off the edge of the stone bench and took a seat in the vacated space.

Eros' heels hit the ground; a growl rolled from the back of his throat. He swung upright, dark hair sticking in every direction.

"Ugh, Octavia," he grouched.

I laughed and twisted so that he could see my face. I waited until his gaze scanned my mouth and said, "How do I get out of here?"

Eros blinked. "What?"

"How do I get out of here?"

"To go where?"

"Down the street? Back to the Infra." I waved a hand. "Back into the competition that I need to win?"

His mouth sloped downwards. "You don't."

"What?" I asked.

"No going back."

An incredulous huff rolled from my chest. I leapt to my feet; hands planted on my hips. "But I only have seven days left in the trial!"

Eros shook his head. "Everyone thinks you're dead. Why would you go back to a series of trials you can't win?"

Shocked silence filled the courtyard. It was the longest sentence I'd heard him say.

"I . . ." I said. "Of course, I could win."

He shook his head, wearing the same sad expression my mother did when she decided I was hopeless beyond repair. My gut twisted.

"I can win," I repeated firmly.

"Octavia . . ."

"The devil likes me!"

"The devil doesn't like anyone," Eros rumbled, standing quickly. "The devil dominates our world and tortures us for his pleasure. This sick competition is just for his amusement, not so you can win. Just little humans scurrying to please him."

I was so taken aback by his vehement speech that I stepped back. Something ugly twisted across Eros' face. I swallowed the lump that had developed in my throat and reminded myself he was not my friend. Of the few I had, one was dead, one I had betrayed, and the other . . . I didn't know what she was doing. Helina had stood up for me so that Envy didn't mount me on his iron gates as a punishment as a warning, sent me into a head spin, so I tried my hardest not to think of it.

"Have you ever met the devil?" I asked.

Eros' lips thinned. "No."

"Have you spoken to him?"

"No," he growled flatly. "Octavia . . ."

"Then, you have no idea!"

He stared at me, and I glared back.

"Have you?" Eros asked softly. He stalked forward a step. "Have you met the devil?"

My face flushed pink as I refused to answer.

"I thought not," he laughed.

I huffed, and his eyes narrowed on my mouth, concentrating on my next answer.

"Have you spoken to the devil, Octavia?"

A laugh rang in my ears, low and soft, and it didn't belong to me or Eros. Samael was listening, and his amusement was warning enough.

"I'm going back to my life!" I told Eros instead. His face shut down. "You can stay here, self-soothing and enjoying your comfortable life, but I'm done."

"You think it's comfortable here?" he asked.

I glared at him.

"Do you know what Envy does to us in the evenings?"

I didn't want to know. My boots scraped the stone as I spun on my heel and wove through the gardens towards the gates that cooped up within.

Eros' hurried steps stamped behind me, his arm slid through mine, and he measured my pace, marching with me towards freedom.

It was a silent apology, and I accepted it.

He rounded one of the hedges, marching towards the iron gates, and I realised the guard was not facing us. He was turned towards a man with his head bowed against the cold serpents. Their conversation was too low for me to hear, but the man was familiar.

"Mikhael?" I cried before I could think better of it.

Mikhael's head snapped up, and shock rolled across his face. "You're alive?"

Time seemed to suspend as I disentangled myself from Eros and ran for the gate.

The cries from the guard were ignored as I slammed against cold iron, wrapping my hands around the bars and his fingers. His skin was cold, his face thinner than it was when we left Ilrea, dark circles drooping beneath his eyes, betraying his lack of sleep.

In his face, I saw his brother, and sadness swept through my soul for the man who had sacrificed himself. As much as I had compartmentalised these past days, I needed to know.

"Is he alive?" I blurted.

"Is she okay?" he asked at the same time.

"Yes." We sighed in complete synchronicity.

It was strange to feel relief that Niklaus Heira was alive. For much of my life, I had hated him every bit that I had craved him, but I still didn't want to see him lost at the hands of an angel.

"Octavia." Mikhael shifted his grip. "Bring her to me."

"What?"

Suddenly, I was all too aware of Eros at my back. Mikhael's eyes bounced over my shoulder; his lips pressed into a thin line.

"Bring the gift to me." Mikhael changed his wording, his face clouded over as he glared at Eros. "I'll take care of the rest."

Eros took a firm grip on my arm and pulled me backwards. He tucked me into the space behind him, and the guard's armour rattled as he shifted between Envy's favourite and Mikhael. Eros was to be protected, and I understood that, but I wished I were important enough to be protected, too.

"I need to go out there," I called to the guard from behind Eros' shoulder.

The man glanced at me; his eyes narrowed on my face in a quick assessment of my worth. "Nobody leaves 'less Envy says so."

He turned his back on Mikhael and stood firmly in place as if to tell me he wasn't going anywhere. I bit down on my lip, desperately trying to work out how to get out, when Eros pushed me backwards.

"Let's go," he said. The guard shuddered at the flat tones of his voice.

I didn't want to go, but Eros caught my arm again, using all his weight to make me move. We walked back to the castle in silence. At the top of the stairs, I glanced back out onto the cobblestone streets. Mikhael was no longer alone, his brother, a copied silhouette standing beside him. Emotion welled behind my eyes.

"What is it?" Eros asked when the doors rolled closed behind us.

We stood in the silence between those too-empty walls. "I don't know how he survived."

"Who?" He frowned.

"Niklaus," I clarified. "He's that man's brother."

Eros hummed, his lips twisted into a thin line, head tilted slightly to the side. When Zeres appeared at the top of the stairs, I realised he had been holding a conversation with someone else.

I heaved a sigh, angry I had been dismissed without him telling me, but when I whirled to leave, his brother placed a hand on my arm to stop me.

"Come upstairs," Zeres directed. "Now."

"Why?"

Eros took my other arm, and I glanced to Zeres' sightless eyes before my gaze scurried away, unsure of if it was right to look him in the eye. His smile turned lopsided, as if he knew what I had done. Although, Eros could have told him. The three brothers had no secrets from one another.

Zeres bundled in close and spoke in soft tones. "Envy is home; you can't let him see you."

A shiver of pure self-preservation rolled through me, and I didn't need any more encouragement to thunder a path back up the stairs. The rest of the afternoon faded as I stared out the window, watching the mass of Invidians and competitors who scurried about the streets like ants, wishing I could see the path to success.

Just before dinner, Envy blew through the apartments early. He stole Nadiya away for the night, and I realised I hadn't seen Aeron all day.

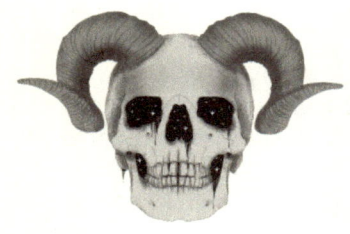

Chapter Thirty-Eight

I woke under the entangled limbs and suffocating heat of other human beings. Disorientation gripped me, and for a moment, I imagined I was at home, in that little room with too many people and not enough space, where I ended up caught beneath the other members of my family.

"Get off!" My limbs flailed at my brother. "Mason!"

"Who?" A lyrical voice yawned.

Another body shoved me to the side. I rolled, finally free, right off the side of the bed and onto the floor. The voice had jarred me out of the fantasy of being home, and the floor catapulted me into awareness.

All too quickly, I knew where I was, in the darkened star-covered room that the triplets shared in Envy's castle. I was still in the competition, exhausted, straddling the line between life or death.

"Nothing," I muttered, finding my feet. "Go back to sleep."

Zeres mumbled beneath his breath but didn't need encouragement as he succumbed to unconsciousness again. I watched them, tangled around in each both physically and mentally, and thought it must have been an exhausting way to live, with no private thoughts and always carrying the burdens of your family. I had hated having even a fraction of the misfortunes and responsibilities that my family needed.

I crept back out into the main room.

Viktoria and Margot sat at the breakfast table. The fiery-haired woman was not in her usual chair and instead sat next to Margot. Their heads were bowed close, conversation hushed. Both looked up as I pulled a chair back and dropped heavily into it.

"What's going on?" I asked, buttering a slice of toast.

They both frowned. Viktoria's mouth puckered with distaste, but Margot answered softly. "Nadiya is not back yet."

When their eyes swerved to the door again, I looked as well. "Is that unusual?"

"Envy . . ." Margot sighed his name. "He usually returns us by the first drop of light."

My gaze flickered to the high windows, and I realised the sun was half up already. "Ah."

Annoyance flashed across Viktoria's face.

With a drink in hand, I steeled myself to ask, "What happens when you go with him?"

They shared a look. Irritation licked at my spine, but I tried to hide it behind drinking my tea. The two women lingered long after they had drained their teacups and wiped the crumbs from the edges of their mouths. Stubbornly, I stayed at the table, too.

"Don't you have something you need to be doing?" Margot asked me pointedly.

"Nope."

Annoyance flashed across her face. I wondered if Margot hated she needed me as much as I hated she could get me killed.

We waited in tense silence. Tomas appeared, ate, and disappeared once more without any sign of Nadiya.

The sun had risen high over the spiral city by the time the doors crashed open, and the woman staggered inside. Her arm sat at the wrong angle, too low. Tears streaked through smudged golden makeup, and blood dripped from her nose. Worst of all, Nadiya's eyes looked haunted. She had transformed a proud woman into a broken doll overnight.

My chest squeezed tight at the sight of her, iron bands of worry firmly back in place. I remembered Eros' words about it not being comfortable there, and I burnt to know what had happened.

Was it only Envy's influence that had them all bickering and preening to be chosen when they came back in tatters? Was his silently poisonous power so great?

Margot and Viktoria rushed to their feet. They cried out, and the triplets' bedroom door flung open.

"You!" Margot hissed at me. She gestured me over as they crouched in front of the woman, smoothing springy curls from her face. Viktoria whispered something, but when they lifted her arm, Nadiya's eyes rolled back in her head, and she crumpled to the ground.

"What?" I asked stupidly. My desire to know had given away to alarm.

"Find the crone," Margot ordered. She frowned when I hesitated and drew herself to her full height. Before I could register her movements, she had slapped me hard across the face.

Pain lanced through my cheekbone, tears itching my eyes, and my fingers raising to touch tender skin. Margot caught my hand; she squeezed my fingers punishingly to hold my attention.

"The crone. *Go!*"

Find the crone. Find the crone. Find the crone.

It would have been an easier task if I knew my way around the castle. I stumbled up and down the stairs desperately to find her until I was completely and utterly lost. On the ground floor, I ran past a man. He was quicker than I had expected, twisting the back of my dress in his fist.

"Hold it," he commanded.

I spun, gaze frantic, eyes glassy.

His attention drifted to my cheek, and I knew Margot's hand had marked it.

"What's going on?"

When I took a second to breathe, I realised it was the chancellor from the first night in Invidia. His name escaped me, the silver streak in his beard recognisable. I had no time for pleasantries and tried to shake myself free.

"The crone," I said. "I need the crone."

The chancellor – Seamus, I recalled – glanced at my wrist, and his expression tightened at the cuff that sat snug against my skin. He shook me hard by his grip on my clothing.

"How did you get in here, trial rat?" he hissed.

"Envy brought me here."

"Tell the truth."

"I am!" It wasn't a lie, but Seamus didn't seem to trust me. I found my tongue again. "Please, Margot wants the crone."

He released me so suddenly I almost fell.

"Ah." He rubbed his wiry beard, cheeks red. "Miss Galatea sent you? Then, we'll find the crone."

I blinked, shocked at his sudden change of heart.

He beckoned me to a side door. I wondered just how many people Margot Galatea had wrapped around her slender fingers. The chancellor strode through the doors, and I scurried behind him, stopping dead when I saw a throne wrought of serpents with jewelled eyes, and an angel sprawled across it. He'd brought me to the angel.

My heart withered in my chest.

Envy had his feet kicked on one arm, one boot over the other, his wings tucked behind his back as he stretched back on them. A silver circlet sat on his brow, and I wondered if he fancied it a crown. The crone stood, stooped beside him, shaking a small bottle before her thumb popped the cork free.

Shakily, I backed towards the door. I didn't want him to see me, but he didn't look up as the chancellor strode forward.

"Seamus!" Envy called, making a mockery of the man's name with his tone, proving even the favoured were not safe in Envy's circle. The young angel would be at the top of everything, and he would cut down anyone who came close to rising up. "Tell me about the Wrathlands' front."

"Sir." The chancellor paused to bow low. I was poised to flee as my heart hammered in my chest. "Our soldiers at the Wrathlands are making grand progress, but if I might borrow Eadlin for a small moment . . ."

Envy shifted, as fast as a snake, and all his attention shifted on his chancellor. One smooth question at the edge of his lips. "Why?"

By now, the crone had noted me, and she frowned from beneath her heavily lined brow. I tried to make myself as small and unnoticeable as possible. Seamus cleared his throat, and I wondered if he would mention Margot. His chin lifted, however, and his lie came out smoothly. "One of the new guards appeared to have stabbed himself. A young fucker playing around."

Envy glanced to the crone.

"Go." He waved his hand, silky wings rustling at his back. "Kill the fool and return for your trial report."

The crone moved in no hurry. In slow and measured steps, she approached me. "Bah!" She hustled me out of the room, whirling on me quickly in the hall. "You disrupted that for a crack to the cheek."

"No!"

"What is it, then, girl?"

I tried to pull my scattered thoughts together, but they slipped this way and that. My hands fluttered in front of my chest as I tried to explain. "Nadiya came back and –"

"From where?"

"She was with . . . Envy? I don't –" I pressed gnarled fingers to my lips, silencing me, and the old woman took off and outpaced me back up the stairs.

Envy's collection stood in the apartment, hovering around Nadiya when we arrived. Aeron was covered in bruises of his own, leaning heavily on a chair. The crone swept them away with practiced ease and knelt on the floor for a better look at the woman. She obscured my view as I hovered to the side, and when she tilted Nadiya's head, I realised her tattooed throat was covered in familiar bruises. The life had nearly been squeezed from her recently.

Eadlin clicked her tongue.

Margot nodded softly. "It's getting worse."

"It's this nonsense with his sister." The crone scoffed. "Sins bleed across borders, and Envy has always been jealous of her above all the others. She has what he cannot ever have."

The collection murmured in agreement.

Eadlin gestured to the triplets. "Carry her gently to her rooms. I'll help her there."

They crouched around Nadiya, communicating between themselves before carrying her away.

"Bah!" The crone chided as she followed. "I said gently!"

When the triplets returned, we all waited for the return of the crone. Lunch sat untouched and was removed after Margot snapped at one of the servants. I tried to stay out of the way and ended up sandwiched between Ciris and Zeres, like they were a protective shield, while Margot's discontent grew.

When the crone returned and closed Nadiya's door behind her, the tension in the room doubled. It felt like everyone was going to shatter, and I became weary of the deafening sound of my own breathing.

"Bah! She'll be fine!" Eadlin announced. Instantly, the tension burst, relief sweeping through. "That arm'll be sore for a few days. I'll bring up salves for the bruising, but she'll do well to stay out of Lord Envy's way for a good while."

Margot nodded tersely. "Thank you."

Eadlin's aged face twisted into something stern. She paused to inspect Aeron. "Whomever he picks tonight . . ." She shook her head. "Be compliant, be careful."

They agreed, and she exited as fast as she had arrived.

I nudged the men on either side of me, and they turned their dark heads in my direction.

"What's he do?" I asked urgently.

"Nothing for you to worry about."

"Zeres!" I snapped. "I'm serious. What's he doing?"

He shifted. His slender, cold fingers pressed against my cheek. "So am I. It's best you don't pry. Don't look at him, don't let him find you interesting . . ."

"Why?" I pushed. My hands found his chest, and I pushed him backwards. Both brothers were quick to help him stay upright. "Why not? I want to know; I *need* to know what's going on. Why can't he find me interesting?"

Margot grasped my arm; her fingers pinched my skin in punishment.

"Because –" Her voice was shrill, emotion colouring her cheeks. "Envy likes to take the things he finds interesting apart.

Physically. Emotionally. Mentally. He pulls us to pieces, and when the fun is gone, he does a horrible job at putting us back together again."

I stared at her, and as I glanced to the triplets, who said nothing, my head spun.

"What?" I squeaked, understanding enough and nothing all at once. I tried to imagine how he took them apart, but Nadiya flashed in my mind, and I shivered. A young lord breaking his toys.

Margot leaned close and hissed in my ear. "Get me out of here."

Less than an hour later, the doors blew open again. We all turned, and I expected the crone to be back with the elixirs she had promised. But instead, Envy prowled into the room. Ciris abruptly shoved me. I collapsed onto one of the cushioned couches with a sharp gasp. All of Envy's treasures, aside from Nadiya, lined up by the window as they had every other night.

The angel appeared agitated as he strode inside, his face darkening with rough emotion, his wings rustling. When he rolled his back and let his power loose, I nearly fainted.

Emotion was bitter in my throat, my lungs only allowed shallow breaths as I drowned in the need and desire to be up there for the picking, to have this angel's eyes on me. His influence wove around his collection in the same way.

Tomas and Aeron argued, shoving each other out of the line. Each of them preened for his attention, and before I could rethink it, I had rolled off the couch. Rationally, I knew I shouldn't draw his attention. The idea of being taken apart by an angel should have sent me skittering back to the relative safety of obscurity in the dungeons, but I dragged myself across the floor towards them all instead. Each of the treasures too focused on their own obsession to notice me, and that only stoked my jealousy further. I was so focused on what I wanted I didn't hear a word Envy was saying.

I would make him notice me.

When I was halfway to the line-up, Envy chose, his fingers threaded in Zeres' hair. Roughly, he dragged him off, barely taking note of me. His sinful influence dimmed, taking the air from my lungs with it, and I crumpled to my knees.

Margot burst into tears and fled.

Eros and Ciris shared pained and panicked looks with one another. They stumbled forward and helped me to my feet. "He took Zeres," I said dumbly, finally registering what that meant. Zeres was not going for a grad dinner and a satisfying nap. I fretted that he would come back just like Nadiya, and these triplets were too thin, too breakable, to be manhandled like that.

The men shared looks, and they led me to their room, dinner forgotten as we all crawled onto the bed. Exhausted, I drew my knees to my chest. The men stripped from their shirts, they moved slowly, pausing at times, eyes vacant, and I realised they were communicating. I hugged myself tighter.

"Don't cut me out," I pleaded.

They didn't owe me a thing. It had nothing to do with me, but I didn't want to be alone.

Eros sighed and climbed onto the bed. "It's going to be a long night."

–

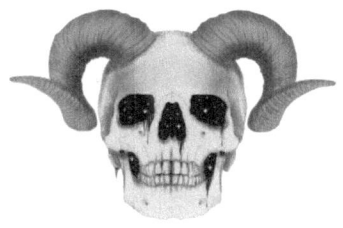

Chapter Thirty-Nine

It started with soft moans in the middle of the night. Gentle sounds that brushed against my skin and pulled me from the depths of sleep. Eros and Ciris rolled in their sleep and curled on top of me from both sides. They were tense, corded muscle and soft breaths against the side of my neck, their arousal pressed hard against me.

I had never shifted into awareness so quickly, smothered beneath their dual body weight and the suffocation of the heat that rolled off their bodies. Blearily, I blinked at the soft lights on the ceiling.

"Envy . . ." Eros whispered against my skin.

"Eros," I croaked, forgetting he couldn't hear me.

A pair of soft lips skimmed up the column of my neck, pulling the breath from my throat.

"Ciris." I gasped.

Fingers trailed up the back of my thigh, eliciting a shiver. I twisted, attempting to writhe free of them, but they were heavy. Their eyes were closed, faces battling shared dreams, sound asleep.

I couldn't tell which brother was which.

"Wake up!" I begged the brother, whose fingers wound through my hair. "Wake up!"

Their faces clouded over, legs tangling around mine, as they wound me close. Escape felt impossible. I lashed out with closed fists, and panic clawed up my throat as the hand on my thigh crawled higher.

"*CIRIS*!" I screeched.

Dark eyes snapped open. A glimmer of pleasure gave way to horror, and Ciris snatched his hand out of my hair. His dark eyes appeared dazed and rolled back, flashing the whites of his eyes.

"What's happening?" I squeaked, trying to get out from between them.

The man wrestled with his own subconscious, fluttering in and out of awareness. Beneath the icy fear that licked at the base of my spine, I wondered what nightmare I was missing.

His hand shot out, fingers curling across my lips, silencing me, suffocating me.

Behind me, Eros moulded himself against me, keeping me anchored beneath his thigh, no matter how hard I kicked. Reactively, I bit down on Ciris' flesh.

Hard.

Ciris' mouth opened in an unspoken shriek, and his gaze focused. He stared at me, wide-eyed, and scrambled backwards.

He dropped from sight as he fell from the bed. I lunged for the space he had created.

Eros twisted faster than me, rolling me beneath him. His brother reappeared in my peripheral vision, face an expression of horror. Ciris reached for my arm, and failing that, grasped at my flailing legs.

Terror shot through me as he gripped me firmly, my skin crawling, but he heaved me sideways with all his strength. He dragged me from my position of vulnerability beneath his brother, and we collapsed on the floor.

Pain laced up my arm, and my head cracked against the floor. Ciris pushed me off him, and I scrambled towards the far wall. My eyes hopped to the door, and Ciris moved into a crouch. He shifted towards me, both palms raised. His lips moved, wordless, soundless placations falling short between us. I watched frustration wash over across his face.

Between one breath and the next, his face went vacant. On the bed, Eros thrashed, limbs flailing everywhere, a terrifying scream rolling from the back of his throat. It sounded like pure agony.

Ciris twisted, his attention diverted.

He leapt for his brother, and I ran towards the door. My heart felt like it was beating in my throat. Bile stung my mouth as I snagged my boots and fled.

The sound of a hand smacking against skin made me pause, and I glanced over my shoulder to the two men. Ciris' hand was fisted in the front of his brother's shirt, his clenched first rearing back again, but when he swung, Eros caught his fist.

Their cheeks were tracked with tears. The men stared at one another before Eros tuned his dark gaze to where I stood, halfway out the door.

"Octavia . . ." My name rolled flat from his lips.

I shook my head.

"I'm sorry," Eros gasped, face haunted by the horrors in his head "I was stuck with Zeres. We . . ."

His excuses were lost as I stumbled away through the main rooms and out into the cold castle corridors. I didn't look back, and the haunted men didn't chase me. I ran through the halls and down the stairs. I had no real concept of where I was going, my head spinning, panic igniting an urgent fire in my veins until I was standing in a vaguely familiar place.

A guard dozed in the corner of the room; his scaled breastplate sat crooked. Iron bars ran down the halls. It smelled so strongly of rot and urine I gagged, pressing my palm across my nose and mouth.

The dungeons, I realised.

The same filthy dungeons where I had been left to rot. A face appeared in the cell nearest me, and I startled, backing away.

"Hey!" a girl called.

I shivered at the sound of it. Despite myself, I crept forward a step, then another, until I was standing at her cell. She leaned heavily against them, looking no more than eighteen years past. She had tawny skin, caked with blood and dried mud. She wore the colours of Ira, deep black with the bold red lion across her chest. Although, someone had shredded through that symbol, revealing flashes of scarred skin. Her pin-straight, inky black hair had been braided away from her face, strands of red cotton threaded through them, an identifier of the war camps that guarded the Wrathlands' borders.

The girl watched me closely, pain twisting her slender features. My gaze fell to the large gash across her thigh. It didn't bleed, but the edges were red and puffy, the skin surrounding it tight and glossy. I could smell the stench of infection.

This girl, she was dying.

"Who are you?" I asked.

"Aieke." Her name was a sigh on the end of her lips.

She knew she was dying, whether from the rot in her blood, the food that came too infrequently, or from being forgotten here, just like I had been.

"Why are you here?" I was curious, even though I had no place to be. I had been a prisoner in these dungeons, and nobody had pried as to why. Her thick, dark lashes fluttered, and Aieke groaned as she shifted, her forehead pressed to the cool iron.

"Because . . ." She murmured so softly I strained to hear. "I'm on the right side of a deadly war."

Her answer yielded nothing about why she was in Envy's dungeons – at least not to me, but I nodded as if I understood. My fingers uncurled from the bars, and I stepped back.

"Wait!"

I froze.

Aieke lifted her head, giving me a better view of the dried blood crusted on her skin. "Help me."

"I . . ."

"Help me," she begged, again.

"I can't."

"Yes," she groaned. "You can."

"I can barely help myself," I admitted.

The guard shifted in his sleep, his armour rattling, and I flinched away. Nervously, I looked over at him, then back at the girl doomed to die. If I was caught, I would join her in wasting away.

"I'm sorry," I whispered. "I'm not your hero."

I fled before I could get caught, before the guard could recognise me as someone who belonged in the forgotten cells and throw me back inside, losing the key permanently this time. It was easy to lose my way below ground levels of the castle. One moment, I was twisting my way out of the dungeons; the next, I was halfway down an unfamiliar tunnel, pausing to put on my shoes, when I realised, I could hear the whisper of voices.

I tucked the laces of my boots in without trying them and crept farther along, squinting in the low light and darting around wooden crates.

"The war front is becoming a dangerous place . . ." an unfamiliar voice stated.

I crouched behind one of the boxes, biting down on my lips and straining to hear their conversation.

"If the angel becomes any more obsessed" – That voice, I knew, the Chancellor of Invidia – "he'll start sending the nobles to the frontline."

Someone else clicked their tongue, a damning sound. "We won't last a day out there, Seamus, I won't have it!"

Murmurs of agreement bounced off the cold walls.

"Talk some reason into him!"

"You think angels can be reasoned with?" Seamus boomed. I cringed back against the wall. It was cold, wet.

"Talk to the devil, then!" someone else barked. "You're his chancellor! Stop this madness before Envy gets us all killed. The devil is supposed to control them!"

Footsteps scuffled. I listened as one of the men spat on the ground.

"I'll not lose my son to an angel's mad war. It's got nothing to do with us."

The declaration seemed grand and bold for people who spent many of their lives trying to one-up each other, to earn that same angel's favour. Seamus shifted, pacing down the tunnel, close enough I caught sight of him and the weariness that shadowed his face.

"Chancellors are not the advocate for humans to the devil. We are the hand of the devils' decree," he told them, and I wondered what that meant. I made a mental note to ask Samael next time he wanted to chat.

"You could try," came a protest.

Seamus sighed heavily again. "Take the tunnels back to the Infra and get home before your wives miss you, men. I'll find a way to keep us off the front lines for now."

The men murmured bitterly; their feet scuffed against the floor, but they shuffled away. Seamus strode right past me, not looking for eavesdroppers, not noticing the woman pressed against the side of the crate in his preoccupation.

Despite my discomfort and my confusion about the conversation I had just overheard, my heart was signing. Elation left me warmer than I had been since I had fled the triplets' rooms. The night was not just a horrifying disaster.

I had found a way out of the castle; I just needed to find my way back.

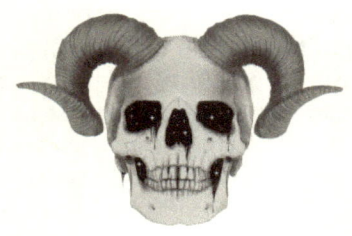

Chapter Forty

The path to freedom was marked with scraps torn from the hem of my dress. I marked my way back to the dungeons, where the guard still slept, and Aieke uttered soft groans as I passed through.

I couldn't get her out of my mind while I climbed the flights of stairs, my naked, cold thighs burning by the time I found familiar bearings. The collection was quiet; Margot stood by the window, alone, and the triplets lay sprawled around the room. Half of Zeres' face was swollen and bruising, an icepack in his hand. They sat in eerie stillness as if they'd shared the ailments and none of them could see, hear, or speak.

I stared but couldn't bring myself to speak to them after the night before. Wherever Zeres had dragged their consciousness, it haunted them, and I still felt a glint of instinctual fear at the thought of being close to the men who had so easily pinned me down.

Instead, I found myself at Margot's side, peering through the great glass window.

"They'll be like that for days," Margot murmured. "Envy can break three of them in a single night with one."

"Oh."

"He makes you want it." She sounded sad. "He makes you want to do better than the idiot who didn't survive the night before. You envy them for being picked. You resent not having the chance. He tells you how they did better. He likes to boast about how they bent for him without breaking. If you manage it, then you feel special. It's like nothing else. Your vile, unstoppable personal envy appeased when he smiles at you, when you can take it. And for a flickering moment, he seems pleased . . . But only for that single moment."

I swallowed roughly.

The sharp angles of her snowy face looked as severe and haunted as the triplets. "The things we do out of envy . . . , and we're stuck here, enduring it, night after night. Wanting it over and over again. Letting this monster break us to pieces, never sure if we'll be put right again."

I knew what she was doing. I knew she was telling me for sympathy so that I would try harder to free her from this place. But for all the torture she had endured, I still envied her position, and the person I truly felt pity for was the girl in the dungeon.

"I found a way out," I said. "Let's go now."

"I'm not ready to go yet."

"What?" I gasped.

"Go too soon, and he'll hunt me down again. We can't go until the day before the trial ends."

I shook my head, spluttering. "That's stupid."

"It's the best plan," Margot argued.

"Why not just —"

"Mikhael is at the gate," Margot spat. I pouted. "Go organise it with him."

Margot turned her pitying gaze on the three identical men before disappearing into her room, the door slamming the door in her wake.

I had nothing better to do than to meet Mikhael. Quickly, I broke into one of the rooms, Nadiya's. I realised when her sleeping form still lay curled in the bed, springy curls spread around her head like a halo. Serenity overtook her slumber, a peacefulness on her face.

I crept to her closet and rifled through it. Finding something to wear was difficult since I knew nothing of the draped styles she favoured, but eventually, I was clothed enough to brave my way back to the gardens, at least with a cloak wrapped around my shoulders.

The guards didn't stop me as I stood by the fence, once again betraying my insignificance. I may have been allowed to live and remain in the castle on the whim of the collection, but I was assuredly unimportant.

As Margot had predicted, Mikhael was waiting. I wondered how many days he had lost waiting for her to come to the iron bars and declare her affection for him. The disappointment that registered across his face that it was me and not Margot felt wildly offensive, and I struggled to overcome it enough to remain civil.

"Did she give you a message for me?" he asked quickly.

I shook my head, and Mikhael looked crestfallen.

"She told me to work out a plan with you," I admitted. His chin jerked up, green eyes brightening. "A plan to get her out. I have a way, but she said not yet."

"How?"

I glanced nervously at the guard, but he wasn't paying attention. "There's tunnels leading from the Infra to the castle."

Mikhael winced. "The Infra isn't the safest place at the moment."

"Why?"

"A harpy got in."

I gasped. "What . . . What happened?"

"It tore apart the encampment," he muttered darkly. "Slaughtered near a quarter of us, decimated the marketplace. We're scattered."

"Where are you staying now?"

"Nik, Helina, and I are safe."

I hesitated. "And Nash?"

He nodded. "Him, too. Keeps asking if I've seen you."

My relief was almost palpable. I wondered idly if the remaining members of my own team thought about – or cared about – my livelihood. Probably not.

"Anyway," Mikhael continued. "Nik and I will find the tunnels that lead to the castle. Put something down there to mark a meeting spot so we can find it and know we're in the right place."

"Like what?"

Mikhael's hands skimmed over his pockets, and he found a piece of Nash's favoured pink chalk. He stared at me for a second. I shrugged. I had nothing to contribute. I couldn't read or write, so chalk was useless to me.

"Hand me that rock." He pointed to the garden. A quick glance told me there was well over a hundred rocks there, but he didn't clarify which one. I picked a rock the size of my fist, carried it back, and forced it through the bars to him.

Mikhael took a moment to turn it over, then etched eyes and a wonky smile.

It was horrifying. He was no artist.

He pushed the rock back through the bars, and I almost dropped it, fumbling for it at the last moment, and smudging the edge of its manic smile. If anything, it looked worse.

"Give me the chalk, too," I demanded.

Mikhael's brows rose, but he didn't argue and handed it over.

"How will I know if you've found it?" I asked.

"I'll . . . I'll change the face on it," Mikhael said seriously. When he stepped back, he reminded me of the man who had been destined to be the next Chancellor of Ilrea. Calm and in charge. He had a plan, and somehow, Mikhael had faith in it, even if I felt it was foolish and destined to fail.

"When does Margot want to leave?" he asked.

"The second last day of the trial."

"Nik and I will see you, then."

Strangely, I looked forward to that. I paused on my way back to the castle and glanced back at him.

"Why do you like her?"

Mikhael didn't miss a beat. "Why did you follow my brother to every single party in Ilrea from sixteen to nineteen?"

I blushed scarlet; I hadn't realised Mikhael had been paying such close attention. He smirked at me through the iron bars. "We do funny things when the heart is involved."

"I never loved Niklaus," I assured him.

He laughed. "I know."

As I climbed the castle's cold stone steps, I wondered if that meant he thought he loved her, the grandest of Envy's treasures. It seemed like a dangerous thing to do, loving a woman like Margot Galatea.

I repainted the path to the dungeons with grand swipes of pink chalk. I was no artist, either, but the pink marring the dark stone walls left a strange pleasure brewing in the pit of my stomach, then let it scrape continuously along the cold tunnel walls until I came to the last scrap of my ruined nightgown.

I stared down into the darkness, shivered in the damp, and realised I'd leave right then and there. All it would take was to start moving, one foot in front of the other, and I could walk, stumble, run, and be free of the castle. I could sneak into the Infra and hide away until the end of the trial. I could take my chances with Envy, his judgement. If I failed him, would I not just end up there again? Or dead, which seemed the most likely of all my options. The soles of my boots scuffed on the concrete as I shuffled forward. I set the rock the crooked smile on top of one of the crates, turning him to grin down at the Infra. All while I weighed up my odds of life and death. I could spend my final days playing dice, listening to the skitter across the mat, feeling the thrill of the win. I could bundle up all the coins I'd earned and hold it tight as I faced judgement and die as a winner. It would certainly be something.

Or I could ask Samael to save me, since he had done it before, and I was half certain he would do it again. Even if he hadn't stopped Ophelia, Monika, and others from dying along the way, even if I wasn't sure exactly what he wanted from me.

I blew a small breath from between pursed, cold lips.

"Would you do it now?" I said, the words echoed softly down the damp tunnel. "Samael, would you save me?"

He chuckled; I shivered.

'*What was it you said to that Wrathling*?' Samael asked, proving he listened in, even when I couldn't feel his presence, even in the quiet moments when I thought I was alone.

"Which part?" I asked.

'*I am not your hero . . .*' He quoted me with complete confidence, and I couldn't even remember having said it.

"But you're the devil," I argued, emboldened by my strange familiarity with him in these small snippets of conversation. "You can save anything and anyone you want."

'*You entered my trials knowing the risks and rewards, Little One.*'

My heart squeezed painfully in my chest.

He was half right: I had no real idea what I had been getting into, no concept if I would be constantly switched into a place of frantic adrenaline, fighting for my life. I didn't realise how badly I wanted to live until I was almost always on the precipice of death.

"Save me," I all but begged

He growled. The hair along the back of my arms stood on end. I shifted my weight and wrapped my arms around my body.

"Fine." I swallowed. "I'll save myself. Give me a clue."

'*I owe you nothing, Little One.*'

"But you'll give it to me, anyway."

'*Why is that?*' He sounded amused, thankfully.

"Because I think you like poking at your trials and seeing what trouble you can make for the sins . . ."

Samael was so silent for so long I thought he had forgotten me.

I turned back towards the castle, the thought of fleeing no longer an option because, to save myself, I needed to help Margot and take her piece of akelda. I needed to win the Heist of Haures because I was at the mercy of the fickle game of angels. It wasn't until I passed by the dungeons again, one foot on the bottom-most stair, that he rumbled in my mind.

'*Benevolence has a variety of faces.*'

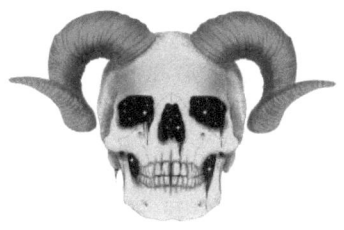

Chapter Forty-One

Aieke lingered in my mind much more than Samael's unhelpful clue. I sat at the dinner table with Envy's collection and watched them all, thinking of the girl who would turn to dust beneath the stone floors, and they would never know. They would never care.

Nadiya had re-joined us, quieter than usual, but her chin still tilted up proudly whenever she was addressed. Some of her spirit seemed to have returned, although her gaze zoomed nervously to the door. I wouldn't be able to help but look, too, each time she did, waiting for the inevitable.

I sat between Aeron and Tomas, distancing myself from the triplets, even though they barely seemed to notice. I knew it wasn't personal, but it still hurt. Zeres didn't eat. They didn't speak, just stared through us and out the window. I could feel pity for their shared brokenness, but my skin still crawled at the thought of being trapped beneath their bodies and their nightmares.

They abandoned the table, once again moving to change and ready themselves. By now, I could feel it coming, the irritation that zipped across my skin, the scorching of my blood in my veins. The first leak of Envy's power, ensuring his little treasures would stand tall in front of him, vying to be picked, to beat one another.

With shaky hands, I remained planted in my chair, watching on as even Nadiya peered into a mirrored surface and fixed the gold applied to her lips. Even after being broken, she was so accustomed to his influence she vied for more attention, vied to do better than everyone else and be the one to bend without breaking for the mercurial angel.

I picked at the edge of a bread roll, then tugged the entire basket in my direction, piling slices of meat into the side of it and covering it with a cloth.

Servants watched on, but they didn't stop me, so I bundled it beneath one arm. When I glanced at the triplets, I knew I couldn't stay in their quarters that night. I wouldn't sleep, lost in the fear their ghosts would haunt me, too. I needed to find an alternative.

Envy did not affect my heart and my spirit. It sung to join the line of people far more beautiful and unique than I. It burnt with the need to have what they had, and by the time I walked out the doors of the apartment, a bead of sweat trickled down my spine. It was exhausting to push through Envy's call.

The dungeons were a cold contrast to the apartment. Envy's influence was not so prominent there. I could breathe a little easier. The guards ignored me, which I should have expected. My knees landed on the stone floor outside of Aieke's cell, and she lay on her back, unmoving.

"Still alive in there?" I whispered. I wasn't sure why I cared, but my chest felt tight until she moved fractionally. Each shift of her limbs was slow. She seemed to take an age to sit upright, chest heaving, as she dragged herself to the front of the cell.

"Why . . . are . . . you . . . here?" Aieke said through panting. Her teeth grit hard while she found a more comfortable position. I could smell the stench of urine on her, but she didn't seem ashamed. She was surviving as best she could.

"I . . ." The words stuck in the back of my throat. I didn't really know, only that when I looked through those bars, I could see myself, shivering with infection on the cusp of perishing. "I brought food."

Piece by piece, bread and meat was forced through the thin gaps in the cell bars. Aieke took it all, and it piled in her lap, but she ate very little of it. I bit my lip and watched closely for when she would eat.

"Thanks," she sighed. It felt more obligatory than appreciative.

"You're not going to . . ."

"Later." Her eyes closed. "Do . . ."

My entire body leaned in, until my head rested against rusted, cold bars. It took time for her to form the whole sentence.

"Do you know what happens when you die?"

I blinked. "Sort of . . ."

Aieke's dark lashes fluttered, and she lifted her amber eyes in my direction, begging for an answer. I sighed softly and settled to sit a little more comfortably.

"My mother" – I picked at the edge of my stolen cloak – "she used to say you soul goes to Eternis, and the devil looks through memories of your life and decides if you are worthy of a second chance. She said the richest and the poorest are all the same when it comes to final judgement, and that Samael looks past our status and sees, as what we truly are . . . just human."

Aieke's breath came in concentrated, short pants. When she shifted, she groaned. "My mother was from Ira City. And there . . . there, they say if you die in battle, you receive no judgement and only eternal peace." She spoke quickly, pain in her expression. "You deserve the long sleep."

"So, you think you'll sleep?" I asked.

Her eyes opened slightly, a frantic light glimmering in it. "This is still my battlefield, and it might take a long time, but I will die here."

A tear rolled through the dirt on her face. I removed the napkin from atop the food and pushed it through the bars, but Aieke didn't take it. Still, she had no shame.

I used the iron bars that kept her in to hold my balance and stood. Aieke watched me through drooping lids. I didn't know that the food was a good idea.

"Are you going to help me?" she asked again, just like last time.

"I can't . . ." I said once more. "But I'll visit again."

"Don't." The word was harsh. "Not unless you're going to help."

That single word haunted each step I took back into the main castle.

Help.

What did help really mean? I didn't know what Aieke expected me to do, not when I was almost as much of a prisoner here. I had no keys to her cell. I just had my way out, and I was waiting for the right time. My feet led me on an ambling path through the castle. I found myself outside of a half open door, the crone mumbling within the four walls of her workspace.

Without hesitating, I pushed my way inside. The crone spun, aggression etched into her wrinkled features, and launched the contents of her hand in my direction.

I ducked. It sailed over my shoulder and shattered with the soft tinkle of glass on the wall behind me.

"Bah!" the crone huffed. "Heard of knocking, girl?"

I grimaced but didn't apologise. "I need your help."

"Everyone needs my help all of the time."

"It's urgent."

"It's always urgent." She fixed her wizened stare on me. "What makes your request special?"

I hesitated. "There's a girl in the dungeons."

The harsh lines of her face softened. "Ah."

"That's all you have to say. Ah?"

"Yes, girl."

"You already knew she was there? Dying?"

"People die every day," she muttered. "All over Kaida."

"Well," I spluttered. "You should help her like you helped me."

"Death is common. You're not a fool, Octavia, you know that. Babies are born screaming with the pain of previous lives that were cut short to make way for them. That is the balance of the world."

I swallowed, indignation pricking between my shoulder blades. "You healed me."

"Galatea asked it of me."

"I'm asking this of you."

The crone shuffled forward and straightened, her spine crackling. She gained an inch of height, and she used that to stare me down. "It's not the same."

"You mean I'm not as important?" Bitterness coated my words, along with soft envy that Margot could make demands and I could not.

"Help me." I sounded like Aieke.

The crone grasped my shoulders and forced me to sit in that lumpy armchair. "No."

"She's dying."

"She is, but we can't save everyone. Bah! If we could, I'd be a better woman."

I shook my head, denying her choice. "She's just a kid."

"Even children die, Octavia."

"But she's suffering . . ."

The crone rubbed her hand across her face, and she looked as if she were carrying the fatigue of too many years. I didn't know if she was tired of me or of the world, but it showed.

"Bah!" she huffed, and I glanced at my hands. "You can still help the girl."

I scoffed; unbidden tears welled in my eyes as emotion tingled my nose. "How?"

The crone shuffled forward, her wrinkled hand pressing my cheek before strong fingers wrapped beneath my chin. She forced me to look up and meet her gaze. In her eyes, I could see the pain of her curses. As she stared me down, I wondered what she saw in my mind, what she saw beneath the scars and the bitterness.

How could she tell when I had no idea who I truly was beneath it all?

The crone sighed heavily.

"There is kindness in mercy," she announced. "Would you want to suffer?"

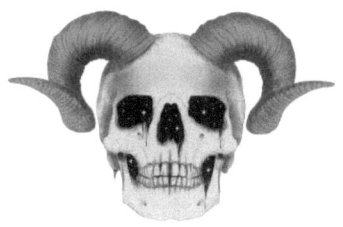

Chapter Forty-Two

Nightmares ravaged my sleep. Images of Erlkangs and Gluttony shifted and melted into the faceless image of the devil himself. Samael, who I knew but didn't know, who helped me but reminded me often he was not here to save me.

Even though the triplets had warned me away from him, the devil in my dream stretched on his throne of human skulls and beckoned me closer. I couldn't see his face properly, but I could tell he was smirking at me, waiting to see if I could accept before I moved closer. And of course, I did.

I sat on a pedestal by his side and above all others, indulging in many sins my envy satiated as I looked down and saw the blurry figures of my fellow Ilrean's below me. Pride, as I knew, I stood above them, at the devil's right hand.

Samael bowed his horned head and whispered in my ear in the same husky tones I had heard through the past weeks of these trials. His breath soft against my skin, shivers rolling down my spine. The devil glanced at the humans below and told me of their sins. He wove in secrets and tales, and I was eager for more.

Then he asked me for my opinion, to look down into familiar faces and render punishment for their transgressions, for the sins in their hearts and souls. I preened to be considered so special, lifting my chin and damning them all to death.

The dream ended, bathed in blood.

When I startled into awareness, curled on a rug in a forgotten room of the castle, I didn't know which of Samael's words to trust. What had been a dream, and what had been the devil whispering his teasing clues in my ear?

In a hurry, I found my way back upstairs to find everyone else in a flurry of activity. Aeron was missing, and when I asked where he was, their collective gaze dashed to his closed door. It was enough said without actual words.

I watched with my back pressed to the wall as they all dressed in their finest. Nadiya, grumbling she couldn't find her plum dress, narrowed her eyes when she noticed the hem of it beneath my cloak. I didn't apologise. She didn't accuse, but I imagined if she had true magic, I would have been cursed into next week.

"What's happening?" I asked.

Zeres paused and reached for my wrist. I flinched, and he faltered, his face twisting with unhappiness. "We didn't mean it, Octavia."

I ignored him and repeated the question.

"We're going out," Margot said before strolling out of her room. Her dress swirled around her legs, literal gems snug around the column of her pale throat dripping in emerald green.

"We're going out?" I repeated dumbly.

She laughed. "Not you."

"Why not?" I pushed off the wall, frowning.

"Envy is taking us out to make an announcement," Viktoria explained from across the room as she stood in front of one of the grand mirrors and fussed at her hair. "You're not part of the collection. He won't take you with us."

"Besides." Margot had drawn close, too close. She snatched at my wrist, squeezing tight. The sharp edges of her nails bit into my flesh. I gasped. "Can't have you running off without me."

"I won't," I protested, unsure of whether it was a lie. "I won't."

The scathing look Margot offered told me she didn't believe me and given I had stood in that tunnel and debated running away, I didn't blame her. I wouldn't trust myself, either.

"I want to come with you . . ." I hated how desperately I wanted to go back out into the spiral. Worst of all, how envious I felt that they were able to go out there.

Zeres' eyebrows pulled together. "It's not safe."

"Nothing is safe here."

"You need to stay behind."

"So, I'm out of the dungeons but still a prisoner." I sounded hysterical, and Zeres glanced at Margot. With that look, I knew it was true: I had never stopped being a prisoner, even if my cage had become a little nicer, and the people within it had tried to be friendly.

Nadiya knocked on Aeron's door, and it opened slowly. The man walked slowly, and I tried not to wince at the pain that flashed across his face. We had silenced as he emerged, and I no longer felt like talking. They filed past me, and the door slammed, dread pooling in my stomach. I wrapped my arms around my middle and shuffled to the window. From there, I watched them leave.

Envy walked first, his white shirt shifting in the wind, but the way he stretched and refolded his wings distracted me. He beckoned one of his treasures forward, and I squinted to see it was Margot.

She was perfection, swathed in green and wrapped her arm through his, leaning into the angel. When the gates shifted, I could almost imagine the iron snakes groaning to allow them passage.

I wished, more than anything else, that I was down there with them.

The only way to pull myself out of it was to force myself not to look. I turned from the window and into the room, re-entering the castle to find a distraction. Unexplored hallways took me to the west wing of the castle, and I pushed through grand onyx doors and into a bedroom. My heart hammered as I took in the oversized bed, with rumpled black sheets. Nervously, I tiptoed inside and noticed feathers on the ground. I picked one up, fingers dragging along the silky edge of it, and my heart raced as I realised it had come from an angel's wings.

I let go of it before it could burn me.

'*You should leave*,' Samael murmured to me, and I startled.

"I am in Envy's room, right?" I asked, dumbstruck. I edged farther inside of it and glanced around at the discarded books, and a strange map sprawled across the table.

'*Yes, Little One*,' Samael confirmed. '*An angel's space is sacred unless invited in. You must leave. You have other things to do today.*'

"Like what? He's not even here." My body flashed with a scorching heat. I liked defying Samael. "Besides, I need to find a piece of akelda."

The devil hummed. His annoyance brushed my skin, pushing against me as if that alone could influence me to do as he bid. My face flushed hot at the feel of it, but I tried to ignore him.

If there was anywhere, I thought an angel would keep his most important valued possessions, it would be within his secret space. I moved quickly, wrenching open drawers to his dresser. Pulling a pin from my hair and fidgeting at the lock of the large chest at the end of his bed. All while I coiled tight and tighter with tension, my muscles locking, eyes always scanning over my shoulder, just in case he came back early.

"What other things do I have to do today?" I asked Samael, my voice loud to try and drown my nerves.

'*What was discussed last night, Little One?*'

I thought back to the conversations of the night before, with Aieke, the crone, and the snippets I could remember of my dream.

"What did we discuss?" I fished for clarity.

Samael growled. '*Get out of here.*'

"Soon," I said. "I promise."

'*Your promises are worth less and less by the day.*'

Soon, I thought I'd found every hiding spot, and instead of an akelda, I had found a handful of loose feathers, a discarded copy of the trial card, and a small knife, the handle carved from a long piece of green gemstone. I kept all three.

I fled the entire west wing and turned the card over in my hand. The scrawled words meant nothing, but I tried to recall what had been said. "Deep beneath the dark city . . ." I recited and frowned, having lost the rest of it. I didn't pay attention to where I was going as I tried to get it back.

"Deep beneath the dark city, where humans fight to survive. Our lord invites you to a game, best played in a team of five. The Heist of Haures; where true nature thrives."

It made as little sense as it had a month before. Except that I knew the Heist of Haures was a game of trying to steal a coveted item from an enemy, a feat so difficult it required the skills of more than one person. Yet, there I was, alone, always alone, trying to get a piece for myself.

In three days, I was likely to still be empty-handed and find myself failing this task.

In three days, the devil would abandon me.

A wave of emotion left me breathless, and when I glanced up, I realised my feet had taken me to the dungeons. Still a cold and quiet place. I stepped inside and peered around the corner; the guard was missing.

"He . . ." My eyes bounced to Aieke. I shuffled forward. "Went . . . to the . . . parade."

The parade, I realised, was Envy showing off his treasures. Protecting them must have been more important than watching a girl die. I didn't have the keys to her cell, and I stood on one side of the iron and watched as she lay on the ground, staring vacantly at the ceiling. Her tawny skin had taken a pale, greenish tinge, and her face dripped with sweat. The odour coming from her leg was enough to make me gag.

I wrapped my hands around the iron bars, tears sliding down my cheeks. I had never been a compassionate person – not really, but I struggled to watch the way she breathed. It was shallow, the hollow at the base of her throat sucking in with each gasp. My eyes dropped to the floor, and I resolved to stay. Just like Monika in the Infra, nobody deserved to die alone.

The thought came to me as I mulled over the fragments of Eadlin's advice and Samael's encouragement. I should have been ashamed of how long it took me to understand, but I realised I was not without some skill. Although I had been called useless before, it was not always the case.

Strands of my hair fell as I slid the pin free and withdrew the thin knife from my pocket. Between the two, I worked at the lock on her cell door until it clicked.

The sound felt jarring in the quiet, especially as I sniffled through my tears.

The cell door swung open, and I foolishly hoped that Aieke would jump to her feet and run free, but she didn't move, just struggled to breathe, the sound raspy and grating as it rattled around us.

With a deep breath, I climbed into the cell, shuffling across the dirty floor, and sat cross-legged beside the girl. I grasped beneath her underarms and pulled her dark head into my lap.

She was shivering, and in the throes of a slow peril, she looked younger than she had before. Just a child in a bad place. My heart felt like it was cracking in two, where it had been racing before. It beat at an ominously slow pace because I knew what I had to do.

"Aieke," I whispered.

Her eyes fluttered open, and I brushed her dark hair from her sweaty face. "What do the red strands mean?" I asked, distracting her and myself in one hit.

Her lips moved fractionally.

No sound came out.

Then, softly, "Kills . . ."

Horrified, I swallowed, counting the strands of red woven into her hair. Aieke had killed over seventeen people, and she still didn't deserve this, a slow and forgotten death beneath Envy's grand castle.

"Aieke, I'll help you," I sniffled finally.

"Please," she whimpered.

"Will you forgive me for this, Samael?" I didn't wait for him to answer. In case I had misunderstood, and he talked me out of it. Worse, in case he damned me.

I smoothed Aieke's hair out of her sweat-soaked face, soft fingers tilting her chin up. The gem-carved handle was cold beneath my fingers, and anxiety thrummed in my veins. I was no hero, no help. I was not brave or thoughtful. I was scared and alone, and what I had decided to do scared me more than anything else.

Swiftly, I dragged the sharp edge of the knife swiftly across Aieke's soft throat.

Her skin split open, and crimson blood bathed us. The last of the light flickered from her tawny gaze, and the shallow, strained attempts to breathe halted.

Envy's pretty knife clattered to the floor.

I stared at my blood-soaked hands with horror as I choked on a final prayer. They had implied it would be kind and helpful, but I stood by my statement. I was no hero. Instead, I was her death. Still, I wished her soul a safe passage, one mine would no longer receive.

"Suffer no more. May your spirit rest a lifetime in Eternis."

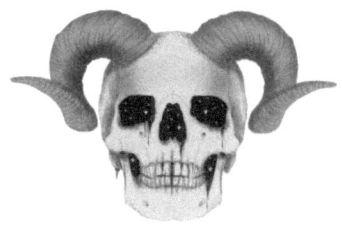

Chapter Forty-Three

When the collection returned, I struggled to contain my tumbling emotions. Samael had been whispering in my ear while I sobbed in the cell, alone and a murderess at last. I left the single glossy feather on her chest, a strange message to the guards who would return, and fled for the safety of the apartments. I had burnt Nadiya's cloak and dress and washed myself in cold water. I had scrubbed the blade's-stained edges, nicking small cuts into the edges of my fingers, tiny pains I deserved.

I redressed in dark clothes stolen from the triplets' closet, rolling the pants at my ankles, and strapped the knife to my thigh with a tightly knotted strip of cloth, unsure of what to do with it. It felt awkward and uncomfortable.

The collection was elated, high on having been out of the castle, but I could only see the drops of blood I had missed on the edge of my boots and the murder I still perceived to be on my hands. I had killed a woman, and it would haunt me forever, but in the face of Envy's favoured eight, I had to force a shaky smile back onto my face.

"Are you okay?" Zeres rushed in front of me and knelt between my legs, his face tilted up with concern. It was easy to imagine he really cared, easier still not to admit to what I had done.

My lips thinned, and I let him draw his own conclusions.

"I'm sorry we couldn't take you, but we have good news," he said and glanced over his shoulder towards his brothers. They huddled close, and I knew they had something to say.

"What is it?" I sounded as exhausted as I felt.

"Your friends are coming here."

"Here?"

"To the castle," Zeres clarified. "Envy announced that the devil's competitors had been here for a month, walking amongst us on a trial he had set. He invited the entire city to dress in their best and attend the castle in three days' time for your judgement."

My judgement.

My heart sank, and even though Samael had whispered sweet words that I had done the right thing and that I would survive, I couldn't help but think that I would have been a better candidate for Eternis if I managed to get through the entire trials without bloodying my hands.

I didn't understand how wanting too much and coveting what was not yours was a sin but stealing the light and life from another was not.

"Three days," I repeated

"Doesn't that make you happy?" Zeres asked, brows pulling together in confusion. "I thought you wanted to see them."

I forced a smile and pulled myself to my feet, almost knocking him. "Yes," I said through a lie.

Margot intercepted me as I tried to leave. She paused and pretended to straighten my collar. I cringed, imagining she could see blood there, and see right through what I had done.

"I saw Mikhael," she murmured.

Of course, she had. Margot's world revolved only around what she wanted and when she wanted it, which was getting out of the castle. I couldn't help but wonder how she had seen him, even with Envy by her side.

"They found the stone."

I nodded. What was there to say?

"The day before judgement. After the sun sets, we'll go."

Hesitation warred at me. "You'll give me the akelda?"

Margot nodded sharply; her lips pressed in a thin line. I was sure she didn't like me questioning her honesty.

"What if Envy picks you?" I asked.

"What?"

"What if that night is your night to be broken?"

Margot cringed away from the words, fury in her eyes, the corner of her mouth twitching. "It won't be."

Margot didn't give away her secrets as to how she was so sure and instead marched away, wrapping her arms around Nadiya and Viktoria as they discussed what they would wear in three days' time.

I envied that they knew and grieved nothing of the dead woman downstairs.

Hours later, I stood in front of Eadlin's door, my fist raised to knock, but still I hesitated, unsure if I wanted to confront my actions. She opened the door to reveal me but didn't look surprised. The crone beckoned me inside. "You breathe louder than a hellhound, girl."

I didn't take offence; it was probably true.

Without a word, I settled into the same uncomfortable armchair and waited for the old crone to speak.

"Does the girl still suffer?"

I shook my head.

She set down a cup. "You'll be needing something to settle those nerves, then."

Tea splashed into the cup, followed by a soft blue liquid, and the crone stirred it twice. It seemed that was all there was to be said. The twice-cursed crone didn't judge me for anything except for my hesitation in drinking her brew.

Then she chatted about everything except the girl in the dungeon. She told me about where she had grown in the Greedlands and how she come to live with Envy, who found her unique enough to keep but too cursed to live in his collection, so she had rooms halfway between the point of prestige and the dungeons, which she grumbled suited her just fine.

"Vanity," she advised. "Goes hand in hand with Envy . . ."

My eyelids were drooping with fatigue as the adrenaline of my actions finally abandoned me, with some help from Eadlin's tea, but I forced myself to sit up straighter.

"You've met the devil!"

The crone blinked. "Of course."

I leaned forward, fingers curling around the arm of the chair. "What was he like?"

Her face clouded for a moment. "Charismatic."

"What does that mean?"

Samael laughed in my ear. '*It means, Little One*,' he purred, '*that she loved me even when she hated me.*'

Pure envy was acrid on the edge of my tongue, and my breath felt tight in my chest as I struggled with an irrational resentment of the person the crone was over one hundred years ago. I missed what she had said entirely, blinking rapidly, suddenly close to tears.

'*Shhh*,' the devil crooned. '*She is the past, Little One. You are the future.*'

His words soothed me enough my body relaxed, and when I glanced back to the crone, she looked stricken. Her wrinkled face tensed with concern.

"Octavia . . ." Caution laced her voice, the same warning Eros had when he had thought I considered Samael a friend.

"What?" The single word was harsher than I intended.

The crone shuffled around the table, rubbing an ointment into her wrinkled hands. When she stood in front of me, she bowed her head. "May I?"

"May you what?"

"This."

The crone pressed her cold hands to my skull. For a moment, it felt as if she were burrowing her fingers beneath my skin, but it quickly soothed, and I felt nothing. I stared into her face, watching on as her brows twisted, the corner of her lips drooping.

Panic gripped at me as I wondered what she could see: my attempts to rob Nash, betraying a friend, the sorrow I had felt that Niklaus might die or even the way the blood had bubbled up from Aieke's throat, and my worry I hadn't cut deep enough.

"Octavia." The crone breathed when she finally let go.

"Yes?" I asked.

She reached into a cupboard for a bottle of brown liquid when she popped the cork with her spindly fingers. I could smell the sharpness of fermentation. It splashed into the bottom of our teacups. In the aftermath, I felt dizzy. I hadn't felt her inside of my head, but I could feel the space she left behind as she vacated my mind.

"Drink," she urged.

The liquid burnt a path down my throat. I coughed. She poured more into the cup before she tossed back a mouthful of her own.

"Listen to me." The old woman fell to her knees by my side, the strange action capturing my full attention. My fingers trembled around the teacup. What had she seen? I could see the wild panic in eyes. Was I so damaged that it caused her to fret?

"I'm listening," I confirmed.

"Stop letting him in."

I recoiled from the statement. The directive to reject the devil was not uncommon from one of the few people I knew to be cursed. But what had they done for me in comparison to Samael? The crone had saved my life. Zeres, Eros, and Ciris had been kind?

Samael had kept me sane, an unexpected friend in dark times.

My lips thinned, and I glanced away, unwilling to acknowledge her comment. The crone sighed and pulled herself slowly to her feet. The sounds of her bones creaking filled the silence between us. She poured from the bottle again and handed me the alcohol as a peace offering.

I took it.

"Sleep," the crone demanded. "You have a big few days coming."

My body obeyed. As I realised how exhausted I was, my heavy lids dragged me into unconsciousness. At the last second, in a flare of panic, I realised the crone had seen all my plans. She knew I was about to aid in stealing one of Envy's true treasures.

She knew I was a traitor.

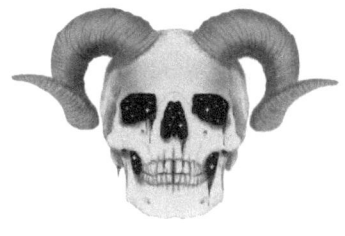

Chapter Forty-Four

Only one day remained before I would steal Margot, two days left until the end of the trial, and I spent a majority of it fretting where the treasures of Envy's collection preened and readied themselves to the rare event of visitors to their castle. It was a moment where everyone would envy them, and Margot never let on she wouldn't be attending.

Instead, she stood tall as one of several tailors took her measurements and reeled off instructions for her dress as if she would be there to stand tall and show it off. At the end of her session, she reached for me, fingers pinching at my flesh in a demand for compliance as the woman pulled me into the small platform.

"Take my friends measurements, too," she demanded, and I fought not to deny that we were friends. The repercussions of embarrassing her seemed too high.

"For what?" the tailor asked nervously.

His nerves left me feeling awkward. Margot frowned, lips pursed and foot tapping until he complied. It was only as he pulled the tape around my waist that she decided to speak.

"The dress we spoke about last month," Margot stated. "Make it for her to wear to the announcements."

I glanced at the tailor as he measured my chest. He looked startled.

"You want me to make that piece?" he asked, his eyebrows disappearing into his hairline. "In one day?"

Margot nodded. She reached to the back of her neck and pulled a single red jewel that hung in the hollow of her throat and showed it off to us.

"A rare flarite from the Greedland mines," she murmured, pressing it into the tailor's hand. "It's yours if can assure me that you'll have both done in time for lunch tomorrow."

The tailor glanced down as she curled his fingers around the stone, the pad of his thumb drifting over it. His throat bobbed, and I felt acutely uncomfortable to witness her bribe.

"Of course." Margot's voice had changed slightly, sleek enough that I shivered in response. "If you fail to deliver, I will tell Envy that you stole it from me."

The tailor shuddered. I could see the war on his face, the need to have the gem and be elevated and envied amongst his peers, and risk that he could be crushed, too.

It disappeared into his pocket; his decision made. "It's done."

Margot smiled, and he came to life beneath her gaze. I could see how she manipulated others. She smiled in a way I could never manage, as if she truly believed that the person were the most important in the world. If she believed it, then it was easy for them to believe it, too.

The tailor scuttled away, and Margot dismissed me just as quickly.

I spent the rest of my day in the gardens, daydreaming of the moment she would put the piece of akelda in my hand the same way she had bestowed her jewels on the tailor.

One more day, and Margot would grant me my freedom.

I missed dinner and the following fanfare, sitting in the cold gardens as the sun set, wishing someone I knew would come to the iron gates and wish me luck for the end of the trial.

It never happened.

That night, I crawled back into a bed filled with three pairs of identical limbs and an overwhelming amount of body heat. I listened to the soft curl of relief in Zeres' voice as he thanked me for a silent forgiveness. I couldn't blame him for his demons when I carried too many of my own.

Sleep washed over me, and in my dreams, I danced in slow circles with Samael, listening to him talk of the way Envy was born, forged of the bitterness he had seen in our hearts. Within his embrace, I thought of every time I had burnt with desire for what others had, especially my brothers and friends, and realised how truly serpentine and poisonous Envy could be.

The second last day of the Envy trial came too fast. I slept in, tangled around the three cursed brothers, until someone beat at the door, hollering my name. One of the triplets pushed me from the bed and onto the floor, promptly evicting me, and I stumbled out into the main chambers with my boots in hand.

Margot stood in the centre of the room with her arms folded across her chest. "Anyone would think you weren't taking this seriously."

"Want to bet?" I grumbled. "You'd lose."

She shook her head, as if I were the source of every problem in the world and beckoned me to follow. "It's past lunchtime. The tailor has come and gone."

Margot swung open her closet and gestured to one of the hangers. The dress was covered in a soft cloth band, a piece of paper pinned to it. I could just make out the whorls and shapes that made up my name on the slip. I reached for it, and her fingers slapped harshly against mine.

Automatically, I recoiled.

"Don't open it before tomorrow," Margot bossed.

"Why?"

"I want it to be a surprise." She shut the closet door so abruptly I almost got caught. "Are you ready for tonight?"

I nodded.

She sighed in disbelief and glanced at the humble replica of her village home. I wondered if she would be sad to leave it behind, when it had meant so much that Envy had picked it up and brought it there.

I didn't miss my home, not as much as I missed the safety of what I had known. Although, sometimes, I worried I didn't remember the lines and shadows of my own mother's face.

"After dinner?" I confirmed. "That's when we go?"

"After Envy comes." She nodded. "Stand in line with us tonight for his selection."

"What?!" I squeaked.

"You heard me."

"What if he picks me?"

Margot laughed sharply. "He won't."

Bitterness overwhelmed me. "And he won't pick you?"

"Not tonight, he won't."

"Why not?"

She tugged at her sleeves, exposing the motley blemishes of black and blue across her arms. Only then did I realise the bruises on her face were covered with some sort of paint. "He never takes us two nights in a row. Envy wants to see us bend and break, but not irreparably. He has some level of conscience; it's just lost to this fool's war."

I fidgeted, nervous about the idea of joining the row to be selected from because of some fragment of arrogance I held, some envy of them telling me I could manage it – I could be picked by an angel, too.

When Margot didn't say anything, I turned to leave.

She called out as I opened the door, "Your akelda is part of the dress. I'll be watching it until we leave, but you can retrieve it once I'm safe."

My fingers trembled, and I wanted nothing more than to snatch the dress now, but I forced myself to nod. "Okay."

I could wait.

Deliver the demanding princess to Mikhael, make her his problem, and run back to steal my piece of success. Once she was with him, she was no problem. I didn't have to worry about whether Margot Galatea died. It would be easy peasy in the devil's speakeasy. Or so I hoped.

It took every ounce of my will to stop my trembling hands to reach my knees when Envy swept inside the apartments. His dark wings cast an ominous shadow at his back.

Sandwiched between Ciris and Zeres, I felt like my legs would fail me, and I would crumple before him. On the end of a shaky inhale, I forced myself to straighten my spine, lifting my chin to wait. Envy wouldn't want me if I couldn't prove my worth, and his influence made me want it. To be picked, better than all of them.

Envy's full mouth curved into a wide smile. I watched him closely. The young angel must have every old man in this city tied in knots. All of them wanted to be him, younger and more powerful, in control. He was an angel that men wanted to be, with whom women wanted to be, even in this line of glittering jewels, where every one of his treasures new the risk in the reward of his attention.

Still, they smiled, fluttering their lashes. They would stick each other with pins to be selected into the envied place as the angel's companion.

The angel's otherworldly gaze slipped across us.

I inhaled sharply as his eyes flicked over me, but he barely seemed to pause. My heart squeezed in my chest, keening to be noticed. I wanted him to notice me in the same way I had wanted nothing to do with Gluttony. It was a magic woven into my blood and affecting everything in my blood, my breath, my brain.

He stalked back and forth, inspecting his collection of unique people.

"Are you excited?" Envy's voice was casual as he rubbed the pad of his thumb against Viktoria's rouged cheek. "A ceremony to show off my treasures."

His voice stroked the edge of my nerves.

Displeasure tasted bitter and stung my throat at the fact that he hadn't asked me.

I felt myself leaning forward, leaning towards him in an impulsive and desperate need for the angel's attention. I wanted to push Viktoria out of the way and step into the space between his gaze, but even then, it wouldn't be enough. I wanted to be her, unique enough to have him pluck me from my life and keep me for himself.

A tear rolled down my cheek; my fingers brushed against it, confused it was even there. I swiped the wetness with the back of my hand and forced myself to stay still until Envy undoubtedly turned my way.

Each night, he had inspected them all so thoroughly, each of his treasures, even the ones he didn't want to pick. Surely, he would see me, even if only for a second. He moved slowly down the line, pausing to inspect and whisper to each of them, his words for their ears alone.

Except Eros. As the angel stood tall before him, he raised a single brow, the corner of his lips twitching. He tipped his chin, eyes widening a fraction before his tongue darted over his lower lip. Envy tracked the movement. A chuckle of dark desire rolled from his chest and stirred within my belly.

As Envy moved on, he whirled on Margot, gripping her chin. His thumb swept her face, smudging her makeup, white powder giving away to the dark bruise beneath.

When the angel chuckled again, the sound twisting my guts into an apprehensive knot, this sound was dark, laden with envious obsession. It left no questions as to what would come in the night ahead.

I was so focused on the icy, foreboding feeling that crept from my skull to my toes I missed the moment Envy focused on Ciris, and before I knew it, he stood in front of me.

The air disappeared from my lungs. There one moment, gone the next. My chest ached in mourning of it. When Envy glanced down at me, his wings rustling at his back, I was lost.

His green eyes could have been forged of akelda and transported me to the old world. They flickered with shadows of memories and illuminated me with the bright wish that I could have seen the worlds before as he had.

"Who are you?" Envy murmured.

My skin tightened, lips parting. Beneath his attention, I could believe I was as beautiful as any of his other treasures. I could believe I would win his devotion.

"Octavia . . ." I murmured.

"Is that so?" Envy's eyes dropped from my head to my toes.

When his eyes fell to the devil's cuff secured to my wrist, all the interest within them flared and died. His gaze cut away, landing on Zeres, and I was all but forgotten as he moved on to the treasure in my collection.

My knees trembled. More tears dripped from the curve of my chin. I couldn't tell if I was disappointed or relieved that Envy had no interest in me.

"Viktoria," Envy called silkily. "Come here."

The fiery redhead stepped forward from the line, her lips stretched into a wide grin, clear eyes sparkling with a proud joy. Not for the first time, I realised that many of the sins truly intersected. There was pride in meeting the desires born of envy and wrath when you fell short.

Envy curled her against his body. Viktoria sighed loudly and melted against him. Once a choice was made, Envy rarely looked back to the line, and we were left in their wake as they swept from the room, swept up in each other.

They had barely left before Margot reached for my wrist, her grip a vice-like shackle.

"Let's go."

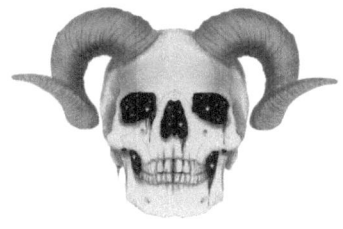

Chapter Forty-Five

My heartbeat roared in my chest as my feet thundered a path down the stairs and into the belly of the castle. With every turn of the banister, I risked falling headfirst down the next flight to look over my shoulder and glanced back to ensure we weren't being chased by an angel. Only idiots would steal from one of the seven Angels of Sin, and I, it seemed, was the biggest idiot of all.

"Hurry," Margot hissed. There was a strident edge to her voice that belied her own fear. "Stop looking and start moving."

"Shh." I chastised as we raced across the ground floor.

I pushed through a set of plain wooden doors, marked by the bright slash of chalk I had scraped across them. They led to more stairs that wound farther and farther down until the floors levels out and the dungeons came into view. It took everything in me not to look to see if Aieke still lay there, not to sob with the memory of my actions.

The temperature had dropped, unlit by fire like the main castle and tainted with the permanent chill of Invidia. Margot paused to pull up her cloak. I was sure I was running only on adrenaline at this point, when I nodded and gestured to what appeared to be a crack in the wall big enough to fit a person and marked with a stroke of chalk.

"Here?" Margot sounded suspicious.

"Just go," I said, eyes flicking back to the stairs again.

Nerves swirled in my gut, a foreboding forewarning.

"You go first," Margot insisted as she stepped aside.

"Fine."

"Fine," she mocked.

Teeth gritted firmly, I pushed past her and squeezed my way through the crack in the wall, stumbling into the tunnel that paralleled. Margot appeared, huffing and puffing a second later. As we twisted down the corridors, she stayed one step behind me the entire time, until a familiar silhouette came into focus up ahead.

"Nik?" I breathed.

"Mikhael!" Margot shrieked, and his name bounced both ways down the tunnel, petering out as an echo. A strange disappointment rolled through me as Mikhael spun, more recognisable at a few paces closer in the way he held himself, taller with subtler arrogance.

The stance of a man who truly believed he would rule the world.

He caught Margot as she flew at him, strong arms gripping her waist, lifting her feet from the ground, and he spun her in such a carefree manner that, for a moment, I was Envy personified. They didn't feel the fear of being caught, not in the sharp acute way I felt it, gnawing at my gut. Instead, they revelled in each other's presence, and I could almost believe that Margot Galatea cared for him.

I edged back from them, even as Niklaus appeared in the shadow. My job was done, and I wanted nothing more than to go back upstairs and claim my piece of victory.

Still, my gaze flew back to them, fingers trembling as the feeling inside of me turned raw and sparked into a fire. I wanted to be that happy. I wanted it so badly I had slipped forward a step, fingers twitching to rip Margot from the embrace and take it for myself.

I couldn't breathe for all that I wanted it, I couldn't inhale, and I skittered forward another step, my fingers wrapped around the thick, rock with the crookedly painted smile. She had what I wanted, and it would be so easy to take it.

I weighed the rock in my hand and tightened my grip on it to lift it higher.

Margot went rigid. "Oh, shit . . ."

Mikhael moved so quickly, swinging her out of the way, that my heavily, clumsily swung weapon missed entirely. It flew from my fingertips and clattered against the opposite wall.

"What is it?" Mikhael asked Margot, too concerned with her soft plea to notice my ridiculous attack.

Niklaus had noticed, though, he gripped my arm tightly and hauled me to the side, his gaze wild, focused not on me but on Mikhael. He hissed in my ear, "Stay away from my brother! I swear—"

"He's close," Margot murmured.

"Who?" Mikhael prompted.

"Who else?" she whimpered. "Envy's coming. Can't you feel it?"

When she said it, the strange weight of my own blood pulsed with the bitterness of his magic. A shudder worked through me as my stomach threatened to overturn.

"How?" Mikhael growled. His jaw tightened, and his narrowed eyes landed on me.

"I didn't—"

"Octavia!"

"I swear it," I gasped, lips curling back in a snarl. "How is sacrificing her to Envy going to get me what I want?"

He pushed Margot behind himself, shielding her with his body. "And what do you want, exactly?"

My blood felt like it was boiling, pounding deafeningly in my ears until I felt dizzy. I wrenched myself from Niklaus' grip and stumbled forward. He followed me cautiously.

"I want to live!" I hissed.

Margot was right. I envied the way they had loved the sight of each other. I envied her beauty. I envied her perfection, but above all else, I envied the fact that she was guaranteed to live safely, even if Envy caught us.

Shadows shifted at the end of the tunnel, and Envy's influence threatened to send me to my knees. Mikhael still bristled with suspicion, wound tight with tension, but he had gone pale in the face of the force that approached.

"Go," he shouted, twisting to Margot. His hands skimmed up her shoulders, and he crushed her in a hug. "Go with Niklaus to safety.

She blinked, frozen.

Mikhael shoved her toward his brother.

Niklaus stepped forward and caught her in his arms. They looked so alike, coiled with tension, staring at each other as if both wanted to flay the other alive.

"Without you?" Margot asked.

Mikhael flinched. He reached for her again, strong hands framing her face, while she stood in his brother's gasp.

"You have to go alone, before Envy reaches us. Niklaus will see you to a safe place." The twins shared a look, a conversation we were not privy to.

"Come with us!" Margot begged, her voice cracking. "We'll be safer together."

Mikhael shook his head. "I'll distract Envy."

"Don't be stupid! This is ridiculous!"

Mikhael frowned. "I said go."

Margot swiftly changed tact. "That's not fair!"

Mikhael whirled on Margot quicker than I had ever seen him move. One of his hands slid up her spine until it cupped the back of her neck, the other roughly grasped at her chin, tilting her gaze until she looked him in the eye.

"Fair isn't about getting all of the same things," Mikhael told her roughly. "Fair is everyone having their needs met. What you need, Margot, is to be free and safe, as you deserve. What you need is to go with my brother. *Now*. So that I know that Envy will only find me here, so I know you'll survive this . . . And that's my need, to know you're safe." His green eyes burnt with wild determination. "Fair for both of us, Margot, is your survival."

He glanced over her shoulder at Niklaus and nodded.

His brother twisted back to the two of them, and when Mikhael let go, he swept Margot up and over his shoulder. She shrieked as her feet left the ground. As Niklaus turned to keep marching on, she pounded her fists against his back, pushing herself up until she could see Mikhael. The last vestiges of her control had shredded, and devastation shattered her once perfect features.

"No, that's not fair," she shrieked as Niklaus carried her further and further away. "Not if you don't live, too."

They disappeared, and I twisted to look back at Mikhael. He was usually the calmer brother, rational and more composed, but that night, he looked as if he wanted to burn Invidia to the ground to find her again. Bitterness twisted in my belly, unwanted but undeniable, as I realised that Margot was like that. Everyone either wanted to have or to be her, and the rest of us were nothing in comparison.

"Go." Mikhael turned his broken gaze towards me, fractured emotion bright in his green eyes. He clenched his fists tight by his side. "Before Envy catches you here, too."

He left me with very little options of where to go through, with the angel fast approaching. I skittered back from him and realised that, if I followed Margot and Niklaus, I would never get my piece of the prize, and if I went back towards the castle, I was in the path of an angel, having just helped his favourite escape.

When I glanced, panicked, back at Mikhael, he was staring past me, towards the sound of footsteps, determination set in his jaw.

My hands fluttered uselessly in front of my chest, my teeth rattling in my skull from the way my body trembled with fear. In an impulsive moment of panic, I slipped towards the same boxes I had hidden behind before. The rough ends of my nails snapped as I grappled the top of the wooden container and pushed it aside, squeezing through the smallest gap I could manage.

Cradled in a load of armour, my knees aching as they pressed against hard metal, I noticed the crate was dark. The sharp edge of a short blade sliced against the palm of my hand, and I whimpered softly, waiting to be discovered.

Wings rustled, the push of power as Envy used it to incapacitate. The jealousy I felt left me so breathless that I crumpled. From inside the crate, I heard a thump and groan of Mikhael hitting the floor, the scrape of his body against concrete as he shifted, and the pained noise from behind his clenched teeth.

Through the smallest of cracks in the crate, I saw Envy stop in front of him. Neither said a word, Envy's power filling the tunnel, pressing down around us, until I had to press my fingers into my mouth, biting down on my fingers to stop myself from crying out.

I could only hope my will to live was stronger than his power.

"Where is she?" Envy had never sounded more like a snake. Anger rolled through the air like a hiss. Shadows flicked through the cracks in the crate as the angel moved, and I was frozen, as instinct threw a trickle of warning down my spine.

My view of Mikhael was obscured, but I could almost imagine him, chin held high, lips twisted in the corner with his near condescending, all-knowing smile.

"Gone." He didn't even try to lie.

The angel's growl rattled the city above us. The ground trembled, the armour within the box with me clattered together with the tremors of the Earth. My blood turned cold.

"She's already outside the walls of your pathetic city." Mikhael sneered. "Margot is free of you."

The thud of flesh and bone against concrete left me sick to my stomach, and I squeezed my eyes closed, trying not to picture Mikhael Heira as a mess of broken bone.

"Read him." Envy's hiss surprised me. Tense, I waited, straining to hear who he was talking to. "Tell me what's inside."

"Yes, my Lord." Eadlin's aged voice bounced down the tunnel.

It felt like an attack, and a pang of hurt flowed through me. She was how the angel had known to find us, I realised. The crone, cursed to know the true nature and intent of man, had known all my intentions and whispered them into the ears of an angel.

She had sold us out, and Mikhael would pay the price.

There was the sound of shuffling against stone and the low hiss of words as the crone spoke. I wished I could hear exactly what she was saying and bear witness to the poison on her tongue.

"Huh." Envy scoffed, sounding like the teenager he had taken the image of, angry and petulant. "*Humanity*. I loathe it."

Their footsteps drifted away, but even after they were gone, I couldn't bring myself to move in the quiet. Fear kept me locked inside that crate as the hours passed, and when I did find the strength, pushing away the lid, unfolding and stretching into the cold tunnel, I moved with caution.

A hiss rolled from my lips as I wiped the shallow cut on my hand against my stomach and noticed the splash of crimson blood on the stone near where Mikhael had been standing.

Freshly spilt blood. I had expected to find him still there, broken and wearing the vacant eyed stare of death, but a smear of blood led me to believe he had been dragged away.

Warily, I glanced in the direction Niklaus had taken Margot, then back towards the castle again, once more faced with the same impossible choices about how to best survive.

My sigh lingered in the tunnels long after I had slipped out of the cold and crept back into the dangers of Envy's castle, unprepared for the final day of the trial.

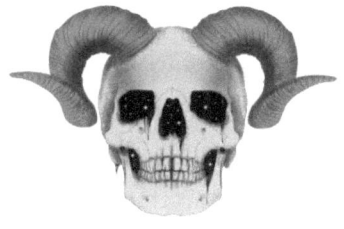

Chapter Forty-Six

Eros' face filled my vision, shaking me back into consciousness. Exactly where I had passed out, I sagged against their carpeted apartments, overwhelmed by the way my heart raced. My head spun, and the tears did not stop falling.

Margot Galatea was likely halfway across Kaida by then, but I still envied her. I wanted nothing more than her freedom.

"The castle's alive," he stated, and I blinked as I realised that his flat, toneless voice didn't jar against my nerves as badly as it had a week prior. "Servants everywhere . . ."

"Oh." I scrubbed my cheeks with my palms. "So?"

Eros held out his hand, expectant. I watched it for a second, then glanced up at his dark features. When I took it, he slowly helped me rise to my feet. They were strange, the three cursed men, and Eros had never tried to hide his opinion that I should just remain with them, forgotten by the competition and presumed dead.

"So," Eros sighed. "We know you're going to go to the ceremony . . ."

I nodded slowly, cautious to confirm it. Eros' hand tightened around my fingers. "And?"

"know what you did for Margot, too."

This time, I flinched. "Eros . . ."

My breath seemed to catch in my throat, and I choked on it, spluttering. He shook his head, and one slender finger pressed against my lips to hush any excuses I could come up with.

"We don't care," he muttered. "We'd all escape . . . if we could."

It was jarring to realise that, even the people who seemed to have perfection, to have everything that others wanted, still weren't happy in their lives. I knew why. I had been trapped in the castle long enough to know each piece of Envy's collection was just twisted into impossible versions of themselves by the envy that was now woven into their souls and waiting to die at the hand of a monster.

I watched the way he shuddered and straightened, pulling himself from the memory of lived and shared trauma and anchoring himself to the present.

"Vik and Nadiya have been getting ready for hours now." His eyes dropped to the shining face of an expensive timepiece that hung from his wrist, then back to me. "You only have two hours."

A breathless scoff burst from my chest. "Two hours is a long time to get ready."

Eros' lips twitched. "We saved your dress."

"Saved it?"

"Envy destroyed her room." My eyes widened a fraction. The emotions of the night before had been so overwhelming, the tension that leaked from my muscles so intense I hadn't even thought of the dress before I had passed out.

Slowly, my chin dipped. Eros turned us both in a slow movement until we faced the triplets' rooms. Behind the doors, Ciris and Zeres were in a chaotic state of half-dress, pants tied loosely around their hips, shirts strewn everywhere. Eros laughed flatly at the sight of them – my benefit, I realised a moment later, because he would know what they were doing through their shared consciousness. He placed a warm hand against my back and pushed me around Zeres, towards the bag winging from the closet door.

The metal zipper felt rough beneath my fingertips, pressing against my flesh as I tugged it down.

"It's very . . ." Zeres bit down on his lip as I lifted the dress from the bag. Ciris snickered silently. The humour in his face showed in the distorted reflection of the mirror. I watched him there for a moment.

"Very what?" I asked, cringing at the sight of it.

"It's very Margot."

I turned with the dress cradled over one arm, daring him to continue. Zeres' dark eyes were brighter than I had seen before, and the three of them watched as if they were waiting for me to crack.

My attention dropped to the slinky, silky material in my hands. The dress was practically serpentine, which I suspected was the point. The material was patterned like the dark scales that protected the city. A metal, silver snake ran down the spine, connecting the neckline to the low, swooping back. It was daring, attention-seeking and had been designed for Margot's soft curves instead of my sharp edges. I studied the dress, once, twice before a growl of frustration pushed through my clenched teeth.

"She said it would be here!"

"What would?" Eros edged a step closer.

"The akelda," I said. "The cost of my freedom."

The three cursed men shared a look. Eros came closer and carefully turned the dress in my grip, inspecting it. After a moment, he laughed and took my hand. He pressed it against the silver serpent. Our fingers slid down the length of what would slither my spine, curving over the triangular head of the snake, before he tipped the jaws up.

Secured between the snake's locked jaws and behind the safety of the sharply pointed fangs was a glittering piece of an angel's old world. It blazed with soft green fire.

Relief left me weak in the knees.

Eros' arms wrapped around me, muscles caging me in tight as he squeezed. "If you want to leave . . ."

Zeres stole the dress and hung it back against the wardrobe. Eros relaxed his grip, and I twisted to glance over his shoulder at their silent third brother.

"Thank you," I said, "you three didn't have to be nice to me. I was just a part of Margot's plan . . ."

Zeres scoffed. "We're more alike than you think."

"What?"

"Zeres," Eros chided. Firmly, he pushed me towards their bathing chamber. "Ignore him."

His words lingered with me through the afternoon, long after my skin turned wrinkled from the bathwater. Even as I stood, I felt like an imposter in someone else's dress. The soft material wrinkled between my fingers as I fidgeted with it. The snake lay cold against the length of my spine. I could feel Eros watching me carefully from the corner of the room, where he leaned against the wall, arms folded firmly against his chest. All three had mastered the skill of being silent and waiting out the rise and fall of emotion. They waited and waited until a huff burst from my chest.

"This is ridiculous!"

"We can stay here," Eros was quick to say, his gaze still caressing the movement of my lips as I swore beneath my breath.

"You can't!" I shot back. "Envy just lost Margot; he's not letting the rest of you out of his sight."

It was half the reason I felt so riled. We had all been able to feel the pressure of the angel's influence, his dominating presence, as he stalked through the corridors outside the apartments in wait.

Eros pushed off the wall, his slender hand outstretched again. "Come to the ceremony with me . . ."

He was roughly shoved sideways, and Ciris stretched out his identical hand. It glittered with silver rings. The offer was implied.

"Oi! Octavia wants to go with me," Zeres protested, jumping on his brother's back.

Ciris twisted, and before I knew it, all three of them were brawling, their carefully pressed black shirted rumbled beneath one another's fists.

"Likes . . . me . . . better . . ." Eros' voice was muffled as Ciris sat on top of him and reached for me again.

A laugh bubbled up from my throat as I danced back out of reach, not wanting to get pulled down into their mess. At the sound of my laughter, they stopped, hair messed in every direction, clothes rumbled, and identical cheeky grins stretched across their faces. All three shuffled and stood.

"That's better." In a fluid movement, they all offered their left hands. "Come with us."

"I feel so awkward," I admitted.

"It's going to get worse," Zeres supplied. "The rest of the trial competitors are going to look and smell like they lived underground for a month. At least you've had a bath."

My hair fell into my face as I shook my head, lips pressed together as I realised, I had unwittingly stepped into the privilege I had envied, and when I walked out there, between the three cursed brothers and on the tail of the reigning angel of Invidia, I, too, would be envied.

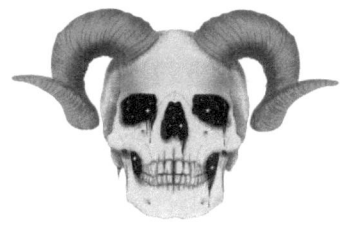

Chapter Forty-Seven

The doors swung open to reveal a ballroom filled with half the city. Undeniable terror gripped me. It was more than the grip that Envy held over his collection, who crowded around me as we walked. It was the deep vestiges of my insecurities.

Two steps behind Nadiya, I felt completely inadequate. Her skirts swished at her ankles, her chin held high, gold paint swirled against her skin. She looked like a temple queen. Her skin glowed as if she truly had magic and had enthralled an angel with it.

Behind her, I paled into nothing. I would be as unseen in the ballroom as I was when Envy had counted his treasures before leading them down here. His otherworldly eyes glowing with a possessive, dominating edge.

The crowd parted as the young angel stalked towards his throne, the snake circlet at his crown sitting low on his brow. Viktoria and Tomas followed closely behind and didn't pause to acknowledge the citizens of Invidia, nor the competitors that had invaded their world.

Nadiya and Aeron held the gazes of some, and I could hear the low hiss of human prayer as they passed. Some people, it seemed, in the depths of the city, believed that humans could, in fact, take magic for themselves and rise above the creatures that had decimated us. For them, these two were a sign of hope.

The triplets moved single file down the path. Eros kept a tight grip on my hand as we filed through. Words rippled through the crowd, jarring me as they turned into a soft chant.

"Hear no evil, see no evil, speak no evil . . ."

I blinked. "Are they . . ."

Eros' lips twitched downwards, but as he started to reply, a meaty hand wrapped around my other arm.

"Octavia," Benton Rumley hissed. He ripped me from the crowd, and I staggered sideways. A cry of pain on my lips where his fingernails ripped against my skin.

All three of the cursed men turned in unison, their pale faces stormy, sharp jaws clenched as they advanced. Zeres stepped into the middle of the three, and where they had once looked slender, strange and breakable, they came together in intimidating solidarity.

Rumley's grip faltered, and the crowd skirted away from us as they advanced.

"Leave your little pet." Envy hissed from the dais that held his throne. A thread of warning rolled into his voice. The three cursed men froze. Unable to avoid it, I glanced past them to the angel. He watched me with narrowed eyes, his gaze glowing, his lips thinned. He tilted his head, a blood-chilling warning.

He had always known I was there, I realised, but was indulging his treasures. I swallowed roughly, realising that I had to help them, too.

"Go on," I whispered. "You heard Lord Envy."

Their faces crumpled with confusion. Eros broke formation and stepped forward again.

"Go to him," I repeated, dropping my gaze. Unable to look at them, unable to look past them and bear witness to Envy's satisfaction. The three heartbeats that it took them to move seemed to take forever. Rumley's nails still dug into my skin; his foul breath hot against the naked skin of my shoulder. He waited until Zeres, Ciris, and Eros were by the angel's side.

"Do you have it?" he demanded.

My throat felt like it was closing in. "No."

"Don't lie to me," Rumley growled. "Or I'll gut you right here, right now."

Emotion, born of hopelessness, prickled at the back of my eyes. Envy had begun addressing the crowd, but I couldn't focus, all too aware of the threat of Benton Rumley, all too aware that Eros had not yet looked away, who intently watched the movement of my face.

"I don't have it," I said, watching the stony faced, cursed men on the dais. Rumley looked, too. "I was . . . I was hoping they would save me . . ."

Eros smiled softly, his head ducking in a tiny, encouraging nod.

Rumley scoffed, loud and disgusted. "Stupid women. Always thinking someone's going to save them," he muttered.

I pursed my lips tight against the desire to argue. His calloused hands shoved at the exposed skin of my back, and I stumbled forward, tripping over the toes of my own boots to hit the floor.

Envy stopped speaking; his irritation was palpable.

My entire body felt like it had been set aflame at the attention. I could feel curious gazes on me but stared resolutely at the floor. Unmoving. If I didn't acknowledge my own shame, I could pretend it didn't exist.

"As I was saying." The angel sounded annoyed, the roll of his words a hiss from the end of his tongue. "The Devil's Trials have come to Invidia, where foolish must face me to continue on and the most envious of all will find themselves forfeit to my desires . . ."

Envy paused, and in silence, his citizens clamoured to be the loudest to cheer, the sound deafening, each one of them craving the attention of the reigning angel. A pair of boots came to a halt beside me, a hand gripped my arm, and Niklaus Heira wrenched me roughly to my feet. By the time Envy commanded their attention again, Niklaus had given me a swift, assessing glance and disappeared back into the crowd.

"Quiet," Envy snapped. The room went silent, and I was conscious of any noise I made. "What you don't know is that these trials are ending, not commencing. These competitors, disgusting trial rats, have been amongst you for the past thirty days."

Whispers rippled through the crowd. The Invidians seemed to separate themselves from us, as if becoming conscious – for the first time – of the dirty appearances and tired demeanours of half the crowd.

A tense feeling, suspicion laced with distrust, seemed to fill all the available space in the room.

Nervously, I glanced to Eros and found him distracted. The three brothers had their heads bowed together; brows sunk low. Curiosity burnt bright within me, wondering what had caught their attention from their position above us all.

Envy cleared his throat, folding his arms across his chest and lifting his strong chin as he stared down the length of his nose at all of us. "The Heist of Haures is my favourite game. A game played by angels and half-gods of the old world. Haures were scavenger demons known for their treasure hoarding, and the winners of the game braved their lairs only to return with the most valuable of treasures."

The crowd stayed quiet as the citizens pieced together the meaning of the story. Tension coiled around my chest, the ever-present corset of worry that I wore tightening in place. I had a feeling they wouldn't take kindly to the news coming next.

"These challengers were given the task of playing for my amusement. The richest of Invidians are our Haures, and their goal was to obtain one of the most precious rewards I have given you . . ."

A beat of silence lingered. The crowd murmured, then the murmurs broke out.

"My Akelda! You sent them to steal back the akelda you gave me when I became a noble of this city?" One man sounded outraged. A short, pot-bellied man stepped forward, and the crowd parted around him. "I worked hard for that! And you sent scum to relieve me of it?"

The fury in his voice led to reason that someone had, in fact, stolen his prized possession. Envy turned, a swift movement, and skipped down the few steps until he towered over this man. Young, arrogant, and powerful, where this man suddenly looked old, worn out and utterly human.

They stared each other down.

The corner of Envy's thin lips twisted up into a sly smirk, and he laughed. "Pathetic human." The angel sneered. "You think you actually had power in *my* city?"

A dangerous silence followed, and the man deflated. Envy grit his teeth and cast his gaze to the room at large. "Lord Shree's entire estate is available to the first person to remove him from my presence."

His influence was suffocating, enhanced by the way the humans of Invidia came alive, their envy identified. They wanted to be lords and ladies in rich estates near the castle. In a stampede, they rushed forward, each one clamouring towards the short man, who had paled at the angel's words. He was lost to view as others reached for him, a feral light in their eyes. Until one woman wrapped herself around him and roughly stabbed his heart.

As he crumpled, the crowd scattered.

She stood, panting heavily in the angel's presence and croaked, "Removed."

Envy smirked. "Who are you?"

"Kat . . ." The woman wiped her hands down the front of her worn pink dress. I marvelled at the way her hands stayed still, even though mine still felt like they shook with the guilt of taking a life. "Katerina Lalara."

Envy's sly smile widened, and he nodded swiftly. "Lady Lalara shall move into the now vacant estate. All that was his is now hers."

The angel rolled his wrist, and when he uncurled his slender fingers, a piece of glowing, green akelda sat in the palm of his hand. Every competitor in the room shifted. Katerina snatched it away before anyone else could steal her chance and scurried into the crowd. Benton Rumley shifted through the crowd after her, still set on obtaining his piece of victory.

Envy walked up the stairs, and as he lounged on his throne of snakes, three people came to stand beside him. Chancellor Seamus, the devil's representative in Invidia. Cyn, who twirled a slender stamp between their fingers and appeared bored with the theatrics, and the crone, who stood on the right-hand side of Envy.

Envy sighed heavily; the room fell swiftly silent. "The late lord was not incorrect; these humans have scurried above and below ground for pieces of akelda, but that is not the entirety of their trial . . ."

My spine stiffened, my heart racing. He was about to present a hurdle I hadn't seen coming. My eyes trailed to Zeres, Eros, and Ciris, but their faces remained carefully blank. The angel waved an imperious hand at Seamus, who nodded gruffly, his fingers running through his wiry beard absently before he stepped forward.

"The Trial of Envy is not just about whether humans can obtain what is coveted by all. It's about their grip on themselves and how they act as they do it," Seamus explained. "To pass the trial of Envy, you must be judged on your true nature."

It felt like my heart had lodged itself in my airway, and breathing had become difficult. My eyes stayed glued to the twice-cursed crone, the woman who could see into the head and heart of men and see their true nature. She could be my judge, my jury, and my executioner.

My fingers had begun to shake as I thought of the dying warrior girl in the dungeons below the city, and the way her hot blood had bubbled up from her throat and spilled across my hands. Nausea crested in my stomach. I had risked my life so many times in this trial for nothing.

"Let us see how they did . . ." Envy said, his voice boomed across the room.

Seamus pulled a folded piece of parchment from his pocket and smoothed it out. His eyes dropped to the words scrawled across it, and he began to read the first team of five. Five competitors detached themselves from the masses and moved forward. They shared a look, formed a line, and approached Envy on the dais. The angel glanced at them without interest, but they pressed forward.

Each one revealed a fragment of the angel's old home.

Envy shifted on his throne and spared them barely a glance as he beckoned Nadiya in his direction. She moved swiftly, and Envy pulled her into his lap, his hand snaking beneath her skirt. His free hand waved, and the pieces of akelda flew in his direction. The angel's throne came alive. The snakes shifted and slithered. I could see the way Nadiya's eyes closed, blocking them out, as the snakes changed the shape of the throne, and created a well in the arm. The crowd took two steps back from the blatant display of magic. Envy dropped the akelda into the bowl, and it glittered there, beneath the light of the ballroom, a dare to all who attended.

Power was there for the taking if they coveted it badly enough.

The competitors watched the angel wearily, waiting for his judgement, and he scoffed loud. He swung his booted legs up onto the arm of his throne, curling Nadiya closer to his body and beckoning to Zeres to join them next.

"The crone will judge you."

Very little could be discovered by watching the crone smear a silver substance across the brow of each competitor, her spindly hands pressed against their temples before she rendered judgement in her loud, unshaking voice.

All five passed. They moved onto Cyn, who seared the mark of Envy against their wrists. There was a pause when the competitors didn't know what to do next, but Seamus dismissed them back into the crowd quickly and turned back to his list.

Three more groups went through.

The fourth split in half as some failed to bring forth pieces of akelda.

"Finley Nightingale, Narelle Gardener, Aidon Reid, Billie Cowan, and Nash Wickham."

Too many people were between me and the dais, but I pushed forward, struggling my way to the front of the crowd as these five presented themselves at the base of the stairs.

"Nash," I called. "I –"

He glanced over his shoulder, but there wasn't time for us to speak, for anything more than the sympathetic glance he offered me. Seamus demanded a presentation of the akelda, and I sagged in relief as nearly all of them presented a piece.

As they walked up the steps, they dropped the pieces into the bowl beside the distracted angel, who was running his mouth along the column of Nadiya's throat, with Zeres pressed close against him.

A hand circled my wrist, and I startled. Twisting, I found Eros by my side. His body was warm as he stood by my back and leaned into whisper in my ear. Somehow, I found his presence reassuring.

"Do you want to know what's happening?" he asked as Narelle stepped forward, who was empty-handed, taken aside by scale-armoured guards.

The crone stood before Finley, her hands brushing his curls from his forehead, and my heart hammered.

"Safe," Eros whispered, before explaining. "Zeres can hear what she's saying."

"Is Zeres, okay?" I asked.

Eros stayed silent.

"Oh." I breathed as I realised, he couldn't see my lips from my back. He couldn't tell I had spoken.

Eros cleared his throat. "He showed kindness nearly every day of this trial. He fed the street kids from his own coin. More and more of them each day."

It was strange to hear him speak so much.

The crone moved on.

"Aidon fails," Eros stated. Aidon joined Narelle to stand with the guards.

Nash was next.

My chest felt tight.

"Nash will pass," I told Eros. He said nothing again. He didn't know I'd spoken.

"Nash passes. He forgives a betrayal that hurt him deeply."

Guilt flowed through me.

"Billie passes . . ."

I stopped paying attention, my breath shortening, panting until my head spun. I wasn't sure my legs would hold me up anymore. Eros wrapped an arm around my waist and pulled me back a step, anchoring me against him and tilting my head so that he could see my face.

"What is it?"

"She's looking for kindness," I whimpered.

"So?" Eros frowned.

I huffed, unwilling to admit aloud that I couldn't think of a single time in the past month that I had been kind. This was the task that would fail me.

Seamus cleared his throat. "Oskar Wallace, Hollie Vale, Adam Leeds, Helina Archer, and Niklaus Heira."

They stepped forward as a group and paused at the base of the stairs. Hollie, Adam, Helina, and Niklaus all turned their attention to Oskar, who searched the crowd for something.

"Ma," he called out.

A woman stepped forward, well-dressed, with a small chandelier of jewels hanging heavily from her earlobes; she had the same round face and small eyes as Oskar. I watched, amazed as she reached into the depths of her purse and pulled out a handful of glittering, glowing akelda and handed it to the boy.

The mystery of why Oskar Wallace needed to be protected had finally been solved. He came from the Invidian elite and had had the akelda all along. All they had to do was wait the month out. They had hunted it from others for fun.

All five approached the crone.

"Which ones are important? I can tell you what Zeres hears," Eros said quietly, his breath hot against my ear. A sharp inhale left my ribs aching against the anxiety that bound me tight, and I shook my head; even though I burnt to know why and how Niklaus, and Helina had been deemed kind, I knew the answers would only eat me up inside. Helina Archer deemed kind, and I wouldn't be. It would be a comparison that would live rent-free in my mind for eternity. My eyes lingered on them as they walked away.

I twisted so he could read my lips. "None of them."

378

"Really?" Eros sounded surprised

"Really." I lied.

Seamus folded the paper in half. "Next, we have Benton Rumley, Octavia Nox, Kyra and Aureen Willett, and Monika Oster."

Eros squeezed my waist, and his hand fell away so that I could move. I twisted, breathing rapidly. My eyes squeezed closed.

"Thank you," I said, my voice strangled and high-pitched.

Eros studied my mouth intently, then nodded. When he stepped back, people moved out of his way. Behind his shoulder, I noticed a familiar face. Rowan blinked at me from a distance. I tried to stave off the overwhelming emotion I felt. I wanted to tell her that I was sorry, that I had screwed up her life for nothing at all.

Four of us stood at the base of the steps. Rumley's face had turned puce, his knuckles cracked with the tightness in his fists. Aureen barely bothered to look at me, although Kyra offered a small smile.

Seamus gestured us up the stairs. The sisters went first, dropping small fragments into the bowl of akelda as an offering. I hesitated long enough that Rumley stood in front of the angel, red faced and empty-handed before me. The guards shuffled him to the side.

The heat of the crowd's attention burnt at the back of my neck, and I was sure they could all hear the rapid, thundering beat of my heart. Nadiya straddled Envy, and I watched her for a breath, her face vacant, detached. My eyes zipped to Zeres, and he nodded.

One of my hands shifted to my spine, feeling the length of the silver scales, just as I had with Eros, in a far safer moment. Over the head of the snake before one of the pointed fangs pierced into the flesh of my thumb, and I prised the gem from its jaws.

Zeres smiled, catching Envy's interest, when I flashed the gem.

The angel studied me through narrowed eyes as I dropped the akelda, stained with drops of my blood, into the bowl by his feet. "Face your judgement."

At his command, I nodded, turning to the crone before I could whisper my goodbyes to Zeres. Unable to deny a command from an angel of sin. Aureen already stood, head bowed and painted, beneath Eadlin's hands. If I had thought I could relax in the moments between offering up the precious stone and facing the crone, then I was nothing short of stupid.

Tension coiled between my shoulders, and a hot flush of pending shame seemed to trickle down my exposed spine. After the crone had moved on to Kyra, everyone would soon know I was not enough.

The crone shuffled over and stood before me.

"What's the liquid?" I asked.

She ignored me, shifting so that her back crackled and popped with the movement.

" Eadlin?" I used her name for the first time.

"On your knees, girl."

With a heavy sigh, I dropped to my knees in front of the crone, bowed my head, and stared at the floor in wait. The silence rubbed my nerves until I couldn't hold it in anymore.

"I know you told him." I whispered. "Sold Margot out."

"I never claimed to be her friend," the crone stated and swiped the silver liquid across my forehead. "Margot Galatea has no friends."

The substance smelt like burnt sugar and smoke. It left me breathless and dizzy. As I swayed, the crone grasped the sides of my temples and tilted my head so that I was looking up at her, into the eyes of a woman twice cursed. I waited, wondering if she could feel the beat of my pulse scattering my thoughts.

"Stop talking to him," she warned, hissing low in my ear. "It's the only way you'll survive, Octavia. Don't trust the devil. No matter what he says."

Relief flowed through my body; her warning meant I had passed. A sob rolled unstoppable up my throat. "But why?"

"What?" Eadlin's wrinkled face collapsed in a frown as tears rolled down my cheeks.

"I'm not kind or worthy," I blurted. "I killed a woman."
"I know." The crone tapped my chin to signal I should stand, her eyes gleamed. "But there is more kindness in the mercy of a quick death than you will ever understand, Octavia Nox. Besides, there is power in being the one who decides your fate."

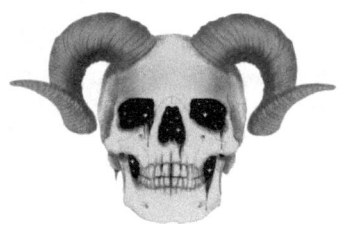

Chapter Forty-Eight

Cyn seared the brand of a snake into my wrist, permanently scarred against my skin in glittering green ink. The mark of Envy, alongside Gluttony, to show that I had passed my second trial. I had no idea how I had managed it. I didn't believe that the murder I had committed truly passed for kindness. Eadlin's words made so little sense. For a while, I might have been merciful, and there was nothing kind about the way I had used Envy's knife to slit the woman's throat. There was nothing kind about the way her body had jerked with a final breath and the light had left her eyes.

"Tristan Timbrell, Mark Meritt, Kale Nihil, Mikhael Heira," Chancellor Seamus called out as I stumbled back into the crowd heading to Eros and intercepted by Nash instead.

"I knew you could do it," he said, arms wound around me as he crushed me in a hug. It replaced the pressure where Envy's influence had been.

"Nash," I murmured, stunned. "I'm sorry. About trying to . . ."

"Devils, Octavia. The next challenge, we all stick together." He pulled back, searching my face. "Promise me?"

I wanted nothing more than to make that promise, but when I studied his face, I knew he was not the same Nash from Ilrea or even from the forests of Gula, and I was not the same woman I had been. I couldn't keep making promises I couldn't hold, not while the guilt of breaking them slowly turned me inside out.

Instead, I pulled back and looked for Eros, but he had disappeared. When I twisted, he was back on the stage and standing beside Ciris, his face impassive and blank.

"Mik!" Niklaus yelled from my left, shoving his way through the crowd. "Mikhael!"

I watched as a body pushed past the armoured guards to join his team at the base of the stairs. The other members barely acknowledged him, bickering between themselves. Mikhael was bruised, and battered, tension curled in his jaw.

"What's the problem?" Seamus called when they didn't advance up the steps.

One of the men flinched and turned his gaze to the chancellor. "We only have one piece."

Mikhael had moved before anyone else could chime in. He shifted to weave his fingers in the hair of his closest teammate. A blade flashed in his hand. My stomach twisted when I recognised the jewelled handle of the weapon I had left in the dungeons.

Before Niklaus reached him, Mikhael had slit his teammates throats. The green jewel dropped from the last one's hand and bounced on the polished marble floor.

The room watched on, hushed, as Mikhael stooped to pick it up.

"That single piece is mine." He sauntered up the stairs, quiet pride in his eyes when he flicked the jewel at the angel. It bounced off Envy's chest, and a collective gasp rippled around the room.

The Angel of Envy dislodged Nadiya and Zeres quickly, the latter barely catching Nadiya before she hit the floor. They skittered aside, well out of the firing line as Envy grit his teeth and drew himself to his full height.

His otherworldly eyes narrowed on Mikhael's face.

It felt like the entire room was holding their breath, waiting for the retribution.

"Face your judgement," he hissed.

The angel crowded in on him as Mikhael turned to the crone. She scoffed in his face. "Bah! I've seen your mind, boy. You don't have a kind bone in your body. You are the most envious man I have ever met."

"Not true," Mikhael protested and swung his hand to point at Envy. "I freed one of his captives. That's kind enough."

The crone narrowed her eyes. "That's not kindness. It's selfishness, boy. You got her out for yourself, for your own desire to have her."

Mikhael shook his head in denial, and the crone circled him slowly. Envy laughed.

"You have more envy in you than most I've seen, boy," the crone announced. "Envy enough to kill four people to stand here. All you want in life is to be recognised apart and above your brother."

Niklaus, at the base of the stairs, flinched back. It drew Mikhael's attention to him, and they stared at one another, a final stand-off.

"You're forfeit to me, little rebel." Envy's wings rustled as he shifted. The room held its breath. Niklaus stepped up towards the dais. When Ophelia had forfeited to Gluttony, he had eaten her heart.

I closed my eyes to block out his impending death.

"However," Envy all but purred. My eyes snapped open to the angel. "I could use the drive of your envy. Stay and become a commander in my army. I promise it will put you in a place of leadership and respect that your brother will never reach."

Mikhael's face tightened. "And if I refuse?"

"Then, I will take you to pieces and feed you to my vipers."

Mikhael glanced to Niklaus before he nodded a silent agreement.

Envy twisted, almost taking out Ciris with the sweep of his wins. He scanned the humans who had failed and stood behind the guards. "All the forfeits will join the front line of my army. With them, we will win the war."

Magic shuddered through the room as he sealed the fate of those who had failed. The cuffs at their wrists cracked loudly and clattered against the marble floor. I glanced down at my own, still firmly in place.

Envy turned towards his citizens, then, dressed in their best, cowered into quiet submission as his eyes glowed with otherworldly envy. "The first child of every family will join them. They march at first light."

Cries of protest raised, then died when Envy's influence flowed through the room, so strong that my knees trembled and I crashed to the floor, clinging to Nash.

"Do you not want to win?" Envy hissed from the stage, and the entire room bowed beneath his whim. Even the crone was on her knees. "Do you not want to be the victors? To triumph and glory over your neighbours, over the vile Wrathlings who threaten to come for your home? You will have everything. The soldiers who secure me this win will be unfathomably blessed in Invidia."

The strained silence was deafening. My lungs felt like they were about to explode. I wanted the glory he mentioned. Even though my rational mind knew I shouldn't, even though my completion of this trial meant I should have been a little more immune to his power.

"Yesss." A hissed groan came from Chancellor Seamus, his face red, fists clenched. "We want that! We want the glory! We want everything!"

Envy let up, and bodies sagged across the room. Citizens breathed heavily in the aftermath of his power. He would make them covet a dream, his dream, whether they wanted it or not.

Nash and I leaned against each other; my hands anchored in his jacket. Finley came close, and the three of us huddled together. At the glow in the angel's eyes, I wondered if he would even let us leave.

It was Cyn who stepped forth, still in a robe that glittered like starlight as they cleared their throat and murmured in low, husky tones to the angel before whispering in his ear.

Envy listened and nodded abruptly. "The victors of this trial have twenty minutes to get out of my city before I kill you all."

I sighed, trembling, sick of being afraid. I looked to the three cursed men who had shown me more kindness than I had ever deserved and waved.

"Go," all three mouthed urgently.

Wisely, I heeded the warning, although I wanted to say goodbye. I took Nash in one hand, Finley in the other, and fled down the black stone spiral that was the city of Invidia.

We tumbled out the gates of the city, stumbling from the stone spiral and into the dirt and grass, where Niklaus Heira had been judged for crimes, he didn't commit. Nash didn't let me stop, all but dragging me along the path until we reached the platform where the train had left us one month ago.

The grass had grown taller. The air felt eerily still, and slowly, the violet and orange painted the sky as the sun dipped beneath the hills. Night was coming.

This time, Charon's Rail didn't wait for us.

Niklaus and Helina arrived some twenty minutes later with a woman thrown over Nik's shoulder. When he set her on her feet and her hood fell back, I flinched.

"You're still here?!" I hissed.

"Of course." Margot's voice was strained, high-pitched. "I wasn't going to walk through the night alone. I'll be going with the rest of you."

I pinched the bridge of my nose; a headache threatened to overwhelm me. "All that struggle, and you're still here?! For the love of –"

"Shhh," Niklaus growled. "We'll get her on the train, like Mik wanted, and then we're done with it."

I stared at him, wide-eyed and accusing. He stared back, the tension in his face daring me to argue with this choice. With a growl of frustration, I strolled to the end of the platform to put space between myself and Margot.

As a group, significantly smaller than before, we waited for the train to come and for Charon to deliver news of our next trial. It never arrived at the station. Time moved too slow and too fast all at once. The sight of the disappearing sun left me in knots over the potential appearance of the harpies.

In the distance, the city quietened. Lights flickered out in preparation for the night ahead. A shadowy figure moved slowly down the road towards us. When they came close, we all watched the old crone with suspicion.

"Bah!" She waved a spindly hand at the platform where I sat, my legs dangling off the edge. "It's not coming."

"What do you mean?" Aureen stepped forward. "We need to be taken to the next trial."

The crone shook her head. Her aged face looked fatigued as she watched us, and I wondered if she was remembering what it was like to be in our places. Having conquered Envy's task and preparing for the next of the seven deadly sins.

The snake on my wrist still stung, and I knew I wouldn't forget my time in Invidia for a long time to come.

"Envy." The crone coughed. "Stopped the train from coming weeks ago. It won't come back if he doesn't have permission from an angel."

"But . . ."

"You'll have to walk," she advised.

"What?!"

"To where?!"

"We don't even know where we're going!"

Groans of dismay rippled through the competitors as everyone shouted. My jaw ached as I grit my teeth and kept my eyes trained on the crone. She was there for a reason; I knew she wouldn't have ventured so far from Envy's side without a point. Her eyes flicked over the crowd, settling on Margot in a moment, who stood behind Niklaus, her hood drawn high.

"Which way do we go, old lady?" Niklaus asked.

One wrinkled finger lifted and pointed towards the hills in the distance, where the sun would rise the next day. "That way. If you walk far enough, you will find the Wrathlands' border."

Niklaus turned and pushed Margot ahead of him. He didn't argue or complain, just marched in the direction she had pointed. I pushed off the platform and landed in the dirt, my fingers rubbed over the slinky material of the dress, inappropriate for walking through the Envylands, and I shivered the cooling air.

"The Wrathlands' border . . ." I repeated, as I approached the crone. She watched me from beneath her heavy brow. "Where there's a war happening?"

Eadlin's face transformed with the sly smile that stretched across her face. She waited until many of the competitors had left before she reached for me, her wrinkled hand a shackle around my wrist.

"Octavia . . ." I glanced over my shoulder at Nash and Finley, who waited expectantly.

"One minute."

The crone watched me intently, dark eyes secured on my face. She pulled me close and pressed a vial into my hand. I glanced down, but her other hand captured my jaw, fingers pinching against my skin as she held my gaze. She refused to let me look, holding my grip tight against the cold vial.

"Get to the Wrathlands, give this to Commander Inaina, and tell him that it's better late than never."

"Why should I?" I asked.

"Bah!" The crone scoffed. "I saved your life, girl. Don't you forget that."

She wasn't wrong: the crone was the reason I lived and breathed right then, in more ways than one. Once again, I had been carried through a trial at the mercy of someone else. I swallowed roughly, and the crone slapped her firm fingers against my cheek to keep my attention.

"What are you going to tell him?"

"Better late than never," I parroted back, twisting free of her grip. I lifted the skirt of my ridiculous dress from the ground and turned back to Nash and Finley, who waited patiently.

"Oh, and Octavia?" The crone called as I retreated.

With a sigh, I glanced over my shoulder. My eyes scanning up and down, and I wished I had never trusted her to begin with.

"What?" I bit out.

"Tell, Samael for me –" She smiled again, sly and unpleasant. She left the words lingering, knowing I wouldn't be able to resist them. I needed to know, and once I knew, Samael would, too.

"Tell him what?" I was eager to know and to speak to Samael. Even as trace amounts of envy bubbled within me at the fact that she had met him and known him enough to be sending messages. "What do you want me to tell him?"

The crone cackled as the sunlight disappeared, shrouding her in shadows.

"History is doomed to repeat itself."

Acknowledgements

Behind every novel is a village of people who helped it come to life. First and foremost, and as always, I need to thank Rhys and Ira for their never-ending patience for my distraction, moods and rambling as I embarked on writing the second instalment in this series, and for soothing the ever-present anxiety that comes with wondering if my second book would be better than my first; and I'm happy to say I think I've achieved that, at least.

Addie, The Devil's Trials beta reader, who is always willing to tell me both the good and the bad about the draft she receives and be honest about what's represented within. Thank you, you're the very first to read these books, and I couldn't do it without you.

Mum and dad, for supporting me and being willing to read these books even if they're not your preferred genre or 'there isn't enough werewolves' – hint, there's never going to be werewolves. The rest of my family, who waited eagerly to see what came next in Octavia's journey.

Lastly, to my fellow writers and authors across all platforms, but especially 'The Second Cup' writers' discord. Our conversation, laughs and the endless support found amongst my peers has been truly invaluable.

About the Author

Stephanie Gluck writes on the traditional lands of the Larrakia people and pays her respects to Elders past, present and emerging.

Stephanie is a fantasy author who likes to imagine worlds beyond her own. When not writing she avidly feeds her coffee addiction and adds to her ever-growing collection of books. She is a registered nurse and lives in the Northern Territory of Australia with her partner Rhys, and Great Dane, Ira.

You can keep up to date with what Stephanie is writing next via her website: www.stephaniegluck.com